A two-time winner of the British Fantasy Award, **Mark Chadbourn** was raised in the mining communities of South Derbyshire and studied Economic History at Leeds before becoming a journalist. Now a screenwriter for BBC television drama, he has also run an independent record company, managed rock bands, and worked on a production line and as an gineer's 'mate'. He is the author of the celebrated *The Dark A The Age of Misrule* and *Kingdom of the Serpent* trilogies. *The S d of Albion* was inspired in part by a mysterious portrait d vered at Corpus Christi College, Cambridge, which may b e only surviving depiction of the playwright and alleged s Christopher Marlowe. It is inscribed with the motto *Quod n urit me destruit* – 'That which nourishes me destroys me.'

M Chadbourn recently completed the next book in th words of Albion' sequence. He lives in a forest in the M nds. To find out more about him and his writing, visit w .markchadbourn.net

# THE
# SWORD
# OF ALBION

## MARK CHADBOURN

**BANTAM BOOKS**

LONDON · TORONTO · SYDNEY · AUCKLAND · JOHANNESBURG

TRANSWORLD PUBLISHERS
61–63 Uxbridge Road, London W5 5SA
A Random House Group Company
www.rbooks.co.uk

**THE SWORD OF ALBION**
**A BANTAM BOOK: 9780553820218**

First published in Great Britain
in 2010 by Bantam Press
an imprint of Transworld Publishers
Bantam edition published 2011

Published in the USA as *The Silver Skull*

Addresses for Random House Group Ltd companies outside the UK
can be found at: www.randomhouse.co.uk
The Random House Group Ltd Reg. No. 954009

The Random House Group Limited supports the Forest Stewardship
Council (FSC), the leading international forest-certification organization.
All our titles that are printed on Greenpeace-approved FSC-certified
paper carry the FSC logo. Our paper procurement policy can
be found at www.r.books.co.uk/environment

Typeset in 11/14pt Bembo by
Kestrel Data, Exeter, Devon.
Printed in the UK by
CPI COx & Wyman, Reading, RG1 8EX.

2 4 6 8 10 9 7 5 3 1

*For Elizabeth, Betsy, Joe and Eve*

# AUTHOR'S NOTE

Credit must go to four hundred and thirty years' worth of authors responsible for the primary, secondary and tertiary texts which provided the research and resources for this work.

On the matter of dates: at the time of this story, England still used the old Julian calendar while the rest of Europe had adopted the new Gregorian calendar, with which we are all familiar today. To avoid any confusion, I have used the Gregorian dates for all events.

*'Spies are men of doubtful credit, who make a show of one thing and speak another.'*

Mary, Queen of Scots

# PROLOGUE

FAR BENEATH THE SLOW-MOVING THAMES, A PROCESSION OF flickering lights drew inexorably towards London from the east. The pace was funereal, the trajectory steady, purposeful. In that hour after midnight, the spectral glow under the black waters passed unseen by all but two.

'There! What are they, sir?' In the lantern light, the guard's fear was apparent as he peered over the battlements of the White Tower, ninety feet above the river. He rattled the staff of his halberd against his gleaming breastplate with a nervous rhythm.

Matthew Mayhew, who had seen worse things in his thirty years than the guard could ever dream in his most delirious fever-sleep, replied with boredom, 'I see the proud heart of the greatest nation on Earth. I see a city safe and secure within its walls, where the Queen may sleep peacefully.'

'No . . . There!' The guard pointed urgently, his features shifting into shadow beneath the peak of his burgonet helmet.

'A waterman has met with disaster,' Mayhew sighed. The Tower guards recognized him as a man apart from their ranks, yet whose word was always to be obeyed. No one was quite sure what role he played there, but his papers were signed by the Principal Secretary himself, Sir Francis Walsingham, and when Mayhew spoke it was with the authority of the Privy Council, and therefore the Queen herself.

Since his temper was as short as his stature, the guards had learned to handle Mayhew with care and made a point of praising the fine court fashions which he took delight in parading, peacock-like. His high-necked, elaborate ruff had nearly six hundred folds, starched so strongly to keep its shape that Mayhew could barely move his head. His doublet had jewelled buttons and a peasecod belly protruding from his ankle-length cloak, which was finely embroidered with a unicorn design, furred at the collar and lined with crimson silk. His beard was clipped to an inch in length and waxed into twin prongs.

Clenching his halberd, the guard gulped the cold air of the March night. 'And his lantern still burns on the bottom? What of the other lights? And they move—'

''Tis the current.'

The guard shook his head. 'They are ghosts!'

Mayhew gave a dismissive snort.

'There are such things! Samuel Hale saw the Queen's mother walking with her head beneath her arm in the Chapel of St Peter-ad-Vincula. Why, the Tower is the most haunted place in England! The two Princes, Margaret Pole, Lady Jane Grey . . . all seen here, Master Mayhew. Damned by God to walk this world after their deaths.'

Mayhew studied the slow-moving lights, imagining fish in the deep with their own candles to guide their way through the inky dark.

The guard's fear made his lantern swing so wildly shadows flew across the tower.

Steadying the lantern, Mayhew said, 'When this great

fortress was built five hundred years gone, King William had the mortar tempered with the blood of beasts. Do you know why that was?'

'No, no. I—'

'Suffice to say,' Mayhew interrupted wearily, 'you are safe here from all supernatural threat.'

The guard calmed a little. 'Safe, you say?'

'England's defences are built on more than the rock of its people.'

The lights veered away from the centre of the river to the Tower of London where it nestled in the old Roman walls, guarding the eastern approach to the capital. Mayhew couldn't prevent a shiver running up his spine; the lights were an arrow driving straight towards him.

'Complete your rounds,' he said sharply, overcompensating in case the guard saw his weakness. 'We must ensure the Tower remains secure against England's enemies.'

'And the prisoner you are charged to guard?'

'I will attend to him.' Mayhew pressed a scented handkerchief to his nose, but nothing could block the stink of the city's filth caught on the night wind, the excrement in the ditches and watercourses, the butchers' offal poured nightly into the river, bloody at first, then rotting where it caught in the shallows, the piles of household refuse, replenished as fast as they were moved, all caught up in the blanket of acrid smoke from the cheap coal the working people burned to keep warm. Sometimes it was unbearable. He hated being away from the court where the pleasures of life were more apparent, hated the boredom of his task, and at that moment hated that he was caught on the cold summit of the White Tower when he should have been inside by the fire.

He cast an eye around the fortress. Pools of darkness were

held back by the lanterns strung along the walkways among the wards. The only movement came from the slow circuit of the night-watch.

The Tower of London was an unassailable symbol of England. Solid Kentish ragstone formed the bulk of its impregnable heart, the White Tower, protected by its own curtain wall and moat, with a further curtain wall, and thirteen towers, guarding the Inner Ward beyond. And there was the Outer Ward too, with a further solid wall, five towers, and three bastions. Everything valuable to the nation lay within these walls – the Crown Jewels, the treasury, the Royal Mint, the armoury, and England's most dangerous prisoners, including Mayhew's personal charge.

As he made his way down the stone steps, he was greeted by the clatter of boots ascending, and the light of another lantern. William Osborne, his youthful face and intelligent grey eyes unsettled, was dressed frugally in muddy browns and greys, his breeches only modestly padded and a felt, waist-length cloak covering his cloth jerkin. An unfashionable stiffened hood kept his head warm.

Mayhew wondered if the fellow now regretted giving up his promising career in the law to join the Queen's service out of love for his country, not realizing what would be asked of him.

'What is it?' Mayhew demanded.

'A disturbance. At the Traitor's Gate.'

*Where the river lights were heading*, Mayhew thought. 'The gate remains secure, and well guarded?' he asked.

Osborne's face loomed white in the lamplight. 'There are six men upon it, as our master, Sir Francis Walsingham, demanded.'

'And yet?'

14

Osborne's voice quavered with uncertainty. 'The guards say the restraining beam moves of its own accord. Bolts draw without the help of human hand. Is this what we always feared?'

Pushing past him with irritation, Mayhew snapped, 'You know as well as I the Tower is protected. Our men are frighted like maidens.' But for all his contempt at his colleague's words, Mayhew's chest tightened in apprehension.

*Walsingham said it could never happen*, he reminded himself. *He told the Queen . . . Burghley . . .*

Trying to maintain his decorum, he descended to the ground floor with studied nonchalance, and stepped out into the Inmost Ward, Osborne at his heels. The white-washed walls of the Tower glowed in the lantern light.

'Listen!' The younger man's features flared in the gloom as he raised his lantern to illuminate the way ahead.

The steady silence of the Tower was shattered by a cacophony of roars and howls, barks, shrieks and high-pitched chattering. In the Royal Menagerie, the lions, leopards and lynxes threw themselves around their pens in a frenzy.

'What do they sense?' There was a querulous tremble in Osborne's voice.

Scanning the Inmost Ward for any sign of movement, Mayhew relented. 'You know as well as I. Churchyard shades. The Devil's horned kin. The very stuff of nightmares. Whatever you fear most, that is what they are.'

Osborne winced at his words. 'Are you not afraid?'

'This is the work we were charged to do, for Queen and country. Raise the alarm. Then we must take ourselves to the prisoner.'

'To arms! To arms!' Osborne shouted as he raced to find the captain of the Tower's defenders, and within moments they were running to their positions. Breathless, Osborne returned to Mayhew and together they peered through the gate in the curtain wall where the string of lanterns kept the dark at bay.

'Nothing,' Osborne said tremulously, his voice almost lost beneath the cries of the animals.

Mayhew focused his attention on St Thomas's Tower in the outer curtain wall. Beyond was the river, and beneath lay the water entrance that had become known as Traitor's Gate, after the enemies of the Crown who had been transported through it to imprisonment or death. The guards had disappeared inside, but there was no clamour.

After five minutes, Osborne's relief was palpable. 'Perhaps we were wrong, and it is Spanish spies on our doorstep. Our men will deal with them in no time.' He looked to Mayhew for reassurance. 'With the country on the brink of war, Spanish spies are everywhere. Yes?'

A guard emerged from St Thomas's Tower, pausing on the threshold for a moment. Mayhew and Osborne watched him curiously. With an odd, lurching gait, the soldier picked a winding path towards them.

'Is he drunk?' Mayhew growled. 'His head will be on the block by noon if he has deserted his post.'

'I . . . I do not . . .' The words died in Osborne's throat as the Tower defender's path became more erratic. His jerky movement was deeply upsetting, as if he had been afflicted by a palsy.

Mayhew cursed under his breath. 'I gave up a life at court for this.'

As the guard neared, they saw that his hands continually went to his head as if searching for a missing hat. Despite himself, Mayhew reached into the folds of his cloak for his rapier.

16

'I am afraid,' Osborne whispered.

'Do you hear music?' Mayhew cocked his head. 'Like pipes playing, caught on the breeze?' As he breathed deeply of the night air, he realized the foul odour of the city had been replaced by sweet, seductive scents that took him back to his childhood. A tear stung his eye. 'And that smell,' he said, 'like cornfields beneath the summer moon.' He inhaled. 'Honey, from the hive my grandfather kept.'

'What is wrong with you?' Osborne demanded. 'This is no time for dreams!'

Mayhew felt a sense of loss as his reverie faded, but he was caught by the sight of the soldier entering a circle of torchlight. For the first time Mayhew recognized that something was terribly wrong with the man's face. Revolted yet fascinated, he tried to see behind the guard's pawing hands. Glimpses came to him, as the man lurched and tore at his skin with increasing panic, of skin unnaturally white, with the texture of sackcloth. *A mask!* Mayhew told himself, knowing it wasn't. When the hands came away for the briefest moment, Mayhew reeled. The soldier's eyes were large and dark, and resembled nothing more than buttons. They didn't blink, they didn't see. Where the mouth had been there was only a row of ragged stitches from which a muffled, desperate mewling issued. *An illusion*, Mayhew tried to convince himself, sweat prickling his scalp despite the cold night, but he couldn't shake off the memory of the dollies the old women sold in Cheapside at Christmastime.

'God's wounds!' Osborne exclaimed. 'What has happened to him?'

Before Mayhew could respond, a blur of ochre and brown burst from the shadows. Amid a terrible roar, the soldier was slammed on to the turf. Claws revealing bones and organs, tearing jaws spraying viscera around the convulsing form. But the most chilling thing was that the man did not utter a sound.

*He cannot*, Mayhew thought, frozen to the spot.

The lion's triumphant roar jolted Mayhew and Osborne out of their shock.

'The beasts have escaped the menagerie!' Mayhew thrust Osborne back towards the White Tower. Drawing their rapiers, they spun this way and that in disorientation at the wild cries growing louder by the second. The iron tang of blood was lost beneath the heavy musk of the approaching beasts caught on the night breeze.

Eyes wide with panic, Osborne appeared to lose all sense of direction until Mayhew grabbed his arm and hurled him against the door. Mayhew fumbled for the handle, glancing desperately over his shoulder. Bounding shadows emerged from the dark. Throwing open the door, Mayhew propelled Osborne inside and slammed it shut behind him. 'Bar the door and defend it with your lives!' he shouted at the two soldiers who waited within. They blanched as the deafening roars and cries drew near to the entrance.

Osborne sprawled on the flags, fighting to catch his breath. Mayhew hauled the younger man to his feet by his cloak and shook him. 'Courage,' he said under his breath so the soldiers would not hear. His scowl underlined the harshness of his tone. 'Do not fail me. Or the Queen.'

Shaking, Osborne threw himself up the winding stone steps behind Mayhew.

They had only climbed a little way when a tremendous crash resounded from the great oak door through which they had entered the tower. Flashing a wide-eyed stare at Mayhew, Osborne took the steps two at a time. As they raced along the ringing corridors, Osborne asked breathlessly, 'What is coming, Mayhew?'

'Best not to think of that now.'

'I knew that man. Carter, a good fellow, with a wife and two girls. What did they do to him?'

'Stop asking foolish questions!'

A scream at the foot of the steps echoed through the tower, cut short mercifully soon.

'Let nothing slow your step,' Mayhew urged.

Reaching the most secure area of the White Tower, they came to a heavy oak door studded with iron, set in walls thicker than a man's height. After Mayhew gave three sharp knocks with the pommel of his rapier, a hatch opened to reveal a pair of wary eyes.

'Who goes?' came the voice from within.

'Mayhew and Osborne, Sir Francis Walsingham's men.'

While Osborne glanced anxiously back the way they had come, hard eyes searched their faces, until, their owner satisfied, the order was given to draw the fourteen bolts that the Queen herself had personally insisted be installed.

'Hurry,' Osborne cried. Mayhew cuffed him across his arm.

Once inside, Osborne pressed his back against the resealed door and let out a juddering sigh of relief. 'Finally. We are safe.'

Mayhew didn't hide his contempt. Osborne was too weak to survive in their business; he would not be long for the world and there was little point in tormenting him further by explaining the obvious.

Six men waited by the door, and another twenty in the chambers within, all chosen by Walsingham himself for their ruthlessness and lack of compassion. Their faces were uniformly hard, their hands rarely far from their weapons. At any other time they would be thieves, slitting the throats of rich sots in the stews of Bankside, yet here they were in the Queen's most trusted employ.

'The cell remains secure?' Mayhew asked the captain, whose face boasted the scars of numerous fights.

'It is. It was examined 'pon the hour, as it is every hour.'

'Take us to it.'

'Who attempts to breach our defences? Surely the Spanish would not risk an attack.'

When Mayhew did not respond, the captain nodded and ordered two of his men to accompany Osborne and Mayhew. Moments later they were marching past rooms stacked high with the riches of England, gold seized from the New World or looted from ships from the Spanish Main to the Channel.

Beyond the bullion rooms, one of the guards unlocked a stout door and led them down a steep, dank flight of steps to another locked door. Inside was a low-ceilinged chamber. Buried so deep in the White Tower that no sounds penetrated through the stone, it was unpleasantly hot, and filled with the vinegary smell of sweat. A brazier crackled in one corner and torches sputtered on opposite walls. Two soldiers played cards at a heavy, scarred table, their eyes flickering towards the arrivals with faint surprise. They had seen Mayhew and Osborne in that room many times, but never at this hour. When barked orders and the clatter of boots echoed from above, the two men jumped to their feet and drew their swords.

On the far side of the room was a single door with a small barred window. Darting across the room, Mayhew peered through the bars into a dark cell. As his eyes adjusted to the gloom, he made out a figure hunched over a rough wooden bench, the hood of his cloak, as always, pulled over his head so his features were hidden. Allowed no naked flame for illumination, no drink in a bowl or goblet, only in a flask, never let beyond the secure area of the White Tower, he had been imprisoned here for twenty years. In all that time, the man had never been known to speak.

But now the light leaking through the grille revealed a subtle shift in the dark shape. It was as if the prisoner was listening to Mayhew, perhaps even considering a response.

Mayhew's deliberations were interrupted by dull bangs and clatters in the mint above their heads. The sound was muffled, but they heard raised voices, and then a low, chilling cry.

'They are in,' he said flatly. Cursing, he turned back to the room.

Osborne was pressed against one wall like a hunted animal. The four guards cast hesitant looks at Mayhew.

'Help your friends,' he ordered. 'Do whatever is in your power to protect this place. Lock the door as you leave. I will bolt it.'

Once they had gone, he slammed the bolts into place with disdain. 'This buys us a little longer, that is all,' he said. 'If they have gained access to the mint, there is no door here that will keep them out.'

'Pray,' Osborne replied, 'for that is surely the only thing that can save us now. These are not men that we face, not Spaniards, or Frenchmen, not Catholic traitors from within our own realm. These are the Devil's own agents, and they come for our souls.'

Mayhew snorted. 'Forget God, Osborne. If He even exists, He has scant regard for this vale of misery.'

Osborne recoiled as if he had been struck. 'You do not believe in the Lord?'

Mayhew's forehead was slick with sweat and his heart was

pounding. Anxiously, he pressed an ear against the door but heard nothing. 'We face a threat that stands to wipe us away as though we had never been, and if there is to be salvation, it will not come from above. It will be achieved by our own hand.'

'Then help me barricade the door,' Osborne pleaded.

With a fatalistic shrug, Mayhew set his weight against the great oak table, and with Osborne beside him they pushed it solidly against the door.

When they stood back, Mayhew paused. Faint strains of haunting pipe music reached him again, plucking at his emotions, turning him from despair to such ecstasy that he wanted to dance with wild abandon. 'That music,' he said, closing his eyes in awe.

'I hear no music!' Osborne shouted. 'You are imagining it.'

'It sounds,' Mayhew said with a faint smile, 'like the end of all things.' He turned back to the cell door where the prisoner now stood, the torchlight catching a glint beneath his hood.

'Damn your eyes!' Osborne raged. 'Return to your bench! They shall not free you!'

Unmoving, the prisoner watched them through the grille. Mayhew did not sense victory or relief in his posture, no sign that he was assured of his freedom, merely a faint curiosity at the change to the pattern that had dominated his life for so many years.

'Go back and be seated!' Osborne bellowed.

'Leave him be,' Mayhew responded as calmly as he could. 'We have a more pressing matter.' They drew their swords and faced the door.

Above their heads, they heard barked orders, wild shouts, running feet and the clash of swords. A muffled boom shook the heavy door and showered dust from the cracks and joints in the stone. Silence followed, and the cloying, sweet scent of honeysuckle grew stronger by the moment.

A random scream became a sound like the wind through the trees on a lonely moor. More noises, fragments of events that painted no understandable picture.

Breath tight in their chests, knuckles aching from the grip on their swords, the two men waited.

Something bouncing down the stone steps, coming to rest against the door with a thud.

A soft tread, then gone like a whisper in the night, followed by a long silence — a stillness — that felt as if it would never end.

Finally the unbearable quiet was broken by a rough grating as the top bolt drew back of its own accord. Eyes frozen wide, Osborne watched its inexorable progress.

The bolt at the foot of the door followed, and when that had been drawn the great tumblers of the iron lock turned until they fell into place with an ominous *clack*.

'I . . . I think I can hear the music now, Mayhew, and there are voices in it.' Osborne began to recite the Lord's Prayer.

The door creaked open a notch and then stopped. Light flickered through the gap. Not torchlight or candlelight, but with some troubling quality that Mayhew could not identify, reminding him of moonlight on the Downs. The music was louder now, and he too could hear the voices.

A sound at his back interrupted his thoughts. The prisoner's hands were on the bars of the cell door window and he had pulled back his hood for the first time that Mayhew could recall. In the ethereal light, there was an echo of the moon within the cell. The prisoner's head was enclosed by a silver skull. A mask of the finest workmanship, it gleamed so brightly that Mayhew could barely look at it. Etched on it with almost invisible black filigree were strange marks and symbols. Through the silver orbits, the prisoner's eyes hung heavily upon Mayhew, steady and unblinking.

The door into the room opened.

# CHAPTER ONE

EVEN AN AFTERNOON OF SOFT SKIN AND FULL LIPS COULD NOT take away her face. Empty wine bottles rattling on the bare boards could not drown out her voice, nor the creak of the bed and the gasps of pleasure. She was with him always.

'They say you single-handedly defeated ten of Spain's finest swordsmen on board a sinking ship in the middle of a storm,' the red-headed woman breathed in his ear as she ran her hand gently up his naked thigh.

'True.'

'And you broke into the Doge's palace in disguise and romanced the most beautiful lady in all of Venice,' the blonde woman whispered into his other ear, biting his lobe as she stroked his lower belly.

'Yes, all true.'

'And you wrestled a bear and killed it with your bare hands,' the redhead added.

He paused thoughtfully, then replied, 'Actually, that one is not true, but I think I will appropriate it none the less.'

The women both laughed. He didn't know their names, didn't really care. They would be amply rewarded, and have tales to tell of their night with the great Will Swyfte, and he would have passed a few hours in the kind of abandon that always promised more than it actually delivered.

'Your hair is so black,' the blonde one said, twirling a finger in his curls.

'Yes, like my heart.'

They laughed again at that, though he hadn't said it in particular jest. Nathaniel would have laughed too, although with more of a sardonic edge.

The redhead reached out a lazy hand to examine his clothes hanging over the back of the chair next to the bed. 'You must cut a dashing figure at court, with these finest, and most expensive, fashions.' Stretching a long leg, she traced her toes across the shiny surface of his boots.

'I heard you were a poet.' The blonde pressed herself gently against his hip. 'Will you compose a sonnet to us?'

'I was a poet. And a scholar. But that part of my life is far behind me.'

'You have exchanged it for a life of adventure,' she said, impressed. 'A fair exchange, for it has brought you riches and fame.'

Will Swyfte did not respond.

The blonde examined his bare torso, which bore the tales of the last few years in each pink slash of a rapier scar or ragged weal of torture, stories that had filtered into the consciousness of every inhabitant of the land, from Carlisle to Cornwall. He had the lithe, powerful physique of a swordsman, a good length of bone – his frame stretched from the top of the bed to the bottom – and a vitality that was evident in his clear skin and shining hazel eyes. Black curls falling to the nape of his neck added a note of sensitivity which offset the hardness carved into his features by a life lived in the shadows. Thrice-weekly visits to the barber on Lombard Street kept his cheeks clean-shaven, and his beard trimmed close to the lines of his jaw in the current fashion.

Aroused, the blonde swung her leg over him for another bout of love-making, then cursed loudly as an insistent knocking began at the door.

'Go away,' Will shouted.

The knocking continued. 'I know you are deep in doxy and sack, Master Swyfte,' came a curt, familiar voice, 'but duty calls.'

'Nat. Go away.'

The door swung open to reveal Nathaniel Colt, shorter than Will and slim, but with eyes that revealed a quick wit. He pointedly ignored the naked, rounded bodies and focused his attention directly on his master's face.

'A fine place to find a hero of the realm,' he said with sarcasm. 'A tawdry room atop a stew, stinking of fornication and spilled wine.'

'In these harsh times, every man deserves his pleasures, Nat.'

'This is England's greatest spy,' the redhead challenged. 'He has earned his comforts.'

'Yes, England's greatest spy,' Nathaniel replied acidly. 'Though I remain unconvinced of the value of a spy whose name and face are recognized by all and sundry.'

'England needs its heroes, Nat. Do not deny the people the chance to celebrate the successes of God's own nation.' With gentle hands, he eased the women away from him. 'We will continue our relaxation at another time,' he said warmly, 'for I fear my friend is determined to enforce chastity.'

His eyes communicated more than his words. The women responded with coquettish giggles as they scooped up their dresses in a half-hearted attempt to cover their modesty.

Kicking the door shut after them, Nathaniel said, 'You will catch the pox if you continue these sinful ways with the Winchester Geese.'

'The pox is not God's judgement, or all the aristocracy of England would be rotting in their breeches as they dance at court.'

'And 'twould be best if you did not let any but me hear your views on our betters.'

'Besides,' Will continued, 'Liz Longshanks's is a fine establishment. Does it not bear the mark of the Cardinal's Hat? Is the land on which this stew rests not in the blessed ownership of the Bishop of Winchester? Everything has two faces, Nat, neither good nor bad, just there. That is the way of the world, and if there is a Lord, it is His way.'

Ignoring Nathaniel's snort, Will stretched the kinks from his limbs and lazily eased out of the bed to dress, absently kicking the empty bottles against the chamber pot. Slipping on his shirt, he struggled into his tight-fitting breeches, then laced them to his black doublet. He motioned to Nathaniel to help him on with boots of the finest Spanish leather.

'And,' Will added, 'I am in good company. That master of theatre, Philip Henslowe, and his son-in-law Edward Alleyn are entertaining Liz's girls in the room below.'

'Alleyn the actor?' Nathaniel puffed as he forced the right boot up Will's calf.

'Acting goes together with whoring by tradition, as does every profession that entails holding one face to the world and another in the privacy of your room. When you cannot be yourself, it creates certain tensions that must be released.'

'You will be releasing more tensions if you do not hurry. Your Sir Francis Walsingham is on his way to Bankside, and if he finds his favoured tool deep in whores, or in his cups, he will be less than pleased.' Nathaniel threw Will his jerkin to end his frustrated searching.

'What trouble now, then? More Spanish spies plotting against our Queen? You know they fall over their own swords.'

'I am pleased to hear you take the threats against us so lightly. England is on the brink of war with Spain, the nation is torn by fears of the enemy landing on our shores at every moment, we lack adequate defences, our navy is in disarray, we are short of gunpowder, and the great Catholic powers of Europe are all eager to see us crushed and returned to the old faith, but the great Will Swyfte thinks it is just a trifle. I can rest easily now.'

'One day you will cut yourself with that tongue, Nat.'

'There is some trouble at the Tower, though I am too lowly a worm to be given any important details. No, I am only capable of dragging my master out of brothels and hostelries and keeping him one step out of the clink,' he added tartly.

'You are of great value to me, as well you know.' Finishing his dressing, Will ran a hand through his hair thoughtfully. 'The Tower, you say?'

'An attempt to steal our gold, perhaps. Or the Crown Jewels. The Spanish always look for interesting ways to undermine the nation.'

'I cannot imagine Sir Francis Walsingham venturing into Bankside for bullion or jewels.' He ensured Nathaniel didn't see his mounting sense of unease. 'Let us to the Palace of Whitehall before the Principal Secretary sullies his boots in Bankside's filth.'

A commotion outside drew Nathaniel to the small window, where he saw a sleek black carriage with a dark red awning and the gold brocade and ostrich feathers that signified it had been despatched from the palace. The chestnut horse stamped its hooves and snorted as a crowd of drunken apprentices tumbled out of the Sugar Loaf across the street to surround the carriage.

'I fear it is too late for that,' Nathaniel said.

Four mounted soldiers eased the crowd back, amid loud curses and threats but none of the violence that troubled the constables and beadles on a Saturday night. Two of the well-armed men barged into the brothel, raising angry cries from Liz Longshanks and the girls waiting in the downstairs parlour, and soon the clatter of their boots rose up the wooden stairs.

'Come, Nat, let us meet them halfway,' Will said, picking up his velvet hat.

'If I were you, I would wonder how your master Sir Francis Walsingham knows exactly which stew is your chosen hide-away this evening.'

'Sir Francis commands the greatest spy network in the world. Do you think he would not use a little of that power to keep track of his own?' Ducking to avoid the low crossbar, Will closed the door behind them and led the way down the winding, uneven stairs.

'But you are in Sir Francis's employ,' Nathaniel said.

'As the Queen's godson likes to say, "treason begets spies and spies treason". In this business, as perhaps in life itself, it is best not to trust anyone. There is always another face behind the one we see.'

'What a sad life you lead.'

'It is the life I have. No point bemoaning it.' Will's broad smile gave away nothing of his true thoughts.

The guards escorted them out into the rutted street, where a light frost now glistened across the mud. The smell of ale and woodsmoke hung heavily between the rows from the inns and stews that dominated Bankside, and the night was filled with the usual cacophony of cries, angry shouts, clamour of numerous simultaneous fights, clatter of cudgels, cheers and roars from the bull- and bear-baiting arenas, fiddle music flooding from open doors and drunken voices singing clashing songs. Every conversation was conducted at a shout.

As Will pushed through the crowd towards the carriage, he was recognized by some, and his name flickered from tongue to tongue in awed whispers. Apprentices tentatively touched his sleeve, and sultry-eyed women pursed their lips or thrust their breasts towards him, much to Nathaniel's weary disdain. But others revealed their fears about the impending invasion and offered their prayers that Will was off to protect them. Grinning, he shook hands, offered wry dismissals of the Spanish threat, and raised their spirits with enthusiastic proclamations of England's strength; he played well the part that had been given to him.

At the carriage, the curtain was drawn back to reveal a man with a fixed mouth that appeared never to have smiled, and dark, implacable eyes. Francis Walsingham was approaching sixty, but his hair and beard were still black, as were his clothes, apart from a crisp, white ruff.

'My lord,' Will said.

'Master Swyfte. We have business.' Walsingham's eyes flickered towards Nathaniel. 'Come alone.'

Will guessed the nature of the business immediately, for Nathaniel accompanied him everywhere, and had been privy to some of the great secrets of state. Will turned to him and said, 'Nat, I ask a favour of you. Go to Grace and ensure she has all she needs.'

Reading the gravity in Will's eyes, Nathaniel nodded curtly and pushed his way back through the crowd. It was in those silent moments of communication that Will valued Nathaniel most of all; more than a servant, Nathaniel had become a trusted companion, perhaps even a friend. But friends did not keep secrets from each other, and Will guarded the biggest secret of all. It ensured his path was a lonely one.

Walsingham saw the familiar signs in Will's face. 'Our knowledge and our work is a privilege,' he said in his modulated, emotionless voice.

'We have all learned to love the lick of the lash,' Will replied with a sardonic note.

Walsingham held the carriage door open and Will climbed into the heavy perfume of the court, the scent of lavender, sandalwood and rose emanating from iron containers hanging in each of the four corners of the interior. They kept the stink of the city at bay, but also served a more serious purpose that only the most learned would recognize.

Hands reached in through the open window for Will to touch. After he had offered his fingers in exchange, he drew the curtain and let his public face fall away along with his smile.

'They love you, Master Swyfte,' Walsingham said. 'As they should. Your fame reaches to all corners of England, your exploits recounted in inn and marketplace. Your heroism on behalf of Queen and country is a beacon in the long dark of the night that ensures the good men and women of our country sleep well in their beds, secure in the knowledge that they are protected by the best that England has to offer.'

'Perhaps I should become one of Marlowe's players.'

'Do you sour of the public role you must play?'

'If they knew the truth about me, there would be few flagons raised to the great Will Swyfte in Chichester and Chester.'

'There is no truth,' Walsingham replied as the carriage lurched into motion at the crack of the driver's whip. 'There are only the stories we tell ourselves. They shape our world, our minds, our hearts. And the strongest stories win the war.' The older man's piercing eyes fell upon Will from the dark depths beneath his glowering brow. 'You seem in a melancholy mood this night.'

'My revels were interrupted. Any man who had his wine and his women dragged from his grasp would be in a similar mood.'

A shadow crossed Walsingham's face. 'Be careful, William. Your love of the pleasures of this world will destroy you.'

Disapproval meant nothing to Will. He did not fear God's damnation. Mankind had been left to its own devices, and in his opinion there was too much hell around him to worry about the one that might lie beyond death.

'I understand why you immerse yourself in pleasure,' Walsingham continued. 'We all find ways to ease the burden of our knowledge. I have my God. You have your wine and your whores. Through my eyes, that is no balance, but each must find his way to carry out our work. Still, take care, William. The devils use seduction to achieve their work, and you provide them with a way through your defences.'

'As always, Sir, I am vigilant.' Will pretended to agree with Walsingham's assessment of his motivations, but in truth the Principal Secretary didn't have the slightest inkling of what drove Will, and never would. Will took some pleasure in knowing a part of him would always remain his own, however painful.

As the carriage trundled over the ruts, the carnal sounds and smells of Bankside receded. Through the window, Will noticed a light burning high up in the heart of the city across the river, the warning beacon at the top of the lightning-blasted spire of St Paul's.

'This is it, then,' he said quietly.

'Blood has been spilled. Lives have been ruined. The glass has been turned and the sands begin to run.' Walsingham's tone was grave, but it was the faint tremor in the usually carefully modulated voice that told Will of the magnitude of what they faced.

'I did not think it would be so soon. Why now?'

'You will receive answers shortly. We knew it was coming.' After a pause, he said gravely, 'William Osborne is dead. His eyes put out, his bones crushed at the foot of the White Tower.'

'So death alone was not good enough for them.' Unable to hide his contempt for their foes, Will peered out of the window at the muddy fields and cowsheds covered with a glistening sheen of frost.

'He did it to himself.'

Shocked, Will looked back into Walsingham's drawn face, and considered Osborne's last moments and what could have driven him to such a gruesome deed.

'Master Mayhew survived, though injured,' Walsingham continued. He pressed his fingertips together so it appeared he was praying.

'You have never told me why they were posted to the Tower.'

Walsingham did not reply. The carriage trundled towards London Bridge, the entrance closed along with the city's gates every night when Bow Bells sounded.

Echoing from the river's edge came the agonized cries of the prisoners chained to the posts in the mud along the banks, waiting for the tide to come in to add to their suffering. Above the gates, thirty spiked decomposing heads of traitors warned of the fate that awaited those who threatened the established order.

As the driver shouted his arrival, the gates ground open to reveal the grand, timber-framed houses of wealthy merchants on either side of the bridge. The carriage rattled through without slowing and the city's defenders hastily closed the gates behind them to seal out the night's terrors.

The closing of the gates had always signalled security, but if the city's defences had been breached there would be no security again, Will reflected.

'A weapon of tremendous power has fallen into the hands of the Enemy,' Walsingham said. 'A weapon with the power to bring about the End-Times. These are the days we feared.'

# CHAPTER TWO

IN THE NARROW, ANCIENT STREETS CLUSTERING HARD AROUND the stone bulk of the Tower of London, the dark was impenetrable, threatening, and there was a sense of relief when the carriage broke out to the green on the north of the outer wall where lanterns produced a reassuring pool of light.

Standing in ranks, soldiers from the city contingent waited to be despatched by their commander in small search parties fanning out across the capital. Drawn from the local community, they were inexperienced and unprepared, with only padded doublets instead of cuirasses, felt hats, and iron gorgets to protect their throats. But they all carried swords and daggers, and knew how to use them. In contrast, Robert Dudley, the Earl of Leicester, strutted in front of them in a light burgonet and gleaming cuirass, loose breeches reaching below the knee and sewn stockings, firing off orders. Though grey-bearded and with a growing paunch, he still carried the charisma of the man who had entranced Elizabeth and seduced many other ladies of the court.

A crowd had gathered around the perimeter of the green, sleepy-eyed men and women straggling from their homes as word spread of the disturbance at the Tower. Alighting from

36

Walsingham's carriage, Will could see anxiety grow in their faces as they watched the grim determination of the commanders directing the search parties. Fear of the impending Spanish invasion ran high, and in the feverish atmosphere of the city tempers were close to boiling over into public disturbance. Spanish spies and Catholic agitators were everywhere, plotting assassination attempts on the Queen and whipping up the unease in the inns and markets, wherever people gathered and unfounded rumours could be quickly spread.

Ignoring the crowd's calls for information about what was abroad, Walsingham guided Will to the edge of the green where a dazed and bloody Mayhew squatted.

'England's greatest spy,' Mayhew said, forming each word carefully, as he nodded to them.

'Master Mayhew. You have taken a few knocks.'

'But I am alive. And for that I am thankful.' Hesitating, he glanced at the White Tower looming up against the night sky. 'Which is more than can be said for that fool Osborne.'

'You were guarding the weapon,' Will surmised correctly.

'A weapon?' Mayhew exclaimed. Bitterness coloured his words. 'We thought it was only a man. A prisoner held in his cell for twenty years.'

Walsingham cast a cautionary glare and they both fell silent. 'There will be time for discussion in a more private forum.' His stern voice left no doubt of the gravity of the situation. 'For now, all that you need know is that a hostile group has freed a prisoner and escaped into the streets of London. The city gates remain firmly closed . . .' he paused, choosing his words carefully, 'although we do not yet know if they have some other way to flee the city. The prisoner has information vital to the security of the nation. He must be found and returned to his cell.'

'And if he is not found?' Will enquired.

'He *must* be found.'

The intensity in Walsingham's voice shocked Will. Who was the prisoner and why was he so important? How could the *weapon* he had been told of be one man?

'Your particular skills may well be needed if the prisoner is located,' Walsingham said to Will before turning to Mayhew. 'You must accompany me back to the Palace of Whitehall. I would know the detail of what occurred.'

Mayhew looked unsettled at the prospect of Walsingham's questioning, but before they could leave the Principal Secretary was summoned urgently by Leicester, who had been in intense conversation with a gesticulating commander.

'They call your name.' Mayhew nodded to the crowd. 'Your reputation has spread from those ridiculous pamphlets they sell outside St Paul's.'

'It serves a purpose,' Will replied. He was used to Mayhew's gibes and would never show the burden he carried with his created life. The Will Swyfte all England knew was an idealized hero, a symbol crafted to inspire comfort. Some of the other spies, like Mayhew, were jealous of the – in their eyes – undeserving adulation he received, but maintaining the façade was exhausting and, occasionally, dispiriting when it was so far removed from the reality of his existence. Fear, sweat, blood, doubt, betrayal, sacrifice – that was his life as he lived it. If he could, he would walk away from it in a moment.

Instead, he flashed a grin that would have been worthy of the public Will Swyfte, but it only antagonized Mayhew more.

'Would they be so full of admiration if those same pamphlets had called you assassin, murderer, corrupter, torturer, liar and deceiver?' Mayhew's mockery was edged with bitterness.

'Words mean nothing, Matthew. It is actions that count. And results.'

'Ah, yes,' Mayhew said. 'The end results justify the means. The proverb that saves us all from damnation.'

Will was troubled by Mayhew's dark mood, but he put it down to the shock of the spy's encounter with their foe. His attention was distracted by Walsingham, who had been listening intently to Leicester and now summoned Will over. 'We may have something,' he said with uncharacteristic urgency. 'Accompany Leicester, and may God go with you.'

At speed, Leicester, Will and a small search party left the lights of the green. Rats fled their lantern by the score as they made their way into the dark, reeking streets to the north, some barely wide enough for two men abreast.

'On Sir Francis Walsingham's orders, I attempted to seek the path the Enemy took from the Tower,' Leicester said, as they followed the lead of the soldier Will had seen talking animatedly to the Earl. 'They did not pass through the Traitor's Gate and back along the river, the route by which they gained access to the fortress. None of the city gates were disturbed, according to the watch. And so I despatched the search parties to the north and west.' He puffed out his chest, pleased with himself.

'You found their trail?'

'Perhaps. We shall see,' he replied, but he sounded confident.

In the dark, with only a single lantern to guide them, Will lost all sense of direction, but soon they came to a broader street guarded by four other soldiers, from what Will guessed was the original search party. They continually scanned the shadowed areas of the street with deep unease. Will understood why when he saw three men dead on the frozen ruts, their bodies torn and broken.

Kneeling to examine the corpses, Will saw that some wounds looked to have been caused by an animal, perhaps a wolf or a bear, others appeared to indicate that the victims had been thrown to the ground from a great height. The victims had been carrying cudgels and knives, most likely common street thugs who had surprised the wrong marks.

'Were these killed by the Enemy?' Leicester asked, his own eyes flickering towards the dark.

Ignoring the question, Will said, 'Three deaths in this manner would not have happened silently. Someone must have heard the commotion, perhaps even seen in which direction the Enemy departed. We should search the buildings.' Will kept a respectful tone, but he knew Leicester would always defer to him in the matter that now concerned them.

As Leicester's men moved along the street hammering on doors, bleary-eyed men and women emerged, cursing as they were roughly dragged out and questioned by the soldiers.

Will returned to the bodies, concerned by the degree of brutality. Those who had taken the prisoner had fought so fiercely to retain their prize that it must have been of the greatest importance to them. Will could only guess that the threat was truly as dire as Walsingham had suggested, although he could not yet see how one man could evoke such a response.

His thoughts were interrupted by a cry from one of Leicester's men who was struggling with an unshaven antagonist in filthy clothes snarling and spitting like an animal. Three soldiers rushed over to help knock him to the frosty street.

'He knows something,' the man's captor said, when Will came over.

'I saw nothing,' the prisoner snarled, but Will could see the lie in his furtive eyes.

'It would be in your best interests to talk,' Leicester said, but his exhortation was delivered in such a courtly manner that it was ineffectual. The man spat and tried to wrestle himself free until he was cuffed to the ground again.

Leicester turned to Will and said quietly, 'We could transport him back to the Tower. I gather Walsingham has men there who could loosen his tongue.'

'If we delay, the Enemy will be far from here and their prize with them,' Will said. 'The stakes are high, I am told. We cannot risk that.' He hesitated a moment as he examined the man's face in the lantern light and then said, 'Let me speak to him. Alone.'

'Are you sure?' Leicester hissed. 'He may be dangerous.'

'He is dangerous.' Will eyed the livid scar from a knife fight that ran from the man's left eye to his jaw. 'I am worse.'

Leicester's men manhandled the prisoner back into his dwelling. Will followed and closed the door behind him. It was a stinking hovel with little furniture, most of which looked as if it had been stolen from wealthier premises. Catching his breath, the man hunched on the floor by the hearth. As Will approached, the rogue threw himself forward ferociously. Will stepped deftly to one side and crashed a fist into his opponent's face. Blood spurted from the man's nose as he was thrown back against a chair, but it did not deter him. He pulled out a hidden knife, only to drop it when Will hit him again. As he scrambled for the blade, Will stamped his boot on the man's fingers, shattering the bones. The rogue howled in pain.

Dragging his opponent to his feet, Will threw him against the wall and pressed his own knife against his prisoner's throat. 'England stands on the brink of war. The Queen's life is threatened daily. A crisis looms for our country.' His voice was a chilling whisper, his expression dark. 'This is not the time for your games.'

'This is not a game! I dare not speak! I fear for my life!'

Will lifted the tip of his knife a notch to reveal a bead of blood, and then pressed a little deeper. 'Then fear me more.' Will's gaze was icy and unwavering. 'I will whittle you down a piece at a time – fingers, nose, ears – until you choose to speak. And you will choose. Better to speak now and save yourself unnecessary suffering.'

Once the rogue had seen the truth in Will's eyes, he nodded reluctantly.

'You saw what happened out there?' Will asked.

'I was woken by the sounds of a brawl. From my window, I saw a small group of cloaked travellers set upon by a gang of fifteen or more.'

'Cut-throats?'

The man nodded, and spat.

'Fifteen? At this time? They cannot find much regular trade in this area to justify such a number.'

'It seemed they knew the travellers would be passing this way. They lay in wait. Some of them emerged only after the battle had commenced.'

Will gave thought to this information. The spy studied the rogue's face, but his fear of Will had driven the cunning out of his features. 'Who were these cut-throats?' Will asked.

The man shook his head. 'I did not recognize them. But if they find I spoke of them they will be back for me!'

'I would think they now have more important things on their mind. What happened?'

'They surprised the travellers.' He hesitated, not sure how much he should say. 'The travellers . . .' He swallowed, looked as if he was about to be sick. 'The sound they made reminded me of hungry dogs attacking a rabbit. And I have never seen any man attack with such disregard for life. When they turned on the cut-throats, I had to look away. Wounding was not enough, nor killing. They took the cut-throats apart. I could watch no more.'

'The faces of the travellers?'

He shook his head. 'They moved too fast. I . . . I saw no weapons. Only the slaughter of three victims. It was madness! The other cut-throats fled . . .'

'And the travellers continued on their way?'

'One of them was different . . . his head glowed like the moon.'

'What do you mean?'

The man began to stutter and Will had to wait until he calmed. 'I do not know . . . it was a glimpse, no more. But his head glowed. And in the confusion, two of the cut-throats grabbed him and made good their escape into the alleys. He went with them freely, as though he had been a prisoner of the travellers.'

'And the travellers gave pursuit?'

'Once they saw he was missing . . . a minute, perhaps two, later. By then, their chances of finding him would have been poor.'

The frightened man had no further information to give. Out in the street, Will summoned Leicester away from the ears of his men.

'The prisoner was in turn taken from the Enemy by a band of rogues,' Will told him. 'Now we have two sides fighting over what my master Sir Francis Walsingham fears is the greatest danger England has ever faced. Put all your men on to the streets of London. This threat may now have gone from bad to worse.'

# CHAPTER THREE

THE SLEEK BLACK CARRIAGE RACED TOWARDS THE PALACE OF
Whitehall, a solitary ship of light sailing on the sea of darkness
washing against the western edge of London's ancient walls.
Through the carriage windows, Will Swyfte watched the
passing of London's silent streets, each jolt over frozen furrows
like the beat of a funeral drum.

Dark fields lined the winding Thames, but the lanterns
hanging from the great palace gates and along the walls
promised some comfort against the night's hidden threats.
Behind diamond-pane windows, candles glimmered across the
great halls and towers, the chapels, wings, courtyards, stores,
meeting rooms and debating chambers, and in the living
quarters for the court and its army of servants. At more than
half a mile square, it was one of the largest palaces in the world,
shaped and reshaped over three hundred years. Hard against
the Thames, it had its own wharf where barges were moored
to take the Queen along the great river, and vast warehouses
received the produce that kept the palace fed. Surrounding the
complex of buildings were a tiltyard, a bowling green, tennis
courts and formal gardens, everything necessary for royal
entertainment.

The palace looked out across London with two faces. One was the image of the sprawling, colourful, noisy pageantry of royalty, of a court permanently at play, of music and masques and arts and feasting, of romances and joys and intrigues, a tease to the senses and a home to lives lost to a whirl that always threatened to spin off its axis; the other face was that of a place of grave decisions on affairs of state, where the Queen guided a nation that permanently threatened to come apart at the seams from pressures both within and without. Whispers and fanfares, long, dark shadows and never-extinguished lights, conspiracies and open rivalries. The palace was a puzzle that had no solution.

Swyfte's carriage came to a halt under a low arch in a cobbled courtyard so small that the buildings on every side kept it swathed in gloom even during the height of midday. Few from the court even knew it existed, or guessed what took place behind the iron-studded oak door beside which two torches permanently burned. The jamb too was reinforced with iron, as was the step.

Will hammered with the haft of his knife, and was admitted into a long, windowless corridor lit by intermittent pools of lamplight. Behind him, the silent guard closed the door and slid six bolts. His echoing footsteps followed Will up one flight of a spiral staircase into the Black Gallery, a large panelled hall. Heavy curtains covered the windows. The room was lit by several lamps and a few flames danced along a charred log in the glowing ashes of the large stone fireplace.

A long oak table stood in the centre of the hall, covered with unfurled maps, and at the far end sat Mayhew, one leg over the arm of his chair. His head bound in a bloodstained cloth and his left arm in a sling, he was taking regular, deep draughts of wine from a goblet, and appeared drunk.

Will had always found Mayhew difficult. He was hard, in the manner of all spies forced to operate in a world of deceit, and had little patience for his fellows. Distracting himself from the stresses of their business with a preoccupation with the latest courtly fashions, he liked his wine, too, when he was not working, but he was a sullen, sharp-tongued drunk.

At Will's arrival, Walsingham emerged from a chamber at the rear, his features drawn. He listened intently as Will told him about the attack on the Enemy and their loss of the mysterious prisoner from the Tower, but passed no comment.

'The Queen has been informed?' Will asked once he had finished his account.

'I advised her myself. Her Majesty is fully aware of the magnitude of what lies ahead,' Walsingham replied.

'Which is more than I.' Swyfte expected a terse response, but the Principal Secretary was distracted by the sound of slamming doors and rapidly marching feet.

Through the door at the far end of the hall, two armed guards escorted a third figure, which, in the swirl of shadows and flickering light, initially appeared to be a grotesque scarecrow. Features shrouded in a deep hood, the man wore a cloak of skins the like of which Will had never seen before. Several animals had gone into the making of it – Will thought he even saw a wolf pelt in the patchwork – and at the shoulders the heads of weasels stared out with black, empty sockets. As the cloak billowed around the new arrival, ruby-coloured robes were revealed, but they were mud-splattered and worn. Scores of small animal bones hung from delicate silver chains crisscrossing his torso, rattling as he walked, so that in the half-light the space beneath his cloak resembled a snarling mouth.

The guards retreated as the new arrival strode across the room to the fire. 'I can never get warm these days.' He thrust aged hands to the flames, the fingers flexing as if he were strangling a child. Blue symbols etched on his skin reached up into the depths of his sleeves. 'It is one of the prices I pay.'

Throwing off his hood, he revealed wild silvery hair, and as he turned to face the room, fierce grey eyes ranged as if they glimpsed things in the shadows that no one else saw. Every move of his body displayed a potency that belied his sixty-odd years.

'Dee!' Mayhew visibly started in his chair, slopping wine in his lap.

Dr John Dee, the Queen's astrologer and alchemist, appeared to notice Mayhew for the first time and advanced on him threateningly, one finger extended. 'You!' he said in a ferocious tone. 'I do not like you!' As he returned to the fire, his mood changed with unnatural speed, so that it appeared another person entirely had taken his place. He cast a disinterested eye back over Mayhew, and added, 'You have not aged well,' before slipping off his cloak and throwing it over a chair.

To the outside world, Dee was a respected scholar and founding fellow of Trinity College in Cambridge. He had been an adviser and tutor to the Queen, and his *General and Rare Memorials Pertaining to the Perfect Arte of Navigation* had established a vision of an English maritime empire and defined the nation's claims upon the New World. Few knew Dee had been instrumental in helping Walsingham set up his extensive spy network, providing intelligence and guidance as well as designing many of the tools the spies used to ply their dangerous trade.

But Will had heard other rumours: that Dee had turned his back upon his studies of the natural world for black magic and scrying and attempts to commune with angels. Will had always presumed this had contributed to Dee's fall from favour.

47

For five years he had been in Central Europe; the last Will had heard of him was from Bohemia a year ago.

'No word must be uttered of Dr Dee's appearance here. He has been engaged on official business in Europe under my orders and will return there shortly,' Walsingham stressed, in full understanding of what was passing through Will's and Mayhew's minds.

'It appears there are secrets kept even from the gatekeepers to the world of secrets,' Will noted as he examined a map of the New World unfurled in the centre of the table.

'That is the way of things, Master Swyfte.' Walsingham poked the fire absently so that showers of sparks flew up the chimney.

'It was fortuitous that I arrived at this time to deliver the information I had secured.' Filled with pent-up energy that revealed no hint of fragility, Dee prowled the room, every now and then glaring and pointing into the shadowy corners. 'Events set in motion one year past are now coming to fruition. The Enemy are about to play their hand. We must divine their secrets quickly before it is too late. Time is short. The Queen's life, and indeed all of England, is at stake.'

Will studied the way Walsingham held himself as Dee moved around the room. To the unfamiliar eye, there was an unruffled indifference in the spymaster's seemingly detached state. But Will had learned over the years that Walsingham was a man whose deep thoughts were revealed in only the subtlest signs: the relaxation of the taut muscles around his mouth, the tension of a finger, a stiffness in his back. Walsingham had been forged in the crucible of the secret war they fought, and was a symbol of the toll that battle took. Though he hid it well, his mood at that moment was grim.

'Where is the Tower's prisoner now?' Dee snapped.

Once Will had spoken his piece, Mayhew added, 'The operation was well-planned and efficiently executed.' He cast a furtive eye towards Walsingham. 'When I was given my post, I was told the Tower was under special protection, even beyond the protection that keeps England safe.'

'It is!' Dee glared at Mayhew. 'And how those defences were breached remains a mystery.'

'That need not concern us now,' Walsingham interrupted. 'Master Swyfte, you are charged with finding the weapon before it can be used—'

'How can one man be a weapon?' Will asked.

Walsingham held up a hand to silence him. '— bringing it back to our control, or destroying it, whichever course is necessary. But first you must be apprised of the facts of the matter.'

Sifting through the charts on the table, he came to one of the New World and traced his finger along the coastline until he came to the name *San Juan de Ulua* in the Spanish territories, the main port for the shipment of silver back to Spain.

'A poor harbour by English standards,' Walsingham said. 'Little more than a shingle bank to protect it from the storms. Twenty years ago, on December the third 1568, John Hawkins put in for repairs to his storm-damaged trading fleet, including two of the Queen's galleons.'

'Into a Spanish port?' Mayhew said.

'Hawkins paid his taxes and more besides. In the past the Spanish had always left him alone once their coffers were full. But on this occasion their spies had told them there was more to Hawkins's visit than the repair of rigging and the patching of hulls.' Walsingham looked to Dee to continue the account.

'Since I first arrived at court, I have been advising the Queen on the threat that has faced England since the Flood,'

Dee began. He plucked insistently at the bones dangling around his waist. 'Every moment of my life has been directed towards finding adequate defences to protect the Crown, and the nation.'

'And you have succeeded. England has never been safer,' Will said. From a jug on a small table near the fire, he poured himself a goblet of sack.

'We can never rest, for the Enemy are wise as snakes, and all of their formidable resources are continually directed towards recapturing the upper hand they once enjoyed. And so, we too search for new defences, new weapons.' In Dee's eyes, the gleam of the candles suggested an inner fire raging out of control.

'My enquiries into the secrets of this world pointed me towards a weapon of immeasurable power that the Spanish were attempting to unlock in the hills not far from San Juan de Ulua.' Unhooking the skull of a rat from its chain, and a small leg bone, Dee began to tap them together rhythmically. Will got the sense it was some kind of charm to ward off evil. 'So fearful were they of the weapon that the King had insisted it be tested far away from the homeland. No one knows its true beginnings, though some say it was forged by the Devil himself, and sent out into the world to bring Hell to Earth. Death follows it wherever it goes. It brought devastation to the great rulers in the far Orient. During the Crusades it was fought over by the Knights Templar and the enemies of Christendom, laying waste, so they say, to armies.' Dee looked from one to the other, now incandescent with passion. 'With a weapon like that, England would be a fortress. The Enemy would retreat to their lakes and their underhills and their lonely moors and we would be safe. Finally.'

Dee's last word was a whisper, and it was followed by a

heavy silence, interrupted only by the crackle of the fire.

'What is the nature of the weapon?' Will asked eventually.

'And therein lies the greatest mystery of all.' Kneading his hands, Dee paced the room. A tremor ran through him. 'It is a mask, a skull rendered entirely in silver, and inscribed with secret incantations. The Devil's words, perhaps. His curse upon all mankind. A mask that must be bonded with a mortal to unleash its great power. But all we have are stories, fragments, hints.' He began to babble, plucking at his robes. 'The nature of that power is not known. All that is known for sure is that nothing can stand before it and survive.'

'So Hawkins was charged with seizing the weapon from the Spanish,' Will surmised.

'That, at least, was England's fervent hope,' replied Walsingham, taking up the story. 'While his fleet was being repaired, Hawkins, Francis Drake and a number of his most trusted crew slipped secretly into the interior. Five men gave their lives to secure the skull from the Spanish, but before Hawkins could set sail with his prize the viceroy, Don Martin Enriquez, took his fleet into the harbour and launched an attack while the English guard was down. Traitorous Spanish dogs! Hawkins, Drake and a few others escaped in two ships, but the remainder of the English party were tortured and killed by Enriquez as he attempted to discover what we knew about the skull.' Walsingham's face grew thunderous with anger, but he kept his voice steady. 'One of the few survivors, Job Hortop, told how the Spanish curs hung Hawkins's men from high posts until the blood burst from the ends of their fingers, and flogged them until the bones showed through their flesh. But not a man spoke of the skull. Heroes all.'

Nodding in agreement, Mayhew bowed his head for a moment.

'Hawkins and Drake returned in two storm-torn ships, Hawkins with just fifteen men,' Walsingham continued. 'Eighty-five stout fellows had starved to death on the journey home. But the skull was ours.'

Dee joined Walsingham back in front of the fire, a little calmer now. Slouched in his chair, Mayhew eyed the alchemist uneasily, as if he were afraid Dee would lash out at him without warning.

Will leaned against the edge of the table, sipping his sack thoughtfully. Several elements of the story puzzled him. 'Then why did we not use this great weapon to drive back the Enemy, and our other, temporal foes? How can Spain be so bold if it knows we hold such a thing?'

'Because the skull alone is not enough,' Dee snapped. 'The stories talk of three parts – a Mask, a Key and a Shield. All are necessary to use the weapon effectively, though its power can be released without direction and with great consequences for the user by the Mask and Key alone.'

Mayhew refilled his goblet with shaking hands. 'And the Key and the Shield?'

'The last twenty years have been spent in search of them, to no avail,' Walsingham replied. 'They were for a time in the hands of the Knights Templar, this we know for sure.'

'And those warrior monks fought the Enemy long before us,' Dee stressed. 'The Templars must have known of the importance of these items and hid them well.'

'Then who was the prisoner in the Tower?' Will enquired.

'Some poor Spaniard who had been cajoled into trying to make the Mask work,' Dee replied with a surprising note of sympathy. 'What he cannot have realized is that, once bonded, the Mask cannot be removed until death. You are a slave to it, as it is to you.'

Will finally understood. 'And so he was locked away in the Tower for twenty years while you attempted to find the other two parts.'

'We could not risk the weapon falling into the hands of the Enemy in case they located the Key,' Walsingham said, 'and brought devastation down upon us all.'

'But after twenty years, the Enemy chose this night to free the prisoner from the Tower. Why now, unless the Key is already in their hands?'

Walsingham and Dee exchanged a brief glance.

'What do you know?' Will pressed.

'The Enemy's plans burn slowly,' Dee replied. 'They do not see time like you or I, defined by the span of a man's life. Their minds move like the oceans, steady and powerful, over years and decades, and longer still. We knew some great scheme was in motion, just not its true nature.'

'When the defences of the nation were first put in place, all was quiet for many years.' Walsingham stood erect, his hands clasped behind his back. 'The hope grew that finally we would be safe. But then there came the strange and terrible events surrounding the execution of the traitor, Mary, Queen of Scots, one year ago, and we glimpsed the true face of the terror that was to come.'

# CHAPTER FOUR

*18 February 1587*

*All through the bitter winter's night, Robert, Earl of Launceston, had ridden, and finally in the thin grey morning light his destination came into view on the rain-soaked Midlands terrain. His fingers were frozen on the reins, his breeches sodden and mud-splattered, and his bones ached from the cold and exhaustion.*

*Launceston was hardly used to such privation, but he could not refuse his orders to be the eyes and ears of Sir Francis Walsingham at the momentous event about to take place. Though but thirty-eight years, he looked much older. His nose was long and pointed, his eyes were a steely grey, and his skin had about it a deathly pallor that many found repulsive and had made him something of an outcast at court.*

*When Walsingham called on him, it was usually to have a throat slit in the middle of the night: perhaps a Spanish agent agitating for Elizabeth's overthrow or assassination, but sometimes a minor aristocrat with unfortunate Catholic sympathies. He had forgotten how many he had despatched.*

*At least this time he would only be witnessing a death instead of instigating it.*

*Just beyond Oundle, Fotheringhay Castle rose up out of the flat,* bleak Northamptonshire landscape on the north side of the meandering River Nene. On top of the motte was the grand stone keep, surrounded by a moat, with ramparts and a ditch protecting the inner bailey where the Great Hall lay alongside some domestic buildings. The gatehouse stood on the other side of a lake crossed by a bridge. Lonely. Well defended. Perfect for what lay ahead.

As he drew towards the castle, Launceston feared he had missed the event. The execution of his Queen Elizabeth's cousin, Mary, had been scheduled for the cold dark of seven a.m. and the hour was already moving towards ten, but he could hear music from the courtyard and the distant hubbub of an excited crowd.

Encouraging his horse to find its last reserves, he pressed on through the deserted Fotheringhay village, across the bridge, and the drawbridge, and into the courtyard.

'A ghost!'

'An omen!'

When they saw his ghastly features peering from the depths of his hood, a shiver ran through the crowd of more than a hundred who had come to see history made. He hated them all, these common, witless sheep, but to be fair he disliked his own kind at the court just as much.

As they slowly realized he was but a man, they returned their attention to the grey stone bulk of the Great Hall. Some waved placards with Mary drawn as a mermaid, a crude insult suggesting she was a prostitute. She had no friends there on the outside, but the long wait had reduced the baying for blood to a harsh murmur. The atmosphere of celebration was maintained by a band of musicians, playing an air that usually accompanied the execution of witches. It could have been considered another insult, except Launceston knew that Walsingham had personally requested the music.

Dismounting, he stamped life into his frozen limbs and approached the hall where his way was barred by the captain of the sheriff's guard in breastplate and helmet, halberd raised. 'Launceston,' he said, 'here at the behest of Sir Francis Walsingham, and our Queen, God save her. I am not too late?'

'The traitor has been at her prayers for three hours,' the captain replied. 'She has read her will aloud to her servants, and prepared for them her final instructions. My men have been ordered to break down the door to her quarters if she delays much longer.'

Launceston pushed his way into the Great Hall, where two hundred of the most respected men in the land waited as witnesses. They had been carefully selected for their trustworthiness, so that whatever happened in that hall, only the official version would reach the wider population.

Though logs blazed in the stone hearth, the fire provided little cheer. Black was the abiding colour in the room – the curtains surrounding the three-foot-high platform that would provide a clear view to the audience, the high-backed chair at the rear of the dais, the kneeling cushion and the executioner's block. It was there too in the clothes and masks of the executioner and his assistant. Bulle, the London executioner, was ox-like, tall and erect, his hands calmly resting on the haft of his double-headed axe.

Launceston could feel the stew of conflicting emotions: the sense of relief that the traitorous whore's lethal machinations would finally be ended, the anxiety that they were embarking on a dangerous course into uncharted waters. Spain, France and Rome watched and waited. The killing of one of royal blood was not to be taken lightly, especially one who many Catholics believed was the rightful ruler of England. But he was in no doubt her execution was the right course of action; Mary would always be a threat to England as long as she lived.

Launceston's reverie was interrupted as a murmur ran through the assembled group, and a moment later the sheriff, carrying his white wand of office, led Mary of Scotland into the hall accompanied by the Earls of Shrewsbury and Kent. Six of her retinue followed.

*Launceston had never seen her before, but in that instant he understood why she loomed so large in the affairs of several states. She exuded a powerful licentious attraction that was most evident in the flash of her unflinching eyes. A glimpse of her red hair beneath her kerchief was made even more potent by the shimmering black velvet of her dress. She would not be hurried, her pace steady as she clutched an ivory crucifix. A gold cross hung at her neck, and a rosary at her waist.*

*Launceston was surprised to find himself captivated like every other man in the room. She was implicated in the deaths of two men, yet that only served to increase her allure; she appeared as a woman who could do anything, who could control any man. She climbed on to the platform and sat in the chair, levelling her gaze slowly and dispassionately across all present.*

*Walsingham's brother-in-law, Robert Beale, the clerk to the Privy Council, caught Launceston's eye and nodded before he began to read the warrant detailing Mary's crime of high treason by her constant conspiracies against Elizabeth, and calling for the death sentence. The Earl of Shrewsbury asked her if she understood.*

*Mary gave a slight, cruel smile, and in her eyes a cold light gleamed. 'I thank my God that He has permitted that in this hour I die for my religion,' she intoned. A hardness buried deep in her features made the words sardonic.*

*No one in the room was prepared to listen to a Catholic diatribe, and the Dean of Peterborough stood to bring her words to a close. For a long moment, Mary stared at him in silence. The room held its breath. Then a twitch near Mary's left eye, the first crack in a frozen pond. Another. And another. The hardness fell away, and Mary suddenly began to sob and wail and shout in Latin, raising her crucifix over her head.*

*Launceston had the strangest impression that he was seeing two very different women occupying the same body: this Mary was devout,*

57

believing herself to be a martyr to her religion; chaste, not threatening, or cunning. The change troubled him for it did not seem natural, and he was reminded of the warning Walsingham had given him before his departure: 'Do not trust your eyes or your heart.'

After she had pleaded passionately for England to return to the true faith, she appeared to change once more, her eyes glinting in the firelight, her lips growing cruel and hard. A faint murmur ran through the assemblage.

As Bulle the executioner knelt before her and made the traditional request that she forgive him her death, she replied loudly, 'I forgive you with all my heart, for now, I hope, you shall make an end of all my troubles.' It was a stately comment, but Mary twisted it when she added in a whisper that only a few could hear, 'But not your own.' As she looked around the room, it seemed that she was speaking about England.

No one in the audience could tear their eyes from her.

Bulle went to remove Mary's gown, but she stopped him with a smile and summoned her ladies-in-waiting to help. 'I have never put off my clothes before such a company,' she said archly.

A gasp ran through the room as her black gown fell away. A bodice and petticoats of crimson satin flared among the dark shapes. It was a bold, almost brash, statement, and in it Launceston once again saw two opposing faces: crimson was the colour of the martyr, but it was also that of carnality, and Launceston could see the effect it had upon some of those around him. Though forty-four, Mary was still a beautiful, alluring woman. She flaunted the heave of her bosom, displayed her cleavage as though she was available for more than her execution.

'Death is not the end.' She held her head brazenly, her tone mocking. 'For me. And there are worse things than death by far, as you will all come to know.'

With a flourish of her petticoats, she knelt, pausing briefly at the level of Bulle's groin and looking up at him before placing her head

58

*upon the block, her eyes open, unblinking. Launceston had the briefest sensation that she was looking directly at him. With another disturbing smile, the treacherous queen stretched out her arms to either side of her, mimicking the cross, and said with mock gravity,* 'In manus tuas, Domine.'

*Candles flickered as if a strong wind had swept into the hall, and the fire flared with a roar. One man began to mutter a prayer in a fractured voice.*

*Bulle's mask hid whatever he thought of this display, if anything. He swung the heavy woodcutter's axe high and brought it down. It thudded into the block so hard Launceston was sure he could feel the vibrations. Blood gushed across the dais. It soaked Bulle's legs, splattered across the flags, more blood than it seemed possible for one body to hold. Crying out, hands clamped on their mouths, the men at the front threw themselves back.*

*Mary made no sound, did not move, continued to stare at the assemblage, still smiling. Bracing himself, Bulle wrenched the axe free and brought it down again. The head lolled forward, hanging by one piece of gristle that Bulle quickly cut with his knife, and then it splattered into the crimson lake.*

*Murmurs of relief broke the tense silence. Men crossed themselves and prayed.*

*Stooping to pluck the queen's severed head by the hair as he had been ordered, Bulle called out,* 'God save the Queen.'

*All apart from Launceston responded,* 'Amen.'

*But Mary had played one last trick on her executioner. Her auburn hair was a wig that now flapped impotently in Bulle's hand. The close-cropped head rolled around the platform, until finally coming to a stop, the queen's dead face in full view of the assembled company.*

*His breath tight in his chest, Launceston kept his gaze upon it. The eyes swivelled in their sockets.*

'She still lives!' *a man at the front cried out. Behind him, the* assembly pressed away from the platform, united by terror. Even the sheriff's guard lowered their halberds and shied away.

Mary surveyed her persecutors, the whites of her eyes glowing like two lamps in the blood-drenched face. Her jaw worked, her lips struggling to form shapes, and then, finally, the words came out, low and harsh, like the wind in winter. 'Two queens now you have plucked in your arrogance. And the third that will fall shall be your own.'

The mouth worked silently for a moment, the eyes continuing to roll. Every man in the room was rooted, every face etched with fear.

'Against you in the shadows, the powers align,' the head of Mary continued. 'Death, disease, destruction on a scale undreamed – all these lie in your days ahead, now long-buried secrets have come to light. Soon, the thunderous tread of our marching feet. Soon, the scythe cutting you down like wheat. The shadows lengthen. Night draws in, on you and all your kind.'

Their worst fears confirmed, a mood of absolute dread descended on the assembled notables. As Mary's eyes continued to swivel, her jaw snapping, Bulle fell to his knees, his axe clattering noisily on the dais. Launceston thrust his way through the crowd until he caught Beale and shook him roughly from his daze.

'Yes, of course,' Beale stuttered, before hailing two men who waited at the back of the crowd. Launceston recognized them as two of Dr Dee's assistants. Rushing to the platform, they pulled from a leather bag a pair of cold iron tongs which one of them used to grip the severed head. It snarled and spat like a wild cat until the other assistant used a poker to ram bundles of pungent herbs into the gaping, gasping mouth. When the cavity was filled, the snarling diminished, the eyes rolled more slowly and finally stopped as the light within them died.

A furore erupted as the terrified crowd shouted for protection from God, or demanded answers, on the brink of fleeing the room in blind panic.

Pushing his way forward and leaping to the stage, Launceston called the captain of the guard. 'Lock the doors. Let none here leave!' Pale and drawn, the captain ran to the rear of the hall to carry out Launceston's order.

Grabbing Bulle's dripping axe, Launceston hammered the haft down hard on the dais, once, twice, three times, until silence fell and all eyes turned towards him.

'You will never speak of what you have seen here today, on peril of your life.' His dispassionate voice filled every corner of the crowded Great Hall, his thin, cadaverous form standing in a pool of blood a sight few there would forget. 'To speak of this abomination will be considered an act of high treason, for diminishing the defences of the realm and putting the Queen's life at risk from a frightened populace. One word and Bulle here will be your final friend. Do you heed me?'

Silence held for a moment, and then a few angry mutterings arose. Launceston's gaze fell heavily on the dissenters. The protestations drained away, and left only the noise of the crowd outside.

'Lest you misunderstand, I speak with the full authority of the Queen, and her Principal Secretary, Sir Francis Walsingham,' Launceston continued. 'Nothing must leave this room that gives succour to our enemies, or that turns determined Englishmen to trembling cowards. I ask again: do you heed my words?'

When they saw the threat in his face, no one was brave enough to deny him. Satisfied, Launceston handed the axe back to Bulle and said, 'Complete your business.' Shaking, Bulle prepared himself to collect Mary's body.

Still trembling, the Earl of Kent stood over Mary's headless corpse and stuttered in a voice so frail few could hear, 'May it please God that all the Queen's enemies be brought into this condition. This be the end of all who hate the Gospel and Her Majesty's government.'

With trembling fingers, Bulle placed the now-silent head on a pewter platter and held it up to the window three times so the baying crowd without could be sure the traitorous pretender to the throne was truly dead.

Finally, the doors were unlocked so Henry Talbot, the Earl of Shrewsbury's son, could take the official news of Mary's death to the court in London. And as he made his way through the towns and villages, proclaiming the news, beacons blazed into life across the country and church bells were rung with gusto.

At Fotheringhay, Launceston approached the nearest gentleman and held his gaze until the man saw the cold determination in Launceston's eyes. 'Do not forget my words,' Launceston intoned. He did not rest until he had done the same with every knight and gentleman in the hall. His silent threat made, he returned to Bulle and his assistant, who had wrapped Mary's body and head in a sheet. 'Take that foul thing to the chapel,' he ordered.

In the chapel, they deposited the sodden sheet next to the altar where Dee's assistants waited. Launceston observed without emotion as they stuffed the remains with more purifying herbs and with their ink-dipped fingers drew defensive sigils on the cold flesh. Everything she had worn, and everything her blood had touched, was burned.

Few beyond that Great Hall knew the truth: that terrible events had been set in motion, like the ocean, like the falling night, and that soon disaster would strike, and blood and terror would rain down on every head.

# CHAPTER FIVE

ONCE WALSINGHAM HAD FINISHED SPEAKING, SILENCE FELL across the Black Gallery, interrupted only by the crackle and spit of the fire in the hearth.

'So the Enemy have been planning the assault on the Tower for more than a year,' Mayhew said eventually.

Will now understood the depths of the worry he had seen etched into Walsingham's face earlier that night. '*Long-buried secrets have come to light,*' he repeated. 'Then we must assume they have the Key or Shield, or both, and are now able to use the weapon.'

'We have spent the last twelve months attempting to prepare for the inevitable,' Walsingham said. 'Listening in the long dark for the first approaching footstep, watching for the shadow on the horizon, every hour, every minute, vigilant.'

'And now all our souls are at risk,' Mayhew said. Upending the wine flask, he was disgusted to see it was empty. 'So that traitorous witch Mary was in the grip of the Enemy. Is no one safe from their sly control? How much of the misery she caused was down to her, and how much to whatever rode her?'

'We will never know.' His mood grim, Walsingham waved a

dismissive hand. 'The past matters little. We must now concern ourselves with the desperate situation that unfolds.'

'It is the nature of these things that the waiting seems to go on for ever and then, suddenly, there is no time at all when the wave engulfs us.' Dee paced the room, running his fingers through his wild hair. 'Yet fortune has given us a gift. The Enemy has lost the weapon almost as soon as it fell into their hands.'

'For now. But they will be scouring London, even as we do. If time has been bought for us, it will not be long,' Will said. With one hand on the mantelpiece as he peered into the embers, he turned over Walsingham's account of Mary's execution. 'You said the thing in Mary's head spoke of *two queens* plucked in arrogance.'

'Elizabeth's father provided ample candidates,' Mayhew said. 'That is of little import. Of more concern are the actions of the Catholic sympathizers and our enemies across the water. Will Spain seize upon our distraction by this crisis to launch an attack upon England?'

'Philip of Spain is determined to destroy us at all costs and will use any opportunity that arises,' Walsingham replied. 'He makes a great play of English *heresy* for turning away from his Catholic faith, but his hatred is as much about gold. He is heartily sick of our attacks on his ships, and our constant forays into the New World, the source of all his riches.'

'But war can still be averted?' Mayhew said hopefully.

Walsingham gave a derisive snort. 'The spineless fools at court who nag Elizabeth believe so. They encourage her in peace negotiations that drag on and on. In the face of all reason, our Lord Treasurer, Burghley, is convinced that peace will continue. He will be advocating gentle negotiation when the Spanish are hammering on his door. Leicester opposes him as much as possible, but if Burghley wins the Queen's ear, all is lost.'

'War was inevitable when Elizabeth signed the treaty to defend the Dutch against any further Spanish demands upon their territories. Philip saw it as a declaration of war on Spain.' Will looked at each of the others in turn as he spoke.

'Now the Duke of Parma sits across the Channel with seventeen thousand men, waiting for the moment to invade England. And in Spain, we hear Philip amasses a great fleet, and plots and plans,' Walsingham continued. 'Be under no illusion, the invasion *will* come. It is only a matter of when. And the Enemy has chosen this moment to assail us from within. Destabilized, distracted, we are ripe for an attack.'

'If Spain and the Catholic sympathizers are in league with the Enemy,' Mayhew spat, 'we will be torn apart by these threats coming from all directions.'

'No, this business is both greater and more cunning than that.' Will turned back to the cluttered table, thinking. 'In this room, we know there is a worse threat than Catholics and Spain. Our differences with them may seem great, but they are meagre compared to the gulf between us and the Enemy, whose manipulations set brother against brother when we should be shoulder to shoulder. Religious arguments mean nothing in the face of the threat that stands before us.'

Chewing his dirty fingernails, Dee nodded in agreement, but Mayhew cared little, and Walsingham was steadfast in the hatred of Catholics that had been embedded in him since his early days at the defiantly Protestant King's College in Cambridge.

'There are threats and there are threats. Some greater and some lesser, but threats none the less, and we shall use whatever is at our disposal to defeat them.' Walsingham's voice was stripped of all emotion and all the more chilling for it. 'Barely a day passes without some Catholic plot on Elizabeth's life coming to light. We resist them resolutely. We listen. We watch. We extract information from those who know. And when we are ready we act, quickly, and brutally, where necessary.'

An entire world lay behind Walsingham's words, and Will fully understood its gravity. Elizabeth had chosen her spymaster well. Walsingham was not hampered by morals in pursuit of his aims; he believed he could not afford to be so restricted. The tools of his trade were not only ciphers, secret writing, double and triple agents, but also bribery, forgery, blackmail, extortion and torture. Sometimes, in unguarded moments, the cost was visible in his eyes.

'This war with our long-standing Enemy has blown cold for many years, but if it has now turned hot, we must do what we always do: trap and eradicate them at every level,' he continued. Will watched the evidence of Walsingham's cold, monstrous drive and wondered what had made him that way. 'We must move quickly, and find the Silver Skull before the Enemy.' Walsingham turned to Will and said, 'Master Swyfte, all of England's resources are at your disposal. Do what you will, but keep me informed at every step. Take Mayhew here, and Launceston.' He considered his options and added, 'Take Tom Miller as well, a stout fellow, if simple, who has just joined our ranks. His strength will be a great boon to you. He has yet to be inducted in the ways of the Enemy, so take care in bringing him to understanding.'

Will attempted to hide his annoyance. Putting an agent into the field without time to educate him in the true nature of the Enemy was cruel and dangerous. More than one spy had been driven out of their wits and into Bedlam after the heat of such an encounter.

'And John Carpenter,' Walsingham concluded. Will flinched. 'I know there has been business between the two of you, but you must put it behind you for the sake of England, and our Queen.'

'I would prefer Kit.'

'Marlowe is your good friend and true, but he wrestles with his own demons and they will be the end of him. We need a steady course in this matter.'

Will could see Walsingham's mind would not be changed. He turned to Dee and asked, 'Have you developed any new tricks that would aid me?'

'Pah! Tricks, you say!' The doctor's eyes flared, and he plucked at the rattling bones with barely restrained anger. 'I have a parcel of powder which explodes in a flash of light and heat and smoke when exposed to the air. A new cipher that even the Enemy could not break. And a few other things that will make your life more interesting, I do not doubt. I will present them to you once I have apprised Sir Francis Walsingham of my findings in Bohemia.'

Will wondered what matter Dee could be involved in that was more pressing than the search for the Silver Skull. But the thought passed quickly; the burden he had been given was large and it would take all his abilities to shoulder it.

'There are many questions here,' he said. Leaning against the table, he folded his arms and reflected. 'Who took the prisoner from the Enemy and why? Were they truly rogues, or were they Spanish spies, and, indeed, is the Silver Skull now in the hands of a different enemy?'

'And can we possibly find one man in a teeming city before the Enemy reaches him first?' Mayhew added sourly.

'Let us hear no more talk like that, Master Mayhew,' Will said. 'Time is short and we all have a part to play.' As Mayhew grunted and lurched to his feet, Will turned to Walsingham. 'Fearful that their hard-won prize might slip through their fingers, the Enemy will be at their most dangerous at this time.'

The log in the hearth cracked and flared into life, casting a ruddy glow across Walsingham's face. 'The next few hours will decide if we march towards Hell or remain triumphant,' he replied. 'Let nothing stand in your way, Master Swyfte. God speed.'

# CHAPTER SIX

WRAPPED IN A HEAVY WOOLLEN CLOAK AGAINST THE CHILL, Grace Seldon waited in the shadowy courtyard outside the Black Gallery. Whatever danger lay nearby, it would not deter her; it would *never* deter her. Surely Will Swyfte understood that by now.

Beside her, Nathaniel shifted anxiously. 'You will have me whipped and my wages docked for this, Grace. Go back to your room before you are seen.'

Easing off her hood, she tied back her chestnut ringlets with a blue ribbon, but her fumbling fingers only emphasized her irritation. 'Because I have a slender frame and a face that does not curdle cream, every man treats me like a delicate treasure to be protected at all times.'

'Will is only concerned—'

'Will is always concerned for me!' she snapped. 'We have both seen our fair share of tragedy and are stronger for it. I will not swoon at the first sign of threat.'

Nathaniel continued to look uncomfortable at her refusal to comply with the order he had been given.

'Besides,' she continued, 'you know as well as I that Will would no more punish you than hurt a dog.'

'I thank you for putting me on a level with a cur, Mistress Seldon,' Nat said tartly, 'but if I am not whipped I will have to endure a day of his lectures and I do not know which I prefer.'

'You are right there,' she muttered to herself, adding: 'If he sent you to ensure I was well cared for, then it is because there is great danger.'

'Yes, such is the nature of his business,' Nathaniel sighed. 'You make my work very difficult, Grace.'

As Will emerged from the Black Gallery alongside a man who seemed unsteady on his feet, Nathaniel tried to restrain Grace, but she slipped past him. Half stumbling in her haste, her hands went to Will's chest, and he caught her at the waist. Embarrassed, they both backed off a step.

'Grace.' His eyes flickered towards Nathaniel, who pretended to scrub a spot from his shirt.

'You would deny me the opportunity to wish you well as you embark on one of your dangerous missions?' she said sharply.

'This is not the time for one of our lively debates, Grace.'

'Did you think I would lock myself away because you told me to?'

He sighed. 'No, Grace. You would never do anything I told you to. I know that.' She saw warmth in his eyes, but it was kept tightly under control.

'Then?'

'These are dangerous times. I would see you safe, that is all.'

'From whom?'

'From yourself, mostly,' he said with exasperation. 'Your capacity for recklessness exceeds that of any person I know.'

'You say reckless. I say fearless. I am not afraid. Of anything.'

'As always, this conversation goes nowhere, and I have urgent matters that require my attention.'

Calming herself, she chose the words she knew would stop him walking away. 'I could not say farewell to Jenny and I have regretted it ever since. I will not be denied this by you.'

He hesitated, softened. 'I am not your sister.'

In the subtle attenuation of his smile, she recognized the ghost of his true feelings. 'You wear your masks well,' she whispered so no one else could hear, 'but I know the true you, as you know me. You are not my sister. Because you live still, and Jenny is dead—'

The blaze in his eyes scared her a little, but she persevered.

'Dead, Will. I spent long months yearning for answers, like you, but I have slowly come to an accommodation. I still need to know who took her, and why, and then I can rest. Then we both can. On that warm, starlit night in Arden, by the churchyard, with the owls hooting and the bats flitting, you told me you had been given the tools to discover the truth, and you vowed to me that the answers we both sought would be forthcoming. I ask now, though you always say one thing with your mouth and another with your eyes: is this mission the one that will allow us to find peace?'

'No.' A moment, then: 'Perhaps.' Frustration laced his words. 'Jenny is in my every thought and every deed, Grace, but these things are not as easy as you would believe. Now . . .'

She caught his arm to stop him leaving, and though he feigned irritation she could see his affection, though whether it was for her or for her long-gone sister she did not know. The other man – she suspected he must be drunk – watched their encounter intently, and then, out of embarrassment or boredom, dragged open the carriage door and lurched inside.

'Let me accompany you,' she insisted.

'And do what?' Will said incredulously. 'Carry my sword? Distract my opponent so I can more easily strike the killing blow?' His mockery was faint, but still she felt her cheeks redden. 'No, Grace,' he continued, softening, 'you must stay from harm's way.'

'You wish to protect me because you could not protect my sister,' she said defiantly.

'I could say the same of you.' He gave a confident smile, a slight bow, and walked towards the carriage.

'A fine pair we are,' she called after him, flushed with the heat of her frustration. 'Both trapped in the snare of a dead woman and neither able to put it right.'

As Will climbed into the carriage without looking back, Nathaniel hurried over. 'Go back to your room, Grace,' he implored. 'I must depart with Will. These times are too dangerous to be abroad at night, even in the Palace of Whitehall.'

He climbed into the carriage and soon the iron-clad wheels were rattling across the cobbles. Grace watched it go with mounting defiance. She would never go as Jenny went. Nor would she see Will go the same way, if it was in her power to prevent it.

# CHAPTER SEVEN

TO SOME, IT APPEARED A MONUMENT TO THE GLOBE-SPANNING power of the Spanish empire. Others saw it as a tribute to the power of God, or a tomb, or a menacing fortress, or one man's grand folly. In truth, San Lorenzo de El Escorial, twenty-eight miles north-west of the Spanish capital of Madrid, was all of them and more. Within the vast mountain of worked stone, its vertiginous walls punctuated by more than twelve thousand windows, its seven towers reaching to the heavens, lay both a palace and a monastery, temporal and ecclesiastical power in perfect union.

Cold, empty, echoing, the sprawling palace was a perfectly sombre reflection of the man who directed its construction: King Philip II. At a cost of three and a half million ducats, it had taken twenty-one years to build, with a floor plan that, too, had a secret face. Many believed its design was chosen in honour of its patron, Saint Laurence, but the truth was that it had been constructed to echo the Temple of Solomon, as described by the historian Flavius Josephus.

Now Philip retreated behind its forbidding walls, cutting himself off from advisers and family so that his relationship with his God could be so much more potent. Thirty-two years on the throne, his empire had spread across every continent. A distant, deeply introspective man who rarely spoke, Philip preferred to dress in black to show his contempt for material things. Always extremely devout, as the years passed he had listened so intently for God's voice that he had become ripe for direction from much closer quarters than Heaven.

Inside the monastic palace, Spain's riches from the New World and the Indies had also provided the means to acquire great works of art, the finest furniture, and the most lavish building materials – rose coral, marble, jasper, alabaster. Yet the long corridors and lofty halls rang with an abiding silence that was only intermittently interrupted by the soft, steady step of cowled monks or the deliberate murmur of priests. No hands of friends touched Philip, no warm words eased his cold, ascetic thoughts.

He lived, and was surely dying slowly, for his faith. His extensive library, which could have held the greatest literature of civilization, contained only religious works. The great church at the heart of El Escorial was second only to St Peter's in Rome. In the Royal Basilica, the reliquary held seven thousand relics, not just shards of bone, but the heads and entire bodies of saints, magic symbols designed to ward off the evils of the world and point the way along the road to salvation.

As dawn broke across the mountains, Philip could be found where he now spent so much of his day: in the basilica, kneeling in prayer before the altar. In his soft, gentle face, his dark eyes revealed only lonely depths. At sixty-one, his arthritic joints ached, but he forced himself to continue his devotions before struggling to the hidden door beside the altar that led to his private rooms.

The sound of no other feet echoed here. It was the King's sanctuary from the rigours of the world, austere, chill, dominated by an office where he spent the rest of each day and much of the night, signing the constant stream of papers from his government and planning the great enterprise that had dominated his thoughts so completely in recent times. The suite was silent and still and empty.

Padding across the cold flags to stand before the fire blazing in the hearth, he smelled her before he saw her. That uncanny heady aroma of sharp lime and perfumed cardamom, with a hint of Moorish spice just beneath. Heat rose instantly in his belly. He felt embarrassed by his body's earthly desire, which suggested troubling unexplored depths of his mind that he always thought well sealed. How did she do that to him, when no one else in the known world could have stimulated him?

'Come out,' he whispered, his voice catching in his throat.

As he turned, he caught a momentary reflection in the ornate mirror she had had installed on the wall: a hollow-cheeked, bone-white face with red-rimmed eyes glaring at him with such malignancy he was overcome with terror. But it was gone in the blink of an eye, an illusion created, he knew, by his troubled mind.

Light shimmering off the glass blinded him, and when his vision cleared she stood before him. She seemed ageless, with a beauty that burned like the sun and was as mysterious as the moon, dark brown hair cascading over bare shoulders, her eyes filled with a promise that made him gasp. She wore only a thin dress tied just below the curve of her breasts, clinging to her hips, her thighs, as she moved, barefoot, towards him.

'Malantha,' he said. 'I would not wish for you to be found here. It would not be seemly.'

'No one will ever find me here. I am yours alone.' Her unblinking eyes held him captive.

And when her cool fingers touched his cheek, he jolted as if burned. She continued running her hands up into his hair, and then down the nape of his neck, her eyes all the while never leaving his, never blinking. Deep inside, at that moment lost to all conscious thought, he hated what she did to him, but could not spurn her. Later he would be filled with so much revulsion and self-loathing that he would make himself vomit.

'You do not want me here?' she asked, knowing the answer.

'You know that I do. Since you came into my life, you have haunted my every waking hour, my every dream. I hear your honeyed words when you are not with me. I feel your hand in mine when you are not at my side. How could I not want you here?'

She appeared to sense the furious competition of desire and loathing, but all it brought was the faintest smile. She leaned in close, her warm breath playing against his ear. 'The enterprise of England. How goes it?'

'The monetary cost is high, but I have support for my God-given endeavour from across Europe. Emperor Rudolf has agreed to send troops, although no coin. The Doge stands beside us, though may not say so publicly. The English continue with their peace negotiations, blind to our true intentions.'

'And the armada?'

Now it was Philip's turn to smile. 'Formidable. Our success is assured. One hundred and thirty ships. Thirty thousand men. Near three thousand cannon.'

'And England will be defeated?'

'Broken on the rack of Spanish might. The English will attack our ships no more, nor steal our gold and silver, and the true religion will return to that land. It did not have to be this way. If Mary had not been executed. If Elizabeth had married me—'

Malantha pressed a long, pale finger to his lips. 'If Elizabeth had married you, you would not be here with me.'

'Yes . . . yes . . .' he stuttered. Her scent, her beauty, filled his senses, speaking of other lands far from Spain.

'The English are devils,' she breathed in his ear. 'They cannot be trusted. They think themselves higher than all others, but there are things that are higher by far.'

'Yes. God.'

She smiled.

'I will do all in my power to break the English.'

He was happy that his words pleased her. Releasing the tie on her gown, she let it fall from her, presenting her body to him for a moment before pushing him back to a divan and climbing astride him. Her skin was luminous, her scent heady. Pressing her breasts against his chest, she kissed him as no one else had, deeply and slowly, with the subtle probing of her tongue. Her groin gently undulated against his, up and down, up and down. Every sensation was so potent, his thoughts broke up and he was cast adrift in the moment.

He perceived only flashes – of her removing his clothes, working down his body with her lips, using her hands and her mouth, and then climbing astride him once more to slide him inside her – before he was overwhelmed.

When he awoke later, Philip II, King of Spain, was alone, as he always was in the aftermath, but it seemed fragments of memory had mixed with his dreams. He thought he recalled Malantha standing naked in front of the ornate mirror, and speaking to it. The mirror was smoky, but reflected flashes of sunlight.

And she was saying, 'All proceeds well. Spain readies its forces. The pieces move into place.'

And then another voice came back, decadent and sly. It

spoke briefly about something being lost and something else being found, and another close to being found.

Though Malantha used the term *brother*, her voice was laced with the lewdness, the desire he knew so well. 'And how is life in the night-dark city, Cavillex?' she enquired.

'Here, they call us the Unseelie Court,' the voice came back.

'Unseelie?'

'Unholy,' the voice explained.

Her laughter filled his senses and it all slipped away from him once again.

A dream, nothing more.

# CHAPTER EIGHT

'THESE ARE DARK TIMES.' STILL SUFFERING THE EFFECTS OF drink, Mayhew stared out of the carriage window with a dazed expression that revealed a depth of troubles. The White Tower was silhouetted against the rosy sky, the first rays of the sun gleaming across the rooftops as London slowly stirred.

'Take charge of your tongue, Master Mayhew,' Will cautioned. 'A man in his cups says the strangest things.'

Mayhew flashed Will an apologetic look for speaking out of turn with Nathaniel in the carriage.

'Worry not about me,' Nat said tartly. 'I have no interest in the affairs of Sir Francis Walsingham's great men.'

Returning his gaze to the wakening street, Mayhew sniffed. 'You should watch your servant. A sharp tongue mixed with an independent mind is a dangerous flaw.'

'Nat keeps me honest, Matthew, and I will hear no word against him,' Will said as he watched the first market traders spill on to the street, bleary-eyed and yawning. Soon the streets would be crowded with all the noisy life of London, the parading gentlemen, the apprentices, the cutpurses and coney-catchers, the women seeking the day's food for the family pot, and the merchants eager to complete a sale, all heading for

Cheapside, the broadest of the capital's thoroughfares, where the market sprawled along the centre from the Carfax to St Paul's. There it was possible to buy produce from all over London and the many rapidly growing villages just beyond the city walls: pudding pies from Pimlico and bread from Holloway or Stratford, as well as root vegetables and sweet cakes, horses and hunting dogs, peacocks and apes from the foreign traders.

The danger was apparent with each face Will saw. London was the boom town of Europe. The population had more than doubled since Elizabeth came to the throne, and the city elders struggled to cope with the problems caused by the influx: the over-crowding, the crime, the beggars, the filth, the disease. Larger now than the great cities of Bristol and Norwich, London was eating up all the settlements that lay outside the old walls. In that thick, seething mass of life, an emboldened Enemy could bring death on a grand scale.

*What was the nature of the missing weapon? Was it truly as dangerous as Walsingham feared?*

'You have your instructions?' he asked, turning back to Mayhew.

'I will wait amongst the rabble on Cheapside for the others to join me while you attend your assignation. We question the market traders about the gangs who prey on the innocent near the Tower, and meet again at midday to exchange what we have learned.'

'Very good, Master Mayhew. I like a man whose brain stays sharp even after wine.'

Mayhew didn't attempt to hide his displeasure. As Will stretched an arm out of the window and banged a hand on the roof of the carriage, the driver brought the horses to a halt with a loud, 'Hey, and steady there!'

Half stumbling, Mayhew clambered out of the carriage without a backward glance and wove his way towards the shade at the side of the street.

'Master Mayhew has a choleric disposition,' Nathaniel noted. 'And he likes his wine even more than you.'

'Life is a constant struggle between virtue and vice, Nat. We cannot all be as worthy as you. Master Mayhew has served the Queen well across the years, but what has been asked of him has taken its toll. Do not judge him too harshly.'

Will banged the carriage roof again and the wheels lurched into motion. After a pause, Nathaniel enquired with an air of studied disinterest, 'This business is truly pressing?'

'You know I cannot say more.'

'Yes. Better I remain in ignorance than be dragged into duplicitous affairs that could cost me my sanity or my life. The view from the poles above the gatehouse tower at London Bridge is not one to which I aspire.' He paused. 'But still. An assistant's work is better carried out with a little light.'

'You do your job well enough, Nat. I have no complaints. I would not add to your burdens.'

Nathaniel shrugged, but Will could see the curiosity burning inside him. It was difficult to move so close to such a secret world without peering too deeply into the shadows; it was an urge Will understood well and had learned to control within himself. But to know more about Will's work truly would threaten both Nat's life and his sanity. The less he knew, the safer he would be. In his ignorance, Nathaniel did not understand, of course. He thought – or so Will hoped – that the only threat was from a few Spanish agents, and for all his barbed comments he remained an obedient assistant, and had worked much harder than Will had anticipated when he promised Nathaniel's father that he would employ him, and keep him well.

Their carriage rattled north away from the cobbles of Cheapside into the rutted, narrow tracks that formed the majority of London's streets. Soon the choking stink of the city swept in through the open windows, the dung and the rotting vegetables and the household waste deposited morning, midday and night from doors and windows of the ramshackle and rundown houses and hovels into the narrow thoroughfares. Even the mayor's order to burn each home's rubbish three times a week appeared to have little effect. Nathaniel coughed and spluttered and clutched a kerchief to his mouth and nose, futilely banging the pomanders hanging within the carriage to try to extricate more scent.

By the time they arrived at Bishopsgate it was growing warmer. The Bull Inn was a three-storey building, the stone black with the soot of London's fires, its overhanging eaves sagging and in need of repair. Rows of tiny, diamond-paned windows looked out from dark, low-ceilinged rooms.

Without breaking its pace, the carriage jolted through the arch to the cobbled yard at the rear of the inn where plays were regularly performed. In one corner, members of the resident acting troupe intoned loudly and performed tumbles, pausing now and then to rub their bleary eyes or heads aching from the night's drinking. A pair of carpenters worked lazily at a temporary trestled stage.

Will instructed Nathaniel to wait with the carriage, and, after a brief exchange with the vintner, made his way to a small back room set aside for 'private affairs', usually gambling or the plotting of some criminal activity or other. Smelling of stale beer and sweat, it was uncomfortably warm. While two men snored loudly in drunken sleep on the floor, a third wrote at a table.

Dark eyes that appeared old and sad stared out of a young, pale face framed by long black hair. A small moustache and close-clipped chin-hair attempted to give him some appearance of maturity, but his sensitive face still made him seem much younger than his twenty-four years.

'Kit,' Will said. 'I thought I might find you hiding here.'

Lost to his imagination, Christopher Marlowe blinked blankly until his thoughts returned to the room and he recognized Will. He smiled shyly. 'Will, good friend. I am currently not in my lord Walsingham's favour and thought it best to lie low to avoid his wrath. He has a cold face, but a terrible fire within.'

'As have we all, Kit. For good reason.'

Understanding, Marlowe nodded and motioned to a stool. 'Shall we drink as we did at Corpus Christi on that night when you inducted me into this business of fools and knaves?' He caught himself. 'I am sorry, Will. My bitterness sometimes gets the better of me. This is not the life that was promised me, and there is no going back, but you have always been good to me.'

'No apologies are necessary, Kit.' Tossing his cap on to the table, Will stripped off his cloak with a flourish and pulled up a stool. Pain lay just beneath the surface of Marlowe's face and Will knew he was complicit in embedding it there. 'We are all lost souls.'

'True enough. Beer, then. Or wine? Some breakfast?' Marlowe laid down his quill and pushed his beer-spattered work to one side.

'Information is all I require.'

Marlowe sighed. 'Work, then. One day we shall drink like

brothers. I see from your face this is a grave matter.'

'The gravest. All England is at stake.'

'The Spanish. Those stories of a fleet of warships, an invasion planned—'

Will shook his head. 'The true Enemy.'

'Ah.' Marlowe's eyes fell and for a moment he pretended to arrange his work materials. 'My tale of Tamburlaine the Second is all but done. I have drained myself with these stories of endless war and strife.' He smiled. 'What is it, coz?'

Will checked they would not be overheard, and then said in hushed tones, 'Last night, from the Tower, the Enemy stole a magical item whose origins are lost to ages past – a silver skull, unmovably attached now to an unwitting victim.'

Filled with the intellectual curiosity that Will admired so much, Marlowe leaned across the table. 'I have never heard of such a thing.'

'It is one of the mysteries of antiquity, a great weapon once guarded by the Templar Knights.' Will smiled. 'Sir Francis Walsingham and our ally Dr Dee saw fit to keep knowledge of it well away from ones such as you and I.'

'And that is why they are our masters. For sure, I would only have sold it for beer and a night of pleasure. And what is the purpose of this Silver Skull?'

'Our betters have spent nigh on two decades trying to divine that very thing, but its mysteries remain untouched,' Will said with a note of regret.

'Yet if the Enemy has need of it, it must be a great threat to our well-being indeed,' Marlowe said.

Will nodded slowly. 'Within a short time of taking the Skull, the Enemy lost it. Stolen by a gang of thieves and spirited away, like a shiny bauble snatched by magpies. The Enemy searches for it even as we speak, and so do we. It would seem whosoever finds it first wins everything.'

'And so this thing is an Act of God, waiting to be unleashed on the dumb populace.'

'Our Sir Francis Walsingham and Dee fear the Enemy know the key to its use. But more, who is to say one of the rogues who took it could not stumble across it by accident and unleash death in the twinkling of an eye? All our lives hang by a thread while this Skull remains beyond our grasp.'

Leaning back against the smoke-stained wall, Marlowe swung one long, scuffed boot of Spanish leather on to a stool and pondered. 'I have many questions, about how the Enemy plan to use the Skull when England's defences against them still stand, and the timing of this act—'

'And I have no answers. There is mystery here. But we are out of time.' As one of the drunken men on the floor stirred, Will leaned across the table and lowered his voice. 'You are our eyes and ears in the underworld, Kit. You know of things that lie far beneath the notice of men of good standing. Think. Who would have the Skull? Where would it be now?'

The brightness faded from Marlowe's face. 'So Walsingham did not send you.'

'No.'

'Even in this hour of need he cannot bring himself to deal with me.' A flicker of fear rose in his eyes. 'He does not trust me, Will. And in our world what is not trusted often meets a bloody end.'

'It will pass, Kit.'

Angrily, Marlowe put the toe of his boot under the stool and flicked it across the room so it crashed against the opposite wall. The man who had stirred looked up with bloodshot eyes.

'Out!' Marlowe yelled at him. 'Fetch me the ordinary! I am hungry.' Once the man had lurched away to ask the vintner for the Bull's daily stew, Marlowe rounded on Will. 'As children we walked in summer fields and dreamed of the wonders that lay ahead. Yet we sold those dreams, and our lives, to defend England against something which can never be defeated, which waits, quiet and patient and still, until we let our guard slip, as it always will, and then we are torn apart in a gale of knives and teeth, unmourned even by our own. Mistrusted by our own! Look at what this business has made us, Will! See what we have become! We cannot trust those closest to us. We fear death from enemy and friend alike. We are alone, waiting for that moment when it all ends. Where is the comfort in this world?'

'There is little for ones such as us, Kit. We live our lives so others can sleep soundly in their beds. You know that.' Will watched the hopelessness play out across his friend's face and it troubled him. He had seen it many times before on others and in every case it ended the same way, in an insidious despair that found its roots in the very nature of their Enemy, spreading like bindweed until every part of a person was choked by it. He had seen men kill themselves. Others throw themselves into danger with no care for their lives, and revelling when they met their end. And yet more simply setting in motion their own demise through their quiet actions. 'If this matter were not so grave I would not have troubled you, Kit. Time away from this business – a lost week or more in one of your dens of iniquity – will help you regain your equilibrium.'

'Yes, of course, Will,' Marlowe lied. 'I am tired, that is all. Forgive me.' He took a deep breath and let his head nod to his chest as if he could no longer support its weight. His face was drawn and the skin appeared to have grown more ashen during the time Will had sat with him.

Though he feared the repercussions, Will pressed his friend for information. Marlowe was right: their business allowed little softness or compassion. The war was everything, and everyone was a victim.

Marlowe ran a hand through his hair as he steadied himself. 'A gang of rogues near the Tower overnight? No. There are no gulls there for them to prey upon. They would be near the stews or ordinaries, the baiting rings and taverns and theatres.'

'They came upon the Enemy as they slipped away.'

Marlowe shook his head; it still did not make sense to him. 'The villains of London are an army, with generals and troops who march to order and follow detailed plans and strategy. They do not wait for their next meal, or they would starve.'

'You are saying they knew the Enemy would be passing by?'

'Perhaps. As we have spies everywhere, so do those rogues. A guard at the Tower, sending word as the Enemy took their moment. A silver skull would be a valuable prize, even if they did not know its true worth. I pity the poor sod who wore it, for they will have cut it free by now.' Marlowe made a slitting motion across his throat. 'Who was he?'

'I do not know. This was not a random occurrence, then.'

Marlowe shook his head slowly.

'Then who is the general? Who could place an agent in the Tower?'

'The gangs of London are countries within a country. They have their own spies, yes, and their own forces to keep them secure. They even have their own land where a criminal can find refuge, and no one – not even the Queen's own men – can touch them. In Damnation Alley and the Bermudas and

Devil's Gap. By the brick kilns in Islington, and Newington Butts and Alsatia. Cutpurses and cut-throats, pickpockets and tricksters, coney-catchers and head-breakers. Who would dare such an act? Why, all of them, Will.'

Glancing through the window to where Nathaniel waited by the carriage, Will saw the inn yard now bright as the sun moved high in the sky. 'Time is short, Kit. You run with these rogues. Give me a name. If you were to point a finger at a likely culprit, who would it be?'

His shoulders hunched as if carrying a great weight, Marlowe thought for a moment and then said, 'There is one they call the King of Cutpurses. Laurence Pickering. Every week he holds a gathering at his house in Kent Street for all the heads of the London gangs, where they exchange information and drink and carouse with doxies. If Pickering is not behind this, he would know who was.'

'I have not heard of this man.'

'Few have. He has faces behind faces, and no one is quite sure which one is the real one, or if that is his true name. But I know one thing – he is the cousin of Bulle, the Tyburn hangman. Bulle himself admitted it when he was cupshotten one night.'

'Bulle?'

Marlowe raised an eyebrow at Will's sudden interest. 'Why is that brute important?'

Will reflected on Walsingham's account of the execution of Mary, Queen of Scots, and the events that followed. Bulle hacking away at the neck of Mary was as clear in his mind as if he had been there. 'Because there are no random occurrences in this world, Kit. And Kent Street is where I should find this Pickering?'

'No. That is just one of the fronts he presents to the world. If

88

he has something of value, it will be in one of the fortresses his kind have built for themselves, secure from any lawful pursuit.' Marlowe turned over the possibilities and then announced, 'Alsatia, below the west end of Fleet Street, next to the Temple. There is no safer place in London for the debauched and the criminal.'

Will understood. 'It has the privilege of sanctuary. Only a writ of the Lord Chief Justice or the lords of the Privy Council carries any force there.'

'And even then, not much. No warrant would ever be issued in Alsatia. I told you, Will – a country within a country. The citizens of Alsatia are, to a man and woman, criminal, and they will turn upon and attack any who come to seize one of their own. Have caution. If there is another way to achieve your ends, take it. You will not emerge from Alsatia with your life.'

Will held his arms wide. 'If we took no risks, Kit, how would we know we are alive?'

Marlowe laughed quietly. 'How secure I feel knowing the remarkable Will Swyfte is abroad to keep the land safe.' With a surprising release of emotion, he leaned across the table and took Will's hand forcibly. 'Take care, Will. You have been a good friend to me, and my life would be worse if you were not in it.' Tears shone in Marlowe's eyes. His tumbling emotions were a clear sign of his inner turmoil.

'You should know that taking care of myself is my greatest attribute. I will not be led gracefully towards the dark night, not while there is wine to be drunk and women to romance.'

Marlowe was one of the few men who could see through Will's words, but he was kind enough not to say anything.

Rising, Will nodded his goodbye, adding, 'Heed my words, Kit. Take time to find yourself.'

'If this business ever let me, I would.' He gave a lazy, sad smile, but when Will was at the door, he added, 'I have an idea for a play in which a man sells his soul to the Devil for knowledge, status and power. What do you think of that, Will?' His eyes were haunted and said more than his words.

Will did not need to answer. As he left the room, he wondered, as he did with increasing regularity, if he would see his friend alive again. But his mind was already turning to the trial that lay ahead – an assault on the most notorious and dangerous part of London: Alsatia, the Thieves' Quarter.

# CHAPTER NINE

AS THE BLACK CARRIAGE RATTLED AT SPEED THROUGH THE archway and out of the Bull Inn's yard, Grace stepped from the shadows by the east wall and dropped her hood, ignoring the lecherous stares from the carpenters at work on the temporary stage. Her own carriage waited a little further along Bishopsgate. She hadn't had to follow Will's carriage to know his destination: Marlowe had been one of his few confidants since Will had recruited him after Sir Francis Walsingham received reports of a particularly brilliant and daring student at Cambridge.

Her heart beat fast as she hurried across the cobbles. Will would be angry if he knew she was following him, but she had recognized the glint in his eye at the Palace of Whitehall. She always felt that the business in which he was engaged had something to do with Jenny's disappearance. His work remained a mystery to her, as it should, but she would not find peace until she understood the truth of what had happened to her sister and she feared Will would never tell her even if he uncovered it, under some misguided sense of duty to ensure her protection. Marlowe would tell her everything; she had always been able to wrap him around her finger.

*Good Kit*, she thought. *Too gentle and sensitive for the demands placed upon him.*

At the back of the yard, around the temporary stage, the actors delivered their speeches in declamatory fashion, something about lost love and fairies stealing hearts under cover of the night. It distracted her briefly so she did not see the four men arrive in the shade beneath the archway. Their well-polished boots were expensive Flemish leather, their cloaks thick and unblemished, their hoods pulled low to mask their features, gloves tight on their hands.

They had followed Grace at a distance from the palace, where they had observed her meeting with Will from the shadows.

Blood was on their minds, and righteous vengeance in their hearts.

The end was drawing near.

# CHAPTER TEN

WILL'S CARRIAGE ROLLED TOWARDS ST PAUL'S, PAST THE CROWD
thronging through Cheapside market. Rival apprentices
spilled dangerously close to the wheels as they beat each other
furiously, and respectable gentlemen darted wildly to avoid
randomly thrown blows.

Amid the cacophony, traders loudly competed with each
other to ensnare the attention of passers-by, focusing most of
their efforts on the smartly dressed servants from the grand
four-storey houses that lined the street.

St Paul's, with its blasted spire towering five hundred feet
above the rooftops, was the heart of the city and a stone anchor
in a rapidly changing world. In the bustling, sun-drenched
church precinct, Will found Walsingham, like a black crow, his
beady eyes flickering over the men that Leicester marshalled
before the puzzled gaze of booksellers, merchants, lawyers,
servants looking for work, and those who had come simply to
parade their expensive, highly fashionable cloaks and doublets.
Beside him, Dee was wrapped in a cloak with a deep hood to
hide his distinctive appearance, still maintaining the public lie
that he was in Bohemia.

Mayhew had assembled the members of Will's team nearby:

Launceston, his ghastly complexion and saturnine disposition unsettling many in the churchyard, John Carpenter, whose handsome features were marred by a jagged scar that ran from temple to mouth on his left side, and one who was clearly Tom Miller, the new recruit, as big as a side of beef with hands that could encompass a child's head and an expression of edgy confusion.

Mayhew and the others passed among the crowd swarming around the church, and with the aid of a constable identified and questioned known cutpurses, cut-throats, beggars and coney-catchers, who were as numerous as the respectable tradesmen who sought business around St Paul's.

Nathaniel cast an eye on the proceedings as he followed Will from the carriage. 'These are dark times indeed for so many of the great and good to be gathered in public away from the security of their halls of privilege.'

'The people should be comforted that these men are active in the defence of the nation.'

'England's greatest spy is not comfort enough?' Nathaniel replied archly. 'The talk in the taverns and ordinaries is all of a Spanish invasion. Since Mary's death, people are afraid. They see Spanish agents everywhere. Swarthy-skinned men are attacked in the street, and foreigners threatened over their meals. Will all this activity calm them, or frit them more?'

As Walsingham approached with a grave expression, Will said to Nathaniel, 'Fetch the items we discussed in the carriage. And hurry. From Sir Francis Walsingham's face, I fear that time is shorter still.'

When Nathaniel had departed, Walsingham drew Will in close and whispered, 'The Enemy is abroad. Stories circulate hereabouts of a fearsome black dog with eyes like hot coals that leaves claw-marks in stone.'

'Are we to be afraid of a dog, then?' Will replied. 'We could toss it a bone and be done with it.'

'I am pleased to see your spirits remain high, Master Swyfte, for we appear to be no closer to discovering the rogues who have taken the Silver Skull.'

'Do not give up hope yet,' Will told Walsingham. 'I have a chief suspect in mind. One Laurence Pickering, known as the King of Cutpurses, who carries out his business from Alsatia.'

'And how did you uncover this information?'

'From one who knows the shadowy world these thieves inhabit.'

Will could see Walsingham suspected the informant was Marlowe, and that there was still little love lost for Will's friend, but the spymaster did not press the matter. Instead, clearly concerned by Will's suggestion, Walsingham said, 'Alsatia is a dangerous place. There will be bloodshed if we send in an army, and no guarantee this Pickering will not escape with his prize.'

'Then we do not send in an army,' Will replied. 'A few men, moving secretly, can achieve more, and faster.'

Walsingham nodded in agreement. 'Even so, you will be strangers in a place where most are known to each other. And I am told they speak their own tongue down there – the thieves' cant. One wrong word could be your undoing.'

'The sooner we are in, the sooner out.'

Realizing there was no choice, Walsingham gave his approval before guiding Will to a secluded part of the churchyard where Dee waited in the shade of a yew tree. 'The doctor has some gifts that may aid you,' the spymaster whispered.

From the depths of his hood, Dee's eyes glimmered. 'Two items for now,' he said. Making sure they were not overseen, he withdrew from a leather bag a handful of small muslin packages like the bundles of herbs a cook would drop in a stew. 'Take care with these,' he said, depositing the packages in Will's cupped hands. 'Hold the loose knot at the top and shake them open. But be careful to look away. They will release a flash of light that will blind, and a loud noise to disorient the senses.'

With a shrug, Will deposited them in the pouch at his belt.

Annoyed that Will was not more impressed, Dee delved into his bag once more. Producing a length of leather with two fastening buckles, he proceeded to strap it to Will's left forearm with a roughness that showed his irritation.

'What is that?' Will asked. 'A forearm shield for archery?'

'Yes,' Dee spat. 'Clearly I would waste my time inventing something which already exists.'

Will felt the weight of the strap and knew it was more than leather. As he began to investigate it, Dee knocked his fingers away and touched a hidden catch. A seven-inch blade burst from a hidden pouch with such speed that Walsingham took a step back in shock.

'There will come a time when you will be separated from your sword,' Dee growled, 'but you will never be separated from this weapon. You can wound and kill at close quarters, and with stealth.'

Will flexed his wrist down so the blade protruded, and then swung his arm in an arc, bringing the sharp point within an inch of Dee, seemingly by accident. Dee glared at him. ''Twill suffice,' Will said with another feigned shrug. 'What, no codpiece that bursts into flames? I could have had sport with that.'

Snorting, Dee turned to Walsingham. 'We place the security of England in the hands of a coxcomb!'

As Dee stalked away, Walsingham sighed, 'Now you have offended him, and now I will have to deal with his foul temper. Since he started communing with angels, Dee has been like a devil, filled with fire and brimstone.'

Will couldn't restrain his grin any more. 'I am a cruel man for taking such easy sport.'

They returned to the busiest part of the churchyard where Launceston, Carpenter and Miller were helping Mayhew to question a succession of shifty-eyed rogues.

Will scrutinized Miller, who hung awkwardly back from the others. 'The new fellow. He seems . . . slow.'

'He is more quick-witted than he appears. He is a miller's son, shaped by hard labour. His strength will be an asset to you.'

'And his lack of understanding of the Enemy and their guiles may be the death of us. Who does he think we fight?'

'Spanish agents.' Walsingham was unmoved by Will's concerns, even though he knew the risks involved.

Hiding his irritation, Will noted the innocence in Miller's face. 'If the Enemy is encountered, the shock may prove too great for him.'

'Then you must provide a quick lesson.'

'Quick lessons do not work. You know that. It takes time to accept the world is not the way any of us are brought up to believe. The mind and heart are both fragile things, easily broken, repaired with the greatest difficulty, if at all.'

'That is the way God made us, Master Swyfte. He is your charge now. I have faith you will see him right.'

Walsingham returned to Leicester, who was swaggering along the ranks of his men, enjoying the eyes of the public upon him. Summoning Mayhew and the others, Will led them from the churchyard, past the shop where the fashionable

97

London men bought their pouches of the New World tobacco, to a quiet spot beyond the bookstalls.

An incandescent rage appeared to be burning just beneath Carpenter's skin. Unconsciously tracing a fingertip down the pink scar on his face, he said, 'Why did Walsingham see fit to throw us together?'

'I think he feels you will keep my feet on the ground, John.'

'That I will do.'

Turning his attention to Miller, Will shook his hand. 'Tom. Sir Francis Walsingham has only good words for you. I am Will Swyfte.'

'I know you.' A hint of awe laced the young man's words. He was taller than Will by a good hand, with shoulders so broad he could have carried a calf on them, but his pale eyes were bright and intelligent. Both his ruddy cheeks and his plain, home-made clothes spoke of his country life.

Snorting derisively, Carpenter pretended to inspect Paul's Cross where a wild-eyed, grey-haired man prepared to deliver a sermon.

Not wishing to frighten the inexperienced young man, Will kept his tone light, but his grave expression reinforced the seriousness of his words. 'You will have heard of some of our work, but know this: you may well see things in the course of this day that you find . . . puzzling . . . troubling . . .'

'Frightening,' Mayhew interjected, staring at his boots.

'There is an explanation, and you will get it when our work is done,' Will continued. 'Till then, anything you see that makes little sense must be put from your mind. Do you understand?'

Baffled, Miller nodded.

'Let me put it another way,' Launceston added, tone

aristocratic and precise. 'If you fail to keep a steady course, and place us in danger, I will slit your throat as surely as I would that of an enemy, and leave you where you fall for the rats to feast on.'

Miller turned almost as pale as Launceston.

'Steady now,' Will said. 'We must not go bragging about the speed and size of our blades. For I would win. Listen with care, for we have a matter to test even the greatest swords of Albion.'

By the time Will finished explaining the task that lay ahead, Nathaniel had returned with a large, foul-smelling sack. From it, he distributed various items of clothing.

'What is this?' Mayhew clutched a hand to his mouth. 'Foul vinegar rags stolen from the backs of three-day-dead beggars?'

'Master Mayhew, you are known around London as a man of exquisite taste for the finery of your dress,' Will said. 'But if you walk into Alsatia as a gallant, flashing that costly silk lining of your cloak, you will find yourself a honeypot for bees with a deadly sting.'

In the cramped carriage on the road to Fleet Street, they quickly changed into the stinking rags, with much complaining from Mayhew and stoic acceptance from Launceston. Miller was eager, but Carpenter only glared sullenly at Will as he attempted to hide the mass of scars that covered his back and left arm. Will considered attempting to clear the air over Carpenter's long-standing grievance, but decided it would only make matters worse.

When they were done, Nathaniel said, 'I have never seen . . . nor smelled . . . a more convincing group of foul beggars. You wear it well.'

'I hear the buzzing of a gnat, Master Swyfte,' Launceston sniffed. 'I will swat it if I see it.'

The coach trundled to a halt. Drawing back the curtain, Will saw the large, timber-framed houses of the Fleet Street merchants, servant girls returning with armfuls of fresh rushes to scatter across the floors, ignoring the bawdy comments of three barrel-makers shouting over the sound of hammering. In the doorway of the largest house, three gentlemen discussed business, ostentatiously smoking the expensive tobacco now regularly on sale near St Paul's.

Barely noticeable between two of the grand houses was a tiny alley running south towards the river, where rats ran and flies swarmed in shafts of sunlight.

'From here there is danger every step of the way,' Will said. 'We will be surrounded by people who would gladly slit our throats for a shiny button, but they are the least of our worries. The Enemy races to reach the Silver Skull before us.' He glanced down the alley to where it wound away into shadow. 'And they come like the night. We must watch each other's backs.' He cast an eye towards Carpenter, who pretended not to notice. 'Good luck, boys. We go for Queen and country, and the promise of wine and a warm embrace when we are done. Let nothing keep us from our just rewards.'

Leaping from the carriage, he plunged straight into the alley.

The boundary of Alsatia, the Thieves' Quarter where the laws of London did not apply, was clearly demarcated by a piercing whistle from an unseen watchman somewhere near the rooftops. Heads held low by the weight of a harsh life, furtive eyes cast down, Will and the other beggars limped and stumbled in a tight knot, faces now smeared with dirt and grime they had picked up along the way.

While the rest of London was filled with colour, noise and life, on the edge of Alsatia all was eerily still. Stone tenements blackened by smoke and the accumulation of centuries of filth rose up four storeys. Overhanging upper floors on some of the newer buildings meant that little sun reached the rutted, puddled narrow streets where a thin grey light leached the colour from everything. Like a constant fog, smoke blew back and forth along the byways from the blocked chimneys of the many who could not afford the services of a sweep.

On the fringes, the houses appeared deserted, the stink of excrement drifting from shattered windows and ragged doors. But as Swyfte and his colleagues progressed towards the heart of the quarter, human life began to appear, in ones and twos at first, talking in hushed tones in the entrances to alleys, or slumped on doorsteps watching with mean eyes. Their clothes were brown and grey and muddy-green, rough cloth, hard worn, with wide-brimmed felt hats that could hide the features. Pale skin. Stubble and unkempt beards. Filthy fingernails. The women hung out of windows, faces lashed pink by the elements, hair prematurely grey. The doxies barely bothered to dress after each short, grunting encounter, pendulous breasts hanging out of torn, filthy dresses, rouge and powder, applied so half-heartedly it appeared to be the work of children, turning each one into a pink and cream grotesque, a pastiche of sexual attraction. It did not appear to deter the men. The whores carried out their trade on the street, against the walls, or on their backs in hallways, doors thrown wide, skirts pulled high, their faces implacable as the men thrust into them, sweating and cursing.

'Animals,' Launceston said under his breath.

The stink grew more intense with each step. Rubbish was piled as high as a man on either side of every door: scraps of rotting meat, and bones, and vegetables, the dung of animals, and the contents of chamber pots. Every heap was alive with

101

rats. They carpeted the streets, swarming away from approaching feet to return a moment later. Clouds of flies filled the air, and plump, white maggots glistened in the half-light.

As Will led the way, the piercing whistles followed them, but their tone was merely observational and not insistent.

Gangs of men flowed past them, ready for an afternoon's work seeking out the country gulls and foreign visitors who would be less alert to the nip and foist that would relieve them of their gold-stuffed purses. They would prowl St Paul's, all the bowling alleys and ordinaries, the brothels, baiting rings and theatres, seeking out their likely marks.

Everywhere knives glinted and cold eyes stared. Will heard whispers in his wake, but they passed as he knew they would; for earning a dishonest living took precedence over the searching of a few beggars.

'Do you hear that?' Miller held up a hand and brought them to a ragged halt, cocking his head to listen to some sound that escaped the rest of them. All they heard was the wind beneath the eaves, the occasional frightened shout in the distance, and the murmur of conspiratorial voices every now and then.

'What do you hear?' Will had caught sight of the anxiety on Miller's face.

'Music?' He strained to hear. 'The playing of some flute just beneath the wind, or behind it, or part of it?'

'Why bother yourself with that, you fool?' Carpenter growled. 'They make merry here like the rest of us.'

Mayhew had picked up on Miller's unease. 'Why should a flute trouble you so?'

''Tis nothing,' Will interrupted. 'Do not jump at shadows. There are worse dangers to concern you.'

As they moved on they came to a crossroads and paused. An eerie stillness lay across the area. It was as deserted as the first part of Alsatia they had entered. The cold wind had dropped and dense, choking smoke billowed all around them.

It was Launceston who noted the most unnerving aspect. 'Look. The rats have fled.'

Now they could all hear a hint of the flute-playing, fading in and out. Peering down each of the streets in turn, Will tried to discern the origin of the music.

Miller dabbed at his nose where a trickle of blood ran down to his upper lip. 'What is this?' he asked, his eyes widening.

Will urged him to be silent. The flute-playing ebbed away to be replaced by the faint tread of boots, drawing nearer. The dim echoes drifted among the smoke and reflected from wall to wall so that it was difficult to identify the source.

On a deeper level than their five senses, all but Miller understood the nature of what approached. Yet Miller was still unnerved and Launceston slapped a cold hand on his shoulder to steady him.

Turning slowly, Will stopped for the briefest moment at each street. 'Which way, which way?' he muttered to himself.

Then, along the route to the west, almost lost to the swirling smoke, what appeared to be two hot coals a yard or more off the ground moved towards them. Several sounds came to Will from the same direction: a low, growling breath, barely audible but making his stomach clench and the hairs on his neck tingle; the pad of a paw and the slap of a tensing leather leash as something strained against it; and then the measured tread of boots.

Will turned quickly and propelled Miller down the street that led south, the others following at his heels. They only came to a halt when the strained atmosphere had evaporated, and there was no sign of pursuit.

Miller had grown pale. 'What was that?' he asked. 'A ghost?'

'No spectre would haunt this foul place,' Will replied, 'not when there are peaceful churchyards and castle towers sheltered from the elements.' He hoped his grin would take the edge off Miller's anxiety. 'A man with a dog, no more. Probably for the fighting pit. But we could not risk its smelling us out. Even in these foul rags, we are sweeter to the nose than anyone in this place.'

Calming a little, Miller unconsciously lifted his fingers to the dried blood under his nose, but before any errant thoughts could resurface Launceston gave him a rough shove and they were back on their journey.

They had not gone far before Launceston's pale face loomed at Will's shoulder. In a low voice that none of the others could hear, he said, 'Bringing that youth was a mistake. The knowledge of what we face, revealed in one shattering blow, will destroy him, and us along with him if we are not careful.'

'Then we protect him until he can be prepared for the truth.' Will maintained the bullish attitude expected of him, but he was as concerned as Launceston. In ideal circumstances Miller would have gone through the same slow stabilizing process of induction and revelation as the rest of them. But Will understood Walsingham's urge to circumvent procedure: these were desperate times, and they were always short-handed compared to the force arrayed against them. 'This is the hand we have been dealt. We must play it as we can,' he said firmly.

In the icy flash of the glance Launceston levelled at Miller, Will saw that the Earl would not shy from taking matters into his own hands if Miller placed them, or their mission, under threat. None of them was a stranger to shedding blood, but killing came particularly easy to Launceston. Marlowe had once commented that it was as if something was missing inside him. Will would need to pay careful attention, should there be any sign of the Earl's giving in to his urges.

As they pressed on deeper into Alsatia, it became apparent that the residents felt safer from the unwanted scrutiny of the law-keepers. Dice was played noisily on doorsteps, or cards on ramshackle tables at the side of the street. Crippled men and women abandoned by society tried to scrape a living begging, and sometimes the criminals would take pity and toss them a coin.

Outside a tavern, amid the vomit and reeking lakes of urine, people sprawled drunkenly across the street with no one to move them on. The noise from the open doors and windows was deafening, inebriated conversations delivered at a bellow against a backdrop of fiddle music and ferociously contested gambling.

A brawl began, but was swiftly broken up by men armed with cudgels who appeared to keep order among the unruly throng. Will guessed they must be in the pay of the gangs, ready to protect any member of the community at risk of being dragged out to face justice.

One man lay face down in the mud and urine, his skull split open and his blood flowing. Will saw the hands of his own men going instinctively to the swords hidden inside their rags, knowing what they would face if they were found out.

He was about to enter the tavern when an uproar echoed from the end of the street. He turned and saw men and women run towards the entrance to one of the tenements.

'Someone is in danger,' he hissed to the others.

# CHAPTER ELEVEN

WHEN SWYFTE AND THE OTHERS TOOK THEIR FIRST STEPS INTO Alsatia, Grace was already making her way through its filthy, smoke-filled streets. Marlowe had always liked her, and it had not taken a great effort to worm Will's destination out of him. His refusal to speak directly of the nature of Will's business in the Thieves' Quarter only added to her suspicion that it had something to do with Jenny's disappearance. Over the years she had learned to read Will's nuances well, and when they had last met, at the palace, she was sure he was hiding something both dangerous and important from her. Jenny was the most important thing in both their lives. Any potential dangers faded into insignificance against possible answers to her sister's disappearance.

Marlowe had been keen to warn her of those very dangers, to a young woman alone in Alsatia – it was not the court, and it was certainly not Warwickshire, he had stressed. Grace had smiled sweetly and told him she would heed his words.

But as she stood on a street where a man at a table took receipt of purses, jewellery and silk handkerchiefs from four rogues who stared at her too long, too hard, she cursed her ignorance. She was not naive; she recognized the hunger in their eyes. She thought she would be able to find Will easily – he was often recognized and hailed by upstanding men and women – yet here there was no trace of his passing, and she was lost, and her perfumed handkerchief could not keep the foul smells from her nose.

At least a woman alone was no threat and she had not been troubled by the majority of the other unsavoury characters she had seen. She began to retrace her steps to the London she knew, only for the men to follow her.

Her heart beat faster, but she tried not to give in to panic that she knew would only attract more unwanted attention. With her head down, she skipped a stinking puddle, keeping one eye on the open doors of the tenements for hidden threats. She kept up a fast pace, deciding that she hated this place more than anywhere she had been in her life. Every face had either a hint of cruelty or the stain of life's crushing ills. She saw no hope anywhere.

She glanced back at the four men loping in her wake, elbowing each other and flashing lascivious grins, their eyes furtive and hard, and saw they would not give up easily. *Do not cry*, she told herself. *Be brave.*

The street to her right was wider and had more traffic, and Grace turned into it in the hope that the men would leave her alone under the gaze of others. But she had not gone more than twenty paces when a rough hand grabbed her arm.

The youngest of the men, who had sandy hair and a ruddy complexion covered with pox scars, said hoarsely, 'Walk with us, lady. These are rough parts and you need strong arms to keep you safe.'

'I fear the cure will be worse than the disease,' Grace said, hoping her bravado would deter them, though she was more scared than she had been in her life. 'Leave me. I would walk alone.' She tried to throw off his hand, but he only held her tighter, and suddenly the other three were moving to surround her.

'Aid me! Please!' Grace called to the people moving along the street. A man with grey hair and hollow cheeks only winked at the men and moved on. A fat woman threw back her head and guffawed, her friend thrusting her fist up provocatively.

'You will get no help round these parts,' the pox-scarred man laughed.

Grace launched a sharp kick at his shins, and as he yelped and staggered back to his associates, she ran. Along the street, jeers and encouragement to pursuit rose up loudly. Catching her quickly, the men bundled her through the open door of one of the tenements.

Grace careered across the mud floor to come to rest against a damp wall. The place was bare apart from a table and chair, and a fire stoked with cheap coal smoked into the room.

Laughing, the four men ranged across the room, blocking her escape.

'Come near me and I will tear out your eyes,' she hissed, but she could no longer hide her terror. The men only laughed harder.

Sliding up the wall, Grace hooked her fingers like claws as her attackers approached. She glimpsed movement through the filthy window and a moment later the door crashed open and four cloaked men burst in. Grace had as little time to react as her attackers before a rapier was thrust into the heart of the pox-scarred man, and just as quickly withdrawn and slashed across the throat of another. Relief flooded Grace. She had only ever seen one person exhibit that degree of skill with a blade.

'Will,' she murmured with relief.

Her remaining two assailants had only seconds to plead for their lives before they too were despatched. Shocked by the cold efficiency of the kills, Grace turned away, but she was also troubled that a part of her was triumphant.

When she turned back, her saviour stood before her, only for an unfamiliar face to be revealed when the hood was thrown off: aristocratic, with an aquiline nose and dark eyes that were as charismatic as Will's, a waxed moustache and chin-hair, swarthy skin.

'Greetings, mistress,' he said. 'I am Don Alanzo de las Posadas, and you will now accompany me.'

'Spanish spies,' Grace gasped.

Don Alanzo gave a curt bow.

# CHAPTER TWELVE

PASSING THROUGH THE FLOW OF DRUNKS FROM THE TAVERN, WILL and the others joined the rear of the crowd at the entrance to the tenement. As people jostled for a view of the mysterious spectacle, Will eased his way past sharp shoulders and elbows until the laughter and quizzical shouts gave way to sudden silence. A moment of confusion ended in panic, shrieks and barked warnings, as those near the front tried to drive back into the flow of the ones joining the crowd.

When Will broke through the mob with renewed urgency, at first he couldn't see anything out of the ordinary. Across the step against the door jamb was slumped what looked like a scarecrow, straw protruding from the sleeves and neck of worn clothes, head lolling on the chest beneath a wide-brimmed felt hat. Yet something about the well-stuffed shape held Will fast.

A moment later, the scarecrow shifted.

'A game!' Miller chuckled under his breath. 'I have seen this before, in my village. A child hides inside it!'

'Away,' Will urged as gently as he could, trying to push Miller back against the weight of the crowd at his back.

It was then that the scarecrow lurched to its feet, stumbling and swaying on the step, straw hands going to a face that was at once twisted knots of straw and hazel switches and also completely human. Terrified eyes rolled insanely. Twig fingers clawed at the place where the mouth should have been, and a mad mewling came from deep inside it. With a pleading arm, the scarecrow reached out to the crowd, but as it staggered around the arc everyone moved back, unnerved, trying to believe it was some joke, knowing in their hearts they were seeing something which went against all earthly wisdom.

Miller's eyes widened. Grabbing his shoulder in an attempt to drag him back, Launceston urged through clenched teeth, 'Get him out of here!' But Miller threw Launceston and Will off, and stepped towards the scarecrow.

Flailing desperately, its puppet-like movements drove the crowd to silence until an old woman whispered, 'The Devil has been here.'

That was enough. 'The Devil! The Devil!' jumped from mouth to mouth as the mob fell apart in uproar.

One bull-necked, bald-headed man was not convinced. Stepping forward, he brought the scarecrow's flailing to a halt and tore open its jacket, ripping at the straw beneath. The scarecrow's desperate mewling grew louder.

Golden straw rained across the street as the bald man's frenzied search for the hidden occupant tore through the insides. Finally his fingers scraped the back of the jacket and the expression of appalled realization that crept across his face was devastating to see.

'There is nothing in it,' he croaked. 'It is the Devil's work.'

Falling to its knees, the scarecrow clawed up the straw and stuffed it back inside. Its mewling was now a loud whine that set the teeth on edge.

'It is one of Pickering's men,' someone else said, 'taken by Old Nick for his sins.'

The horror that had gripped the crowd began to turn to anger, then cruelty. With cudgels and boots they attacked the scarecrow as it flopped and flailed and emitted muffled whines on the ground. The bald-headed man emerged from one of the tenements with a burning stick pulled from the hearth.

'Here will be an end to it!' he called.

The crowd parting so he could drag the scarecrow to its feet, the bald man thrust the blazing stick into the gaping belly. The straw caught immediately. With roaring flames engulfing the figure in moments, greasy, black smoke billowed up between the tenements. Women clutched their ears to keep out the high-pitched whine as the scarecrow at first ran back and forth, then staggered and finally fell to its knees and grew silent as the blaze consumed it.

Finally, nothing remained but black ashes, half-burned boots and remnants of clothing. Kicking through the ashes with a fury that revealed his secret fear, the bald man searched for any blackened bones, and only calmed when he saw there were none.

As their anger dissipated, a deep unease fell on the silent crowd. Miller tore off the hood of his cloak, tears of fear streaking his pallid face.

'What happened to him?' he croaked.

Will and Launceston did their best to bundle him away, but the damage had already been done.

'Strangers.' A pointing finger was levelled at Miller.

'Strangers,' another repeated.

'They did it.'

Hands tore at Will's cloak. Carpenter's rapier was revealed, and Mayhew had his hood ripped from his head.

'Strangers!'

It did not matter whether they were agents of the law or responsible for the terrifying event that had just unfolded, the crowd was eager to forget the scarecrow and Will saw that he and the others were a vent for churning emotions. Throwing off the men attempting to grip his arms, he barged enough space to draw his rapier and carved an arc around him with the tip of the blade.

The others were not so quick. 'The Devil!' quickly gave way to 'Spies!' and 'The law!' followed rapidly by the call to arms of 'Clubs!' which was soon ringing out loudly along the length of the street. Men rushed from the tavern and the buildings all around, armed with whatever they could pick up to defend their illicit livelihoods, quickly joined by women and children too.

A cudgel clattered across Mayhew's temple, sending blood spattering in a wide arc. Stunned, he staggered back until Carpenter caught him. But the crowd surged in such numbers there was no room to use his blade, and soon he was swamped in bodies, fists and sticks and bottles raining down on him.

In the space he had carved for himself, Will kept the mob at bay with his flashing sword, but he could not see a way out. Overhead, the whistles rang out from the rooftops, and more people ran to the disturbance from all around the area. Daggers were drawn and razors pulled from the lining of cloaks. The anger and fear of the people of Alsatia would only be sated when five torn bodies were found on the edge of the Thames at daybreak.

Miller, Launceston, Mayhew and Carpenter were lost to him beneath the roiling sea of bodies, but he could hear the thwack of wood on flesh, and the slap of boots and fists. In the turmoil, Will recalled the small packages Dee had given him

113

at St Paul's. Sheathing his sword, he plucked one of the parcels from his pouch and unfurled it, turning his head away as he did so. As the powder within met the air, the resounding bang made his ears ring and the flash burned through his closed lids, but it brought turmoil to the already anxious crowd. With yells and shrieks, the attackers fell back. Dazed and covered in blood, Miller quickly came to his senses as Will dragged him from the mud. Mayhew, Launceston and Carpenter staggered towards him, similarly bloody and bruised.

As their eyes and nerves recovered, the mob circled warily. Will knew it would only be a matter of moments before they rediscovered their courage, and sheer weight of numbers would bring his band down.

'Follow my lead,' he quietly instructed the others, 'and do not tarry, for if you fall behind they will be upon you like wolves.'

Spinning, he kicked open the door that had been at his back and pushed into the smoky, damp-smelling shade. He sped through the tenement and out of the back door on to another street with Launceston, Miller, Mayhew and Carpenter behind him.

They ran west along the street, the mob slowed by the narrow passage of the tenement. But as the whistles blasted urgently from the rooftops, more figures streamed from alleys into the street ahead, trying to block their escape.

'They will not rest until we are dead,' Carpenter said.

Gripping his sword tightly as he ran, Mayhew said fiercely, 'I will take a hundred of them with me when I go! Damn the Spanish, and the Enemy – sometimes I wonder if the real enemies are within.' He ducked his head low as bottles and stones rained down around them.

Breathless, hearts pumping, they sprinted, with the baying

of the mob always close behind. 'We must find a place to lie low,' Will shouted above the din.

'Where?' Carpenter snapped. 'They will ransack any filthy hovel we choose to make our castle.'

'And did you accept defeat so easily when we fled across the snows of Muscovy with Feodor's men at our heels?' Will yelled. 'Or did I dream us hiding like foxes in the roots of a tree?'

'I wish it *had* been a dream,' Carpenter spat. 'At least then I would not have these scars to itch morning, noon and night.'

With a bellow, a man wearing a butcher's leather apron erupted from a door, swinging a bloodstained cleaver directly towards Will's head. Ducking beneath the arc, Will brought the pommel of his sword crashing against the back of the assailant's neck. That was enough to deter him, but Launceston stepped in swiftly and slit the butcher's throat. Gurgling, and attempting to stem the arterial spurt, the man plunged to the ground.

'A warning to the others,' Launceston said. Will cursed the Earl's brutality, but the mob slowed a little when they saw the blood.

Kicking his way into another tenement, Will called to the others, 'Bar the door behind us!' as he ran to open the rear door on to the next street.

Mayhew and Carpenter jammed what little furniture they could find in front of the door, and were making for the back door when Will summoned them to follow him up the stairs.

'Has God taken your mind?' Carpenter shouted. 'We will be trapped up there!'

'Follow him,' Launceston said with cold insistence. 'He is no fool.'

He and Mayhew propelled a dazed Miller up the stairs after

115

Will. At the bottom, Carpenter hesitated for a moment until the sound of their pursuers drew towards the door and then he reluctantly followed. As he reached the top of the creaking stairs, he heard the front door burst open and the torrent of angry voices flood through the tenement and out of the back door.

Forcing his way through a door into a room filled with detritus and a bedroll on the bare boards in one corner, Will pointed up to where a hatch led to the loft. Mayhew and Launceston boosted him up and then he helped the others scramble into the dusty dark space, which was filled with the flapping of disturbed birds and the scurrying of rats along the rafters. Here and there, missing tiles allowed shafts of afternoon sunlight to punch through into the gloom.

Below, the muffled sounds of the mob washed around the tenement.

Keeping his head low, Will loped along a rafter to the end of the loft, where a crawlspace led through to the adjoining tenement. Followed by the others, he continued along the row of tenements to the end house where they made their way down to the ground floor. While the hubbub continued further along the street, they took advantage of the drifting smoke to slip across to the opposite tenement and make their way rapidly up the stairs and into the loft space of the next row.

They came to rest where the roof was missing enough shingles to give them a view across Alsatia. Strands of cobwebs hung down, white with the thick dust that carpeted the loft. A dead bird lay among the vermin droppings, half eaten by rats. Sheathing their weapons, they sprawled on the rafters, finally drawing breath and composing themselves. Any relief was restrained by the sound of the crowd milling in the street below.

'Now we wait. They will soon find better things to do,' Will said.

Leaning in close, Launceston nodded towards Miller, who was huddled off on his own, head bowed. 'The boy was a mistake,' he whispered. 'It is not his fault, but that does not matter now. Look at him. He will break at any moment. That makes him a danger to what we do here.' Pausing, Launceston attempted to show a modicum of compassion, but all Will saw was cold efficiency. 'We should despatch him now and be done with it.'

'Let me talk to him,' Will said. 'We all recall our introduction to this world. He may find his feet quickly.'

'Or he may not. And what then?'

In Miller Will saw the innocence that the rest of them hardly remembered; he recalled the pleasant days of his rural upbringing, and he regretted the toll taken by the hard business of life. Stepping cautiously from rafter to rafter, he made his way to the young man. Miller didn't look up.

'Was that the Devil's work?' Miller's voice was a ghostly rustle. The country burr was clear, and Will realized the youth had been suppressing it, probably to appear more sophisticated to his new associates.

'Not in the way you mean. But it is certainly devilish.'

'I heard stories of these things, in the tavern, and around Swainson's hearth one winter night, but . . .' He chewed at his lip. 'They were just stories. Not real. But that . . . That should not be!' Finally, he looked up at Will with wide eyes stung by tears.

'You are right. It should not.'

'They burned him alive! Whatever happened, the poor soul was still inside somewhere. And they burned him!'

'People do terrible things when they are scared. We are

117

taught to see the world a certain way. An ordered place, where the sun rises in the morning and sets at dusk, and all happens as it should. The world is not like that.'

As Miller wiped away his tears, Will saw a hint of defiance that gave him hope. Perhaps that was what Walsingham had recognized. 'What is it like, then?' Miller asked.

'It is a place where night can fall at noon, and cows give blood not milk. Where mothers can find strange creatures in the cribs where their babies lay only a moment before. Where mortal men do not rule and never have.' He cast an eye towards Launceston, Carpenter and Mayhew, who were whispering conspiratorially on the far side of the loft. 'I will tell you the truth of these matters,' he said quietly, squatting next to Miller. 'Listen carefully, and then I will answer any questions you have, as well as I can. But you must not cry, or rail to the heavens, or give any sign of fear. You must accept these things like the man that Sir Francis Walsingham saw when he chose you to defend our Queen and country. Do you understand?'

Miller nodded.

'Good man. These secrets would have been revealed to you at the Palace of Whitehall over time, and they would have been allowed to settle on you, so they did not disturb your mind. But there was no time for that, and so you must hear them now, hard, and cold, and painful.'

'Tell me. Make sense of what I saw.'

'Sense? No, there is no sense to any of this, but I will help you understand. The stories that you heard at Swainson's hearth are true. Every story that you laughed off in the light of day, but feared deep in your heart at night, is true.'

'The Devil . . .'

'Yes, by other names. Devils. A race of them. As long as we have walked on this earth, they have preyed on us, for sport,

118

out of cruelty, for malign purposes. They have transformed us, like that poor wretch you saw in the street, tormented our nightmares, twisted our limbs, stolen our children, driven our old men to their graves, slaughtered our young men, and drunk their blood, and bathed in it. No forest was ever safe for us, no lonely moor, no quiet, moonlit pool or river's edge or mountaintop, for they would come from under hill and mound and treat us like cattle, or, worse, like rats, forced to play for the mouser's enjoyment before one swipe of a claw bears innards to the light.'

Will paused to allow what he had said to sink in. Even after all he had experienced, he felt queasy when he contemplated the potential threat of their age-old foe. He had learned long ago that it was best not to examine their existence too closely, for no enlightenment lay there, only madness.

Disbelief and the hint of a smile flickered on Miller's face. It was the first sign, Will knew from experience, and it would pass. There would be worse to come, not just then, but for many nights after, if not a lifetime. Outside, the cries and whistles of Alsatia punctured the unsettled atmosphere in the loft.

'You have had an education in the history of this land?' Will asked.

'A little.'

'Then let me tell you the true history, the secret history. England has always been at war—'

'Always?'

'Not with the Spanish, or the French, the Scots or the Welsh or the Irish.'

'With that race of devils?' Miller's disbelief had already started to turn.

'I dress it up in fine clothes to call it a war,' Will continued,

119

'but really we have been in rags, 'pon our knees. The Enemy did what they wanted with us. Killed, stole, tormented. And we could not fight back for they were too powerful.'

'They have magic?'

Will thought for a moment before answering. 'Let us just say they can do things we cannot. They have guile and secret knowledge. Is it magic? It seems that way at times, but I am but a humble spy and do not know about such things.' Will spoke calmly and carefully, smiling to make his words appear simpler than they were. 'In truth, they are more cunning than wolves, see like eagles, swim like fish, are stronger than bears, and can strike more swiftly than snakes. They are there and gone in the twinkling of an eye. Most important, they value our lives not a whit. In their eyes, we are as far beneath them as the sheep of the field are beneath us.'

'And this Enemy . . . you say they have been attacking us for ever? Then why have I not seen nor heard of them?'

'You have, in stories, in whispers. They are always known by other names. You called them the Devil yourself. But our kings and queens have always ruled that their existence should be kept a secret from the common man as much as possible. For if the good men and women of England knew the terrors that could pluck them from their lives at any moment, they would be driven mad with fear, and all we have tried to build here would fall into an abyss.'

In the street below, it seemed the clamour had ebbed away as the mob returned to their plots and plans. But in the silence there was little peace.

'Tell me what they do,' Miller said.

'I will tell you some of what they do,' Will replied. 'A flavour, but there is no time to tell you all.' *And I would not see your hope extinguished*. 'In Chanctonbury Ring, in Sussex, the Devil appears every Midsummer Eve, the local people say, and plucks one poor wretch from his hearth to take beneath the clump. In Tolleshunt Knights in Essex, not far from your quiet home, these people of the dark engaged in carnal displays on the banks of the bottomless pool in the place known as the Devil's Wood. One year, a local landowner attempted to build a house there, and the unholy crew ripped out his heart, screaming that his soul was lost.'

Numb, Miller bowed his head and covered his eyes as he listened to Will detail the atrocities: the blood-soaked fields, the devastated lives and stolen children, the changelings, the disappeared, the hunted and the haunted and the corrupted. His litany of misery covered every quarter of England, and reached back as far into the past as the historians had documented. It was what Will himself had been told in the days after he had been recruited by Walsingham, and Miller's reaction was the same: the disbelief shading to shock, then to a creeping, cold devastation at the realization that there was no safe place. The others had fallen quiet, drawn in by Will's litany of the terrors that circled their lives.

Stretching his legs, Will watched the clouds blowing across the afternoon sky as he completed the first part of his account. 'In Atwick, in Yorkshire, no one dares drink at the local spring. In York . . . at Alderley Edge . . . at Kirkby Lonsdale and Castleton Fell . . .' His words dried up, but the silence that followed said enough.

'My grandfather disappeared in the marshes at Romney, following a mysterious light. We never found the body,' Miller began hesitantly.

'They are everywhere, Tom Miller. In every part of this country, and beyond too, I would wager. We have all been touched by them, though we might not realize it. They may exist on the edges of what we see, but they are always there. They have always been there.'

'What are they?' Miller asked. 'Are they—'

With a reassuring smile, Will held up a hand to silence him. 'The farmers do not speak their name, lest they answer. They call them the Fair Folk or . . .' and here Will grimaced, 'the Good Neighbours. You know who they are.'

'My mother said they helped.'

'Some did. But there is a cruel group among them who find us game for hunting, or sport when they are bored.' As he looked out of the broken tiles across the smoky city, Will could feel the eyes of Launceston, Mayhew and Carpenter on his back, all waiting to see how Miller would deal with the news. He had revealed to him the problem and brought him down; now it was time to uncover the solution. 'But no more,' he added.

'But . . . the scarecrow in the street. They do not leave us alone,' Miller said, puzzled.

'No. There are other accounts, but fewer now. Mere skirmishes, to let us know they still exist. The hot war we fought with their kind has blown cold.' Will struck a defiant tone as he turned back to Miller. 'We found a way to fight back.'

'Against a power like that? How?'

'Your thanks should go to Dr Dee. When our Queen came to the throne some thirty years ago and received the truth of these matters, passed down across the years through royal channels, she decided it was time to take a stand. The people of England could no longer be the plaything of an outside power. Determined to end generations of suffering, she turned to her teacher, adviser and confidant, Dr Dee, and brought him close, charging him with the task. Through his esoteric studies, Dee came upon a solution, and after a night in which it is said storms tore England apart and ghosts walked in every churchyard, England's defences were secured.'

'How did Dr Dee achieve such a thing?'

'In this business of secrets, Dee keeps his closer than any. Whatever he did . . . whatever price he paid . . . it changed everything overnight. The Enemy could no longer attack us with impunity. They retreated to their distant homes, seething that those they considered so lowly had now risen up to challenge their rule.'

'If we have locked them out, how do they return to torment us?' Miller asked.

Arms folded, Will leaned back against the slope of the roof, his defiance tempered by the reality of the threat. 'Over time, they find a way through here or there, a quick blow, but it is nothing like before. Yet in their absence they are even more dangerous. Their loss of power has wounded them. Always arrogant, they refuse to accept they now have equals and are determined to bring us once again to our knees. Now, instead of seeing us as sport, they see us as a threat, and they are determined to destroy us for all time. And so they plot, and bide their time, and search for a way through our defences. We must be ever vigilant, for we do not know where their decisive blow will come. And it will come, sooner or later. Their intellect, and their anger, burns hot. They have been spurned, and they want a vengeance that will clear us from the world.'

'And this business with the Silver Skull?'

Will was pleased to see that Miller's unease appeared to have dissipated a little. His brow was furrowed as he turned over the information, weighing options, realizing, Will hoped, that there was no need to be fatalistic.

He squatted next to Miller. 'They have never launched

such a bold attack before. That suggests this artefact is of the greatest importance to them. And the only thing they consider important now is our destruction.'

'So . . . so . . . we do not fight the Spanish?'

'We do. We are in a bitter struggle with our earthly enemies for our continued existence as a nation. That is how it always has been, though our lot was made more difficult by Henry's decision to break with Rome. But now the Enemy stirs and manipulates our Catholic opponents. Indeed, not just Spain, or France, but all the foreign monarchs. We should stand shoulder to shoulder against a common foe, but religion is a formidable wedge. Catholic? Protestant? It means nothing to me. We are all brothers in our skin. But the Enemy are skilled at finding weaknesses and exploiting them to their own advantage.'

Launceston made his way across the rafters, his gaze heavy on Miller, searching for signs of weakness. When he stood beside the young man, he nodded, happy with what he saw. 'At times it appears the whole world is against us, with the Enemy manipulating all to crush us,' the Earl said. 'But we have risen up off our knees and now we have gained freedom, we shall not let it go again. We will do whatever it takes to survive.'

'And this is our job, then?' Miller asked.

'This is the true reason for our network of spies,' Will agreed. 'Yes, we have agents in the foreign courts and we continually gather information against our earthly enemies, but the real reason for our existence is our fight against the true Enemy.'

'We operate in the shadows, always presenting two faces to the world,' Launceston continued, 'but the true nature of our fight, and the Enemy we face, must never be known. For the people of England would lose hope if they knew the scale of the forces ranged against us.'

'After Dee's defences were secured, the first plans for a secret service to oppose the Enemy's renewed attention were laid by Elizabeth's Chief Minister, William Cecil, Lord Burghley, and in turn he summoned Sir Francis Walsingham to enact the strategy that we now see through today.'

Miller clutched his forehead. 'My head is spinning. I can no longer tell what is truth or fiction. This all seems like a dream. A nightmare.'

'A nightmare indeed,' Launceston replied, although he appeared as dispassionate as ever. 'And we continue to take those bad dreams back to the Enemy's door. We have fought them to a standstill in the twenty-two years since Sir Francis came to court, and there have been casualties on both sides. The battle will continue, cold, and hard, and fought for ever in the shadows. I cannot see an end to it.'

'We cannot defeat them?' Miller asked.

'They are like the sea.'

'And if our defences ever crack, they would wash us away in the flood,' Will said. 'We cannot let that happen. Our guard must not fall for an instant.' He paused and looked at the younger man. 'You see now the importance of the work we do?'

'It is all down to us?' Miller's voice had grown thin and reedy.

'England, and our Queen, demands the best of us,' Will said. 'We shall not let her down.'

Outside, a flock of crows rose suddenly into the darkening sky, cawing discordantly as they swooped across the rooftops. It was a strangely desolate sound that touched them all.

'I would be alone with my thoughts for a moment,' Miller said quietly. 'You have given me much to ponder.'

Once again, Launceston fixed a dark eye on the youth.

'Take your moment,' Will said, 'but our business is urgent. It is time to act.'

# CHAPTER THIRTEEN

*Branches tore at Will's face and brambles ripped at his ankles as he crashed through the trees in search of the watcher. It was cool in the twilit world, the trees so densely packed in the ancient forest that he could barely see more than ten feet ahead. After a moment, he came to a halt against a twisted oak and listened intently. Only the sighing of the wind reached his ears.*

*After a moment's hesitation, he picked his way back along the trail he had made. It would be too dangerous to go any deeper. Near impenetrable in parts, the Forest of Arden sprawled for mile upon mile across the Warwickshire countryside and was home to bands of cut-throats and robbers.*

*In the high summer heat, Jenny sat on the grassy slope falling away from the forest's edge, the whole of their world spread before her. She greeted him with a wry smile. 'Starting at shadows again,' she teased.*

*Will was caught by a moment of pure clarity. Her dress, the blue of forget-me-nots, the tumble of her brown hair across her shoulders, features more delicate than those of the other village girls', green eyes more intelligent, the faintly quizzical nature of her smile. Some element, or combination of elements, brought forth an acute awareness of the tumble of time: from the moment the tomboy pushed him into the pond on the green when he was ten, through the fights and the arguments,* the slow surfacing of respect, emotions and perceptions shifting and coalescing across the seasons. At no point could he have predicted it would lead to here, now. But it had.

'Some of the girls hereabouts dream of a valiant protector who would fling themselves into danger at the slightest provocation,' he sniffed.

'Then you should seek them out.'

Lounging languorously next to her, he feigned aloofness, but his gaze was continually drawn back to the trees and the shadows that lay among them. Someone had been watching them, he was certain.

'Though I am now filled with confusion,' she mused. 'I thought I was stepping out with a poet. Who, in recent times, had also found fame in the debating chambers of the university at Cambridge. A scholar, and a dreamer. A writer of beautiful sonnets mapping the landscape of his heart.'

'A man can be many things, Jenny.'

'You would not hurt a fly,' she laughed. She toyed absently with the locket at her neck.

'What do you keep in there?'

'A fresh rose petal every day during the summer. To remind me of my one true love.'

'He is a lucky man.'

'He is. I hope he knows it.'

Excitement and nervousness fought within him. Everything was changing so quickly. Good fortune had brought the patron to his door, and it now seemed certain his verses would be published. At first there would only be a small stipend, but his future appeared assured and he could finally consider marriage.

With his hands behind his head, he pretended to watch the clouds, while surreptitiously eyeing the girl who sat next to him. Was this the right time to ask her?

Jenny cuffed him on the arm. 'I can see you watching me,' she said.

'Making sure you are safe.'

'I need no man to keep me safe.' She arched one eyebrow at him. 'You should know that by now, Will Swyfte.'

He did. She was strong-willed and fearless in the way she lived her life, and she kept the men of the village at bay with a quick wit that left them slack-jawed. Many of the locals found her too independent, but these were the very qualities that had drawn Will to her.

He weighed telling her of his intentions, and then decided it would wait until the afternoon. He wanted to ensure the moment was perfect, shaped like a sonnet to capture the emotion for all time, and soon she would be away to help Grace prepare the midday meal for their mother.

'When does your father return from his business in Kenilworth?' he asked.

She eyed him curiously. 'Why do you ask?'

'No reason.'

'Well, Master Without-Reason, I must be away to my chores. Let us meet again in an hour. And I will give you my opinion on your latest sonnet, should you require it.'

'As always.'

She surprised him with a kiss on the forehead. 'My heart is yours,' she whispered. And then she was gone.

He spent the next few moments planning the proposal in his head, and then fell asleep beneath a rowan tree, confident in the knowledge that there would be no more momentous day in his life.

When Will awoke, it was well after noon and the countryside was held beneath a languid heat. Afraid that he was late, he hurried down the baked track towards Jenny's house. The wind stirred the golden sea of corn into gentle waves that rippled around the hedgerows, where clouds of butterflies fluttered over the meadow fescue and birdsfoot trefoil. Birdsong and the drone of bees was a languorous accompaniment to a day for lazy walks, not momentous events.

*Across the field, he could just make out the thatched roof, and beyond it the dense, dark wall of the Forest of Arden stretching as far as the eye could see. Jenny's mother would undoubtedly be tending the garden with Grace at her side after the morning's tasks had been completed. And Jenny would be free to spend the afternoon with him.*

*His thoughts of a lifetime with Jenny, of writing, of love and art, were interrupted by the sound of her voice calling his name. On the far side of the field, she pushed her way through the corn towards him, smiling and waving, the blue of her dress sharp against the gold. Her face was aglow with the joy of seeing him. There was something so perfect in that moment he was sure it would stay with him always.*

*Climbing the stile, he set off across the field to meet her halfway. Before he had taken ten paces into the crop, the black clouds of a summer storm swirled out of nowhere on a sudden blast of wind. Puzzled by the strange sight, he paused to watch the clouds sweeping towards the sun, wondering why the image troubled him so.*

*In no time, it had grown almost as dark as night. Disoriented by the buffeting gale, Will was shocked by a crack of thunder directly overhead, and then the clouds dissipated as quickly as they had arrived.*

*With the sun blazing once more, he returned his attention to the cornfield and prepared to hurry on to Jenny. Yet she was nowhere to be seen. He slowed to a halt and looked around the rolling, golden waves.*

Playing a game, *he thought with a smile.* No one took such joy in teasing him.

'You cannot hide from me,' he called. 'I will find you.'

She must have ducked down below the level of the corn and was circling to surprise him from behind.

Calling her name, he ploughed a furrow through the swaying gold, but when he reached the point where he was sure she had been standing, he came to another puzzled halt. Her trail was clear through the field back to her house. But there was no sign of any other path leading *away. He knelt down to examine the stems of the corn around him, but none had been bent or broken.*

*He felt his heart begin to beat faster, still without truly realizing why. He was suddenly cold. Jenny was playful, and clever, he told himself, trying to find an answer to the puzzle.*

*He searched around the field, but when he glanced back he only saw a confusion of his own furrows crisscrossing the corn. It was impossible to move without leaving a path. But Jenny had left none.*

*He called her name loudly. He tried to call brightly, but he could hear the edge of desperation in his voice.*

*Only the sighing of the wind returned, as it had in the forest. A feeling of unaccountable dread descended on him. He knew then that Jenny was gone.*

*Turning slowly, he tried to find answers that would not come, and after a moment he heard himself whispering, 'I will find you.'*

# CHAPTER FOURTEEN

BOW BELLS RANG OUT AS NIGHT FELL AND THE CITY GATES WERE
slammed shut. From the ragged gap in the roof, Will heard the
bellman set out to patrol the streets, calling the hour followed
by his familiar refrain:

> *Remember the clocks,*
> *Look well to your locks,*
> *Fire and your light,*
> *And God give you good night,*
> *For now the bell ringeth.*

'Now?' Carpenter prompted as he listened for any sounds
from the street below. All appeared still, finally.

'Now,' Will replied. He led the way down from the loft.

In the street, the chill of the spring dark had done little
to dampen the stink. As they waited in a doorway for a pair
of smartly dressed coney-catchers to pass on their way to
finding a naive gull or two they could cheat out of their
money at the theatre, Launceston whispered, 'Let us hope
Pickering has not disposed of the Silver Skull, or the Enemy
has not located it while we hid like mice. If the boy had not

been so weak we would not be in this position.'

'But we are, so let us hear no more of it,' Will replied.

He eyed Miller, who waited with Mayhew, now even more subdued since night had fallen. The young man's eyes continually flickered from side to side as if searching for an imminent attack.

The dark cloaked them as they moved along the now empty streets, the only illumination the glimmer of candles and lamps through dirty glass. At the tavern, they hid in an alley where they could observe the door. A drunken man with a thick black beard and broad shoulders reeled out across the rutted street. Will and Carpenter caught him beneath the arms, clamped a hand over his mouth and steered him into the alley, where Launceston's knife at his throat helped loosen his tongue. Slurring his words, he told them the location of a house where Pickering's men took daily delivery of prizes stolen by cutpurses.

Leaving the drunk unconscious, they dodged down alleys, moving stealthily from doorway to doorway to avoid scrutiny. It took them a short while to find the house. Of all the rundown tenements in Alsatia, it was at first glance one of the worst, windows covered with planks, no signs of life within. A second glance revealed a surprisingly solid-looking door with a large lock, and in the shadowed doorway of the next property the dark shape of a sentry, arms folded, unmoving.

'Master Carpenter?' Will whispered.

Withdrawing a knife, Carpenter measured the distance and then let the blade fly. It thudded into the guard's throat and with a short gasp he pitched forward into the street.

Mayhew gaped at the fallen body. 'God's loaves! Where did you learn that trick?' he said in hushed tones.

'Why should I not have natural skill?' Carpenter hissed,

adding sullenly: 'It was taught me by one of the natives brought back from the New World.'

After they had hidden the body in a water barrel, Launceston and Carpenter kept watch while Mayhew dropped to his knees and unfurled a roll of purple velvet on the step, revealing a set of locksmith's tools.

'A steerpointe three-chamber,' he murmured. 'The lock of kings. A somewhat grand addition to such a hovel.'

'Pickering lives among the greatest thieves in all of England, and there is no honour among them. Of all places, here he would need the best protection,' Will replied. 'You can open it?'

With a theatrical sigh, Mayhew's skilful fingers swiftly manipulated three of the tools in the keyhole until the lock turned.

Aside to Miller, Will whispered, 'It is time now to put all doubts behind you, Tom. We face only mundane foes here. Pickering will have guarded his riches with the strongest arms in Alsatia. We will have to fight to reach him. Are you ready?'

'You need not doubt me, Will,' Miller replied. His smile was strained.

Easing the door open a crack, Will slipped inside and drew his sword. The hall was dark, but he was instantly caught by the scent of lavender pomanders, and bowls of spice to keep the smell of the street at bay. From high above them came the dim sound of revelry.

Putting a finger to his lips, Will beckoned the others in. He had expected there to be at least one of Pickering's lackeys on the other side of the door. Finding that the hall was deserted made him uneasy.

A blast of chill, smoky air reached him. As his eyes adjusted to the gloom, he saw, further along the hall, the door leading to the cellars hanging open. Muffled noises came from the dark below. Carpenter was about to climb the stairs to the rooms above, but Will motioned to him to stop. The cellars would make a secure place to store riches or prisoners.

Cautiously, he approached the open door. Rough stone steps led down past walls glistening with damp to where a ruddy glow was visible through the smoke, as though a furnace roared beneath. The voices were louder, but still indistinct, yet something in the tone gave Will pause. Motioning to the others to stay behind, he edged down a step at a time, covering his mouth against the noxious smoke. As he moved below the level of the hall, he dropped low until he could peer into the room.

Through the fumes, he saw a blazing stove, door open, with burning clothes, purses, and other unidentifiable objects spilling around the floor. What Will perceived to be the next bundle for the fire was revealed by the shifting smoke to be a body, tossed against one wall, still leaking blood.

The murmur of voices continued in the drifting acrid cloud, a susurration ebbing and flowing, now and then joined by a low, throaty rumble. Will saw two hot embers suspended in the smoke.

From the wreathing grey emerged a black dog that was unlike any cur Will had seen before, bigger than a calf, heavy-set with muscle. What Will had thought embers were its eyes. It turned its huge head slowly from side to side, a low rumble emanating from its throat, ready to attack in an instant. Lips rolled back from teeth that could crush a man's bones. A leather leash ran from its thick neck to a shape still partly obscured.

Will waited.

The dog's growl grew louder as if it sensed his presence.

Again the smoke shifted. An instinctive warning chill ran through Will before he had even realized what he was seeing. Squatting hunched over in a menacing posture was a lithe, powerful figure. Though Will couldn't see his face, the stranger's presence burned as hot as a furnace. Brown hair fell across his shoulders, and he was dressed in a shirt and breeches of a timeless cut in deep forest shades. Brown leather boots reached to his knees, and at his belt were a curved knife and the hilt of a sword shaped into a dragon's head. The dog's leash was held loosely in his hand.

In front of him lay another of Pickering's men, eyes flickering on the brink of death. His stomach had been torn open by the dog. The poor wretch was suspended by one powerful hand wrapped in the folds of his shirt, and was being quietly questioned even as he died.

When the timbre of the dog's growl changed, the intruder paused. Slowly, he turned his head towards the crouched spy. Slipping back before he was seen, Will was sure he had caught a fleeting glimpse of eyes as glittering and intense as the dog's red glare. The threatening mood in the cellar was palpable, and it had only increased his sense of urgency. Easing back up into the hall, he closed the cellar door and turned the iron key that protruded from the lock, although he knew it would only slow the one who waited below for a moment at best.

Miller read Will's face. 'What is down there?'

'Nothing of note,' Will lied. 'They are burning the leftovers of Pickering's ill-gotten gains.' As he moved past Miller, he whispered to the others, 'Time is slipping through our fingers, men. We must find what we came for, and quickly, and be gone in a twinkling.'

Darting silently up the stairs, Will slowed as he neared the top of the first flight. Round the turn two men waited halfway along the landing. They were rough and unshaven in their poor clothes, and their numerous scars detailed their violent life.

Withdrawing, Will motioned for Miller to ease by him, and then he rapped on the wall. A second later the shadows of the men loomed across the top of the stairs. Miller burst forth, and before the guards could raise the alarm he cracked their heads together and they fell to the boards unconscious.

After they had found all the rooms empty, they moved up the next flight of stairs. Four more men argued noisily as they drank ale, too many to eliminate without a fight.

Bounding from the top of the stairs, Will and the others took them by surprise. Will and Mayhew ran their rapiers through the first two men. Launceston rammed his dagger under the ribs of another, withdrawing it with a flourish to slash his victim across the throat.

The tip of Will's rapier brought the final man to a halt. 'More guards?' Will asked in a quiet, commanding voice. Frightened, his prisoner shook his head.

'Pickering is up there?'

'He is making merry with his copesmates for his bene fortune.'

'He speaks the thieves' cant,' Carpenter said. 'Prick him some more until he recalls the Queen's English.'

'Pickering celebrates a fine day's thievery with his men,' Will translated. He brought his sword hilt up hard against the guard's head and knocked him unconscious.

From below, the cellar door rattled, clear in the stillness of the house. The others looked to Will questioningly. Another rattle, more forceful. Raising his rapier, Carpenter prepared to despatch what he presumed was another of Pickering's men, but Will shook his head insistently, and pointed up the final flight of stairs. They saw the truth in his face, and cast uneasy glances back as they climbed. Will was acutely aware that the one he had seen in the cellar would soon stand between them and their only route out of the building. He would face that problem when he came to it.

He took the remaining steps two at a time, with the others close behind. The sound of festivities emanating from the room at the top was so loud that Will understood why no one had investigated the disturbance. A woman's giggle. The smash of a broken bottle. Frenzied music and raucous cheers.

'Some wine would be good now,' Mayhew said.

'You can have all the wine in the Palace of Whitehall if we can recover the Silver Skull from this den of thieves.' From the top of the stairs, Will could see through the open door.

The large room was ablaze with candlelight. Men in gaudy costumes and masks sat at tables arranged in a horseshoe, the roughness of what features were visible at odds with the delicacy of their outfits: gold and silver, black and red diamond patterns, green velvet, purple silk. The masks had long beaks like birds, or resembled devils or farmyard animals. Piled high on the tables were beef and pork, cheese and bread and honeycakes, and numerous jugs of wine and ale, on the finest tableware Will had seen outside the Queen's dining hall. Gold platters, silver goblets. In the space within the horseshoe, a buxom, half-naked woman frolicked with a jester who barely reached to her waist.

From his narrow view, Will estimated twenty men were present, but he guessed Pickering's inner circle would comprise the hardest, most violent cut-throats, who had sealed with blood their ascension to the upper ranks of the gang.

On the edge of his view was a grand, high-backed chair that resembled a throne. In it sat a fat man with a booming laugh.

His manner was confident, and the others appeared to be paying deference to him.

Will turned to his men, who waited for his orders in the shadows on the stairs. 'We are about to step into a pit of vipers, outnumbered by four to one,' he said, 'but we have surprise on our side. Cause as much disturbance as you can. I will seek out Pickering. The others will calm once I have a knife at his throat. Agreed?'

Nodding, the others drew their rapiers.

Bounding through the open door, Will leapt on to the nearest table, booting a platter of meat into the face of one of the guests. Amid the deafening outcry that erupted, knives were drawn and cudgels pulled from beside seats. Shrieking, the woman scrambled beneath the tables.

As two men pushed back their chairs to attack, Carpenter and Mayhew ran them through. By the time the other cut-throats had thrown off the effects of their drink and food, Miller and Launceston were among them. Blood sprayed across the floorboards as Walsingham's spies carved a swathe through the drunken underworld lords.

Running along the tables, Will avoided the fray and went directly for the King of Cutpurses. With one boot on the back of the throne, he propelled himself behind Pickering, turning fluidly to press his rapier against the man's neck. 'One word or movement and you are done,' Will whispered in the man's ear before shouting to the room, 'Hold now, or your master dies.' With his free hand, he tore off Pickering's mask to reveal a red-faced man, hair lank with sweat, piggy eyes roving fearfully.

Slowly, the cut-throats came to a halt, gazes flickering between Pickering and the door.

'Any attempt to leave this room will ensure you leave your life,' Will continued.

Then, through the open door, came the creak of the stairs and the unmistakable advancing rumble of the dog's growl.

'Matthew.' From his cloak, Will pulled one of the small leather pouches that all the spies carried, and tossed it to Mayhew.

Slamming the door, Mayhew poured the contents of the pouch — salt and a mixture of herbs — along the floorboards from hinge to lock. 'Now we shall not be disturbed,' Will said, gesturing to the concoction that lined the bottom of the door. As he had many times before, he silently thanked Dr Dee for his help.

'Now, Pickering, I presume?'

Rolling his eyes towards Will, the red-faced man looked frightened enough to faint.

'All we want is the Silver Skull.' Will flicked the tip of his rapier along Pickering's cheek for emphasis, raising blood. 'You have overreached yourself this time. This is not some purse from a poor country visitor or a necklace from some dowager fresh off the ship from Flanders. The price you pay for this prize will be your life.'

Pickering opened and closed his mouth like a beached fish.

The slow, steady tramp of boots echoed from the top of the stairs. Candles flickered, and Will was sure the room had grown a notch colder. Spies and cut-throats alike glanced uneasily towards the door, and when the dog's throaty rumble rose up, loud in the sudden silence, several men blanched. Blood trickled from the nose of the rogue closest to the door.

Spinning Pickering round roughly, Will pressed the rapier harder against his neck. 'Speak, now!'

'I . . . I . . .' Pickering stuttered, 'I am not who you think I am!' His eyes darted towards his associates.

'He lies,' Launceston said. 'Cut him a little more. It will loosen his tongue.'

But Will could see the fat man was too scared to lie. He scanned the faces of the other cut-throats and saw puzzlement there. 'So, even you did not know this was not your master.' The stand-in tried to scramble away, but Will caught him and dragged him back. 'So the King of Cutpurses keeps his identity a secret from those closest to him for protection from rivals and injured parties. Who is your master?'

'I do not know.'

'He hired you.'

'He wore a mask!'

Throwing the fat man to one side, Will stepped back on to the table and walked slowly round the perimeter so he could study the rogues. 'Take off your masks,' he ordered.

Reluctantly, they obeyed, revealing sullen, brutish eyes and unshaven jowls, scars and missing ears, teeth and eyes.

'The court of the King of Cutpurses,' Will mocked. 'It is a poor king who deserves a court like this.' He watched for any sign of offence, but all eyes were downcast.

Outside the door, the canine growl became a low howl that had a chilling, hungry quality. Everyone in the room flinched.

'What, you would feed us to your dog once we speak?' cried one of the rogues, a sallow-faced man missing an ear. 'We know nothing. That one there is Laurence Pickering.' He pointed to the fat man. 'He gave me ruff-peck and shrap every time I brought the lifts.'

'Feeding to the dog? A good idea,' Will said. 'Matthew, John, what say we toss one out of the door at a time until we find the real Pickering?'

140

'A good idea,' Mayhew replied with false bravado. 'Our dog has a frightful hunger.'

Mocking laughter rose up from the back of the group of cut-throats. Unable to see who had made the sound, but suspecting the real Pickering was there, Will jumped from the table and advanced. The rogues moved away from him.

In the middle of the room, he scanned the faces slowly. A faint click reached his ears, and a second later the boards fell away beneath his feet.

# CHAPTER FIFTEEN

AS WILL SURFACED FROM A DEEP, DARK POOL IN HIS HEAD, THE first thing he saw was the ruddy, grinning face of Pickering's jester filling his entire vision. 'Life is an illusion,' the jester sang with a slight sibilance. 'Laugh now, for there will be none of it when you are gone.' Pain lanced through the spy's wrists. He had been bound to a wooden frame.

When the jester tumbled away with an insane giggle, Will was overwhelmed by the colours, sounds and smells of his surroundings. Fiddle music soaring over a hundred drunken, clamouring voices. Woodsmoke and roasting pig, fat sizzling and spattering in the darting flames. Lanterns dancing on the awnings of stalls, the brightly coloured canvas glowing in reds, greens and golds, banners on the tall poles flapping in the breeze. Jugglers and fire-eaters moved among the crowd, alongside the vendors selling hot pies and sausages. The Thieves' Fair had transformed a dirty courtyard constantly thrown into shade by the crumbling tenements into a sea of colour and life that raised the spirits of people dragged down by day-to-day survival.

Glancing around, Will wondered how long had passed since he fell through the trapdoor, but there was as yet no hint of dawn's light. Where was the Silver Skull now? Memory of the dog and its master came back to him sharply, and he searched the crowd for any sign of the threat.

Seeing nothing, Will turned his attention to Miller, who was bound to a wooden frame beside him. Beyond, Carpenter, Mayhew and Launceston hung from a beam by their wrists, toes just resting on the cobbles. Their faces bloomed with bruises and cuts from a harsh beating.

'Tom, are you well?' Will called.

'No bones broken. When you fell through the trapdoor, they rushed us and beat us with their cudgels. We took several of them with us as we went down, but that only inflamed them more.'

Around the market, the thieves' strong-arm men patrolled with cudgels and daggers clutched in meaty hands. Glowering eyes watched for any sign of trouble. Sizing up the force, Will saw they were a formidable barrier to any way out of that enclosed space.

'What now, Will? They mean to do us in, I fear,' Miller said in a low voice.

'Keep steady. An opportunity will present itself.'

'I am not afraid. Better to go this way, looking a man in the eye, than facing up to those things that should not exist in any sane world.'

'The dog and his master—' Will began.

Miller interrupted. 'Gone when the door was thrown open.'

Miller held himself defiantly, despite the bonds. Will decided he liked him, and admired the way he fought to keep his equilibrium in the face of knowledge that filled him with dread, but the fatalistic note in his voice was a concern.

'Tom, you must trust me,' he said. 'I have stared into some

dark and dismal holes in my life, and yet here I am.' He kept his tone light for Miller's sake, but his body ached from the fall and what he guessed had been subsequent rough treatment at the hands of Pickering's men.

A commotion on the far side of the fair caught their eye as a torchlight procession made its way among the stalls. Cheers rose in its wake. When the parade drew near, Will saw the torches were held by young women in fine dresses who flirted and joked with the rogues they passed. They were accompanied by four men in the colourful masks and costumes worn at the feast – a devil, a harlequin, a wolf, a boar. At the head of the procession was a tall, wiry man in a robe embroidered with so much silver and gold thread it gleamed like a lantern in the reflected torchlight. He wore a white mask with a long, cruel bird's beak that arced down at the end, and several peacock feathers sprouting from an elaborate headdress. It was flamboyant and unthreatening, but through the eyeholes Will felt he glimpsed an aloof, menacing persona.

'Is that him?' Miller whispered. 'Laurence Pickering?'

'We forced him to step out of the shadows,' Will replied. 'But he still wears his mask.'

As Pickering led the procession forward, Will saw more prisoners trailing behind them, bound with ropes and covered in blood and bruises, and at the back a cloaked figure accompanied by two guards, but unbound. From the epithets – and occasional missiles – hurled at the prisoners by the crowd, Will guessed they were Spanish.

The man who was Pickering came to a halt in front of Will and looked him up and down silently.

'Life is an illusion,' Will said wryly. 'Laugh now, for there will be none of it when you are gone.'

'You are far from the fields you know. This is my court now.'

Pickering rolled the words around his mouth like pebbles. A note of at least rudimentary education shaped his tone, which was a dangerous thing for a man brought up in the rough criminal class of London where the skills of cutting purses and handling a knife or a razor were taught at the mother's apron.

'You appear to lead a grand life. I am surprised your fame has not spread further afield,' Will said.

'I do not seek attention. Indeed, I detest it. I am a private man—'

'And the work you do does not thrive in the full light of the sun.'

Pickering hardly blinked, which added a strange, detached nature to his manner as though he were examining another species. 'I would not appreciate more of your kind crawling round here like beetles on a dung-heap. And that is why I cannot allow you to return to your masters to tell them what you know of my business.'

'You think very highly of yourself. I have no interest in you, whatever title you give yourself, nor in your society of rogues. All I require is the return of an item that belongs to our Queen.'

'I think not. I know your kind. Your pride has been hurt.' Pickering motioned to the wooden frame and the taut bonds. 'You would have to return to teach one such as me a lesson.'

'I have far better things to do.'

Pickering flinched as though Will had slapped him. His voice was suddenly cold and cruel. 'I am king here. I rule. I command men and women to do my bidding. I have riches at my disposal. I may act upon any whim. I have my own army. Your kind would prefer I did not exist. You think I – and all these good men and womenfolk – are the dirt beneath your feet. But you cannot dismiss me. And especially now, for I hold your life in my hands.' Pickering fought to hide a quaver in his voice. Will gave a knowing smile that only angered the King of Cutpurses more.

Raising one hand imperiously, he snapped his fingers. From behind the prisoners, two of Pickering's men brought out a tall figure in a black robe. The hood was thrown back to reveal the Silver Skull glowing like the moon. A gasp ran through the crowd, and Will and the others too were transfixed by the striking mask. With great bearing and dignity, hands clasped calmly in front of him, the Skull looked directly into Will's face.

'Fine workmanship indeed, but that is little silver for a man of your standing,' Will said. 'Why, I would give you the same amount in gold to buy that entertaining mask.'

'So, you think me a fool too.' Pickering frowned. 'The value of the thing lies beyond the silver.'

Will looked deeply into the shadowy eyeholes of Pickering's mask. 'And what did your cousin Bulle the Hangman tell you of this thing?'

Pickering waved a dismissive hand an inch from Will's nose. 'I know that it is more than a mask. That some think it has a great power hidden within it. And I know interest in it reaches far beyond our shores.'

Will's attention fell on the Spanish prisoners, glowering among the armed guards. 'That is an interesting way to negotiate a sale to Spain.'

'Do you take me for a traitor?' Pickering snapped. 'Again, you show your contempt for me. I am as good a man as you, a true Englishman.'

'Then I admit I am confused.' Will was playing Pickering carefully to draw out the information he needed.

'It was my intention to arrange an exchange with the

Spanish, and then to steal their gold. However, they proved their untrustworthiness and attempted to trick me first. Like you, they did not give me the attention I deserved, and so paid the price.' He turned to examine the Spanish spies. 'Or will before the hour is out.'

Since he had awakened, Will had been testing his bonds, but they were fastened with the thieves' reek-wort knot, considered to be unbreakable. 'English gold would be much more rewarding,' he said.

'And that will be my next port of call. Once you are dead, and there is no one to trace this business to me.'

'You will not escape so lightly. You have woken the beast now.' Will's hard smile only emphasized the weight of his words.

'Do you fear death?' Pickering asked sharply.

'There are worse things than death. I have seen them.'

'Will?' A woman's voice drifted out from the back of the prisoners, quizzical and slightly dazed. Will knew it at once.

'Grace?' He immediately regretted showing any sign of recognition, for Pickering snapped one of those black, unblinking eyes towards him, and Will got the impression that beneath the mask he was smiling.

Pickering motioned for the guards to allow Grace to come forward. Throwing back her hood, she revealed eyes glistening with tears. 'I am sorry, Will. I persuaded Kit to tell me where you had gone. The Spanish knew you and I were friends and they followed me here.' She appeared dazed.

'Did they hurt you?' Will asked. He fought back his anger.

'No . . . no . . . They thought they could offer me in exchange if you acquired the item for which they were searching, but then we were all taken.'

'Let her go,' Will said quietly. 'She has nothing to do with this business.'

Pickering didn't answer, but Will could see he had no intention of freeing Grace. No one who had witnessed the role Pickering played could be allowed to leave Alsatia in case they brought the authorities back to his door.

'Free her now,' Will continued, 'or, God help me, you will pay a price far in excess of anything you plan to do to us.'

'You are in no position to make demands.' The surrounding mass of criminals began to shout Pickering's name. Basking in their adulation, Pickering stood for a moment with his arms raised to the sky. 'Is it time for our entertainment?' he called across the fair. The crowd bayed its response. 'Is it time for good sport?' Howls now, feverish eyes gleaming in the torch-light. 'Let us celebrate our good fortune. We are the masters here. We can do anything.'

Drumming their cudgels on the cobbles as they pressed in on every side, the mob appeared on the brink of rushing forward to tear the prisoners limb from limb. The crowd parted as Pickering marched in a parody of stateliness. At a snap of his fingers, four guards released Will and the others and re-bound their hands behind their backs. The procession set off again, and the five men were guided behind the Spanish prisoners through the fair. Shattered barrel staves and stones rained down from all sides and the noise of bloodlust became deafening. Fearful, Grace eased herself close to Will's side, head bowed, hands pressed together in prayer. She was pale, her features appearing even more delicate against the rough faces of the rogues. She was trying to appear strong, Will could see, but her hands trembled.

On the far side of the fair, Pickering led the procession up the steps of a circular wooden arena about twenty feet across. The crowd eased around the perimeter, resting against a fence. 'It is time for you to shake hands with Hob!' Pickering announced with a theatrical flourish.

In the pit below was a brown bear. It appeared to be blind in one eye, with patches of fur missing and covered in scars, but it threw itself around with ferocious energy, ripping at the air with its claws in response to the crowd's raucous baiting, and when it tore its jaw wide and roared, those closest to the edge of the pit grew pale and backed away. In the centre of the small arena was a post used to tether the beast with a chain, but this bear had been set to roam free.

On the edge of the pit, with a prime view of the activity below, was a wooden platform with a raised dais underneath a flapping canopy supported by poles. Gold tassels hung around the edge and red banners fluttered from poles in a poor attempt at regal grandeur. On the dais under the canopy was a long wooden table with a high-backed chair behind it – a throne for the King of Cutpurses. The crowd milled on either side, roaring in excited anticipation of what was to come.

As he stepped on to the dais, Pickering gave a kingly wave, and the crowd cheered him wildly. He took his seat and a plate of hot pork and a flagon of ale were quickly laid before him by attentive hands, and then the crowd began to chant. 'Hob! Hob!'

Will watched the bear crash around the pit, swatting at the taunting spectators just out of reach of its claws. *I have danced with some ferocious partners, but that is the worst, no doubt.* Inside, he steeled himself for what was to come, quickly scanning the pit for any paths to escape.

Pickering pointed to one of the Spanish prisoners. A guard cut the man loose and before he could protest he was thrown into the pit. The bear fell upon him. One sweep of the claw took the Spaniard apart, organs cascading into the sawdust. Snapping jaws tore at the still-twitching torso. Inflamed by the blood, the crowd cheered loudly.

Regally, Pickering waved for a second Spaniard to be tossed to his death. He went silently and defiantly, with a proud bow to the companion who was clearly his leader.

Sobbing, a third prisoner pleaded in babbling Spanish. It amused Pickering for a while until he became frustrated by his inability to understand, and gestured for the man to be sacrificed. With a scream, he plunged into the whirl of snapping jaws and raking claws.

Will watched the spectacle, taking in the muzzle now caked in blood, the stained teeth when the bear threw its head back and roared, the power and speed of it. But two important things struck him: at times the bear moved awkwardly, the result of an injury to its left leg, and the blind eye also hampered its movements.

'My time is being wasted! Commit me now before I die of boredom!' he called.

Grace cried out and then began to sob at his folly. Knowing how much she was suffering, Will couldn't bring himself to look at her.

The crowd fell silent and looked to Pickering. Under their scrutiny, he seemed to flinch, as if fearful of losing face. 'I accept your offer,' he responded. 'But the bear appears to be winning this bout. Shall we give it more competition?' The crowd cheered its response.

As Will was released, Pickering ordered the final Spanish prisoner to be set free too. He was as tall as Will, with the same strong, graceful movements of a swordsman. There was an aristocratic tilt to his head; Will could see by his confident manner that he was used to commanding respect. His beard was waxed, his black hair shone in the torchlight, and his black and gold doublet and jerkin were of a stylish and expensive cut. Rubbing his wrists, he approached Will and gave an elegant bow. 'Don Alanzo de las Posadas,' he said.

'William Swyfte.'

Pausing, Don Alanzo fixed Will with a quizzical eye. 'England's greatest spy?'

'If my assistant, Nathaniel, were here, he would have a quick reply. But . . . I have been called worse names.'

Don Alanzo bowed again. 'And I am the world's greatest swordsman.'

'And a spy too. We have much in common. Though I would be forced to challenge your title, in another place, at another time.'

'For now, we are associates in battle.' Don Alanzo turned to the bear pit. 'Though I would have preferred more equal competition.'

'We could give the beast a sword?' As he stepped towards the edge of the pit, Will whispered to Don Alanzo, 'Stay on his left side.'

Before Pickering's men could throw them in, Will and Don Alanzo jumped into the gore-splattered arena. In the enclosed space, the creature's roars were magnified, and the baying of the crowd faded into the background. The bear lunged with a massive swinging paw. Will ducked beneath it, the claws tearing chunks from the wooden planks of the walls. Taking Will's advice, Don Alanzo danced into the bear's blind zone.

'Do you have a plan?' the Spaniard called.

'Yes. Not to die.' Will avoided a heap of torn flesh and bones that had once been one of the Spanish spies. A severed head stared at him with glassy eyes.

'I expected something more detailed from someone with

such an impressive reputation.' Don Alanzo darted behind the bear as it turned.

'Your patience will be amply rewarded.' Will briefly recalled a snowy landscape not so long ago, and another bear threatening to end his life, but the image was lost as he leapt to stay ahead of the claws.

The bear was fast, but its age and injuries had taken their toll. Even so, Will's concealed blade was too small to cause any real harm to the beast, and he was afraid the weapon would only serve to enrage it. Will and Don Alanzo continued to dart left, forcing the beast to flail around in a continuous circle. Every time it attempted an attack, they put the central tethering post between them and it. Its frustration drove it to lash out towards the crowd hanging over the restraining fence and bellowing their dissatisfaction. Will caught sight of Pickering's beaked mask as he leaned forward, his posture rigid. Will flashed a grin and bowed, which provoked Pickering to yell and shake his fist.

As they continued their baiting, Don Alanzo lost his footing in the bloody flesh of his companions and skidded into the path of the maddened beast. The bear roared and dropped its head low, throwing all its weight into a ferocious attack. Sprawled before it, Don Alanzo was unable to move.

Reacting instinctively, Will spun himself round the central pole and swung both booted feet into the side of the creature's head. As it lumbered and slipped in surprise, Will dragged Don Alanzo out of its path.

'Best not toy with him,' Will said with a grin.

Barely had Will scrambled halfway across the pit when the bear returned furiously, its jaws torn wide. Will flung himself to one side. Teeth snapped air a mere inch beyond his heel. Angered by Will's blow, the beast seemed to have found a new reserve of speed and strength, and it was all the two men could do to keep away from its jaws and claws.

Recognizing that their luck had almost run out, Will barked a quick order to Don Alanzo, but had no time to check if the Spaniard understood. Luring the beast towards him, Will suddenly turned and darted back. He was relieved to see his ally waiting with cupped hands for a boot, propelling Will up on to the bear's back. The wild din of the crowd even drowned out the creature's roars.

Will clutched an arm across its throat. It took all his strength to hold on as the beast thrashed wildly from side to side, its jaws snapping in rage. Again and again it swatted at him. Claws ripped within a whisker of his face. Then, in its frenzy, the creature almost crushed him against the side of the pit, but still he held tight.

Finally, Will managed to exert more pressure on the bear's throat with his flexed arm. At first, it only served to enrage it more, but after a moment its swats became more feeble.

The crowd's exultation turned to fury as they saw what Will was doing. Eventually the bear stumbled, and then fell to all fours.

Will rolled off its back to be met by an unsettled stare from Don Alanzo. 'You are insane.'

'We only know we live when our heart beats faster,' Will gasped. 'Now, I think we are done here. Shall we be away?'

Before the bear could recover, it was Will's turn to cup his hands for Don Alanzo, sending him to the top of the central pole. Around the arena's edge, the mob became frenzied. Half slipping, the Spaniard steadied himself and then leapt to the edge of the platform. Two of Pickering's men rushed him, but he ducked beneath their grasping hands, turned and thrust both of them into the pit. As they shrieked in terror, he reached an arm down and hauled Will to safety.

In their brief glance was a mutual acknowledgement that the truce was over, and as Will turned to his men Don Alanzo disappeared into the mêlée. Three of Pickering's cut-throats came at Will with cudgels and daggers. As they neared, confident in their numbers, Will decided it was finally time to use the hidden knife Dee had given him. The blade burst out of its sheath along his forearm, and with one fluid swing he slashed the throat of the first man and planted the point into the chest of the next. Startled, the third man fell before an elbow rammed into his face.

Bounding to Launceston and the others, Will slashed at their restraining ropes. As they quickly freed themselves and turned to fight, Will forced his way through the crowd to where Pickering was rapidly disappearing into the throng, bundling Grace and the Silver Skull along with him.

'Grace!' Will called, too late.

Before he gave pursuit, Will put his weight against the long table and heaved one end into the pit. The bear hesitated for only a second, and then launched itself up the ramp.

Chaos erupted across the fair as the bear crashed over the edge of the pit and into the crowd. The screams and shrieks were drowned out by roars as it tore through flesh and bone.

Will rammed his way through the fleeing people, throwing bodies right and left, but Grace, Pickering and the Silver Skull were lost in the swell.

In the confusion, stalls were overturned, their owners fighting furiously with their former customers. Shattered lanterns sent flames leaping to canvas and wood and then up into a blazing column that only added to the panic, for in the city fire was the greatest threat.

Through the whirling bodies, Will glimpsed a glint of silver bobbing towards the other side of the courtyard. As he neared, he saw Don Alanzo leading the Silver Skull through the throng towards one of the alleys heading off the courtyard, but the cry of 'Clubs!' was already rising up from Pickering's men as they surged towards him.

Will sprinted across the cobbles, but he had not got far when the chilling howl of a hunting dog echoed over Alsatia. The milling crowd slowed, faces growing unsettled. Even the bear came to a momentary halt.

The dog, and its master, were close and drawing closer.

# CHAPTER SIXTEEN

WITH HER HOOD PULLED LOW TO HIDE HER FACE, GRACE sheltered behind the wreckage of a stall from the yelling crowd of cut-throats and customers washing back and forth between fire and the rampaging bear. The howl of the dog had chilled her unaccountably, but she had quickly forgotten it when she saw knots of Pickering's men beating paths through the mass as they searched for her. Soon she would be discovered and her skill at giving the King of Cutpurses the slip would be for nothing.

Roaring furiously, the lunging bear was finally surrounded by several men with staffs. Shrill screams echoed as raking claws tore one open from throat to groin, but within a minute the others forced the beast over the edge and back into the pit. A cheer went up, and as the bear's rage subsided, the panic receded.

Keeping low, Grace edged round the stall until she glimpsed a path to one of the four alleyways leading off the courtyard. Before she could move, a heavy hand fell on her shoulder.

Her startled cry was stifled by a hand over her mouth, and her head turned to see a huge man, smiling kindly down at her. Almost weeping with relief, Grace recognized him instantly as one of the men who had been held prisoner alongside Will.

'Mistress, we must get you out of this danger,' he said.

'Please,' she begged, 'Will is in great danger. You must help him.'

'Will can take care of himself.'

'No,' she pressed. 'I saw him go in pursuit of the Spanish spy. The Spaniard will lead him into a trap – the Don has other allies in London. And the King of Cutpurses has despatched his murderous crew on Will's heels. You must help him!'

As Miller looked into Grace's face, he softened and said, 'Very well. But stay here. I will fetch the others to help you—'

'Go!' she interrupted. 'I will call if I need them.'

With a hesitant nod, Miller threw his great frame in the direction Grace had indicated. Glancing around, Grace spied Launceston, Mayhew and Carpenter. They had now claimed cudgels and knives and were carving a path through Pickering's men with cold efficiency, too occupied to help her.

Determination blazed inside her. She would not be beaten down, or afraid. Jenny's death had convinced her that life was hard, easily cut short, and that living in fear only diminished it further. Setting her jaw, she waited for the way to the alley to clear again, and then darted from her hiding place.

Few women were in the courtyard, and most of them were doxies or members of the criminal gangs, but she moved deftly, not wanting to draw attention to herself. She was involuntarily caught up in a hectic attempt to put out the blazes, but the alley appeared within reach. Yet even as her heart leapt in anticipation, out of the corner of her eye she caught sight of a bird-mask fixed upon her, and for the briefest moment she was caught in Pickering's unblinking stare. With no cronies close to hand, Pickering gave chase himself. Barging through the crowd, he closed the gap so quickly that Grace knew that even if she reached the alley he would be upon her soon after.

The clatter of his hob-nails upon the cobbles rang at her back. With her breath burning in her chest, she slipped into the dark of the alley and only when her eyes adjusted realized it was occupied. Her startled shout faded at the sight of a familiar face.

'Kit!' she cried. 'And Nathaniel!'

With a small group of the Queen's men at their backs, Marlowe and Nathaniel advanced on the courtyard. Marlowe had his sword drawn, but Grace almost fell into his arms in relief.

'Thank God,' she gasped. Glancing back, she saw Pickering come to a halt when he saw the new arrivals, and then turn and push back into the crowd.

'Nat urged me to bring help when Will did not return by the appointed hour,' Marlowe said. He turned to the men. 'Seal off this courtyard. Let no man escape, for we will have an army of rogues on our back if word gets out that we are here.'

'Will pursues a Spanish spy, and another of your men has gone to help,' Grace said. 'You must aid him—'

The words died in her throat as the chilling howl of a hunting dog rose up again, this time laced with an insistent bloodlust. It had located its prey.

# CHAPTER SEVENTEEN

THE TWISTING ROUTES AMONG THE TENEMENTS WERE IM-
penetrably dark, the buildings too high to allow the moonlight
to reach the ground. Only the occasional glimmer of candlelight
gleamed in the black, sackcloth-covered windows. Will's
footsteps seemed to echo off the walls like stones dropped on
ice. From somewhere ahead of him, a similar noise resounded,
and from behind came the tramp of many boots as Pickering's
men followed him through the maze of byways. Their lanterns
flickered like fireflies as they searched doorways and side
alleys.

Reaching a crossroads, he realized the footsteps ahead
had slowed. Keeping close to a wall, he edged forward until
whispering voices emerged from the gloom. They were
speaking Spanish. Another voice responded, mellifluous
but with an unsettling note of menace. It came to Will like
some half-remembered nightmare, involuntarily unlocking
unsettling thoughts that gradually filled him with dread.

Following the low conversation along an alley to another
courtyard large enough to be filled with silvery moonlight,
Will saw Don Alanzo and the Silver Skull with the one he

now thought of as the Hunter. Beside him, his dog's red eyes sparked.

Keeping well to the shadows where he could not be seen, Will spied on the scene. Within moments, the dog's hackles rose and it released a low threatening growl. Will's breath caught in his throat. At the dog's warning, the Hunter paused and then turned in Will's direction with a knowing smile. The dread Will had felt at the sound of his foe's voice was magnified tenfold. At first the Hunter's face appeared strong and handsome, with a square jaw, defined cheekbones and almond eyes, and clear skin that had a soft, golden hue. But Will had the unsettling impression that he was looking at a mask, and that something terrible squirmed behind it. This true nature spoke to Will on a level beyond his five senses, teasing out thoughts of death and despair, failure, sickness and pain. There was something undeniably of the churchyard about this being, with the only real glimpse visible in the fierce eyes, which were as black as coals and devoid of any compassion.

Will expected the Hunter to set his dog loose, but instead a hand moved to the pouch at his belt and he seemed to remove something which he then kept hidden in his palm.

Stepping out from the shadows, Will said, 'You keep dishonourable company, Don Alanzo.'

Don Alanzo eyed the one beside him. 'A mercenary from Flanders.' Will couldn't tell if the Spanish spy was truly blind to the Hunter's real identity, or if Don Alanzo had convinced himself of a lie as the only way he could do business with the Enemy in good conscience.

'More than that. And worse.' Will strode forward, keeping his left arm and Dee's blade hidden behind his back.

'Leave here, Will Swyfte, as quickly as you can,' Don Alanzo said. 'I offer this advice as a courtesy. In return for your saving my life in the bear pit, I now save yours.'

'I cannot leave without the Silver Skull.' Will kept one eye on the Hunter as he spoke. 'I have been entrusted with the task of returning it to the Tower.'

'Him,' Don Alanzo snapped. 'Not it. There is a man beneath this mask, and he has been held prisoner in this godforsaken country for twenty years. You claim to be the civilized defenders of the true way, righteously holding back the conspiracy of barbarians beyond your borders, but you commit atrocities without a second thought. You persecute good Catholics—'

'Because you persecute us. You and your allies will not be happy until Elizabeth's England is but a memory.' Passion rose up in Will's voice.

The dog strained at its leash, but the Hunter only watched Will with wry amusement.

Scowling, the Spanish spy replied with a note of anger, 'Arrogance finds a good home in this country. You believe any action you take is justified, and so you are capable of anything, without even a glimmer of guilt. You are blind to the blood on your hands, and the brutality that lurks behind every sneering face in your court. You have turned away from God and Rome, but your sins run deeper by far.'

Aware that earthly enmities were drawing him away from the most dangerous threat, Will restrained his emotion and said calmly, 'The one who stands beside you is more dangerous than any Englishman, and capable of worse things by far. He smiles and calls you friend, but he plays you like a lute.'

'That may well be,' Don Alanzo replied, calming. 'But for now we have a common enemy, and so we walk shoulder to shoulder.'

Will was distracted by Miller emerging from the alley on

the other side of the courtyard. The young man sneaked along the wall, only to be brought up sharp by the sight of the dog and his master. In that single moment of hesitation, Will saw all Miller's fears play out across his face, but then the man Walsingham had put his faith in pushed those doubts to one side. Gripping his dagger, Miller attacked.

Though he didn't make a sound, he'd barely got halfway across the courtyard when the Enemy sensed his presence. Will watched a smile flicker across the Hunter's lips, but there was no time to call out. Their foe didn't move until Walsingham's man was almost upon him, and then he whirled and grabbed Miller's wrist before he could use his knife.

As Will moved to help, the leash was slipped and the giant hound prowled forward, its deep, rumbling growl turning the pit of Will's stomach. Will held the blade before him, but the dog didn't attack; it seemed to be simply marking a line between the Hunter and Will and moved back and forth along it, holding Will at bay with the snap of its huge jaws every time he tried to round it.

Still smiling, the Hunter pulled the boy towards him with slow, relentless ease. And then he leaned in and whispered in Miller's ear.

Instantly, Miller grew still, his eyes widening. A tremor crossed his face, and a moment later a pool grew around his boots where his bladder had loosened. Pulling back, his smile now crueller, the Hunter let go of the young man's wrist, which remained aloft for a second before his arm slumped to his side.

'Tom! Pay him no heed!' Will called, unable to get past the still-prowling dog.

Miller appeared unable to hear. His shoulders slumped, he walked as if in a trance away from the Hunter, Don Alanzo and the Silver Skull towards the dark shadows on the edge of the courtyard. Sliding down the wall, he came to rest with his head buried in his hands.

'I will exact a harsh price for any harm you have caused him,' Will said.

Eyes glittering, the Hunter turned to stare back at Will, silently mocking.

As the hound returned to its master's side, the tension broke. Thirty of Pickering's men suddenly surged into the courtyard from different alleys and surrounded them. Turning slowly, Don Alanzo looked directly at each of them as if searching for something he couldn't find. Despite the overwhelming force, he appeared completely at ease.

Turning back to Will, he said in a cold voice, 'This is my final warning. Move away from here and do not look back.'

His words were filled with such weight that Will walked slowly backwards until rough hands grabbed his arms and held him tight. He continued to study Don Alanzo and the Hunter, trying to anticipate what was to come; but if one thing convinced him of the extent of the potential threat, it was their complete calmness in the face of cudgels and knives.

'This Spaniard is an Abraham-man,' the leader of Pickering's men said in the thieves' cant. The ragged scar that ran from his left temple to his right cheek only emphasized the contempt in his voice. 'Or he's been too long in the boozing ken. You know I cut bene whids – he carries no sword and there are thirty of us good copesmates! Let's have him!'

He beckoned the others with a hand missing two fingers and together they advanced on Don Alanzo and the Silver Skull. Will had expected his foe to let slip his terrifying hound, but instead the Hunter opened the palm of his hand to reveal what looked like a blue jewel as big as a coin. It shimmered with the reflected light of the moon.

'See, lads! They offer us their riches to buy their lives. We shall have that . . . and their lives!' The scarred man gave a mocking laugh.

As the rogue stepped forward, the Hunter fluidly reached out to the Silver Skull and pushed the jewel into an almost invisible indentation on the ghostly mask. An unnaturally loud click brought the scarred man to a suspicious halt. Will watched his foe whisper in the ear of the Silver Skull, who started to wring his hands and turn away, but the Hunter caught his arm and held him tight. Don Alanzo whispered in the Skull's other ear, which seemed to soothe him a little. After a moment, the Silver Skull began to shake, and Will was convinced that beneath the mask he was trying to control deep sobs. Then, with what seemed like resignation, he raised one hand to his temple, and half bowed his head as though in deep thought.

The actions were strange enough to bring the band of now baffled thugs to a halt.

As Will looked on a barely perceptible change came over the Silver Skull, perhaps a slight change in the quality of the moonlight it reflected, and he thought he heard a barely audible noise like a single-struck fiddle string.

The scarred man flinched, his hand involuntarily going to his throat. He coughed once and spluttered. When it passed, his mocking smile returned. But only for a moment. Within seconds he was reeling, tearing at his face and arms and fighting for breath, eyes bulging and wide with panic.

The rest of Pickering's thugs were rooted in horror. The hands holding Will fell away, and, keeping his eyes on the scene unfurling in front of him, he slowly edged back through their ranks to the shadows on the edge of the alley.

The scarred man's skin blackened as if burned by an invisible fire that spread quickly across his face, then down his arms, and his skin cracked like a muddy track beneath the hot sun. Blisters erupted everywhere, covering every part of him, forcing his eyes shut and deforming his lips. One by one they burst to release foul, yellow pus. As blood streamed from the corners of his eyes, and out of his nose, and his ears, so his flesh began to liquefy. Falling to his knees, the unfortunate man began to claw at the parts of him where sticky bone was now visible.

Sickened by the hideous sight, Will was transfixed.

Watching their colleague's death throes, Pickering's men crossed themselves, eyes wide in horror, and whispered prayers, but the spectacle kept them fixed.

At last, what remained of the scarred man pitched forward on to the cobbles and lay still. Will was reminded of something similar, in a village not far from Darmstadt when the plague had struck. But there death had come slowly, over days, not a matter of moments. Now he understood what the Silver Skull really was: a creator of disease, powered by the will of the one who wore it. All it required to operate was the Key: the blue jewel which the Hunter had fitted to it.

As he looked around him, a second, then ten, then all of the cut-throats showed similar symptoms. In no time at all, the magicked disease had leapt among them, driving them to their knees as they experienced an agonizing death.

Will felt numb as he realized with horror why the Enemy was so determined to gain the Skull: if thirty men could be brought down so quickly, where was the end of it? A street? A city? An entire country? Perhaps even the greatest army could be wiped out in the blink of an eye. With this vile mask under their control, all Dee's defences amounted to nought, and England was left naked and on the brink of becoming a charnel pit.

A tingling began in the tips of Will's fingers and his throat began to close. The Silver Skull was looking directly at him. Dread formed in the pit of Will's stomach, but as its icy touch reached into every part of him he realized he didn't fear his own death. Indeed, a part of him secretly yearned for it, for then he would know the truth about Jenny, and all the desperate worry and doubt would finally be over.

But before the disease could rush through Will, Don Alanzo caught the Skull's arm and guided him away with a gentle tug. The Hunter and his monstrous dog were nowhere to be seen. Don Alanzo gave Will a slight bow, the scales now balanced, and hurried across the courtyard into the dark beyond, with the Skull beside him.

Will lurched after them, but his head was swimming and his legs were like jelly. Staggering, he fell to his knees, and could only watch Don Alanzo and the Skull disappear into the maze of Alsatia. Anger at his failure surged through him, driving out the last remnants of the Silver Skull's lingering touch, and he hammered one fist on to the cobbles and cursed. Within moments, the whinny of a horse was followed by the crack of a whip and the rattle of carriage wheels.

Miller stumbled over, unscathed, but with a deep-seated horror burned into his eyes. 'Will, I failed you,' he croaked.

'You did what you could, as do we all. Come.' As they headed back, Will added, 'Whatever he said to you, ignore it. They lie. That is what they do.'

His face haunted, Miller couldn't meet Will's eyes.

At the scene of the Thieves' Fair, Will was surprised to find that Marlowe and a group of the Queen's men had rounded up a collection of rogues, who were being held at sword-point in one corner of the courtyard. The bodies of those few who had resisted lay on the cobbles as a lesson to the others.

Grace ran over and took Will's hand so tightly it was as if she would never let it go. 'You are safe,' she whispered. 'I prayed for your return.' She tried to smile, but it only emphasized the tears of relief in the corners of her eyes.

Her concern touched him, but it was not the time to show it. 'You should not be here, Grace,' he scolded her. 'But I am glad to see you well.' He motioned to Nathaniel to take Grace to one side.

'She only wished for knowledge of her sister,' Nathaniel said quietly. 'Do not treat her harshly.'

The weight of what he had witnessed lay heavily on Will. With the mask in the hands of the Enemy, time was rapidly running out. He sought out Marlowe. 'Kit, I thank you for coming to my aid. Now, bring me the so-called King of Cutpurses. I have some hard questions for him.'

Marlowe motioned to Pickering's costume, topped by the bird's mask, lying in a heap on the cobbles. 'Mistress Seldon tells me this was his disguise.'

'Then once again he hides among his people.' Will cursed as he eyed the sullen mass of rogues.

'If you do not know his looks, you will never find him among that rabble, Will.'

Will considered his options, and then said, 'Bring the men to me one at a time.'

As the pageant of glowering men trailed past, Will studied the size, the gait, and most important the eyes; for Pickering's unwavering stare was unforgettable. Many he dismissed immediately: too squat, too large, too grey. A few he spent a moment considering. But there was one who at first appeared wrong, until Will realized he was feigning a limp and walking with his left shoulder stooped. He kept his gaze down, until Will forced him to look up. The unblinking black eyes were coldly familiar.

'The King of Cutpurses,' Will said wryly. 'I fear your nobility is about to be tested.'

Pickering responded only with a defiant stare.

Will turned to Marlowe. 'Take him to the Tower.'

# CHAPTER EIGHTEEN

'A LADY, IN ALSATIA, AMID THE GREATEST ROGUES OF LONDON? What did you expect?' Will said angrily as he strode down the Long Corridor from the State Rooms to the wing set aside by Walsingham.

'And this is where I hear your lecture about recklessness again, I suppose?' Grace responded without flinching.

He could see her temper was hot and she would fight him every step of the way, as always. 'You risked a great many things, including death.'

'If you kept me informed, I would not have to take risks.'

'So it is my fault?' he blazed.

'Stop treating me like a little girl.'

'Then trust me.' He paused. 'If I discover anything about Jenny, I will tell you.'

She grew sullen. 'It is not simply about Jenny, and you know that.'

His own anger drained away as he saw clearly the pretty young girl who raced to him through the garden whenever he visited Jenny. 'You cannot protect me in the work I do,' he said, his voice softening.

'And you cannot bring Jenny back by protecting me. Nor

can you erase the pain of her loss. But we cannot help ourselves, can we? We are both cursed to repeat our mistakes over and over, trying to save the one person who reminds us of that time when all was right with the world.'

She looked away sharply. He knew it was because tears had sprung to her eyes, but she would not show him what she perceived to be a weakness. Much of what she said was true, he knew, but Grace was more to him than a symbol of what had been lost. In the midst of his own grief, he had been devastated to see the effect of Jenny's disappearance on her. It had torn out her heart at first, and then replaced her happiness with a slow-burning bitterness. He cared for Grace deeply, and he would not have her suffer any more.

Grace saw him wrestling with her account of his motivations and she too softened. Resting a hand on his velvet-clad arm, she said, 'Jenny haunts us both. The manner of her passing . . . here one moment and then gone, no body to bury or grieve over, no truthful account, only guesses and hints and what-might-have-beens . . . Neither of us can find rest while there are so many questions still, and no likely answers forthcoming.' She bit her lip and looked away out of the window to where the servants carried cuts of ham to the kitchens from the back of a wagon, ready for the day's meals.

The warmth of her hand on his arm soothed him. 'This is not the life either of us would have chosen, but it is the one we have,' he said, gently brushing her cheek with the back of his hand. 'You have accepted Jenny is gone for there is no evidence to show otherwise. That is sensible. I believe she is still alive because there is no evidence to show she is dead. Perhaps less sensible, but it is all I am capable of doing. Whatever happened that day is lost to us. Now. But I have seen . . .' He caught himself. 'I do not believe the world is as simple as most people accept. There are spaces in it for strange things to happen.'

'For Jenny still to be alive?' she said, unable to believe.

'Perhaps.'

'You hold on to a ghost and it slowly draws the life from you. You will never find peace, or happiness, while you look back, and grip so tightly to such fantasies, and ask question upon question. Will, you are here, now. You must take some joy . . . some love . . . or all will be wasted.'

'I only ever wanted my Jenny. She was right for me. There will be no other.' His voice was so hushed it almost disappeared into the stillness of the corridor.

Grace turned away from him, pretending to examine the servants once again.

'Whatever happened to her, she is still with me every day,' he continued, 'here and here.' He touched his temple and his breastbone. 'I would not give up that to dull what pain I feel.'

'If one of us is the child here, wishing and hoping, it is not I,' she said brusquely. 'I will continue to search for answers in my own way. And if you continue to keep secrets from me, I will be forced to go to even greater lengths.'

Will watched her march back along the corridor, head down, cheeks burning, defiant. He felt a deep sadness for what she had lost, and a determination that she would, at least, have a happier life ahead. If he failed Grace, he failed Jenny; he failed in everything.

Putting aside his emotions, he made his way to the Tryst Rooms, where Henry had secretly wooed the Queen's mother. They were now set aside for Walsingham's use, and lay on the first floor above the hall that Dee had christened the Black Gallery.

Nursing their wounds, Mayhew sat gloomily in one

corner, drinking wine despite the earliness of the hour, while Launceston and Carpenter ate bread, cheese and sausage as they turned over the previous night's events.

'Where is Tom?' Will asked.

'Away brooding,' Launceston replied. He skewered a piece of cheese with the tip of his knife and popped it into his mouth, chewing slowly.

'I would not have him on his own after what he saw.'

Mayhew let out a theatrical sigh. 'We cannot mollycoddle the boy. He must learn to deal with these things, as have we all.'

'He did not have the benefit of a slow admission to the secrets of the world, as we had,' Will replied. 'Find him and bring him here.'

Cursing to himself, Mayhew levered himself from his chair and sloped out.

Carpenter pushed his plate away and growled, 'At least with the failure of this mission no one was left dead. Or scarred.'

Will turned on his colleague. 'There are no failures, and no victories either, you know that. Just a constant shifting back and forth, with casualties on both sides. That is the true tragedy of our war: it will never be won.'

'Defeatist,' Carpenter sniffed. 'I presume Walsingham will want to hold someone accountable for our failure to recover the Silver Skull.'

Will tore a chunk of bread off the loaf in the centre of the table and gnawed on it absent-mindedly. 'Again, John, no failure, however much you might want to apportion blame. This struggle continues. We have simply reached a turn in the road, and it seems we must take another direction.'

'Yet we still do not know what this Silver Skull does, and why it is so important to the Enemy. Perhaps it is simply meant to distract us from the real threat,' Launceston said.

'All will become clear in time,' Will replied. So far he had only told Walsingham what he had witnessed of the Skull's terrifying capabilities, and Miller had been sworn to silence, although the power of the mask appeared to be the last thing on his mind.

Nathaniel appeared at the door to the Tryst Rooms and beckoned Will over. 'Sir Francis Walsingham is ready for you now,' he said. 'Should I be prepared for fanfares and fawning crowds?'

'Not this time, Nat. This matter is still a tangled web, which requires some unpicking.'

Nathaniel held the door open. 'A case not concluded in time for an ordinary in the tavern? Your reputation is in danger.'

'We all have our bad days, Nat, and I fear this one will get worse before it gets better.'

They made their way outside and took Walsingham's black carriage, following the cluttered, noisy streets east to the Tower. As was so often the case, Nathaniel pretended to show no interest in the matter under investigation, all the while asking oblique, circuitous questions in an attempt to assuage his curiosity. And as was usual, Will pretended not to notice, and batted them away with an infuriatingly insouciant manner. It was a game of friends, but with serious intent: in his ignorance, Nathaniel rattled the cage door, but Will had made it his business never to let him realize what beast lurked within.

The carriage passed through the main gates of the Tower into a furious hive of activity, the like of which Will had not seen before. Soldiers dressed in shining burgonets and cuirasses, brown breeches and white stockings carried pikes, arquebuses, arbalests and broadswords from the Tower's armoury, while other groups escorted bruised and battered prisoners to the cells for interrogation.

Will instructed Nathaniel to stay with the carriage, and went in search of Walsingham in the White Tower. In a room filled with charts and documents, Will found England's spymaster in deep discussion with a small army of his advisers. Will overheard part of the conversation, about the parlous state of England's defences in the face of a rumoured Spanish invasion. The atmosphere was tense, the advisers failing to grasp the urgency of what Walsingham requested. They knew that an invasion could take weeks, and his paymaster's suggestion that disaster could strike within hours or days made mouths gape with incredulity. Surveying the scene, Will realized he had never seen Walsingham lose his temper, but there was an intensity about him that was frightening; in such moments he appeared capable of anything.

Once the advisers had been dismissed, Walsingham led Will along a maze of corridors and down the winding steps that took them into the bowels of the White Tower.

'It would be easier if you could guide them with more than hints and innuendo,' Will suggested.

'That is our burden, and you know that well, Master Swyfte,' Walsingham replied. 'Only a very few understand the true nature of the war we fight. The rest must accept our guidance on faith alone.'

'No sign of Don Alanzo or the Silver Skull?'

'Our informants watch all the highways out of London, and the ports of Kent and Norfolk, Sussex and Dorset. Yet they seem to have vanished like the mist.'

'You have informed the Queen?'

His brow furrowed, Walsingham paused and looked Will in the eye. Though he was marginally shorter, the spymaster's cunning-bright eyes carried authority. 'In the most basic details. One must walk a line between providing an adequate summation of the threat facing the nation, and leaving the monarch paralysed by fear.' Walsingham waited for guards to unlock a large, iron-studded door before continuing. 'We have struggled with disease many times during our Queen's reign. The thought that such devastation could be unleashed by an enemy in the blink of an eye, in one of our cities, perhaps even in London itself, is beyond the comprehension of most minds. But we know the depths to which the Enemy will stoop to destroy us. And the Spanish, of course, would seize upon such internal chaos to launch an invasion from across the seas. We are in a state of high alert – England's fate hangs by a thread. Never have matters been so critical.'

'Then we cannot afford to delay here,' Will said. 'Our King of Cutpurses, Pickering, is our only link to the mask, and the Enemy's plans.'

At the foot of the stairs, in the deepest part of the White Tower, they were confronted by another oaken door flanked by two guards, who unlocked it, and closed it swiftly behind them. The room beyond was vast, and unpleasantly gloomy. A handful of torches at large intervals created a permanent twilight that obscured many of the workings of that place. Occasional moans or cries emerged from the shadow, like the haunting voices of lost souls, and there was a heavy stink of excrement, urine and blood.

A tall man in his early forties, fair-haired, with bright eyes and an easy smile, walked out of the dark to greet them. He clasped his hands before him in an expression of continual glee. Jeremiah Kemp, England's Torturer-in-Chief, enjoyed his work. A constant succession of Catholic spies and potential spies, criminals, traitors and informants passed through his doors, among them Jesuit priests, minor aristocrats, lawyers, farmers, gentlewomen and wealthy merchants. Kemp treated them all with equal care and attention.

'Welcome, Sir Francis, Master Swyfte,' he said with a shy smile and a deep bow. 'All is ready for you.'

'Pickering?' Walsingham asked.

'He has been softening. Please see.' Kemp led them past every imaginable device of human torture to one of the wooden posts that supported the ceiling of that underground chamber. From near the top of the pillar, Pickering hung from iron gauntlets fastened to an iron bar supported by staples in the wood. It was a deceptively simple instrument. The weight of the suspended body caused the flesh in the arms to swell so that it created the agonizing sensation that blood was about to burst from the end of every finger.

His face drawn and badly bruised, Pickering watched in a daze.

'Are you ready to confess?' Walsingham asked him.

'I am but a lowly thief,' Pickering croaked. 'I know nothing of these matters of state.' His weak voice sounded truthful, but Will saw the briefest shadow flicker across his face.

'You like games?' Will asked. 'Chess?'

Pickering eyed him with hatred.

'The pawns are removed from the game early. There is little to be gained by extending their life.'

'Unless they are clever pawns, with aspirations to rise to be the true power on the board,' Pickering spat from bruised, bloody lips.

Will nodded. 'Then we know where we stand.' Turning to Kemp, he said in a clipped, icy voice, 'Let us introduce our guest to the Duke of Exeter's daughter.'

'Certainly, Master Swyfte.' Kemp clapped his hands to

176

summon the guards to bring Pickering down from his perch. Though he had only been on the pillar for a short while, his legs were too weak to support his weight.

The guards dragged him to the end of the chamber where the rack stood before a row of candles, a wooden bed stained with bodily juices, a ratchet system for turning at one end.

'The Duke of Exeter was an inventive man when he was the Constable of the Tower, and he devised this method to ensure full truth and honesty from those he entertained,' Will said. 'You are aware how his "daughter" works?'

Pickering shook his head, but his expression suggested his imagination was already hard at work.

'The arms and legs are fastened thus,' Will continued, his voice clear and precise. 'This winch is turned, which extends the rack here, and here, and so the guest's limbs are stretched. I am told the pain is very great indeed, in the joints in particular. If the turning of the winch is continued, the limbs are dislocated, and eventually torn free.'

'I will tell all you wish to know,' Pickering said. His eyes widened, and tremors ran through the taut muscles of his features.

'Unfortunately, it is already too late,' Will replied. 'The moment has long since passed for caution. We can no longer risk time wasted on dissembling and mistruths in the hope that you might find some small advantage for yourself.'

Pickering's face drained of blood as he realized what Will was saying. 'You will torture me, even though I will tell you what you want to know?'

'Every act we perform in this dark room destroys our humanity a little more.' Will pressed his face close to the rogue's ear, his voice harsh, barely above a whisper. 'We strip our soul by degrees. But we are small men, all of us, and meaningless in the vast sweep of the nation's life. When we are gone, we shall be forgotten, but now we have a part to play. The men and women of England deserve to live free, and earn their crust, and laugh and play, and sleep easy every night, free from fear. I gladly sacrifice my life to buy that liberty for them.' He paused. 'And I would gladly sacrifice your life for the same.'

Walsingham nodded to the guards. Pickering's feeble struggles were quickly restrained, but his mounting cries reverberated off the stone walls. Calming a little once he was strapped to the rack by his wrists and ankles, he began to babble everything he thought his captors wanted to hear.

Will stood back until the rack had been tightened to the point where every increment of the winch released a cry of agony from Pickering. 'You are inhuman!' he screamed.

'We are,' Will said. 'No good man should ever submit another to these deprivations. It would behove neither of us to say you brought this upon yourself. Nor should we consider it a punishment, for I pass no judgement on you. But at this point all men and women in England are at risk of the worst death imaginable. I weigh my own soul, and your agonies, against that. Now, let us proceed slowly and carefully, so there is no room for doubt. You are the cousin of Bulle, the Tyburn hangman. Is that true?'

'Yes, yes, yes!'

Walsingham watched Will, curious to see where this line of questioning would take him.

'I am always troubled by seemingly random connections,' Will said. 'This business began with the execution of Mary, Queen of Scots, at the hands of Bulle. Now his cousin is involved in the next stage. By chance?' Will shook his head. 'What did Bulle learn at Fotheringhay?'

It took a moment for Pickering to stifle his sobs, and then

he began, 'Mary . . . Mary delayed her execution for hours, through pleas, and prayers, and lies, and deceit.'

'That is true,' Walsingham said.

'There was nothing to gain by extending her execution. She was not afraid to die.'

'Then why?' Will pressed.

'She was waiting. For . . . for news of the discovery of the Key to the Silver Skull.'

'No news could reach her in Fotheringhay,' Walsingham said. 'Guards were at the door of her chamber continuously. All letters in and out were carefully scrutinized.' He nodded to Kemp to turn the winch another notch.

When Pickering's screams had died, the King of Cutpurses cried with a raw throat, 'What I say is true. She did receive news by . . .' He looked from face to face fearfully. 'You will not believe me, but it is true!'

'Go on,' Will said.

'By a mirror. A magic mirror!' He screwed his eyes shut and waited for the pain to lance through his joints. Kemp was poised, one hand on the winch.

'A magic mirror,' Will mused. 'That is how the Enemy communicates?'

'Their own mirrors? Or all mirrors?' Walsingham wondered aloud. 'Should we remove every looking-glass from the Palace of Whitehall? My God, do they spy on us as we look into our own faces?'

''Tis true,' Pickering gasped, relieved. 'That is how Bulle told it to me. He spied upon Mary from the secret passage that ran behind her chamber.'

'He knew of that?' Walsingham asked.

'He bribed the captain of the sheriff's guard,' Pickering continued, eager to please. 'Many of the women brought to

179

execution offered their bodies to Bulle in return for their freedom, or at the least a quick end. He took them regardless. This time, he thought . . . perhaps . . .'

'With a queen?' Walsingham said, disgusted.

'Mary was renowned for her skills between the sheets.'

'So, while Bulle spied on Mary in the hope that he could steal favours from her, he saw her speaking at the mirror?' Will enquired.

'Yes! As my cousin told it to me, the glass grew cloudy as if the smoke of a great fire billowed within it. From his vantage point, he could not see any face within it, but he could hear a voice.'

'What kind of voice?' Walsingham asked.

'A man. Or something that purported to be a man. It told Mary that the Key had been recovered . . . from the crypt beneath the Holyrood—'

'The palace in Edinburgh.' Will wondered how long the Enemy's plan had been in motion; when had they first seized control of Mary to manipulate their way into the Palace of Holyrood to search for the Key? Months? Years? Had she always been under their control, as they slipped into the spaces and the weaknesses between human prejudices?

'—and then the voice proceeded to tell Mary about the plot to steal the Silver Skull from the Tower, and the date and the time.'

'And Bulle passed this information on to you, for you to find some way to gain financial advantage from a blow against England itself,' Will said sharply. 'You did not pass this on to the authorities. You sought only your own personal gain. That is treason in and of itself.' He nodded to Kemp to tighten the winch another notch.

Pickering's shrieks ended in a series of juddering sobs. 'I

did not seek to harm my country or my Queen!' he sobbed. 'I simply saw an opportunity.'

'As all men of business do,' Will said sardonically.

'I planned to return the Skull to the authorities—'

'Once you had played England and Spain off against each other, and grown fat on the proceeds. What else did Bulle tell you?'

'Nothing.'

'Nothing that you remember?'

'No.'

Will gave the nod to Kemp, who tightened the rack another notch. Briefly, Pickering lost consciousness from the pain, and when he finally came round, Will said, 'Jog your memory, while your limbs are still attached.'

Babbling incoherently, the King of Cutpurses eventually attempted to run through everything his cousin had told him, one drunken night in the Bear in Alsatia. It was only after two more turns on the winch that he recalled something new.

'The voice said . . . they still search . . . beneath the palace,' he gasped.

'For what?'

'I do not remember! I . . . I . . .' Kemp moved a hand on to the winch. 'A shield! Yes, my cousin said a shield!'

'A shield,' Walsingham repeated.

'Thank you for your time,' Will said to Pickering. 'You have been most helpful. Now, I believe, Master Kemp has some further questions for you on other matters.'

From a brown leather bag, Kemp removed a sheaf of documents two fingers thick. Pickering began to sob gently.

As Will and Walsingham made their way back to the light, Walsingham mused, 'The Shield. The third and final item required for the Silver Skull's operation. It lies . . . or lay . . .

181

beneath the Palace of the Holyrood. The Enemy searched at the time of Mary's execution, but do they now have the object they sought?'

'If the Enemy had the Shield, the Hunter would have used it in Alsatia,' Will replied. 'As it was, the Skull's power was only released briefly, the display stopped before it could do harm to all present. It was a warning to us . . . mockery, perhaps . . . nothing more.'

'My agents beyond the city walls reported a black carriage moving north at great speed, all curtains drawn. It did not stop at the usual places,' Walsingham said.

'Then I will be away to Edinburgh within the hour,' Will announced, pulling on his gloves. 'There may still be hope if we act swiftly.'

'God speed,' Walsingham said. 'But remember, Scotland and England may now have a steady relationship, but Dee's defences do not extend beyond the border. The Enemy has always thrived on the lonely moors and misty mountains of that northern land, aye, and in their cities too. A desire to gain some protection from our common foe is one reason why James of Scotland is so keen to bring England even closer in his embrace. It is said he rants nightly to his advisers about yawning graves, straw dolls in babies' cribs, and the threat that waits for him and all Scotsmen under the Hill of Yews. You must watch your back at all times.'

'Nathaniel will do that for me. Our spies in Edinburgh are to be trusted?'

'As much as any. I will alert them to your arrival.'

'No,' Will said. 'Let my arrival be a surprise. I will contact them when I reach the north.'

In the carriage on the journey back to the Palace of Whitehall, Will ordered Nathaniel to pack his bags to accompany him on the journey to Edinburgh. 'Scotland,' Nathaniel sighed. 'I hear it is a place of hard, grey skies and a constant drizzle that dampens the spirit as much as the clothes.'

'But you have the joy of my company, and such learned and witty discourse that many would pay for such a privilege.' Will watched the faces pass the window, afraid with every one that he would see some sign of disease starting to flower.

'My heart sings already,' Nathaniel replied.

In the courtyard next to the Black Gallery, the carriage pulled into a stream of activity, with several servants accompanying the court physician and bystanders whispering in doorways. Almost as ashen as Launceston's natural complexion, Mayhew dashed from the Black Gallery and tore open the carriage door.

'What is wrong?' Will enquired. 'The Queen—'

Mayhew shook his head. 'The boy.'

He led Will at speed from the Black Gallery through the Tryst Rooms and into a loft where pigeons cooed. The physician was just leaving as they arrived, his face grim.

Miller hung by the neck from one of the rafters.

Sickened, Will could not speak for a moment as he tried to comprehend what must have tormented the youth after his encounter with the Hunter. He cursed himself for not doing more to ease Miller's pain, and for failing to protect one in his charge.

'Cut him down,' Will ordered.

'I searched for him as you said,' Mayhew stuttered, 'and could not find him anywhere until one of the servant girls came here for a tryst with her love and—'

'Cut him down!'

Mayhew hastily complied. Once the youth was laid on the dusty boards, Will collected him in his arms and carried him down to the Tryst Rooms. Although he had only known Miller for a matter of hours, he felt the death more personally than any he had experienced in recent months.

'We failed him,' he said to Mayhew as he laid the body on a table.

'We did what we could,' Mayhew replied. 'The knowledge of the Enemy affects all of us in different ways. We cannot predict the outcome. We can only hope.'

'We did not do all we could,' Will stated, his face set. In anger, he hammered one fist into an open palm. 'He was thrust into this battle too soon, without proper precautions.'

Mayhew held out his arms. 'Desperate times—'

'Quiet!' Will snapped. 'Many people killed this youth and they will all have to carry it on their conscience – our side, who engaged him in activities beyond him; those who stole the Silver Skull and ensured he would be forced to battle too soon; but most of all, the Enemy . . . the Hunter.' Will recalled the Hunter whispering in Miller's ear, the grinding expression of confusion, then horror, that bloomed in the boy's face at whatever had been said. 'He was murdered at that moment, though it took some time to take effect. But know this: there is a price to be paid here, and I will ensure it is exacted from that Hunter the next time we meet. So do I vow!'

Will studied the dead boy's face, which even in death contained the innocence that he had carried like a torch. He tried to recall the last time he had felt that warm innocence himself, but it had long since been driven out of him.

'Fetch me parchment and a quill,' he said, his voice hollow. 'I shall write to his father myself.'

# CHAPTER NINETEEN

'CAN THIS THING NOT GO ANY FASTER?' WILL BELLOWED OVER
the thunder of the carriage wheels on the rutted lane winding through the night-dark Scottish Lowlands. Hanging out of
the window, he clutched the rail on top of the carriage to stop
himself being thrown clear.

'Not unless you want to risk pitching down the bank into
the valley,' the driver yelled back. He cracked his whip and
the horses increased a step, but the carriage slewed on to one
wheel, skidding sideways across the mud before crashing back
with an impact that threatened to shatter the axle.

The road had been treacherous ever since they had left
England behind, winding around the side of the great hills
that were still touched by snow on the top, or ploughing across
valley bottoms beside sucking bogs. Horseback would have
been quicker, but the carriage allowed them to sleep while
travelling, and to remain out of sight of prying eyes.

Glancing behind, Will could just make out the silhouettes
of their pursuers against the star-dappled sky as they crested a
ridge: there were three of them on horseback, riding as if Hell
were at their backs. Will had known the Enemy would attempt
to prevent his journey at some point, but when the riders had

185

appeared from the trees in the carriage's wake four miles back, their arrival had still felt like a winter storm.

Cloaks billowing behind them like bat-wings, the riders moved inexorably closer. Recalling the maps he memorized before their journey began more than seven days ago, Will peered into the dark landscape flashing by to try to get his bearings. Away in the valley was the River Esk, and he could see the bulk of Rosslyn Castle rising up from the dense forest. That meant Edinburgh was only six miles away, but the riders would have caught them long before then.

He threw himself back inside the carriage where Nathaniel was clinging on for dear life. 'Spanish or highwaymen?' Nathaniel asked.

'Being a poor fellow, you have nothing to offer either of them, so do not alarm yourself.'

'I suppose you will be playing the hero at some point,' the younger man sniffed. 'Have some regard for my life while you seek to bolster your own fame.'

'Nat, you are first and foremost in my mind, as always.'

The carriage careered to the left as the road followed the contours of the hill. Once again the right wheels lifted, this time so high it seemed the carriage was going over. Bags and cases flew around the interior, and Nathaniel crashed across the leather seats. As the wheels went down, it threw him back the other way.

'Damnation!' he shouted. 'I could drive this carriage better myself!' Exhausted and hungry, his temper had deteriorated during the long journey from London, on which they had stopped only briefly to change horses and eat, sleeping in the carriage as it bounced north over the lanes of England.

'We will soon be in Edinburgh, Nat, where there will be all the wine, women and hot food that you need.'

'You think about yourself. All I want is a good bed and a long sleep.'

Always a hair's breadth away from a disastrous crash, the carriage plunged on, round the steep sides of hills, through dense woodlands, where it felt they were floating in a sea of black, and then across the valley floor while the moon painted a silver trail ahead of them. Finally they began the ascent of the hills that rimmed Edinburgh.

The deafening storm of the horses' hooves had become the familiar music of their journey so they were acutely aware when the note changed: the disturbing syncopation of more hooves had joined the steady beat.

From the space beneath the seat, Will removed a length of rope from among the tools the driver stored within the carriage, and tied one end to his wrist, leaving the other to trail free.

'Nat, I ask this of you now: whatever happens, do not look out of the windows,' Will said, his face stern.

'Why? You are afraid I will see you fall like a jester upon your bony rump?'

'Heed me now, Nat. This is important.'

Nathaniel recognized the tone in his master's voice and nodded. 'Whatever you plan, take care.'

'Those who take care never experience all the wonders life has to offer.' Will pushed his head outside where the wind tore at his hair and made him deaf. The nearest rider was just behind the rear wheels of the carriage and to one side. Though the face was lost to shadows, Will could see the fire of the eyes burning through the dark. He had noted the strange, shifting quality of the eyes' inner light before – sometimes green, sometimes gold, sometimes red as now – and though he had no idea what it meant, it sealed their unnatural nature.

Grasping the roof rail, Will hauled himself out of the window, placing one foot on the sill to push himself on to the roof. As the carriage rattled into another area of dense woodland, it bounced so furiously that only the strength in Will's arm prevented him from being hurled off.

The other two riders were close on the further side of the carriage, riding in an uncannily effortless manner.

Will gained purchase with the toes of his boots and held himself fast within the area defined by the rail. With an effort, he tied the free end of the rope at his wrist to the rail, an anchor that should keep him from being thrown off the carriage. But if he fell it would drag him into the wheels.

When the carriage burst out of the wood, Will hooked his toes under the rail and carefully raised himself upright. The wind tore at him even more fiercely, and although the rope allowed him to steady himself, he had to keep shifting his weight to maintain his balance.

As the rider closed in, Will drew his sword. Gripping the rope with his left hand, he hung out over the void and sliced down. The rider dropped back to avoid the blow and drew his own sword. Pulling his mount alongside, he launched a series of duelling strokes, attempting to slash through the rope that held Will fast.

Secured by the rope, Will parried every blow the rider made. Thrown wildly about, he caught only glimpses of his foe: a face that in the gloom seemed little more than a skull with those fiery eyes burning in sunken sockets, bone-white hands making powerful slashes and thrusts with the sword. All three men were relentless, seemingly tireless, with unnatural strength and grace. Yet the way the shadows clung to them left Will chilled, as if they could control the very darkness itself.

The dark rider dropped back a way before stepping up

easily to balance on the saddle. Still clutching the reins in one hand, he drove his mount forward, leaping for the carriage and slashing as he flew through the air.

Stumbling back on one knee, Will brought his sword up high to take the brunt of the attacker's blow. Even up close, the Enemy's face was lost in shadow, as if it drew all light from the vicinity. His sword darted, towards Will's heart, his neck, the supporting rope, switching rapidly.

Just as Will thought he was gaining the upper hand, the carriage crashed over a fallen branch in the road and all four wheels left the ground. When it slammed back down, Will was thrown on to his back.

Seizing the moment, the Enemy swordsman thrust down with his weapon. Will tore his head to one side at the last moment, the blade driving a fraction past his ear and through the carriage roof. Nathaniel's cry of surprise rang out.

Before the Enemy could withdraw his sword, Will thrust his weight on to his shoulders and jammed his feet into his opponent's gut. The impact flipped the Enemy swordsman over the end of the carriage into the road.

Will had no time to catch his breath. One rider was preparing to attack the terrified driver, who lashed out frantically with his whip, while the other was ready to leap on to the carriage roof from his saddle.

As Will threw himself towards the driver, another lurch knocked him off balance. When he next looked up, the Enemy was on the seat. Even with his whip, the driver didn't stand a chance. His attacker grabbed his cloak and wrenched him up with ease. Holding the now screaming man up over his head for a brief moment, the Enemy flung him from the racing carriage, just as the third rider leapt on to the carriage roof.

Will didn't wait for him to gain his footing. With his sword, he slashed through the rope holding his wrist and in the same fluid movement propelled himself forward, kicking the Enemy from the seat. Plunging down the side of the carriage, Will's foe flew under the rear wheels.

Dragging himself into the seat, Will gripped the reins with one hand while turning with his sword to face the final rider.

At the last, the Enemy was distracted by a loud cry. Nat was hanging half out of the window, brandishing the long iron needle the driver used to repair the horses' bridles.

'Nat, inside!' Will yelled; too late.

As the swordsman fixed his gaze upon Will's assistant, a haunted expression rippled across Nathaniel's features.

Will thrust his sword into the distracted Enemy. Fearing his foe would be as insubstantial as mist, Will was grimly pleased to feel solid flesh and bone under his rapier. Straining, he used his weapon to lever the attacker off the side of the carriage. With relief, he turned all his attention back to the horses, refusing to slow the pace until he was sure any of the Enemy who had survived were far behind.

'Nat, inside, now!' he shouted, afraid his friend had already seen too much. After the devastation he felt at Miller's suicide, Will could not bear Nathaniel to be infected by the same creeping despair. The words he had spoken to Nathaniel's father all those months ago were still heavy on him. He would keep Nathaniel safe.

After another mile, he reined in the horses and called for Nathaniel to sit with him. From his assistant's subdued demeanour, Will could see how greatly he had been affected.

'What was that, Will?' Nathaniel asked quietly once they had set off again.

'What kind of question is that, Nat?' Will replied as lightly as he could muster, though his heart still pounded in rhythm with the hoofbeats.

'The face—'

'Did not have the rugged, handsome features of my own, but that is no reason to pour scorn on a poor, afflicted highway robber. Perhaps those same unsavoury features were what drove him to a life of crime. Why, perhaps we should pity him, Nat! Were he not now a bloody smear 'pon the road.'

'Like the coachman.'

'I mourn him, as do you, but there was nothing that could be done once those bastards had chosen to take his life.' He added in a quiet, respectful tone, 'We will arrange for his body to be collected once we reach Edinburgh, so he can be buried by his family.'

Nathaniel nodded. Will watched the fear and confusion mingle in his assistant's face. He had seen it many times before, in others, as the mind fought to reassert its own state of order on what should never be.

'And they were highwaymen?' Nathaniel pressed. He couldn't help but glance over his shoulder along the dark road behind them.

'What else would they be?' Will laughed, and he hoped Nathaniel would not hear the lie in it. 'You frighten yourself, Nat. I know you are made of sterner stuff than that.'

Will's tone eased Nathaniel a little. 'I felt I saw my own face looking back, though frozen in death . . .' He gave a humour-less laugh at how ridiculous that sounded.

'Exactly,' Will affirmed. 'An illusion. The mind plays strange tricks, especially when it is jolted free of its moorings by a runaway carriage ride.'

'Then it was a highwayman I saw? Nothing more?'

'Nat—'

'Yes, I am a fool! I am sure you will find great humour at my expense when you are in your cups.' Nathaniel feigned annoyance, but his relief was palpable.

Cracking the reins to urge the horses on, Will hid his own relief. At times, it felt as though he was attempting to hold back a torrent that would wash away everything he held dear if he failed for a moment. Every word was a lie designed to create a world that did not exist. It was not surprising that the members of Walsingham's band of spies rarely lived long. Will was convinced many reached a point where they simply gave up, let themselves die – worn down by the lies, and by the harshness of the reality that lay behind the illusion they created.

He put on a grin and showed it to Nathaniel. 'Wine and women are within our grasp, Nat,' he said. 'Let us make haste so we can enjoy the night before it is gone!'

Grumbling quietly, Nathaniel sat back.

Will let his own thoughts drift to what lay ahead. Whatever threat they had faced there on the road paled into insignificance compared to what waited for them in Edinburgh.

# CHAPTER TWENTY

AFTER THE UNSETTLING DARK OF THE WILD SCOTTISH COUNTRY-side, Will was comforted by the torchlight and glinting lanterns as the carriage rattled through Edinburgh's city gates and on to the cobbles of the main street. The boom of the closing gates behind, too, was oddly reassuring.

Though a centre of high art, scholarship, and religious thought, Will could see that Edinburgh was a world away from London. It was a city of shadows, still attached to the old world as London was scrambling into the bright modern future. During the time of Elizabeth's rule south of the border, Edinburgh's population had soared, Will knew. Nearly seventeen thousand people were now constrained within the walls of a city little more than a mile square. Looking up, he could see the result silhouetted against the lighter sky; with no room for building outwards, newer residents had added precarious, poorly constructed storeys on top of tenements – known in the city as *the lands* – designed to carry less than half their new height.

Far below, in the claustrophobic gloom among the dour stone buildings, the overcrowded, filthy streets were a breeding ground for disease and crime, where cut-throats and murderers preyed upon their own and hope was thin. It was the perfect hunting ground for the Enemy.

*No Dee here to keep the people safe. Only the harshness of daily life.*

Will was not blind to the irony of the fact that the city's brooding aspect reflected his own state of mind. He would never reveal it to Nathaniel, or to anyone else, but he felt the world slipping from under his feet as it had after Jenny's disappearance, only this time the stew of emotions was infected with guilt and a sense of his own personal failure to protect young Miller's life.

A cold anger seethed within him, demanding retribution, and answers. Nothing was going to stand in his way.

They abandoned the carriage near Cowgate, where the noblemen, ambassadors and rich clergy made their homes, and slipped quietly to the address that Walsingham had given them, a three-hundred-year-old, three-storey house of solid stone with a fine oaken door and an iron knocker. Will hammered out the coded rap, and after a moment they were admitted by a man carrying a candle. He was exceedingly tall, thin and elegant, with a hooked nose and swept-back white hair.

'Alexander Reidheid?' Will enquired.

'Master Swyfte!' Reidheid shook his hand furiously. 'It is an honour . . . an honour! . . . to have the great hero of England in my home!'

Nathaniel sighed loudly.

'Sir Francis Walsingham speaks highly of you, sir,' Will said, after they had been invited inside. 'He claims you know the comings and goings of every man in Edinburgh, and your understanding of the subtle moods of this city is without peer.'

'He flatters me.' Reidheid's cheeks flushed, but he was pleased with the compliment.

A young woman entered shyly. She was pretty, with delicate features, brown hair in ringlets and green eyes that flashed when she saw the guests.

'My daughter, Meg,' Reidheid said. She curtsied as her father introduced Will and Nathaniel. Will noticed Nathaniel about to register his tart weariness at another woman fawning over *England's great hero* when Meg's eyes skittered quickly across Will and settled on Nathaniel himself. Nathaniel was clearly taken aback by the attention and did not know how to respond.

'Perhaps Meg could show Nathaniel our quarters while we discuss important matters,' Will said.

Discomfited by this new development, Nathaniel followed Meg to the rear of the house while Reidheid led Will into the with-drawing room where a roaring fire made it exceedingly hot.

'I apologize if you find the temperature unpleasant,' he said. 'Increasingly, I have difficulty getting warm. It appears to be an affliction that affects all our kind sooner or later, as though those damnable things suck the life and warmth from us.'

'The nights are still chill. It is comforting,' Will replied with a polite sweep of his arm.

While Reidheid tossed another log on to the grate, Will took in the room: the wooden panels marked with the family crest, the gold candlesticks and silver platters, a tapestry and several delicate embroideries. 'You have a fine house,' Will said.

'Sir Francis Walsingham pays well,' Reidheid said, smiling, 'but I have some investments in ships sailing for the New World.'

'That business brings high rewards, so I am told.' At a gesture from Reidheid, Will took a seat next to the fire. 'We could exchange pleasant talk till dawn, I am sure, but I am here on urgent matters,' he said.

Reidheid's smile faded. As he poured two flasks of amber whisky, he said with regret, 'Our mutual Enemy even intrudes on polite conversation.'

'And you have more trouble with them here than we do in England?'

'They torment the countryside as they have always done, haunting the glens and the lochs, and they move freely through our city. But here they have chosen to play a quiet game in recent years. They can pass for mortals, if they so choose, and they slip between the cracks of everyday life, causing mischief and misery in subtle ways, and only intermittently.'

'Their attention has been elsewhere,' Will said. 'On the search for a key to a great weapon, which was hidden here in the city. Now they hunt for the final thing they need to complete their plan.'

Reidheid's hands shook as he offered Will the flask. '*Uisge beatha*, in the native tongue. The water of life. It keeps me warm when there is no fire in the grate.' He pulled his chair close to the hearth. 'The poor and rich alike have long learned to protect their homes with salt and herbs and cold iron, and to watch where they walk after dark has fallen.'

'You have seen new activity from them in recent days?'

'They call them the Unseelie Court here. It is an old name, coloured by centuries of torment.' He sipped his whisky reflectively. 'There is a place in Edinburgh not far from the castle that is known as the Fairy House. The local people understand it to be haunted, or cursed. It is said that anyone who ventures within never comes out. No one is ever seen inside, although the candles blaze intermittently. The rooms below are said to be guarded by a demonic black dog.'

'They have a house they call their own within the city?' Will said, amazed. 'And no one has raided it?'

'We have an uneasy relationship with the Unseelie Court in Edinburgh.' There was a rueful note in Reidheid's voice. 'A black carriage stood outside two days ago. No one was seen leaving it, or entering the house, and it left shortly after.'

'I feel I need to examine the inside of this Fairy House.'

Reidheid started. 'I have watched that foul place for many days and nights. I can see no safe way in.'

'Then it will have to be unsafe.'

Nathaniel and Meg entered with a platter of cold beef, bread and cheese and some ale. They were both quiet and respectful, but Will saw them exchange glances as they laid out the food on the table.

'I would also have access to the Palace of Holyroodhouse,' Will said as he washed his hands in the silver basin Meg had deposited on the side.

'An audience with the King will not be easy,' Reidheid said. He carved the beef with careful strokes of his sharp knife.

'I do not want an audience. I want to prowl around his private rooms, poke my nose in his closets, go through his clothes, sift his jewels, rap on his walls, prise up his floorboards and generally skulk around and make a nuisance of myself.'

'It is the most highly guarded residence in all of Edinburgh,' Reidheid protested.

'Then I have two impenetrable buildings to penetrate.' Will tore a chunk off the bread and chewed on it thoughtfully.

'And you do like to penetrate the impenetrable,' Nathaniel whispered to him.

'Father?' Meg said. 'The King has a ball tomorrow night.'

Reidheid considered this for a moment, then said, 'Perhaps I could garner you an invitation. A visiting luminary. I am sure

King James would think you would brighten up the festivities and perhaps provide a welcome talking point for the members of the court who find these events familiar. Would that serve your purpose?'

'A palace swarming with people in which to lose myself.' Will nodded. 'Perfect.'

'And wine, and women,' Nathaniel muttered.

Will loaded his plate and poured some ale from the pitcher before settling back by the fire. 'Then let us make haste, for there is little of the night left.'

'You intend to visit the Fairy House this night?' Reidheid spluttered into his beer. 'You have not slept. Surely after some rest—'

'I have fire in my blood,' Will replied in between mouthfuls of beef, 'and an urge to make the Enemy pay for the wrongs they have inflicted upon my friends. Sleep can wait.'

# CHAPTER TWENTY-ONE

SQUATTING ON THE ROOF, WILL LOOKED OUT ACROSS EDINBURGH'S jumbled buildings sprawling around the winding, ancient ways, the grand stone houses glimmering with candlelight, to the soaring backdrop of the great hills silhouetted against the starry sky beyond. The wind tearing at his hair brought with it the salty aroma of the port at Leith two miles distant.

After picking his way past crowded apartments to bribe his way through the window of the topmost lodger, he now stood at the summit of one of the highest lands in the city. Balancing on the ledge with the dizzying drop to the cobbles far below, he briefly wondered if he was as mad as the lodger accused him of being, before hauling himself up and over the edge on to the slick tiles.

'I wish you could see this, Nathaniel,' he muttered. 'The world looks less harsh from on high.'

Steadying himself on the balls of his feet, he loped along the ridge of the roof. Progress was hazardous. The gusting air currents channelling through the wynds – the narrow alleys connecting the larger streets – threatened to pluck him up and cast him down the steep slope to the vertiginous drop at the end. Occasionally the wind direction changed and he was blinded by the choking smoke from the rows of chimneys.

Whenever he came to one of the wynds that broke up the run of housing, he leapt the narrow gap, aware of the black gulf beneath his feet. His landings were always a scramble for purchase, one missed footing or twisted ankle a death warrant, but he kept up a relentless progress towards his destination.

Nearing the Fairy House, he leapt on to the roof of one of the lands and suddenly felt it shift beneath his feet. It seemed the highest storey had been attached only recently, with nailed boards and beams, but no proper joints as far as Will could tell. It felt as insubstantial as a collection of randomly heaped firewood, swaying whenever he shifted his weight, held up by luck and hope more than anything. Dropping to all fours, he edged along the top until he could move to the adjoining roof.

Finally he landed with barely a whisper of a footfall on the roof of the Fairy House. To all intents and purposes, it was a five-storey residence that had long since seen better days. Missing and broken tiles peppered the roof; tufts of grass and elder sprouted.

Creeping to the edge of the roof, he peered down to the street below where a black coach drawn by a sable stallion waited outside the entrance to the house. There was no sign of a coachman. The building's windows were dark. No sound issued from within. He knew his supernatural foe would have defences in place to protect the usual entrances to their house. He had heard rumours of men who had aged years in a heart-beat, or who had turned to stone. But he was gambling that his chosen route would be unprotected, for who else would be foolish enough to attempt such a path?

Crawling back up to the ridge, Will inspected the chimney stack. It was cold, and, as he'd surmised, the vent was wide enough to admit him, though it was a tight squeeze. Falling soot could always alert those waiting below, but the biggest danger was that he would climb down into the maze of flues and become trapped, especially in a chimney that had not been kept in good repair. His rapier, too, presented a problem. He fastened it against his chest with a leather strap, and hoped that would give him enough leeway to manoeuvre. But if it became too difficult, he would have to abandon his sword and rely on his knife alone.

Steadying himself on the top of the stack, he lowered himself into the hole. Amid the suffocating stink of soot, his clothes and skin were soon black, his breath rasping in the confined space. It was impossible to see anything in the dark. He focused on the tips of his fingers and his toes, searching for cracks and footholds in the brick. The gulf below breathed steadily, his heart beating a regular, rapid rhythm in response. Bracing against the sides of the chimney, he edged down a little at a time. His rapier bit into him, and he had to stop regularly to adjust its position. And then his boot slipped and he started to fall. He tore at the brick with his fingernails, finally gaining purchase, though it seared his knuckles and wrists. Taking a moment, he breathed deeply to dispel the pulse of blood in his ears, then continued. Yet however perilous his journey, imaginings of the terrors that waited below were far worse.

As he made his way down, intermittent noise floated up from the lower floors: voices speaking no tongue he recognized, emotions seesawing in an extreme and disturbing manner. There were barks of anger and frightened mewling and what sounded like shrieks of insane laughter and mocking whispers. A blacksmith's hammer on an anvil came and went, one moment echoing dimly, the next resounding near at hand. A dog's growling sounded disturbingly as if it were on the other side of the brick; and then there was the music: pipes and a fiddle, eerie and haunting, fading in and out.

He passed junctions in the chimney that must lead down to the large stone fireplaces in each room. But although the strange sounds continued to rise through the flues, no noise seemed to emanate from any room he passed.

When Will estimated he'd reached the first floor, he slid down towards a fireplace, bracing himself just above the hearth to listen. When he was sure the chamber was empty, he dropped down in a cloud of soot. The room was bare apart from a cracked mirror above the mantelpiece which revealed a white-eyed black figure. Pausing, Will grinned and saluted himself before brushing off some of the grime.

The house was silent now. Darting across the dirty floorboards, he opened the door a crack and peered out into a corridor where a candle flickered in a holder on a small table.

*Not so empty, then.*

He moved quickly along the corridor, checking the rooms on either side. All were bare. But outside the last the boards creaked, and there was a corresponding growl from the ground floor, followed by the sound of heavy paws padding on the stairs. Stepping lightly, Will bolted up to the next floor.

Flickering light on one wall brought him to a halt just before a turn in the corridor. Peering round, he saw a figure – male, he thought – moving slowly away from him, holding a candle aloft. Below, the padding paws reached the first floor. Another deep, penetrating growl. Will's heart beat faster.

Caught between the two, he weighed his choices. Just as he had decided to draw his sword, a door at the far end of the corridor opened and light flooded out. The man paused and spoke to someone within in a low whisper before entering the room. The door closed behind him and the light winked out.

Will darted to the nearest door and listened briefly before opening it slowly. The room was in darkness. He slipped inside.

Closing the heavy oak door, he pressed his ear against it and waited. He could hear the padding reach the top of the staircase and then move into the corridor. The beast paused outside the door and let loose another growl, disturbingly loud in the quiet. Will's breath burned in his chest; one exhalation would be enough to reveal his presence, he was sure. After a second, the dog moved on and silence returned.

Will wondered if it was the same dog that had accompanied the Hunter in Alsatia. *And where that creature was, the Hunter surely was too,* he thought, *and perhaps even the Silver Skull.*

'Who are you?'

Will started at the voice, soft and dreamy, with the distinctive burr of a Scottish Lowlands accent. There, in the dark of the room, he could just make out a man sitting on a chair looking out of the window, his back to the door.

Drawing his sword, Will waited for the alarm to be raised, but the man said nothing more and did not move. After a moment, Will cautiously approached. As the moonlight broke through the window, Will saw it *was* a man, not one of the Enemy. Grey streaked his black hair, and his face had the lines of middle age. Will was struck most by his eyes, which had the faraway look of a sleepwalker.

'Who are you?' Will asked.

'John Kintour,' the stranger replied. 'Adviser to my Queen, Mary.'

'Your Queen is dead,' Will replied, puzzled.

'No . . . no . . . I saw her this morn. So beautiful. The sun made her hair glow like fire.' His voice seemed as insubstantial as the moonlight.

203

Will passed his hand in front of Kintour's face, but the man did not blink. 'How long have you been here?'

'A day? A week? A month? A year?' He paused as if deep in thought, then said, 'They gave me food and drink. The most wonderful food . . . The taste . . . I had never experienced anything like it.'

And Will suddenly understood. During his induction as one of Walsingham's men, one of the first rules he was taught was that he should never eat or drink anything offered by the Enemy, for to do so would allow them to take complete control of you. It was how they lured their prey for their sport, usually simple country folk drawn to hear the music on the hilltops or in the fields at night. But Kintour was clearly not being kept a prisoner in the house for sport.

'You have had a busy time here,' Will said, more gently this time.

'Yes. So many questions.'

'And you answered them all?'

'As best I could. Some were beyond even me. The location of the Shield . . .'

'The Shield? What is that?' Thinking he heard a noise outside, Will glanced to the door. Silence. He returned his attention to Kintour.

'The Shield protects against the foul diseases released by the Silver Skull, of course,' Kintour said lazily. 'It allows a man to move freely among the ranks of the infected and the dead without any mark appearing upon him. That is what the Templar Knights said.'

It was as Will had thought. Without the Shield, the Skull was a blunt instrument, laying waste to vast swathes of an enemy. With it, the attacker could loot the dead, or search for more specific prizes.

'What do the Templar Knights have to do with this?' he asked.

Kintour's head rolled from side to side and he gave a faint smile. 'I was Keeper of Records at the palace. So much to read . . . so many secrets. Among the parchments, I found many relating to the Knights Templar.' His voice was barely more than a whisper, the cadence drifting as if he were lulling a child to sleep. 'At first they made little sense. It was only when I realized they were written using an obscure cipher that the truth began to emerge. It seemed the knights encountered the Silver Skull in the Holy Lands, and were aware of what a terrible threat it was to all Christendom. They had to act to protect all good Christian men.'

'And what did they do?'

'Separated the Skull from the Key and the Shield so it could not be used. They brought the Key and the Shield back here, to Scotland, and hid them well. The Skull . . . I do not know what happened to that.'

'The Key and the Shield were hidden at the Palace of Holyroodhouse?'

'Hidden well. The knights had many strong connections with Edinburgh and the surrounding area, and they were involved in advising King David when he built Holyrood Abbey more than four hundred years ago. There were rumours of chambers hidden beneath the abbey, and extending under the palace west of the abbey cloister. Aye, it was one of the locations across Europe where the knights stored items of vast importance.'

Will recalled the tales of the Templars he had heard told at court, and how the military religious order had brought back many secrets and riches from the Crusades. Dee had even suggested that the disbanding of the order and the killing of many of their number was down to the machinations of the Enemy. *The Enemy's greatest victory*, the alchemist had called it.

'Mary charged me with finding the location of the Key and the Shield,' Kintour continued. 'I searched through the old papers, spent long days and nights breaking the ciphers the knights used. And I found the Key.' His brow furrowed, his eyelids fluttered shut for a moment.

'Yes, the Key was found,' Will responded. He put one hand on Kintour's shoulder to prevent the Scot from slipping back into a dream. 'But you could not locate the Shield?'

'Only that it was hidden somewhere beneath the abbey. But where . . . and how . . .' He shook his head sadly. 'And so you still search.'

'Yes, we still search,' Will said reassuringly. He tried to guess the Enemy's plan, which appeared more subtle than he had envisaged. If the Silver Skull was simply a weapon that would strike like the hand of God, they would be content for it to destroy all who lived in England, with no thought to the man who wore the mask. But if the Enemy needed the Shield to protect themselves it suggested they wished to move through the areas where the disease ran out of hand. Why would they want to do that?

'How close have you got to locating the Shield?' he asked, looking into the older man's face.

Kintour bowed his head in shame. 'I have the reference to the entrance, and the guide to the defences, but I cannot understand it.' He pulled a piece of parchment from a pouch and handed it to Will with trembling hands. Will inspected it briefly before slipping it into his doublet. 'I know you requested an answer by this evening, and I am sorry . . . I am sorry . . .' The dazed man began to sob softly. 'Please do not hurt me any more. Please, just let me dream.'

Will studied the wretched figure and wondered how long he had been a prisoner, without truly knowing where he was or what he did for his captors. 'Why have they . . . we . . . not descended on the abbey and torn it apart to find the Shield?' Will enquired cautiously.

'Why . . . part of it is protected. You cannot walk there,' Kintour replied, baffled.

'So mortal agents are needed to search,' Will mused. 'You will not have to remain here for much longer. Firstly, I must find where they have hidden the Silver Skull here, but then I will return you to your life. Do you understand?'

Kintour nodded slowly until his chin drooped slowly on to his chest and he fell into a deep stupor. Will crept back to the door. The corridor was clear, and he slipped out.

Outside the room, the house was filled with a strange atmosphere that reminded Will of a churchyard after a funeral: a hint of regret, a resonant tone of grief, yet somehow the joy of a new day like the sun breaking through the branches of the yews. Behind it all, though, was an underlying tone of threat, rumbling so deep it was felt rather than heard.

He paused outside the door through which the Enemy had passed, but there was no sound within. He hesitated, thought better of it, and ventured up to the next floor; he could always return to that room if the rest of his search turned up nothing.

Slipping up another flight of stairs, he found a different atmosphere. It was as though he had walked from one season into another. The air was rich with the perfume of a summer garden: he smelled lavender, rose, honeysuckle. The first door was locked, as was the second.

In the third room, it took a second for his eyes to adjust to the deep dark. He saw that thick velvet drapes hung over the window. Pulling them back, he allowed the moonlight to illuminate the chamber. Glassy eyes stared back at him.

Will leapt back, drawing his sword, his heart thundering.

In one corner, rising almost halfway up the wall, was a pile of human heads. Will guessed there were at least fifty: men, women, children. The stench reached him and he fought the urge to gag. Some of the heads were so badly decomposed only traces of flesh remained on the bone; others looked so fresh they might well have been placed there that night.

As his shock subsided, he gritted his teeth in anger. Here was the Enemy's sport, he knew, plucked from the dark, over-crowded wynds where the dregs were all but ignored by the city authorities. Here, in this charnel house, was the entire reason for his life's work, and why Walsingham and Dee, for all their flaws, were right. Biting back his anger, he moved swiftly back into the corridor and continued to search the house.

More doors were locked, more rooms empty, although many held a tantalizing hint that they had only just been vacated, a wisp of scent in the air, or a fading echo.

Then, at last, in a chamber at the end of the corridor, he found Don Alanzo. The Spaniard was asleep, his sword by his side, on a four-poster bed with the curtains partly drawn. In a chair next to the bed, head on his chest seemingly in slumber, was the Silver Skull. The two of them together in the same room, in that position, was an odd sight, and Will couldn't tell if they were under the spell of the Enemy.

The room was furnished with more warmth than the other chambers in the Fairy House, but here too there was an under-lying stench of decomposition. It was then that Will saw the single rotting head on the mantelpiece.

*Even here. A reminder to the occupants of their mortality.*

Searching for any creaking board, he edged across the room

to within a foot of the Skull. But as he reached out an arm to slide round the Skull's neck, the severed head tore open its mouth and began to shriek.

The bloodcurdling alarm rang through the still house.

Shocked awake, the Silver Skull leapt to his feet, knocking over his chair. Grabbing his sword, Don Alanzo rolled off the bed and thrust himself between Will and the Skull.

He yelled the alarm in Spanish, unnecessarily, almost drowned out by the head's deafening shriek.

Deep in the house, doors slammed.

Will saw it was futile to attempt to escape with the Skull. 'I will return to finish this at a later date,' he said, backing towards the door. 'Until then, enjoy your stay in Edinburgh.'

Activity rumbled throughout the house, punctuated by the loud barks of the sentry dog. The sensible option would have been to enter one of the empty rooms and clamber back into the chimney, but Will couldn't leave Kintour. The archivist had already suffered greatly at the hands of the Enemy, and Will felt instinctively that he would become superfluous to their needs very soon.

Racing for the stairs, he selected his knife. He took the steps three at a time, crashing on to the landing below where a shadow on the wall had already warned him of an impending assailant. Dropping and rolling, he brought the knife up sharply into the groin of the waiting figure. The inhuman cry of pain made Will's head ring.

Without looking back, he ran for the next flight of stairs. Four more of the Enemy pounded up the steps to meet him.

On the top step, he threw himself forward, crashing hard into the first attacker who was propelled into the ones behind. They careered down the staircase with Will rolling across the top of them to land on his feet on the next landing. As he fought his way through to the corridor where Kintour's room was, he found the one he called the Hunter waiting in front of the door. Eyeing Will with contempt, he put his fingers to his mouth and whistled. From below, his dog answered with a hunting howl.

Everything Will saw in his foe's face – arrogance, a dismissive regard for a lesser species, cruelty – made him yearn for revenge for Miller's death, but he knew it would mean his own end. Behind him, he heard the other combatants pick themselves up from the tangle at the foot of the stairs and advance towards him.

Will ran. The Hunter's eyes narrowed. He moved with a casual grace to repel the attack, but instead of meeting the supernatural being head on, at the last moment Will leapt to the left-hand wall, propelled himself off it to the right-hand wall and launched himself past his wrong-footed opponent. He felt his knife tear open flesh. The cry of anger-tinged agony brought a surge of black pleasure to Will.

'Something to remember me by,' he said.

The inhuman figure clutched his cheek. Moving by, Will knocked the Hunter off balance, and then he was in the room and sliding the bolt across the door.

'Come, we must leave this place,' Will urged, shaking Kintour from his stupor. He heard bodies briefly throwing themselves at the door. The noise stilled and then the bolt began to slide back of its own accord.

Staggering, Kintour allowed himself to be guided towards the fireplace. It was as if he was a puppet, with no will of his own.

'We climb,' Will urged. 'You first. I will follow to hold off any pursuit.'

Kintour was leaden, his fingers feebly feeling for handholds.

Will put his shoulder to the man's behind and launched him up the chimney, climbing quickly behind him while bracing himself against the sooty brickwork with his legs. Black showers rained down all around.

In the room, the door crashed open and the heavy tread of boots crossed the boards. A wild barking followed.

'Where are we?' Kintour's dazed voice floated down to Will.

'On the road to freedom. Now: climb faster!' He gave Kintour a rough shove as the sound of canine scrabbling echoed from the fireplace below.

In the dark, Kintour began to panic. Will took the time to explain what was occurring as they inched along the flue.

'What if we become trapped here?' The edge of fear in Kintour's dreamy voice was eerie.

'I came down. Ergo, we can climb out,' Will shouted up.

The snarling began to rise up the chimney. Somehow the massive beast was climbing after them.

'No dog at all, then,' Will muttered to himself before calling, 'Climb faster, now.'

As they drove up through the flue system, Will looked down between his boots and glimpsed the glint of the dog's teeth as it snarled only a few feet below him. Finding near-invisible footholds, it climbed with relatively little purchase on the blackened brick, so that it appeared to be gliding upwards.

'What is happening?' Kintour cried. The edge in his voice grew more intense. He was surfacing from the spell.

Finally, they broke out into the chill night. Disoriented, Kintour almost toppled off the roof until Will pushed his way out of the chimney and caught hold of the man's jerkin. The hound wriggled up the final few feet, its jaws snapping like a gamekeeper's trap.

'Along the roofs, now!' Will urged. 'We can be away from here before—'

'No!' Kintour clutched his head as though in pain, his legs buckling. Will held on to him as his feet slipped on the tiles. 'I . . . I remember now,' Kintour stuttered.

Will attempted to guide him along the rooftop. 'Do not look down,' he said. 'Keep your eyes on my face.' The fingers of the gusting wind tugged at them. At their backs, the dog's snarling echoed from the chimney.

Kintour looked up at Will with an expression of devastation. 'They told me . . . I could never . . .'

There was a faint *poof* and Kintour burst into silvery-grey dust. Stunned, Will grasped at the glittering powder, but it drained through his fingers, was caught on a gust of wind and blew out across the city. Within moments, where there had stood a man, there was nothing.

Will stood rooted to the spot, aghast. His incomprehension at Kintour's sudden fate gave way to the certain knowledge that the Enemy – the unholy Unseelie Court – were capable of any cruelty, any atrocity. He was shocked back into the moment by the dog's thrusting its head out of the chimney. Eyes glaring, it thrashed savagely as it attempted to extricate itself.

Will threw himself along the ridge of the roof as he heard the dog crash on to the tiles, slipping and scrabbling until it found its balance. Will knew caution was no longer an option – the dog's speed and strength would punish even the slightest hesitation – but one misstep would mean certain death.

At a wynd, Will threw himself across the gap without slowing his step. Tiles flew out into the void under his heels. He half slipped, caught himself on the brink of careering down and over the edge to the cobbles below, then almost fell the other way as his weight shifted. The dog thundered along behind him.

He landed on the roof of the ramshackle construction he had crossed earlier that night. As it swayed beneath his feet, a notion struck him. Casting an eye towards the hound and the Hunter, loping with supernatural ease in its wake, Will hammered a foot through the tiles and yelled at the two startled occupants he spied inside to vacate their rooms.

At the edge of the next roof, he braced his back against a chimney and pressed his feet into the shuddering one he had vacated. It began to move.

The dog slammed on to the shaking roof. It was too late to escape now. Grunting, Will drove all his strength into his legs and pushed. Tiles began to scatter as the roof shifted away from him, gathering speed as it moved. Then, with a lurch and a loud rending, it tore free from its moorings and slid off the top of the building. Frantically paddling to keep its balance, the hound continued to snap and snarl, even as it fell away, over the edge and down. The cries that rose up from the ragged remnants of the tenements' lower floors were drowned out by the explosive boom of the top storey smashing into the street.

Feet kicking, Will dragged himself up to safety. As he caught his breath, he looked back to see the Hunter standing on the far side of the newly formed gulf. The Enemy watched him with a cold, malicious eye, the gaping wound on his cheek glistening in the moonlight. Will had no doubt that the dog had survived the fall, but it was a small victory none the less, a marker for what he would do the next time he encountered the Hunter.

With a sardonic salute to his adversary, he turned and made his way along the rooftops, filled with conflicting emotions, but sensing he had come a step closer to thwarting the Enemy's plans.

# CHAPTER TWENTY-TWO

TAKING CARE TO WATCH EVERY STREET AND WYND HE PASSED for the Enemy who would soon be in pursuit, a battered and exhausted Will made it back to Reidheid's house on Cowgate within the hour.

'You have protection here?' Will asked, pushing his way over the threshold as soon as Reidheid opened the door.

Gaping, Reidheid was brought up sharp by Will's soot-streaked, bruised appearance. Hesitantly, he indicated the trail of salt and herbs across the lintel. 'Every entrance to this house is defended. The Enemy cannot enter. It is a safe haven.'

'That is reassuring. I fear at this moment the Enemy may well be consumed with a desire to see the inside of your house,' Will said with a wry nonchalance he did not feel.

'Your mission was a success?' Reidheid guided Will into the withdrawing room. There Nathaniel and Meg sat in deep, quiet conversation. Troubled by Will's state, they left quickly at Reidheid's gesture.

'The Silver Skull is here in Edinburgh, as we presumed. Unfortunately, the time was not right to bring him back with me, but it is clear the Enemy is not yet ready to use the destructive force it carries with it. They need the Shield to complete their plan, and they have not yet located it.'

'And do you know what this plan is?' Reidheid asked.

'Not yet. But now I have my own plan,' Will replied, reaching for the flask of fortifying spiced wine that Reidheid proffered.

Reidheid smiled broadly. 'Of course. I would expect nothing else from the great Will Swyfte! Could you enlighten me?'

'I am going to find the Shield myself.'

Reidheid's eyes narrowed as he tried to ascertain if Will was serious. 'But you said the Enemy have been searching for the Shield without any success.'

Will shrugged. 'But I am not the Enemy. And there are places that I can go where they cannot. Do you know a man by the name of Kintour, a keeper of the records at the palace?'

Reidheid nodded. 'He has been missing for a long time . . . since the days of the traitor Mary. Many felt he was loyal to the Queen and fled when she fell from grace. That, or dead.'

'He is dead now, another thing for which the Enemy must pay.' From within his doublet, Will withdrew the parchment that Kintour had given him. He studied the scrawled writing. 'He had found something that pointed to the whereabouts of the Shield, but had not yet broken the cipher.'

'May I see?' the older man said eagerly.

'Perhaps later. Master Reidheid, you have a library? With books pertaining to Edinburgh and the palace?'

'Of course,' Reidheid said. 'I have many books. Come.'

Reidheid led Will through the house to a large room at the rear of the building. The musty smell of great age lay across the shelves of leather-bound books. Reidheid indicated the volumes on local history and left Will to study them at a table by the light of a candle.

When the bright morning light flooded the room, Will had become so engrossed he didn't notice Nathaniel enter until a flask of sweet malmsey wine was placed before him.

'Thank you, Nat. You are thoughtful, as ever,' Will sighed without looking up. 'And I see you have found a friend in the beautiful Meg.'

'It is pleasant to speak to someone who is untarnished by this business of ours,' Nathaniel replied, not rising to the bait. 'She is entertaining and witty. A novelty,' he added pointedly.

Will allowed himself a small, unseen smile. 'Then enjoy yourself, Nat. God knows there are few entertaining distractions in this work.'

His curiosity getting the better of him, Nathaniel leaned over Will's shoulder to examine the book he was reading. 'It is also a novelty to see you with an open tome rather than a woman in your lap and wine in your hand. Which is why I brought you that drink, to right a world that has gone mad. What do you read?'

'The object of our search and the key to our success in defeating our Enemy is hidden at the Palace of Holyroodhouse. A cipher left by the Templar Knights would appear to point to its location.'

'The Templar Knights? Their task was to protect good Christians in a dangerous world. What do they have to do with this?'

'There was more to those holy warriors than the world knows,' Will mused while turning the pages. 'As there is more to everything than the world knows.'

Nathaniel picked up the parchment. 'This is the cipher? *The protection lies where the heart of truth beats, beneath the Holyrood where the martyr stands in black and white.*' He considered the words for a moment and then suggested, 'Under a statue of a martyr in the palace?'

'A good attempt, Nat.' Pushing his chair back, Will swung a boot on to the table and wiped a bleary eye. 'Enlightenment might strike you if you had taken the time to read *The Matter of Olde English* by one Williams, a dour fellow from Cambridge. I presume you have a copy by your bedside table?'

Sighing, Nathaniel motioned for Will to continue.

'If you had, then you would know of *heorot*, the word of our ancestors for deer, which the rough-tongued people of England pronounced *hart*. H–a–r–t.'

'Hart . . . heart,' Nathaniel mused. 'Ah, I see. We search for the deer of truth, who bounds through the glades of faith . . . or is it charity? . . . not far from the fields of hope. In the hunting grounds behind the palace, I presume.'

'Why, Nat, in your sadly familiar mockery you come close to striking the nail upon the head.'

'Is that a copy of *The Matter of Olde English* I spy before you?'

As Nathaniel leaned forward, Will moved the book to the other side of the table. 'Concentrate, Nat! I am here to add to your poor education. Another word for hart is stag. I read here of the early days of the palace, and more important, of the abbey that stands beside it. It was built for the Augustinians by King David in 1128, guided, I was told earlier this night, by the Templar Knights. The location was precise, and chosen by King David following a vision he had of a white stag with the Cross lodged between its antlers – the Cross, or the Holy Rood, from which the palace gets its name.'

'So the thing for which you search—'

'—a Shield, or the *protection*—'

'—is at the abbey, not the palace.'

'Correct. The Enemy presumed the reference to the Holy Rood meant the Shield was beneath the palace.'

'And the martyr in black and white?'

Will sighed and took a draught of the wine. 'Now that still eludes me. But we have a start. And when we are entertained by the King this evening, we shall investigate further.'

# CHAPTER TWENTY-THREE

AS THE SUN SET, THE COACHES ROLLED DOWN THE COBBLES OF the mile-long avenue that stretched from the castle to the Palace of Holyroodhouse, each one awash with peacock feathers, pearly beads and gold banners. Inside were the Scottish nobility in all their finery, the ambassadors and the senior clergy who had amassed great fortunes to match their indulgent lifestyles.

From the Cowgate house, Will, Nathaniel, Reidheid and his daughter travelled together in a less extravagant carriage. Though they were protected, Will kept a close watch along the route for any sign of their true Enemy.

'This will be a fine night,' Meg said. Her eyes shone when they fell on Nathaniel. 'The King's festivities are lavish. I think he likes to take the opportunity to rebel against the preachings of the Church.'

'Yet still no queen,' Nathaniel commented. 'And he is . . . what, twenty-two?'

Eyeing Nathaniel askance, Reidheid added with a strained note, 'The King prefers the company of his male courtiers. His advisers have struggled to find a suitable match, but at least the damnable Earl of Lennox no longer exerts his influence over His Majesty.'

'You know the court well,' Will said, 'and you have some influence to gain an invitation for a well-known English spy.'

'Not influence enough. The King is suspicious of all beyond his immediate circle. The threats that preceded the forcible removal of Lennox from the King's company have made him wary of all. Indeed, he has moved to exert control over his lords. Yet I have been informed that His Majesty was very keen to have you present.'

Will raised an eyebrow. 'Is that so?'

'He has some concerns over mutual enemies. He is mindful – and fearful – of many things.'

Will and Reidheid exchanged a glance while Meg and Nathaniel smiled at each other, oblivious. The carriage rattled past the last of Edinburgh's houses and the crowd of local people who had gathered to watch, to the wild, green land at the foot of the hills that surrounded the palace. The extensive gardens that James had remodelled when he took the throne overflowed with colourful blooms and the last strains of the day's birdsong filled the air. It was a far cry from the oppressive gloom, the filth and the crime of the city. Yet the wilderness that stretched from the hunting grounds beyond the palace was disturbing in another way, for it belonged to the Unseelie Court, and particularly after dark. To Will's eyes, the palace was an island extending into Enemy territory.

The building was much smaller than the Palace of White-hall, though still imposing with its pale stone and red-tiled roof, towers and spires, and vast diamond-paned windows that during the day would flood the interior with light. Just behind King James's residence, to the south, Will spied the solid bulk of the abbey, a dour, brooding, ancient presence beside the bright palace.

There was already a queue of coaches dropping off guests under the protective arches of the large stone gatehouse on the west side of the palace. Greeted by a clutch of the King's busy but deferential servants, Reidheid led Will, Nathaniel and Meg through the gates to the quadrangle, a grassy area surrounded by the three-storey palace buildings, and from there to the State Rooms where the guests were gathering.

King James's court comprised almost six hundred people, now swelled by many other guests, and the perfumed atmosphere was abuzz with conversation. Musicians played a masque specially composed for the occasion, with lutes, both bass and mean, a bandora, a double sackbut, a harpsichord and several violins.

Despite the grandeur of the occasion, Nathaniel and Meg were happy to enjoy their own company on the fringes of the room. Will was elegantly dressed in a black doublet with silver hooks, a jerkin of finest Spanish leather, and a thigh-length cloak in compass-cut, embroidered in black, scarlet and gold and with a purple silk lining. Reidheid clearly took pride in introducing his charge to the guests.

The young wife of the Earl of Angus broke off from her conversation to be presented to Will. She looked him in the eye flirtatiously and smiled. 'I have heard tell of your exploits, Master Swyfte, even here in Edinburgh, and I would know if they are true.'

Will bowed and kissed her hand. 'If all the stories about me were true, my lady, I would be worn down and upon my deathbed.'

She laughed, her eyes twinkling. 'How you evaded the Doge's men in Venice by disguising yourself as a harlequin?'

'True, my lady.' Will hid his weariness at the familiar tranche of questions, smiled and nodded as he answered several more.

'And how you have romanced all the women at the court of Elizabeth?' The Countess narrowed her eyes.

'I have not heard that story, my lady.'

As a ripple of excited conversation went round the room as the King entered, the Countess took the opportunity to whisper in Will's ear. 'I would hear more of your tales, Master Swyfte. Perhaps in a quieter place?'

Before Will could respond, the King swept towards the English spy under the guidance of an obviously unsettled Reidheid, and the Earl's wife retreated with a knowing gleam in her eye.

'Master Swyfte, the King would speak to you in private,' Reidheid said. He was clearly unused to such attention.

The King had inherited his mother's red hair, but none of her good looks or allure. Slightly feminine in manner, he had a weak chin, a lazy eye, a prominent nose and lips which pursed in a manner that suggested he was continuously passing judgement. But as he spoke to his guests in passing, Will could see he had a ready intellect and a bright sense of humour.

Will bowed. 'You honour me, sire.'

'Yes. We do.' James gave a wry smile.

Will followed him to the edge of the room where Reidheid and James's aides kept a respectful distance so the conversation could be conducted privately.

'Master Swyfte, your reputation precedes you,' James said.

'So I have just been told.'

'I would say, first, that the execution of my mother at Fotheringhay last year was a harsh blow, "a preposterous and strange procedure", as I pronounced at the time.' He chose his words carefully, hesitating for a long time at the end of the sentence. 'How strange was it, Master Swyfte?'

'It was in accordance with the law of the land.'

'That is not my meaning.' After a moment's consideration, the Scottish king continued, 'My mother acted strangely for many years. She was not herself, do you understand?'

Will did not respond.

'The circumstances surrounding her execution led me to believe that there was more to her death than perhaps even I knew.'

'Sire, these are matters of state, and I am a lowly—'

'I know what you are,' James interrupted sharply. 'I know the business of Walsingham's men.' His voice dropped to a forceful whisper. 'Do you think me blind to the terrible ways of the world, when I am surrounded by vile things that seek to threaten everything we have built?'

'Then we have an understanding, Your Majesty.'

'But you do not understand what it is like here in Scotland, Master Swyfte.' Emotion rose in James's voice and for a moment it looked as if he might cry. 'You do not understand the trials we face, the secret suffering inflicted upon my people. They feel themselves the victims of a harsh fate, plucked from their homes, murdered as they cross the glens and hillsides. If only they knew the truth!'

'Which is why, I fear, they should never know.' Will's calming voice masked an acute awareness of his own isolation.

James steadied himself, nodding. 'Scotland needs aid, Master Swyfte. We need the defences you have established in England.'

'That is not a matter for me—'

James held up his hand. 'I know. And I know you have the ear of some of the highest in the land. If you could take word back with you—'

'There are proper channels for such communication.'

'And yet they are always closed to me! England does not want to know of our suffering!'

'England has suffering enough of its own. It faces enemies on every side, and from within.'

King James's expression grew taut. 'We need the aid of England. One day, when Elizabeth passes, I will be King. I will save my nation, Master Swyfte.' His tone was defiant.

Will recognized the passion in the Scottish king. The urge to be free of the Unseelie Court's tyranny had consumed him for too long. 'We all wish to see the Enemy defeated,' he assured him. 'This is not a matter of nations, or religion. Those are distractions . . . yes, that is tantamount to treason in some quarters, but it is the truth. We are a brotherhood of man, and we should stand together against the greater threat. Only by recognizing our common humanity can we rise up from our knees.'

James smiled, relief obvious on his face. 'It pleases me that we share this common ground, Master Swyfte. Perhaps change will come in my lifetime. Perhaps—'

They were interrupted as a commotion rose up near the entrance to the State Rooms, and moments later several of the King's advisers ran over, concern marring their features. Ashen-faced, they hovered near their King until one addressed him, 'Your Majesty, they insist on entering. They claim it is their right as nobility.'

With Will close behind, James strode towards the door, the crowd parting before him. The music died away, and the conversation stilled.

As the doors to the State Rooms swung open, the light from the candles seemed to dim, although the flames burned as strong. Shadows fell at strange angles, and a suffocating atmosphere descended. Here and there across the room, blood began to drip from noses.

It was then that ten members of the Unseelie Court stepped in, the terrible weight of their gazes ranging across everyone present. The Scottish king's guests recoiled as one. The strangers approached with languid strides, like wolves among sheep, their emotions, their thoughts, everything about them unreadable. No one could look them fully in the face, and if any caught an Enemy eye by accident the blood drained from them, and they crossed themselves, muttering prayers. Will knew the unease went far beyond the physical presence of the Unseelie Court; it was as if a grave had been opened.

So potent was the sense of threat, it seemed the strangers were on the brink of falling upon the assembled company and slaughtering them where they stood. Their clothes, while of the finest material, appeared to be on the brink of rot, stained with silvery mildew, the style harking back to a distant age. A scent of loam accompanied the ten. Their cheekbones were high, their hair long, their eyes pale, but there was a strangeness to their features that meant they rarely registered on the mind; once they had passed from view it was almost impossible to recall the details of their appearance.

Will went for his rapier, but King James stayed him with a cautionary hand. 'Leave them,' he said, his voice desolate. 'If we dare to challenge them, my people will pay the price for months, perhaps years, to come. Now do you see what I mean? Now do you see?' His voice cracked with emotion.

From his bearing, one of the strangers was clearly the leader. His long hair, the colour of sun on corn, fell around his shoulders, but failed to soften his icy features.

Spying the King and Will, he approached as his companions circled the room, pausing to stare into the faces of those nearby. Some of the guests sobbed or swooned under their gaze. Others took on a fatalistic expression that was painful to see. It was as if they had accepted that the date of their death had been decided.

The leader studied James's and Will's faces for a moment as if examining a lesser species. His eyes were too black, his stare unblinking. 'I am honoured to be in the presence of the great King James of the land of Scotland,' he said, pronouncing each word as if he carried a pebble in his mouth. His voice was low, and quiet, and some quality to it made Will feel unaccountably cold. 'I am Cavillex of . . .' he paused, and then added with a contemptuous nod for the phrase, 'the Unseelie Court.'

'You are the king of your people?' James asked.

Cavillex's eyes narrowed. 'My family guides the court.' His attention had skittered on to Will. 'You trespassed in one of my homes, hurt one of those close to me, took what is mine—'

'I freed a poor soul imprisoned against his will.'

King James flinched at Will's defiance.

'Took what is mine,' Cavillex repeated in a dispassionate tone. 'The disrespect you have shown is unforgivable. I would know your name.'

'You will learn it soon enough. It will be engraved in your heart.'

Cavillex nodded thoughtfully as he searched Will's face. 'You have been touched by us before.'

'Many men have been touched by your kind. There will be an ending to that business.'

Cavillex ignored Will's insolence and continued to peer deeply into his eyes. 'What was her name?' he enquired with a tone of mild amusement.

Deep in his head, Will felt something shift. His thoughts unfolded, rolling away like the mist on an autumn morning, and in the sun-drenched landscape that was revealed he saw Jenny again, coming towards him through the cornfield, her face ablaze with love. His heart pounded with joy. He wanted to feel the touch of her hand in his once more, the sweetness of her cheek against his lips, the perfume of her hair, the melody of her voice, her laughter; her love.

And then the image faded, and he knew it was an echo, fading with each passing day, slowly draining the happiness from his life. A wave of grief washed through him, but he held it back before it broke on his face.

'Would you like to know if she still lives?' Cavillex enquired.

'Why would I listen to your words? They are lies and obfuscations and swamp-lights that lead you on to disaster.'

'Because hope and yearning force you to listen, even when you know it is painful or futile. That is the way of men. You follow the light to try to ease the pain of your existence. You need the promise because you cannot deal with the harshness of the truth.' Cavillex peered down his nose at Will in a haughty, dismissive manner.

'And you take advantage of our weakness.'

A chilled silence had descended on the room, all eyes focused upon the confrontation between Will and Cavillex.

'You carry your own destruction with you,' Cavillex continued. 'Love. Even as it leads you on, it ruins you.'

'And yet we continue,' Will replied. 'And when you divine that mystery you will realize you can never win.'

'I know where she is.' Cavillex nodded as he saw the light rise up in Will's face. 'Alive, yes.'

'With your kind?'

Cavillex's face remained implacable.

Privately, Will cursed himself for responding; he had proved

227

Cavillex right. He forced himself to dismiss Cavillex's revelation as another manipulation designed to inflict pain, but something in his opponent's face, or voice, hinted at a deeper truth.

'We will meet again, when it is time to balance our accounts,' Cavillex said to Will with a nod. He turned to the Scottish king and added, 'We enjoy our time among your people and the sport it gives us.' James winced and again Will sensed he was on the brink of tears. 'Now, you have a choir here?' Cavillex continued. 'I would hear more of your music that celebrates the joys of your short lives. Let them sing the opening verses of the hundred-and-thirty-seventh Psalm, in the setting of Filippo de Monte, *Super flumina*. Please your honoured guests.' He bowed, and moved away into the crowd.

King James wrung his hands. 'I am a king, yet I am a slave.'

'None of us can be ourselves – our lives are not our own. We all make sacrifices for the good of the ones we serve, and that is how it should be.'

'But I would not be a slave to him!'

'Nor shall you, for much longer. We will never be truly free of them, but there will come a time when we have driven them back to the edges of our world, and for most they will become a memory, nothing more.'

'Your words give me confidence. Remember me to your Queen, and, if you find it in your heart, pass on what I have said.' He gave a weary smile, a nod, and went in search of the choir.

His resolve reaffirmed, Will made his way back to Nathaniel, Meg and Reidheid, who had been watching from afar, their faces etched with concern. All the noise of the festivities faded into a dull background buzz as his thoughts coalesced around the image of Jenny in the cornfield. Was Cavillex telling him the truth, or was it a lie designed to cause pain? New hope that would eventually be crushed so brutally it would be worse than not having hope at all? It showed the cold effectiveness of the Enemy: in a moment they had identified his weakness and attacked his most vulnerable area, his heart. He tried to force the picture of Jenny back into the deep, dark place where he had learned to keep it so he could continue with his life, but it clawed its way back, refusing to be subdued. Raw once more, the old questions hit him with renewed force: alive or dead? Salvation or damnation?

Unsettled, Nathaniel wanted to know the identity of the new arrivals, and appeared only partly placated when Will told him they were Spanish agents, although Meg was convinced. 'They are here because they know I have the cipher and they are afraid I will reach their prize before them,' Will said. He watched as the Unseelie Court moved amongst the guests, selecting nervous women and men for dancing partners, and added, 'Though how they knew I would be here this evening, I have not yet concluded. But they must not be allowed to follow us, or prevent us from reaching the object of our search. Nat, you must come with me.'

'You can count on us,' Meg said with a confident smile.

'Do not take any risks,' Nathaniel said with concern.

'We shall not fail you,' Reidheid added, 'though our lives be forfeit.'

'I said, do not take any risks!' Nathaniel stressed. He touched Meg's hand briefly before Will tugged him away.

'She has a brave heart, Nat. Trust her,' Will whispered as they slipped across the room. Nathaniel cast one backward glance as Meg began to complain loudly about the new arrivals. Murmurs of fear ran through the crowd and an attendant ran to silence her, drawing the attention of all. At the door a guard barred their way, but the King caught his eye and nodded. James then exchanged a brief, curious glance with Will, and turned away, accepting that whatever was planned was in his best interests. Will and Nathaniel darted through the door.

'I am in debt to the King,' Will said as they moved into a long corridor with views across the darkening hunting grounds at the rear of the palace. The sky was a deep blue, turning rapidly to black, the trees stark silhouettes, the moon and stars gleaming. 'He is a good man, burdened by the demands of his office.' Will realized he felt a strong affinity with the young monarch.

All the activity in the palace was centred on the State Rooms, and the rest of the corridors and chambers through which they passed were still and silent. Returning to the quadrangle, they found a door on the south side that opened on to a short corridor leading to another door which let them directly into the abbey.

Inside it was cool and dark. The glow from the candles flared up the walls to the vast wooden beams supporting the roof and drew sparkles of brilliant colour from the stained glass windows. The empty abbey was filled with the pungent aroma of incense. Their footsteps echoed on the stone flags as they made their way into the nave and looked up to the transept and the choir where the shadows gathered.

'Where do we begin?' Even though Nathaniel whispered, his voice carried far amid the perfect acoustics of the interior. He shivered and glanced towards the door to see if he had drawn any attention.

'We search,' Will replied. 'A statue. A painting. An icon. An image hidden in the stained glass. A carving in the wood. Anything which speaks of martyrdom.'

Nathaniel moved off to begin his quest at the west end near the tower. Will approached the transept, and saw where King David's original design of the abbey had been altered following an attack by the English army forty years earlier. Will studied the rebuilt eastern wall of the church and wondered if their search was futile. Perhaps a statue of the martyr had not been replaced during the restructuring, or some other clue to the location was missing.

As he continued to scour the abbey, he feared he was right, for there was no sign of a martyr anywhere. Refusing to give up, he returned to the nave where Nathaniel paced back and forth, scanning the walls and floor.

'Anything?' he asked.

Nathaniel shook his head. 'Perhaps we are looking in the wrong place.'

'No, I am convinced the Templars would have hidden the item here, under the protection of God, in the most sacred area of Edinburgh.'

'Then perhaps there is some sign we are missing.'

Will agreed. 'Let us reconsider. We are dealing with a cipher, after all. A martyr may not be a martyr.' While Nathaniel looked up to the heavens for inspiration, Will sank into one of the wooden pews and rested his chin in his hand. Thinking aloud, he said, 'King David dedicated this foundation to the Holy Rood. His mother, St Margaret, brought that precious relic, a fragment of the True Cross, back to Scotland from the land of the Magyars.' He mused, 'Margaret . . . martyr,' then shook his head with frustration.

Craning his neck, Nathaniel continued to examine the ceiling of the abbey, where moonlight through the windows and flickering candlelight made a constantly shifting interplay of shadows and illuminated areas.

'Nat! Concentrate on the matter at hand.'

'There. Do you see that?' Nathaniel pointed at the main arching beam of the abbey roof.

'This is no time to search for bats.'

'There! On the beam!'

With irritation, Will followed his assistant's pointing finger. After a moment of squinting, he spotted it. There seemed to be a badge above the centre of the aisle: a red cross on a square, half white, half black. 'One of the Templar flags,' he said thoughtfully.

'If you had spent more time on your studies of the Christian faith, and less in the stews of Bankside, you would know that the red cross is the mark of a martyr.'

'Nathaniel, you are a constant source of inspiration to me. Disregard all I said about you.'

Will dropped to his knees to examine the stone flags of the aisle. Hammering the hilt of his rapier on the one directly beneath the badge resulted in a hollow echo.

'*Where the martyr stands in black and white*,' he said with a pleased smile. 'I think we have it.' With his knife, he scraped the dirt of centuries out from round the edge of the slab. 'If we had a tool, we could prise it up.'

'Let me look.' Nathaniel hurried off into the gloom of the abbey. Will heard him opening doors and searching cupboards. After what seemed like an age, he returned and shook his head.

'What now?' Nathaniel asked.

Will looked towards the great door that led back to the palace. 'We cannot afford to leave this to another day. Our Enemy could arrive at any moment.' He paused, and said almost to himself, 'Yet Kintour said they could not walk near the entrance to where the Shield was kept.'

'Why could they not walk here?' Nathaniel asked suspiciously.

Will ignored him. 'No, there is no choice. We must break through this stone. Fetch me that.' He pointed to a large single-stem candlestick in front of the altar.

'I fear your constant desire for attention is getting the better of you,' Nathaniel said. The candlestick was several inches taller than him, and he had to brace himself to lift it, which he did with a grunt. He staggered over to Will and lowered it slowly to the paved floor with another grunt.

'You are growing soft, Nat. I must work you harder.' With a grin, Will braced himself and lifted the iron implement as high as he could. When he brought it down hard, the resounding crash reverberated around the walls of the abbey. Nathaniel jumped and looked to the door. At Will's nod, he ran to it, opened it a crack and peered out. Listening for a moment, he said, 'Nothing yet. I can hear the music from the festivities. Perhaps it drowned out your attempts to bring disaster down round our ears.'

Once Nathaniel had closed the door, Will brought the candleholder down again. A few flakes cracked off the centre of the flagstone, but it remained solid. An increasingly anxious Nathaniel looked out of the door again.

The third time Will thundered the candlestick against the floor there was a loud crack, but no sign on the surface of the stone. Then, on the fourth strike, the slab shattered into pieces that plunged into the dark below. Cold, damp air and the smell of great age rushed up to greet them.

Nathaniel glanced out of the door once more. All remained as before. But peering into the void by Will's shoulder, he grew hesitant. 'There is something about that sight that fills me with dread,' he whispered.

'Then let your heart beat slower, Nat, for I would have you wait here,' Will told him.

Nathaniel bristled. 'Are you saying I cannot match the courage and fortitude of the great Will Swyfte?'

'No, Nat, I am saying I need someone here to keep watch at my back,' Will lied.

Placated, Nathaniel watched as Will fetched a single silver candlestick for light and crouched at the edge of the hole, preparing to lower himself into the dark. 'Wish me luck, Nat. Fortune favours fools!'

# CHAPTER TWENTY-FOUR

FROM BEHIND WILL, A SHAFT OF WEAK LIGHT PLUNGED DOWN into the hole from the abbey and he could hear Nathaniel moving around the edge as his assistant tried to follow his progress. Holding the candlestick aloft, Will edged along the stone wall of what appeared to be a tunnel. Although mottled with age and glistening with damp, the floor was perfectly level. But for all the fine workmanship, he was aware that after four centuries collapses could lie ahead, perhaps even drops into the foundations.

The stale air told him that wherever the tunnel led, it was sealed. After a few paces, it sloped down until Will estimated he was at least ten paces beneath the floor of the abbey.

Finally, he came to a raised step. The change in the timbre of his footsteps' echoes suggested a large space lay beyond, but the candlelight barely penetrated into the chamber.

A stone column topped by a plinth stood just inside the entrance. There, carved into the top, was the Templar cross and an image of two knights on a horse, underneath which was engraved *Sigillum Militum Christi* – the Seal of the Soldiers of Christ.

Lowering the candle, Will saw a legend had also been engraved.

> Under God's ever-watchful eye
> A Shield against earthly decay shall lie,
> But the fires of Heaven and Hell consume
> The unworthy seeker who enters this tomb.

Studying this message of damnation, Will was puzzled by the reference to the 'fires of Heaven'. He knew there must be some greater meaning hidden within the words. 'There is a mystery here,' he mused aloud.

Amid the disorienting echoes, Will edged past the plinth into the near-suffocating, almost tangible darkness of the chamber. It was impossible to tell how large the space was, or where the Shield was located, if indeed it was here. As he progressed, the candle revealed that the plain flagstones of the floor were about to give way to ones engraved with the Templar cross, stretching as far as the light revealed.

Reciting the carved legend to himself, Will advanced with caution. Pausing at the line of Templar stones, he took one hesitant step. Without warning, the flag cracked and fell away beneath his boot. He threw himself back as, from above, a stream of silvery powder fell towards a gleaming black liquid smelling of pitch that lay beneath the broken stone. As the powder landed, the liquid burst into flame, a fierce column of fire.

Kicking back several more steps as the heat scorched his face, Will caught his breath and realized how close he had come to being incinerated. The flaming column had died down a little, but still blazed intensely at its base. In its glare, Will looked out across a vast chamber bigger than the floor of the abbey, with the cross-marked flags reaching to the far wall. There, in a niche, rested an object that he couldn't quite discern.

Quickly, Will rapidly considered what had happened. Now he understood some of the meaning of the words on the plinth. *Fires of Hell*, burning beneath his feet. He guessed what *fires of Heaven* meant. Returning to the tunnel, he hefted up a heavy chunk of the original broken entrance flag and hurled it out on to the cross-marked stones. Two shattered. One ignited another hidden pool of the pitch-like liquid. The other released a gush of flaming liquid from above.

Somewhere, he guessed, there must be a path across the floor to the opposite wall that would not end in death – a route the Templars had left should they, or their heirs, ever need to reclaim what he was now certain was the Shield for their own use.

Will was acutely aware that time was against him. Sooner or later, the Unseelie Court would realize he was no longer part of the festivities and would come searching for him. It was likely they were already. But the ferocity of the fire showed he could not take any chances. Even testing the stones with his boot could result in death, and the heat from too many blazing locations would be too much, even if he did find a path across them.

He paced up and down the boundary of the cross-marked flags, searching for any that were different, marked with an angled cross, perhaps, or completely bare, but he knew that that would be too easy. The Templars wanted to protect the Shield from anyone who wished to use it for malign purposes. Yet they also recognized that the Shield could be of benefit, perhaps in protecting against one of the Skull's attacks. Will knew they must have allowed a way to it for someone who wished to use it only for good. But how?

Leaning against the wall of the chamber behind him, he dwelled on everything he had learned about the Templars. He knew of their public works, of course, and of their secret war against the Enemy that had been revealed to him by Dee. He had discovered that they used ciphers to hide true meanings, and that they relished the use of symbols.

Still deep in thought, he returned to the plinth. The key was there, he was sure: a warning to those who wished to use the Shield for evil, that was clear. But a clue to help the needy? He carefully read the legend again.

The second half was specific in its warning. What if the first half was too? *Under God's ever-watchful eye.*

Walking back to the line of cross-marked stones, Will peered up to the ceiling high overhead. It would normally have been obscured by gloom, but the blaze of *the fires of Heaven and Hell* had revealed what was hidden there. Will smiled. Now he understood the minds of the good Christian Templar Knights. The unworthy would focus on the perils of the fires. The worthy would look to the heavens for salvation.

The stones across the ceiling mirrored the ones on the floor, each marked with a Templar cross but for a few that were marked with an eye.

*God's watchful eye.*

If he followed the trail of the eyes, would he find his way through to the Shield? The reasoning appeared assured, but there was only one way to be certain. Placing his foot firmly on the flagstone beneath the first eye, Will shifted his weight on to it. The slab held.

Shying away from the roaring columns of flame, he followed the route. Momentarily, he had to wait for the thick smoke to clear so he could see the eyes, and he realized that if he had cracked any more of the fire-stones the smoke would have completely obscured the way. There was something symbolic in that, too.

The path led him a merry and fiery dance left and right across the entire width of the chamber, but at last he stood before the niche itself. There, resting on an angled plinth, was a silver amulet on a chain. Inscribed on it in black filigree were symbols and words in a language that Will did not recognize.

Snatching the amulet, he turned to make his way back across the deadly floor and spied Reidheid on the far side of the chamber, his sword drawn. Reidheid slowly nodded. Thoughts played out across Will's face as the realization dawned on him.

'Traitor,' Will called out across the flickering, smoke-filled chamber.

'I am not alone,' Reidheid replied with mock sadness. 'There are traitors everywhere among Walsingham's men. Sometimes I wonder if there are more traitors than loyal followers of the Queen.'

Holding the amulet behind his back, Will carefully made his way back along the path. 'How could you betray England?'

'England endures, whatever,' the other man answered. 'The question is: how could you *not* betray the Queen and her government? You have seen what *they* are capable of. We can never win.'

'What have *they* promised you, Reidheid? Riches? Congress with the most beautiful women in the land? A life eternal?' Will snorted in derision. 'They prey on human weakness, and find the spaces in our character that they can prise open from crack to chasm. You know that. They cannot be trusted.'

'They promised me freedom from fear.' A fleeting look of desperation crossed Reidheid's face. 'Imagine what that would be like. No longer glancing over your shoulder in anticipation of death's looming, bony face. No longer waking with bleak thoughts in the morning so that you are unable to appreciate the new dawn, and no longer fighting to find sleep each night as the terrors flood your mind.'

'We are mortals. There is no true freedom from fear. We live with it, and learn to accommodate it. That makes us human. And that is where we gather our strength.' Will's voice echoed around the chamber.

'Yes, we are mortals. We hate each other for being Catholic or Protestant, Jew or Moor, English, Spanish or French. There is no hope for us. We must get what we can from this world, before Heaven beckons.'

'Or Hell.'

Steadying himself, Reidheid pointed his sword towards Will. 'Enough. Our philosophic discourse can be continued at another time. Give me the Shield.' He gestured with his free hand.

'So you can in turn give it to the Enemy?' Will now held the amulet by the chain in front of him. It turned slowly, re-flecting the gold and scarlet of the flames.

'It matters not to you.' Reidheid stepped to the edge of the cross-marked flags. 'Another turn in a war that goes on for ever.'

Will smiled tightly. 'I see the Enemy treats you as a dog, chained up in the kennel and thrown titbits. You do not know what is truly at stake here? You betray not only the Queen and England, but also your fellow men, your own family, your daughter Meg.'

'And why should I believe *you*?' Reidheid snapped. 'Will Swyfte, who lives a lie as the greatest hero England knows. He is but a fairy tale to soothe the nightmares of men and women so they think themselves protected by gods and not, in truth, by an assassin . . . a torturer . . . a man of grey morals. You are no better than me. We each have our ambitions and we pursue them vigorously.'

Clutching the amulet in his left fist, Will came to a halt a few paces before Reidheid and drew his sword, addressing him with cold contempt. 'You speak like a child. Is this some revelation to you? That we all wear masks? Which is the true face? The truth is, there is none. We are all many things, and all of them insubstantial. Good and Evil are elusive. But there is one thing that divides you and me. You do what you do for your own gain.'

Reidheid's cheeks flushed. 'The Shield.'

'It is here. You may take it, or try to.' Will raised his sword.

Reidheid hesitated. 'I am not afraid. The Unseelie Court will be here soon, and you will not escape their attentions.' Yet when he looked at the flames leaping up around his black-garbed foe, who was now sporting a diabolic grin, Reidheid couldn't hide a flicker of fear.

'I think not. It is my belief that this place is protected. No Enemy foot can tread here without risking destruction. It is you and I, Master Reidheid. I hear you were a fine swordsman in your prime. Do your recall your skills?' With poise, Will swished his rapier through the curling smoke, relishing the sound it made.

Reidheid stepped on to the first of the cross-marked flagstones, and by chance it was the one beneath an eye. Hesitating, he looked round at the blazing pools and realized Will was attempting to lure him into a trap.

The Scotsman smiled. 'Clever, Master Swyfte. But it is you who are at the disadvantage. Even now the Unseelie Court prepare to close off your options for escape, and the Spaniard

241

has been despatched to, shall I say, collect your assistant. He will not last long.'

'Then let us end this.' And without warning, Will raced along the true path among the flags, but at the last he stepped on one of the fake slabs nearest to Reidheid. It crumbled under his boot, but his momentum carried him over it as he ducked the wild swing of Reidheid's sword and rolled across the solid stone floor of the chamber's entrance.

As flames rushed up from the black pool, Reidheid reeled back, one arm raised before his face against the blast of heat.

On his feet in an instant, Will spun and planted a kick in Reidheid's gut. With a cry, the traitor doubled up and fell back, but with unexpected agility he rolled across the chamber floor to avoid Will's sword.

He was up quickly, blocking Will's driving thrusts and responding in kind. Their fight ranged along the edge of the cross-marked flags, and they were evenly matched as Reidheid settled back into the duelling skills he had learned in his youth. Resounding off the chamber walls, the clash of their blades sang, thrust and parry, high and low.

But Reidheid was the older man and out of condition and after a short time he began to tire. As he flagged, Will saw the opening he was looking for. He kicked one of the cross-marked stones next to Reidheid, withdrawing his boot sharply as the silvery dust fell. The flames roared up and engulfed the left side of Reidheid's body. Screaming, and now ablaze, he dropped his sword and staggered away.

Moving quickly, Will knocked him to the floor and rolled him over until the flames were extinguished. The skin of Reidheid's face and most of the left side of his body was scorched, the smell now of burned meat, but he was alive. Will dragged the man to his feet and propelled him towards the tunnel. 'You are fortunate I am not the man you thought I was.'

Near the entrance, the flames' shadows danced along the tunnel walls, but soon they were in the dark again, with only the pale light from the abbey above to guide them.

Whimpering in pain, Reidheid offered no resistance. Beyond his cries, Will listened for any sign of threat, but all was quiet.

'Nat,' he called up, his voice hoarse from the smoke. There was no response.

Weak and in pain from his injuries, Reidheid was happy to be helped by Will. Beneath the shattered flag, he managed to claw his way up Will's body, and with Will's cupped hands to propel him, he scrambled into the abbey. Leaping up to grip the edge of the slabs, Will hauled himself up after Reidheid. The church was empty. Had Nathaniel gone to investigate the festivities, to ensure the Enemy was not closing on the abbey? Will hid the Shield in his doublet and prepared for the worst.

'Make no sound,' he said quietly to Reidheid as he gripped him by the arm, 'or I will retract my previous decision and run you through.'

At the door, Will listened. He could hear the distant music from the King's festivities, but there appeared to be no one near. Moving out into the short corridor that linked the abbey and the palace, he saw that the door to the south cloister was open and the quadrangle was now illuminated by the silvery light of the moon. Darkness hung heavily in the cloisters as he led Reidheid to the door.

'Father!' Meg's cry rang out from the cloister along the eastern edge, and a second later she separated from the darkness of a doorway, accompanied by another. Will froze. It was the Hunter. Tearfully, the girl struggled to free herself so she could

243

run to Reidheid, but the Hunter held her fast. As she fought, he raised a cruel, curved knife to her neck.

'See what you have done?' Will said coldly to the wounded man beside him.

'Meg.' The desolation in Reidheid's voice rose up above the pain of his injuries. 'Please leave her be.'

In the moonlight, other figures appeared in the quadrangle. Cavillex stood at the head of the assembling members of the Unseelie Court.

'There may well be places where we cannot walk, but our influence can never fade while we are able to reach into the human heart,' he said.

His rapier glinting in his hand, Will thrust Reidheid away. Slowly England's greatest spy backed to the wall, his eyes darting along his branch of the cloister.

'Kill her,' Cavillex ordered. 'And then the rest of them.'

Reidheid cried out, but before he could make a move, Nathaniel lurched from a shadowed doorway. He manhandled the hefty iron candlestick and brought it down hard on the Hunter, who fell to the ground, his knife spinning across the flagstone floor.

'Run, Nat!' Will yelled. As he turned, he caught a glimpse of Nathaniel grabbing Meg by the hand and dragging her towards the abbey. Cavillex's orders echoed across the quadrangle, but Will was already racing along the cloister towards the tower in the far corner. His hope was to escape through the entrance to the gatehouse, but the Unseelie Court moved silently and stealthily, revealed only by the moonlight throwing their fleeting shadows on the stone.

Reaching the end of the cloister, Will plunged through a door that led to a spiral staircase. As he made his way up, he passed windows which looked out over the formal gardens.

Only one pursuer appeared to be on his heels, climbing the stairs behind him – the Hunter, Will guessed, seeking revenge for the wound Will had inflicted the previous night in the Fairy House.

At the top of the steps, he crashed into the outer chamber of a dark, panelled bedroom. Each ceiling panel carried the royal crest, and the decor suggested its incumbent was a woman. He realized he had arrived in the old quarters of Mary, Queen of Scots. Moonlight broke through the window across the boards. A wooden cabinet inlaid with red hearts and gold stood by a small dressing room and a four-poster bed rested against one wall next to another door.

Will leapt on to the bed, and drew the curtain. Steadying his breathing, he listened, and waited. The thunder of boots crossed the floorboards, and then the pursuer skidded into the room, coming to a halt as though he could sense his prey was nearby. Will listened as the Enemy moved around the chamber. A soft tread, the brush of fingers on wood. The door to the dressing room thrown open. The cabinet knocked to one side. And now the other door torn open, a blast of chill air stirring the curtains around the bed.

The footsteps came to a halt, followed by a moment of searching silence, before they moved towards the bed and stopped on the other side of the curtain. Soft exhalations disturbed the quiet. Will pictured them separated by only one hand's width, looking directly into each other's eyes.

Will felt calm, his heartbeat steady. He was fixed, staring directly at the thick, embroidered drape. A long moment of deathly quiet.

And then the curtains were torn back forcibly and Will found himself gazing into the dark eyes of the Hunter. He saw in their infinite depths a coruscating intelligence, and with

245

a single fluid motion drove his sword through the Enemy's throat.

'For my friend,' Will said quietly.

He watched the eyes flicker in shock, and then roll towards white as the Hunter slid backwards, off the sword, his hands going to his throat. Will leapt from the bed and thrust his weapon through his adversary's heart, and held it tight until the Hunter slid to the boards, dead.

Standing over him, gulping air, Will surveyed the body. He saw something less than the Enemy that had haunted the nightmares of Englishmen; the Hunter was a foe who could be killed, like any man. Then he thought of Tom Miller, dead at the end of rope long before he had begun to reach his potential. And he thought of Jenny.

'Not even a balance,' Will said coldly. He withdrew his sword and wiped it on the cloak of his fallen foe.

From outside came a keening sound that set his teeth on edge, and he understood it for the sound of grief from a world beyond the one he knew. Somehow the other members of the Unseelie Court had sensed the death of one of their own.

The sound of running feet echoed from the spiral staircase, and Will bolted through the other door of the bedchamber into the Queen's Lobby, and then a long gallery. Bounding down a flight of stairs, he encountered a mass of guards rushing towards him, led by King James himself. For all that they held swords and torches, fear burned in their faces.

'Master Swyfte,' James said drily. 'I expected to find you at the heart of this disturbance.'

'Apologies. I fear I have upset your guests.'

A slight smile alighted on James's face.

'They will not trouble you, but I believe they may want to introduce me to an unpleasant end,' Will continued.

'Then I suggest you leave the palace forthwith, Master Swyfte, and we shall do all we can to ensure your pursuers are engaged in entertaining conversation! I hope you enjoyed the hospitality at the Palace of Holyroodhouse. You are welcome here any time.'

With a grin and a bow, Will ran back out into the quadrangle, while James led his entourage towards the remaining members of the Unseelie Court. Will knew the King would only be able to delay Cavillex and his group for a short while; time was of the essence.

Concerned for the safety of Nathaniel and Meg, he found his assistant in the abbey church, armed once again with the iron candlestick. Behind him, Meg tended to her father, who lay sprawled on the flagstone floor.

'Come, Nat. We must take our leave,' Will said. 'Time is short.'

Nathaniel's relief was palpable. 'This is not the fun and games I was promised. I will think twice the next time you invite me to a party.' He turned to Meg and offered his hand, but she shook her head.

'I must stay with my father,' she said. She looked to Nathaniel, the yearning clear in her eyes. Will saw the same emotion in the face of his assistant.

Moments passed, and then Nathaniel gave a restrained nod in parting, and hurried to Will's side. 'There will be time to renew acquaintances another day,' Will said.

'London is a world away.' Nathaniel glanced back briefly as they made their way through the door. With a wan smile, Meg waved goodbye. 'And after this day, I understand why your time is spent in stews, and your heart is your own.'

'That is my world, Nat, not yours. I happen to like doxies.

What they lack in romance, they make up for in vigorous entertainment.'

The cloisters echoed to the sound of their running feet, and then they were through the gatehouse and into the forecourt where the coaches waited, their drivers seemingly oblivious of the uproar that had tainted that night. Will informed Reidheid's man that his master had instructed they be delivered to the house at Cowgate with speed.

The carriage rattled out of the gate in the west wall towards the steep cobbled street that led up to the castle. The city was dark but for the candles burning in the windows of the tall stone houses on either side.

Will glanced back at the receding palace. There was no sign of pursuit, and he settled back into the leather seat. Taking the Shield from its hiding place, he examined the amulet. It glowed dully in the half-light.

'This has been a good night, all told, Nat,' he said. 'We have escaped from under our Enemy's nose with the prize we sought. We have shown them that England is a force to be reckoned with – if they had not realized it yet, they know now they cannot treat us with impunity. And Tom Miller has been avenged. Our time in Edinburgh has been well spent.'

Lulled by the rocking of the carriage, Will put his feet up, closed his eyes and considered the next stage. The Enemy would come looking for the Shield if they needed it to complete their mysterious plan, and that knowledge could, he felt certain, be used to the advantage of England. A trap, perhaps. And then they might turn the tables and recover the Silver Skull and the Key, perhaps even strike a devastating blow at the Unseelie Court in the process.

He realized Nathaniel had slipped into morose silence, and was staring into the pitch-black wynds that ran off the main street. 'Are you thinking of Meg?' Will asked. 'She will be safe.'

The younger man shook his head. 'Our enemies were not Spaniards, Will.'

'Their allies—'

'Who were they?'

'Nat—'

'*What* were they, Will?'

A cold pit formed in Will's stomach. He would rather see Nathaniel dismissed and sent back to the mundane life in the shires whence he came than destroyed by the truth.

Before Will could put Nathaniel's mind at rest, a baleful howl echoed along the street from somewhere behind them, just audible through the sound of the coach and horse on the cobbles. The cries of waking babies, the barks of chained dogs joining with it, the slams of shutters and doors, moved up the street like a drum-roll. Nathaniel started. 'What was that? A hunting dog?' He paused uneasily. 'I have heard no dog like that.'

Will knew exactly what it was, and his frustration mounted and turned to anger. Pulling himself half out of the window, he peered back down the street, but there was only a sea of darkness. 'Faster, driver!' he called up. 'As if the Devil himself was at your back!'

'Yes, sir!' At the driver's whip-crack, the horse picked up its pace.

'What is happening here?' Nathaniel said with an edge of desperation. 'You urge the driver to speed because a dog howls? That makes no sense to me.'

'The agents of Spain do not give up easily, Nat,' Will dissembled. 'We need to reach the house in Cowgate where we will be safe, for now.'

'Why safer there than here? Or at the palace?'

'Not now, Nat!' Will snapped, unable to tell his assistant of the magical protection at Reidheid's home.

Looking out again, Will thought he could now see two sparks of red swimming in that ocean of dark.

'Hold on, Nat! If you thought the journey to Edinburgh was hard, there is a rougher one to come!'

The coach driver glanced over his shoulder and saw something that Will couldn't, for his face grew white and fixed in horror.

'Keep your eyes ahead!' Will yelled. 'Let me worry about what is at our backs!'

As the howling grew louder, the terrified man cracked the whip wildly, driving the horse into a panic. The carriage skewed across the street, and as it careered towards Cowgate it tilted on two wheels and threatened to turn over. Will and Nathaniel threw themselves over to the opposite side using their weight to bring the carriage down with a jolt.

'Damn him!' Will cursed. '*He* will kill us!'

'What scares him so?' Nathaniel shouted.

The carriage raced down the hill towards Cowgate. Will forced himself to look out of the window once more. There, by the side of the door and keeping pace perfectly, was the colossal dog. It turned its eyes upon the spy, and then it leapt, jaws wide.

Will threw himself back just in time. Foul saliva splashed across his face as the motion of the beast's snapping jaws caressed his skin.

Then the creature slammed against the side of the carriage with such force that it felt as if they had been struck by another coach. As the wheels skewed across the road, the wooden side and roof cracked and splintered under the repeated assault.

There was a crash across the roof and moments later the driver released a sickening shriek, cut short.

The carriage spun across the road in the opposite direction, the sound of the protesting wheels lost beneath another terrifying scream, this time from the horse, which was quickly swallowed by a horrifying snarling as the dog tore the unfortunate animal to pieces.

In the frenzy of the attack, the carriage pitched and keeled over. Will and Nathaniel were flung across the interior as it crashed on the cobbles and skidded to a sudden, bone-jarring halt.

Dazed, Will looked to Nathaniel, who lay in a heap, stunned, but alive. From nearby came sickening wet sounds of the hound tearing at the remains of the horse. Conflicting emotions tore through Will. He knew he must act decisively, but could he put Nathaniel at risk of greater contact with this nightmarish world Will had protected him from for so long? What was more important: his friend's sanity and possibly his life, or the secret war? He knew there was only one answer.

'Nat! Nat!' Will whispered insistently, shaking his companion's groaning form. 'No bones broken? Good. I have work for you.'

'N . . . now?'

'Especially now.' Will sat Nathaniel up and thrust the amulet into his hands. Feeling that he was possibly damning his friend for ever, he said, 'Take this and make your way back to the house. You will be safe there.'

In the background, the rending and tearing had ceased.

'I am the one they want. I killed one of them. They believe I have the object they desire.' He pointed at the amulet. 'You will have time to make good your escape before they realize their mistake.'

'But they will kill you!'

A skin-crawling growl seemed to circle the wrecked carriage.

'I made my peace with that eventuality a long time ago. It is as inevitable as the snows of winter – if not now, then later.' He pulled Nathaniel to his feet, and helped him clamber out of the window above his head before flashing him a grin. 'Know that I do not plan to go easily into the arms of the Reaper.'

The dog was near the steaming remnants of the horse. Coming to a halt, it raised its head towards Will, baring its gore-stained teeth.

'Will . . .' Nathaniel began hesitantly.

'You know me, Nat!' Will insisted. 'I will demand my due reckoning. Now go!'

Nathaniel hesitated for only the briefest moment longer, but in that time Will saw the depth of concern and friendship in the other man's face. He nodded and was gone.

As the great black dog prepared to leap, Will Swyfte drew his rapier. Out of the corner of his eye he saw Nathaniel weaving into the relative safety of a dark, foul-smelling close.

And then, with a snarl, the unnatural beast attacked.

# CHAPTER TWENTY-FIVE

AS THE DARK OF THE CLOSE SWALLOWED NATHANIEL UP, FROM behind came a chilling howl that ended in the sounds of slaughter. Will's voice rang out, defiant, the words lost beneath the bestial roars, and then there was only a distant silence against which Nathaniel's running feet sounded like whip-cracks.

He still felt groggy from the knock he had taken when the carriage crashed over, but he was resolute. Will had survived many close encounters with death, and Nathaniel had long since learned there was no point spending time worrying about what might be. Instead, Will had trusted him with a matter of great import to England, and he would not let his friend down by betraying that trust.

Slipping the amulet into his pocket, he sped on into the unfamiliar city. It was the easiest way to lose himself; the closes and wynds ran out from the King's High Street, numerous, narrow, dark, filthy and rat-infested. If he reached out both arms he could touch the walls on either side, the buildings soaring up so high that only a tiny patch of star-sprinkled sky was visible. No moonlight reached the ground. Excrement and urine sloshed under his feet from where it had been thrown from the surrounding houses, and piles of rotting rubbish were heaped everywhere.

Pausing to catch his breath, Nathaniel leaned against a wall and looked back to see if the giant dog was pursuing him. He was sure not, but instead, silhouetted figures were searching near the entrance to the alley.

As the figures darted into the dark close, Nathaniel's skin prickled and he grew sick with an inexplicable fear, one far greater than he should have felt were they just Spanish agents at his back. Instinctively, he knew there was something more here, and much that Will was not telling him.

Pushing himself away from the wall, he ran on in the gloom, but his pursuers were remarkably fleet-footed. And they seemed very much at ease in their task. He could hear them pause as they searched the doorways and hiding paces as they passed, yet still they drew nearer. He knew he would not be able to outrun them. What, then, when he broke out of the other end of the close and into the open?

'Quick! Tell me. They are coming?'

Nathaniel jumped at the hissed voice. A grey-haired old woman crouched in a doorway, peering back along the close.

'There are enemies at my back, yes,' Nathaniel whispered.

'Enemies. That is a good word for them.' The old woman peered at him with black eyes, her brow knotted, but whatever she saw appeared to reassure her for she threw open the door to her hovel and urged him inside.

From the room, a rectangle of light flooded out into the close like a beacon. Behind, Nathaniel could hear the voices of his pursuers rise up.

'They will know where I am!' Nathaniel said.

'Inside! Now!'

Torn, Nathaniel hesitated until the woman grabbed him

254

with a strength that belied her age and dragged him inside. The door slammed shut behind them. Hastily, the woman poured a fragrant line of salt and herbs along the floor at the foot of the door, and then ducked down to floor level, urging Nathaniel to do the same. As he squatted there, he looked up and saw a line of charms hanging above the door and along the length of the wall – animal bones, twisted pieces of metal, feathers and painted jewellery.

'They will sense you are somewhere nearby, but they will not know where,' the woman whispered. 'And even if they come to the door they will not be able to enter.'

'Have you lost your senses?' Nathaniel hissed. 'They saw the light! They will be inside in an instant!'

The woman waved him silent as running footsteps slowed outside. Nathaniel held his breath as he glimpsed movement along the gap beneath the door. He guessed that there were three or four pursuers outside, moving slowly along the close, pausing every now and then to listen. One hesitated outside the door, slow breaths clear in the silence. It was as if whoever was out there was inhaling his scent. Eyes widening, Nathaniel focused on the door handle, waiting for it to turn. Silently, he mouthed a prayer.

After what seemed an eternity, and when he thought his heart was about to burst, his pursuers moved on. The sound of running feet continued down the close until they faded from hearing. Bowing his head in relief, Nathaniel took a deep breath.

When he had recovered, he snapped at the old woman, 'We were fortunate. You could have doomed me, believing in your magic!' He indicated the charms dismissively.

The woman narrowed her eyes at him with equal contempt. 'I saved your life. And you are a fool if you think otherwise.

They prey 'pon our people continually. Do you think we have not found ways to keep them at bay?'

Nathaniel snorted, but the woman's words unsettled him. His mind refused to contemplate their implication. As he turned to examine the hovel, he was surprised to see they were not alone. Twelve others crouched along the far wall of the room, their faces pale and fearful. There was a baby, and children of other ages, too, as well as four adults. They were clad in poor clothes, and their hollow cheeks betrayed their daily struggle for survival. But they, and their house, were clean, and the woman had offered Nathaniel the hand of friendship, at great risk to herself and the others.

'I must apologize for my poor manners,' Nathaniel said to her with a bow. 'You gave me refuge, and it is a truth, I think, that you saved my life. For that I am very grateful.'

'Apology accepted.' The woman hauled her aching bones to a chair near the hearth.

'I will arrange for my master to send you a reward—'

She shook her head forcefully. A cold eye warned him not to continue.

'Then I will be on my way,' he said.

'Are you in your cups?' One of the adults, a man, bounded forward and grabbed Nathaniel's arm forcefully. 'They are still out there.'

'I can slip back the way I came—'

'They can see a rabbit in a field ten miles distant. They can hear the breaking of an ear of corn from the same. They can smell your sweat, your fear, on the wind.'

Nathaniel tried to laugh off the man's concern, but there was no humour in the drawn features so close to his own.

'You do not know what hunted you?' the man asked warily.

'Spanish agents.'

He laughed contemptuously and spat on the floor. 'They are—'

'Hush!' the old woman urged. 'We do not talk of them! Once they notice you, your time is done.'

Hesitating, Nathaniel pieced together the woman's words. 'You say they are—'

'Hush,' the woman said, more softly this time, and turned her attention to the pot bubbling above the fire in order not to have to meet Nathaniel's eye.

'You are welcome to stay for a bowl and some bread.' The man's voice had the edgy tone of an adult talking to a child who has not grasped that a relative had died.

'Yes . . . thank you,' Nathaniel replied, feeling a weight settling upon his shoulders. 'But I must reach a house in Cowgate.'

'At dawn,' the man said. 'It will not be safe then, but it will be easier. For now, take your rest on our bed in the back room. We will call you when the food is ready.'

His thoughts racing, Nathaniel allowed himself to be guided to the dark rear room. As he sat on the bed, listening to the dim, restrained talk through the door, his thoughts returned to that time when everything changed. He was nineteen, and he had been offered work as an apprentice in the nearest town, to start three weeks hence. His lodgings had been found, his plans made, and then he had woken suddenly in the night to find his father missing.

# CHAPTER TWENTY-SIX

The brilliant white harvest moon framed the silhouette of the church steeple and caught the wayward flit of bats from their roost in the bell-tower. Across the churchyard, shadows cast by leaning tombstones and yews gently swaying in the breeze lay stark against the well-tended grass. One yawning grave held the attention of the crowd of fearful villagers gathered around the lychgate. None of them spoke, but it was as if they could not draw their eyes away from the black hole and the earth scattered all around.

Hurrying from their cottage, Nathaniel had found his father, the church warden, standing among his neighbours with the air of someone wrestling with a cruel choice.

'Father,' Nathaniel said, still half asleep. 'What is this? The grave has been disturbed again?'

'Go back to bed, Nathaniel. This is not for you.' His father was distracted, his face grey under the moon's lantern, and appearing much older, as if his features were attempting to catch up with the hair on his head which had turned white overnight after the death of Nathaniel's mother.

'Can this not wait till morning? Then let me help you fill in the grave—'

His father rounded on him, gripping his arm. 'Anne Goodrick is

258

missing. We fear she is within the church, taken there by . . . by . . .' The words died in his throat and he looked away quickly in the hope that his son would not see the horror in his features.

'Then this is not the work of grave-robbers,' Nathaniel said. 'There is more here. A plot.' He considered for a moment, and then said, 'Catholic sympathizers. They do this to disturb our faith. Is that it?'

After a moment, his father replied, 'Yes, Nathaniel. You are correct. And now young Anne's life is at risk.'

'Then we must storm the church to save her! All of us together can overcome any opponents, however well armed they might be—'

'No!' Nathaniel was shocked by the fury he saw in his father's face. He was always such a gentle man. 'You do not venture into the churchyard, do you hear me?' He turned to the other villagers and said loudly, 'Whatever might transpire, do not let my son follow me in there.'

The villagers nodded, but they would not look his father in the eye.

'What?' Nathaniel rounded on him. 'You cannot mean to go alone? If there is danger, it would be wise to enter the church together, and well armed.'

'No arms will help us,' his father muttered. Then, in a surprising show of emotion, he hugged Nathaniel to him and whispered, 'You must take care of yourself, Nat. This is a dark and dangerous world.' The moment he had spoken, he turned and darted through the lychgate and into the churchyard.

Nathaniel made to go after him, but the strong hands of the blacksmith and his son held him back, and however much he fought he could not shake them off. They continued to restrain him as his father entered the church, but after a time their grip eased as they watched in anticipation. No sound came from within. The mood of the vigil gradually became darker, and in the intense silence Nathaniel's anxiety

259

spiralled and turned to fear. He suddenly realized his father was not coming back out; that he was a prisoner, or worse.

Before panic seized hold of him, the crowd was disturbed by the sound of hoofbeats drawing near at a gentle pace.

Confusion at who could be riding into the village at that hour distracted Nathaniel and the others. A man not a great deal older than him rode up. He was dressed all in black, with black hair and black eyes and well-trimmed chin-hair. For all his sombre appearance, there was no dourness to him. Nathaniel recognized a confidence, amplified by a touch of playfulness that in itself was dark, together with a deep, reassuring strength.

'My name is William Swyfte,' the stranger said, rising up in his stirrups, 'sent here from London to aid you with your difficulty.'

'How did you hear of our problems?' the blacksmith asked suspiciously.

'Word of these matters travels quickly. The Queen has good men everywhere who watch and listen for any threat to the nation.'

As he dismounted, Nathaniel pressed forward and said urgently, 'My father has ventured into the church, and not come out. I fear . . . I fear . . .'

The dark rider rested a hand on his shoulder and said, 'We all do. Tell me what has happened here.'

'Three days ago, Nicholas Goodrick was buried.' Nathaniel pointed to the open grave. 'He was . . . not a good man,' he added hesitantly. 'We thought some of his enemies had caused this desecration, but there was talk that Nicholas had been seen abroad, as if he were still alive.'

'Your manner suggests you do not believe these stories.'

Nathaniel shrugged. 'Of course not. Dead is dead. We are not all superstitious fools. This is a time of knowledge and understanding.' He cast an eye over his neighbours and felt the gulf between him and them.

'You have a strong will. I like that. What is your name?' the stranger asked.

'Nathaniel Colt.'

Will Swyfte nodded. Nathaniel could see he was an educated man, storing away any information that might be of use to him. 'And the corpse was gone?'

'We searched for it, but . . . These things happen, sometimes. Nicholas was—'

'Not a good man, yes. So you filled in the grave?'

'And the next day it was open again. There was a space beneath it, and tunnels leading under the churchyard and beyond. Animals . . .' He paused. 'Though bigger tunnels than any animal could make.'

'And more talk of Nicholas Goodrick at large.' Will Swyfte nodded, almost to himself.

Nathaniel explained the notion of a plot by Catholic sympathizers, or even foreign spies, and was rewarded with a reassuring nod and smile. 'And now they have taken Anne Goodrick,' Nathaniel continued, 'a cruel blow when she was finally free of her father.' At Will Swyfte's quizzical glance, Nathaniel added quietly, 'It is common knowledge that he thrust an unnatural relationship upon Anne. Many times I found her crying, but she would never talk of it.'

The horseman's expression darkened, and he looked back to the church. 'And now she is in there, with her tormentor. Tormentors.'

'Help my father, sir,' Nathaniel urged. 'He is a good man, and only wished to aid Anne.'

Nathaniel received a clap on the shoulder that he found oddly reassuring, and the newcomer drew his rapier and set off towards the church. Fearfully, the villagers watched him as he entered the building. At first the silence confirmed their darkest thoughts, but suddenly lights flashed within as though lightning were crackling across the nave. As one the crowd cried out. More lightning, then blood-curdling cries that seemed barely human echoed from within the bell-tower.

261

*As always, Nathaniel found he was torn between the religious teachings of his father and his own faith in reason, between a world that could be mapped and understood, and one filled with terror. Conflicting images of the battle taking place in the church fought in his mind.*

*The crowd pointed and called out as Will Swyfte appeared in one of the small arched windows of the bell-tower, fighting furiously, against whom, none could quite work out. A collision made the bell toll, and then came another inexplicable flash of light. All around Nathaniel, people were cheering the dark stranger on, and Nathaniel was caught up in the passion and the belief that here was a great man, a protector, fighting a harsh battle on which all their lives depended.*

*It was then that Nathaniel caught sight of a shadow slipping out of the bell-tower and passing rapidly across the moon before whisking away across the fields. Or so it seemed. He told himself it was a trick of his eyes, nothing more.*

*Moments later, the church door was thrown open and Will emerged, together with Nathaniel's father and Anne. Overcome with relief, Nathaniel ran to them and grabbed his father, before turning to grasp the swordsman's hand. 'You saved them,' he said with admiration.*

*'I did what I could,' Will Swyfte replied.*

*It was only then that Nathaniel noticed the look on Anne's face – a glassy stare and an expression of abject horror that appeared to run so deep it would never be expunged. Without uttering a word, she trailed away from them towards the lychgate, pausing briefly to stare into her father's empty grave.*

*And Nathaniel's own father seemed deeply troubled in a manner that far surpassed the annoyance he might feel at the activity of some Catholic sympathizers, even if it was on hallowed ground. He pulled Will to one side and engaged him in intense conversation for several minutes. As he looked on, bemused, it appeared to Nathaniel that Will Swyfte was attempting to reject what was being said by his father, but eventually he relented.*

The conversation apparently over, the swordsman approached Nathaniel and took him by the elbow and led him away. 'Your father has found you a new appointment.'

'I have an appointment.' Nathaniel was alarmed but knew not why.

'And now you have a new one. You will accompany me to London, young Nathaniel Colt, to the court of our Queen Elizabeth, where you will be my assistant.'

Nathaniel didn't know what to say. He looked to his father, who had an expression of deep relief mixed with something else.

'Gather your things together and say your goodbyes,' Will Swyfte said. 'We leave tonight.'

'He is scared,' Nathaniel said. 'I can see it in his face.'

'It is a dangerous world, and your father wants you safe.'

'And you are supposed to keep me safe?' Nathaniel turned to look at his new master.

At first, Will Swyfte didn't respond, but what Nathaniel saw in Will's face convinced him that here was a good man, just as his father was a good man. Finally, Will spoke. 'I can see, Nat, that you will no doubt be a terrible burden, with your worryingly quick mind and, I would wager, a quicker tongue. But it is too late to go back on my promise now. It seems we are stuck with each other for the foreseeable future.'

The younger man saw through the words. 'And I would wager the burden will be all mine,' he responded in kind. 'But if nothing else, I suspect there will be interesting times ahead.'

As he headed to the cottage to collect his things, Nathaniel glanced back. Will Swyfte was looking at Anne, concern etched on his face. Nathaniel could sense dark currents that he didn't yet understand, but he was determined to learn all there was to know of the world; and of the world this brave, impressive figure inhabited.

# CHAPTER TWENTY-SEVEN

ACROSS A DESOLATE MOOR WHERE STANDING STONES RAISED high by ancient people stood against a lambent moon in a star-filled sky, Will ran. The muffled sound of fiddles and pipes drifted across the gorse and sedge behind him, and a sickly-sweet smell of honeysuckle blossom drifted in the warm breeze. Under his feet, vibrations ran through the soft ground, accompanied by a dim clanging, like a blacksmith's hammers, never slowing, beating out the shape of his past and his future in dark caverns far below. Then, behind, a dog howled, familiar and blood-chilling, and within moments the sound was moving closer, and he knew he would never escape his fate.

Will woke in a cold sweat and unable to move. He was tied to a chair in a shaft of moonlight breaking through the window. Through the grime-covered glass, he could see tall stone houses, their windows dark. The dusty boards under his feet were bare, the plaster on the walls crumbling. He could smell damp, a hint of human decay, and something else besides. That familiar underlying scent of honeysuckle. He was in the Fairy House.

The last thing he recalled was standing, sword in hand, on

the upended side of the carriage, as the giant black dog attacked. He remembered feeling its hot breath, seeing its teeth stained with the blood of the slaughtered driver and horse, and then nothing.

As his senses came back to him, he realized he was not alone. Presences waited, unmoving, in the dark at his back. He couldn't guess the exact number, but instinctively he felt there were at least three.

'You have me, then,' he said.

After a moment's hesitation, the measured tread of boots revealed Don Alanzo, dressed as though for court, in a ruff, a fine linen shirt, a crimson and gold beaded doublet, padded breeches and stockings, topped off by a velvet hat at a carefully positioned angle. He rested one hand on the pommel of his sword and studied Will.

'You cut a fine figure, Don Alanzo,' Will said. 'If I did not know better, I would think you dressed to keep company with royalty.'

'I return to Cadiz tomorrow,' the Spaniard replied in his heavy accent. 'And then to glory, to the beginning of the end of England. With my prizes in hand.'

'Not all your prizes.'

'No, true. One evades me still.'

'And it will continue to do so.'

'I think not.' Don Alanzo examined his well-groomed nails with theatrical nonchalance. 'Already our agents are closing in. It is only a matter of time before your assistant is located and the Shield returned to us. Edinburgh is not a large city, Will Swyfte, and the people here have no love for an Englishman.'

Will stifled a pang of regret. He hoped that it was some previously unseen Spanish agents pursuing Nathaniel and not the Unseelie Court. As he had always feared it would, his vow to Nathaniel's father continued to haunt him. 'My man has a surprising degree of animal cunning. You may well be disappointed,' he said blithely.

Don Alanzo gave a faint, mocking smile. 'You have not disappointed us yet.'

There was much unsaid in the smile. 'Your meaning, Don Alanzo?' Gently, Will tested the strength of the bonds around his wrist. As he had expected, they held fast; Don Alanzo would not make any mistakes.

'Why, you recovered the artefact for us, of course, where we and our allies had failed.'

Will groaned inwardly at Don Alanzo's implication. 'So you let me discover what Kintour knew.'

'Of course. Your reputation is well known. If there is one man in this world who could break a cipher, and overcome the traps of those Templar Knights, it is the great Will Swyfte.' His mocking smile grew wider and implied, quite plainly, that Will was not at all *great*. 'Reidheid, who plays both sides in this game, fed you the information we required about the existence of this house, and then it was only a matter of waiting for your arrival.'

'A good plan,' Will said. 'One that I would have been proud to put into effect myself. Except . . . one of your allies lies dead . . .'

Don Alanzo's face remained unreadable.

'And you do not have the prize you sought,' Will continued.

'As I said, only a matter of time.'

'Which is what all failures say.' Will was pleased to see Don Alanzo flinch. 'Your allies are a poor choice, Don Alanzo, and do you no credit. Do you think they would not slit your throat, and that of all Spain, once you have served your purpose?'

Don Alanzo's eyes flickered towards the silent, unseen presences behind Will. 'Do you think we are not aware of that? Shared interests cross boundaries of suspicion.'

'Men are judged by the friends they keep.'

Don Alanzo laughed. 'And we should only ally ourselves with people we like? How naive! Why, Master Swyfte, I would think you would struggle to find allies even within your own court if that were the case.'

'We are not talking about the French here, Don Alanzo. Or Venice, or Florence, or the Hapsburgs, or even that weak and feeble Feodor. The Unseelie Court is a half-starved wolf waiting in your parlour.'

'And you think Spain is not such a hungry beast? England is a corruption upon the world. Your arrogance spins out of control, standing against God and Rome, overthrowing laws and truces and order whenever it serves your purpose. You are despised by all free-thinking men, and soon you will see grey sails on the horizon. The dark ship that reeks of rot sails towards your land, and it is already too late to turn it back.'

Don Alanzo looked away from Will to one of those who stood behind him. The Silver Skull stepped into moonlight, the dread mask glowing with white fire. Through the holes in its face, Will saw bloodshot eyes glaring at him.

'Who are you?' he asked.

'His identity is not important,' Don Alanzo interrupted. 'There are many prepared to sacrifice all that they have to ensure England is destroyed. It is the sacrifice itself that matters.'

'Play the hero in your game. We all do the same,' Will said. 'In the end, there are only winners and losers.'

'Sadly, your role is already defined. If you think the lack of the Shield will slow our plans, you are sorely mistaken. This grand weapon here has many uses. While it remains in our hands, you will always be in danger.'

'Then my best endeavours will go to returning it to the Tower.'

'I think not.' Don Alanzo spat and caught the Silver Skull's arm and guided him towards the door. 'I take no pleasure in the suffering you are about to endure,' the Spaniard continued. 'This is war, and the stakes are high, but still . . . You will reveal the whereabouts of the Shield, and then it all ends.'

Don Alanzo and the Silver Skull stepped out of the room. Behind him, Will felt the gaze of the others fall upon him, studying his strengths, his resilience, turning over his flaws and weaknesses, like hunters circling their prey. He knew exactly what was to come.

Finally, Cavillex stepped before him. The superiority Will had sensed at the palace had been replaced by a cold indifference, though Will could almost feel an intense rage burning just beneath the surface.

'I have a question: how many of your kind have fallen by a mortal hand?' Will asked blithely.

Cavillex ignored him. Someone proffered a small silver tray, which he held just above Will's line of vision.

'It was surprising. I found it just like killing a man,' Will continued. 'Or a dog.'

'It has been some time since you have eaten,' Cavillex said. 'Would you like a bite, to fill your belly?' From the tray, long, elegant fingers selected a fragrant, golden biscuit and wafted it under Will's nose. The scent of honey, butter and spices filled his senses, and despite himself Will's hunger magnified unnaturally, and his stomach growled. 'Or perhaps a drink of water?' Cavillex poured a goblet of crystal-clear water from a silver jug. Suddenly, Will's throat was as dry as a summer street.

Overwhelmed by the urge to consume the biscuit and water, his head spun, but he forced himself to resist. He knew what happened to those who accepted food and drink from the Enemy; he could not forget Kintour's fate.

'Thank you,' he said, his voice hoarse, 'but my appetite has fled.'

Cavillex leaned in and said quietly, 'That would have been the easy road.' His breath carried the scent of cloves.

'I would give you the gift of a challenge,' Will replied. 'For life is nothing if it is not tested.'

'No challenge,' Cavillex stated.

Then, behind him, Will heard the sound of metal upon metal, the clink of objects being arranged upon another tray, the clack of items being tested. He began to picture their shape and nefarious uses, and forced himself to stop.

'You will never defeat us,' Will said.

'*Us*?' Cavillex said, his voice suddenly louder and touched with emotion. 'Ah. The brotherhood of man. You think yourself my equal. Of course. In the New World, you treat people like slaves, and slaughter them as if they have no value. As you did with the Moors. As you have done, always, over the steady march of the centuries. We stood in our glades, and by our lakes, and on the hilltops, and watched, slack-jawed and silent, as you tore through your own kind. When the Norman, William, invaded your nation, one hundred thousand fell in the north before his will. Thirty thousand dead of starvation in Ireland under your own Queen's campaign. How many more have died excruciating deaths as a result of your pathetic arguments about religion? You are animals falling on each other in the field. You do not deserve to exist.'

There was the sting of truth in Cavillex's words that Will could not deny. 'That is not the sum of us,' he replied dully.

269

'What makes a man, then? Let us investigate, shall we?'

Hands grabbed Will's shoulders roughly and pulled his chair backwards. Just as he expected his head to slam against the floorboards, it came to a gradual rest. One of the Unseelie Court supported the chair on either side, but he could not see their faces, and for that he was grateful.

Cavillex loomed over him with the water jug. 'This gift is given freely, and without obligation,' he stated ominously.

He poured the water slowly from the spout, down Will's chest, allowing it to flood across his face and into his mouth and nose. It was barely more than a trickle, but Will was forced to inhale it, and suddenly he was overcome by the sensation of drowning. As his limbs thrashed involuntarily, he tried to draw himself up, but Cavillex's two helpers held him tightly in place. Choking, he tried to breathe but was overcome by an overwhelming feeling of water filling his lungs, of slow suffocation. Darkness closed in on him and stars flashed across his vision.

As he felt he was about to die, the water stopped. Coughing and spluttering, he sucked in huge gulps of air. His vision cleared to reveal Cavillex a hand's breadth away from his face.

'This is just the beginning,' the Enemy said, and began to fill the jug out of Will's sight. The meticulous, slow pouring echoed in the room. Will tried to respond, but his throat was raw. The water in his lungs made him choke once more.

Looming over Will again, Cavillex said, 'Once more, before I begin my questions. To soften you.' He poured again.

This time the flow was faster, the water filling Will's lungs in an instant. He choked, thrashed, could not draw a breath.

*I'm dying.* It was his only conscious notion, before the involuntary responses to drowning took over: a wild panic rising from within as the darkness of death rushed in from all sides. Frantically, he fought, but his captors maintained their grip. Fire consumed his chest. His throat was a solid block through which no air could pass. His brain fizzed and winked out.

When he came round, the chair had been set upright once more. Uncontrollable convulsions gripped him, consciousness asserting itself, fighting against the belief that it had died. Each time he recalled it, panic seized him. The horror of the experience had embedded itself deep within him and out of his control.

His heart was thundering so hard the blood in his ears muffled every sound, and it took him a while to realize that Cavillex was speaking. 'I am told that is what it feels like to drown. You should thank me. I have given you knowledge that few men have: of the dark landscape that lies beyond the edge of death.'

'Free me and I will give you an experience beyond that,' Will rasped, his throat raw.

'Where is the Shield?'

Will didn't respond. Shuddering, he filled his battered lungs with air and clung on to the memory of breathing.

The chair was upended roughly, and this time his head did hit the boards. The water followed moments later.

'What do you know of Dartmoor?' Cavillex asked once Will had been set upright.

Wrong-footed by the question, Will fought through the sensations of drowning that still washed through him. 'Dartmoor?'

'And of what happened there.'

'I have heard tell of that wild place in the west, but I have never been there.'

'What happened there!' Cavillex's voice seemed to crack

with emotion. From someone who had maintained his equilibrium from their first meeting, the loss of control was shocking.

'Hunting?' Will ventured. His mind raced to draw some sort of connection. Why was Cavillex interested in Dartmoor? What *had* happened there?

'How do we break the defences that keep us from exerting our will over your land?' Cavillex asked.

'You will have to ask Dr Dee that.'

Taking a step back, Cavillex looked into the street below. 'You know you will not survive this hour. For the remainder of your brief life, there will only be a cascade of pain and suffering, tearing your mind into ribbons. Save yourself. Seek salvation. Tell me what I need to know, Will Swyfte, and you will be spared that misery. I will end your life in an instant. On that you have my word.'

'God granted us memory for those moments when the world gets too harsh. I have much to remember.'

'Very well.'

Chilled to the bone and trying to stop his teeth from chattering, Will waited for the chair to be upturned again, but instead Cavillex nodded to one of his companions, who went to the back of the room and returned with another silver tray. Cavillex placed it on the floor in the moonlight where Will could see it. Lined up across it was a row of cruel instruments so strange that their use was barely imaginable. Will saw gleaming blades, tongs, bands, screws, needles and clamps.

'The question we ask ourselves is, what makes a man?' Cavillex reflected. 'We shall find out. Blood and gristle and meat and bone. This part fits that part. But where in that jumble of raw, bloody mess is the glimmer that thinks and

272

feels? Or is it all an illusion? Are men mere puppets made of meat that imagine themselves something more? Have you told yourself a lie for so long in your stories and mythologies that you have come to believe it?'

He studied the tray of instruments, waving his slim fingers in the air over them until he made his selection.

'We have existed on the edge of your world for a long, long time,' he continued. 'Over the ages, we have probed the mysteries of your existence, plumbed the depths of life, climbed the peaks of experience. We have come to understand the minds of mortals with the eye of an artist. Like wizards, we can conjure miracles from the base stuff of your being. We can distil the finest evocation of pain from the mist of your lives. We have learned to draw out suffering in minute increments, each one blossoming like a flower into something beautiful and delicate.' He turned back to Will and showed what he held in his hand. 'Once you have gained our attention, your time here is over.'

'Get on with it,' Will said. He focused on the information about Jenny with which Cavillex had taunted him earlier. In that, he found hope, and strength.

He woke to find his body was a symphony of pain, his thoughts floating in and out of the rhythm. He had lost track of how long Cavillex had been working on him, but he knew he had not answered a question, and he had not given up Nathaniel. He would stay true to his vow to the end. That could be a long time coming, he knew. But as he had promised, Cavillex was an expert in drawing out suffering, building then releasing the pressure only to build it again. Survival was no longer an option. It had come down to a battle of wills, as Will had always known it would.

'What makes a man?' he said to Cavillex. 'I'll tell you. Defiance in the face of brutality and oppression.'

'The Spaniard was right, you know. You think you are the hero in this play? You are not.'

Will spat a mouthful of blood. 'There are no heroes.'

'You will tell me what I need to know.'

Will sighed. 'Let us dispense with this chat. Your words torture me more than your actions. Boredom is your greatest weapon.'

Cavillex's answer was to select another tool from the tray. Gritting his teeth, Will steeled himself.

Then through the window came the distant sound of voices. Cavillex hesitated, then continued towards Will as he considered which new part of his body to assault. The noise continued to draw closer and it became clear it was a crowd, shouting angrily. Hazy from the pain, Will couldn't make out the words.

The crowd washed up against the house, their clamour so loud Will couldn't hear Cavillex's quiet voice. Somewhere below glass shattered. Objects clattered against the side of the building. Puzzlement briefly crossed Cavillex's face, and he turned to the window. Will watched his body stiffen as he studied the scene in the street below.

'It appears you have gained the attention of the good people of Edinburgh,' Will said wryly.

The rain of missiles continued to rattle against the wall, and a steady boom echoed from the front door as the masses attempted to break it down. When Cavillex turned back to Will, his expression was cold and murderous.

'Does it serve your purpose to stand and fight?' Will pressed. 'Or will you melt into the mist as you always do?'

Cavillex's face was unreadable. He looked to the others and nodded.

'So, your pleasure has been cut short,' Will croaked. 'It appears my life is to end much earlier than anticipated.'

'No,' Cavillex said, his voice like ice.

'No?'

Cavillex levelled a pitiless gaze at Will. 'I told you, our skill at drawing out suffering is unmatched. Your activities in the past were an irritation, easily forgotten, like those of all your kind. But this night you killed one of our own—'

'Who caused the death of one of *my* own.'

'No matter. When you kill a rabbit in the field, do you give it a second thought? But you have slain something unique and wild and astonishing.'

Will was surprised to see tears sting Cavillex's eyes.

'You have stolen from this world something wonderful,' he continued. 'Yes, we have noticed you. And your crime against all there is must be punished.'

'This is never going to end,' Will replied. 'You prey upon us, we shut you out. You attack us, we attack you. You kill one of ours, we kill one back. What is there to gain?'

'It will end, and soon,' Cavillex said. 'And your corruption upon the face of this world will be wiped away, and you will be forgotten.'

The window burst inward, showering glass all around Cavillex, but he didn't flinch. His attention was fixed solely on Will as if there was nothing else in the world that mattered.

'You have gained our attention,' he repeated in a quiet voice that was filled with such emotion it carried above the roar of the crowd. 'You have someone you *love*?' He let the final word roll around his mouth with contempt. 'Not the one we spoke of earlier. Someone close to you now. A friend, perhaps, someone you hold in affection.' His gaze was heavy upon Will.

*Grace.*

Cavillex nodded and smiled. 'I see now. A woman. When we leave this place we will find her.'

'No,' Will said, a shudder running through him.

'We will take her. We will show her the heights of our skills. We will make the fibre of her being ring out with un-imagined agonies. But she will live.' Cavillex gave a brief, cold smile. 'Until we bring you back to us, and then we will slowly slaughter you in front of her, so that everything in her heart that she felt for you is corrupted by her final memory of your suffering. And then we will set her free to live with her misery. A life lived in that manner is usually short.'

'No!'

Cavillex's cold smile was the cruellest tool he had used that night.

'No!' Will roared until his throat burned, and tore at his bonds until his wrists were numb, and threw himself against the chair in a futile attempt to break free. He thought of Grace, and of Jenny, and his anger consumed him. If he could have freed himself, he would have torn Cavillex limb from limb. All the pain he had suffered in his life, and the agony that so many around him had suffered, was to be magnified.

*It will never end.*

And when the fury finally cleared, Cavillex was gone.

Within minutes, the main door burst in and the mob raced through the building, but they found no sign that the Unseelie Court had been there – just an old, deserted house left to its ghosts.

Calling for help above the tumult, Will was finally answered by Nathaniel and another man. When they paused in front of him, concern lit their faces and he realized how he must look, covered in blood, with too many wounds to count.

'They are but small things,' he croaked. 'A physician will

276

stitch them in no time. Help me.' The biggest wound lay inside him.

The other man rejoined the mob. As Nathaniel fumbled to untie Will's bonds, he said, 'I returned to the carriage and when I did not find you there, I knew you must have been brought to this foul place.'

'You disobeyed me, Nat. You put at risk everything for which we fight.'

'You would never have left me behind, if I were in need,' Nathaniel responded defiantly. The ropes fell to the floor, and he helped his master to his feet. Though Will struggled to stand unaided, he was too weak.

'Thank you,' he said. Though only two words, the depth of his gratitude was clear.

'I would be a poor assistant if I let my master die when it was in my power to prevent it.'

'You have undreamed-of abilities, Nat. You raised a mob.'

'Not an easy task. The people here live in fear of . . . your enemy.'

Will winced when he heard the beginnings of understanding in Nathaniel's words.

'But I convinced them that together they possessed a power they did not have alone,' Nathaniel continued before adding quietly, 'That, and a promise of some small reward if they saved your life.'

'Small reward?'

'Quite large, actually.'

'You are giving away the Queen's money, Nat. Walsingham will not be pleased that you have bought such a poor thing with her fortune. Help me out of here, quickly. There is much to do—'

'Not for you. If you lose more blood you will surely die, sir.'

'I cannot rest. They know of Grace. She is in danger.' Will swayed. He was close to fainting.

'You must see a physician first.'

Resting against the door jamb, Will nodded weakly. 'Then I must ask more of you. Leave Edinburgh now. Take whatever money you can from Reidheid's house, and a horse, and ride for London. Find Walsingham and tell him Grace is in danger from the Enemy. She must be protected at all costs.'

'And the amulet?'

Will hesitated. 'I would not wish this upon you if it were not an emergency, Nat.'

'And if you did not call upon me in a time of crisis, I would not forgive you, Will.'

'The amulet must be delivered to Walsingham. It is not safe here. You will be safer once you cross the border into England, but you will still be a target. Keep to the highways. Avoid the moors and the hills and the lakes. If you can, find someone to travel with you at all times. Do you understand me?' Will caught Nathaniel's arm with a desperation that troubled his friend.

'You can count on me.'

As Nathaniel helped Will slowly out of the house, Will dwelt on Cavillex's vile words and wondered if it was already too late.

# CHAPTER TWENTY-EIGHT

IN A COLD, STONE RECEPTION ROOM IN HIS SOMBRE PALACE OF El Escorial, King Philip of Spain and all the Americas sat in silent contemplation of the heat of passion waiting for him in his private quarters. Increasingly, his daily life felt like a troublesome distraction from the only thing he truly valued. At times it seemed almost an unpleasant dream. Yet every wave of desire was accompanied by an equal pang of self-loathing. Now Malantha had started to infect his prayers. She was there, within him, where before there had only been God. There was so much to concern him, not the least the invasion of England, but he somehow lacked the strength or the urge to resist. Only Malantha mattered.

A knock at the door was followed by the arrival of the Seventh Duke of Medina Sidonia, Don Alonso Perez de Guzman el Bueno, a quiet, unassuming man with a greying beard, whose obsession with money had led to repeated claims of poverty despite his great wealth. It was his very retiring nature that had encouraged the Spanish king to place him in charge of the armada; among the many competing, arrogant and cunning personalities in the Spanish nobility, Medina Sidonia had made the fewest enemies. His appointment – at Malantha's request,

Philip had to admit – had offended no one and had cleared all obstacles among his own people to a successful invasion.

'How goes it, Don Alonso?' Philip asked.

'Well, Your Majesty. Our preparations are almost complete and we will be ready to sail by the end of April.'

'Parma's forces are not as great as we had hoped, but he still has a good seventeen thousand men,' Philip said in his whispery voice, 'comprising eight thousand Germans and Walloons, four thousand of our own men, three thousand Italians, one thousand Burgundians, and even a thousand English exiles, ready to heap disaster upon their own land. Parma has made plans to protect our flanks in Flanders, and he will be ready to lead his men on to English soil as soon as you have done your work.'

'I have made arrangements for the blessing of the standard in Lisbon on April the twenty-fifth, the feast of St Mark the Evangelist,' Medina Sidonia said. 'Will Your Majesty be there to oversee the launch of this magnificent enterprise?'

Philip felt a sudden pang of panic. He knew he could not leave El Escorial, and the secret pleasures it held, not even for a night. 'My viceroy, the Cardinal Archduke, will represent me on that day.'

Medina Sidonia was unhappy at this response, but he bowed and said, 'As you wish, sire. My men would have taken some pleasure in seeing you, but they will understand Your Majesty has much to do at this momentous time.'

Philip gave a reassuring smile. '*La Invencible* is all you need. Once England's bastard Queen Elizabeth sees the mighty fleet you have amassed, she will surrender without a shot being fired.'

Philip was eager to return to his private quarters and barely noticed the unease in Medina Sidonia's face. 'There are many across Europe who question the wisdom of the coming battle,' the Duke began hesitantly. When Philip didn't respond unkindly, he took strength and continued, 'Our Catholic allies in the Vatican, and Venice, and Prague, all fear an emboldened Spain. They believe we are too strong already.'

'One can never be too strong.'

'True, true,' Medina Sidonia responded hastily. 'However, I have heard word that Henri of France is afraid that he will be next. That once England is ours, we can starve the Dutch rebels into submission and then move on his country. And once Western Europe is ours, he says angrily to anyone who will listen, Spain will sweep away the Protestant rule in the German states, and across Scandinavia.'

'Then King Henri is very wise.' Philip smiled, but when he saw Medina Sidonia become more troubled he added, 'We *are* strong, too strong for any of them to attempt to throw obstacles in our way, whatever their fears. Wherever we venture – be it here or in the New World – we see victory. We have a brilliant military commander in Parma; we have a great force, filled with fury. And the fleet you have amassed will tear through England's pathetic band of pirates and adventurers. There is no doubt here.' The King held his hand to his heart.

Yet Medina Sidonia would not be deterred. Now the dam had broken, long-held anxieties were rushing out. 'In thirty years, all our fortune and our might have not subdued the Netherlands. How, then, can we hold England? Even if we seize London and remove Elizabeth's head from her shoulders in revenge for what she did to Mary, the rest of that damned country is near lawless. We could be fighting in the north, and the Fens, and Wales and Cornwall, for ever.' He caught himself, afraid he had stepped over the boundary. 'And there is the prophecy of Cyprianus Leovitius,' he added quietly.

Philip sighed and smiled patiently at his anxious admiral, as a father would humour a worried child. 'A prophecy which is in our favour.'

'Based on the numerology hidden in the Revelation of St John—'

'It speaks of the year of wonders. The beginning of the final cycle. Upheavals for all. The end of empires. The end of England.'

Medina Sidonia was not convinced. 'Some say—'

'I say!' Philip shouted. 'The end of England! Do not question me!' Steadying himself, he studied the weakness in Medina Sidonia's face before trying to bolster his commander. 'God is on our side. He will not allow us to be defeated. There is much you do not know, much that must be kept from you if our plans are to succeed.' Philip clasped his hands together tightly, and gave a thin-lipped smile. 'We have a secret ally, and a weapon of great power that will be at your disposal. England *will* fall, and such destruction will be wreaked on that country and its people that there will be no doubt to whom the prophecy refers.'

Curtly, he waved his hand to dismiss Medina Sidonia, and then hurried from the reception room as quickly as his gout-ridden feet would carry him. By the time he reached his private rooms he had already forgotten the Duke, the armada and the invasion.

Malantha was waiting for him, naked, sprawled on the couch, so brazen in her sexuality that he could barely look at her, yet could not look away. Much as he desired her, he was unsettled by the way she watched him; and sometimes, when she slipped into the corner of his vision, he was convinced he saw something white and cold and predatory, not Malantha at all.

'I have good news,' she said, without warmth. 'I have spoken to my brother, Cavillex. Our plans proceed satisfactorily. Don Alanzo brings the Silver Skull to Spain.' A brief narrowing of her eyes was replaced by a seductive smile. 'As you acquiesced to his request.'

'He deserves that at least for all his sacrifices.'

'And after that brief respite,' she continued, 'the Skull will be readied to travel with the armada.'

'And the Shield?'

'Not yet under our control, but that is a trifling matter. It is unnecessary, in the end. England will still be devastated by disease.'

'I worry about so many deaths upon my conscience.' Trembling, the Spanish king collapsed on to the couch and covered his face.

Sidling next to him, Malantha breathed into his ear, 'God will forgive that, for the great works you do in His name.' Gently, she pressed her breasts against his arm. The heat rose in Philip. 'And the High Family will ensure no other country stands in your way,' she murmured, her mouth and lips teasing.

'You are sure?' He slipped a hand on to her thigh, his remorse already evaporating.

'My brothers have the ears of the greatest in Europe.'

'You spin your web well.'

'All for you, my love. All for Spain.'

A flash of chalky skin and red-rimmed eyes that held no compassion. He screwed his eyes shut and drove the image out, allowing himself to be pushed back as she climbed astride him. Within seconds he was lost in her and her perfume, like honeysuckle, and all his troubles and doubts and fears were washed away.

# CHAPTER TWENTY-NINE

FILTHY FROM THE ROAD AND EXHAUSTED FROM NEARLY TWO weeks' hard riding, Nathaniel guided his foaming, sweat-flecked horse through the dirty, crowded streets of London. It was not long after midday and unseasonably hot for early April. He had found the city abuzz, as always, but for the first time there was a pervading uncertainty in the faces of the people he passed. In the time he had been away, fear of a Spanish invasion had magnified as visiting merchants from the European ports spread dark rumours and gossip as quickly as they distributed their wares.

At the gates of the Palace of Whitehall, Nathaniel could barely believe he had reached his destination. Since he had left Edinburgh all those days ago, he felt his life had hung by a thread many times. Within hours of his journey's beginning, five hooded raiders had swept down from the hills to pursue him along the valley between the high summits that stretched south along Scotland's Lowlands. He was only saved by a small group of the King's men who had been sent to accompany him to the border. The fighting had been ferocious and many of King James's men had died; Nathaniel had heard their death-screams echoing among the hillsides, and glancing back he had seen flashes of mysterious fire.

Once he had crossed the border into England, the attacks were not so overt, but he had been shadowed by riders near the moors as he passed Carlisle, and again as he made his way through the high peaks that formed the spine of the country. Someone had attempted to break into his room during a terrifying night in an inn, when it had seemed that every time he locked the door it would mysteriously open whenever he was distracted.

A pack of wolves appeared to track him through most of the country. Strangers waited at crossroads, threatening him as he rode by, or urging him to stop for food or drink. On the first occasion, Nathaniel had brought his mount to a halt, thinking the cloaked man needed directions. Soon he had found himself listening to a long, involved story that made him drowsy, and only when he realized the stranger was attempting to search his saddlebag did he shake himself awake and ride on. Just as unnerving was that within a mile he couldn't recall the stranger's face.

Nathaniel had always considered himself a man of reason, but as he passed Oxford the sticky weight of superstition had finally begun to lie heavily upon him. However much he attempted to dismiss the chance occurrences, they piled around him to such a degree that he saw supernatural danger in every shadow. He felt the Devil himself was at his heels. To save his sanity, he knew he would have to question Will when he returned to London, however much he dreaded the answers.

Within the palace walls, activity was beginning to build towards the midday meal after another lazy morning of discourse, sewing, business with visitors from the shires or walks amid the perfumed gardens. Nathaniel guided his mount directly to the Black Gallery, and on weary, shaking legs sought out Walsingham, who had been in conference with a man recently returned from France. Whatever he had heard in that meeting had left him in a dark mood.

Nathaniel quickly outlined the events in Edinburgh, as far as he had been told, and related Will's desperate plea that Grace be protected.

'I do not know this woman, but I will send men to bring her here now,' Walsingham said. 'If she requires protection, we can offer her the best in the land.' He paused. 'If she is still here.'

Nathaniel felt a pang of fear. He had ridden as hard as he was able, but could their enemies still have beaten him to the palace and found the opportunity to capture Grace?

'And the other reason you travelled to Edinburgh?' Walsingham pressed.

From his pack, Nathaniel withdrew the folded cloth and revealed the amulet. 'Our enemies fought hard to retrieve this, and pursued me all the way from Scotland. It must be vital to their plans.'

Walsingham's eyes gleamed, but he would not touch the amulet. He shouted for Dee, who hurried in a few moments later as Walsingham paced the room.

'You must tell no one that the doctor is here in England,' Walsingham cautioned Nathaniel, leaving the young man in no doubt that the punishment for disobedience would be severe. But then he and Dee huddled over the amulet with barely restrained triumph.

'Is this indeed the object we sought?' Walsingham asked.

'See here? The filigree? This symbol here? It is the language of angels,' Dee said. 'This is a true object of power.'

'Then you will study it? Unlock its secrets?'

Dee gave an excited nod. 'The Enemy will be eager to reclaim this. It must be kept in a place of formidable protection. The Tower?'

'No. Its defences have already been breached,' Walsingham said. 'We need to keep it close. Here, at the palace.' He fixed an eye on Dee. 'The Lantern Tower.'

Dee readily agreed that this was the best option and hurried out with his prize, but Nathaniel was puzzled. He had heard much talk of the Lantern Tower, a unique, solitary edifice constructed by order of the Queen at the heart of the palace complex, yet no one appeared to know its use, and few were ever seen entering it.

Eager to return to his business, Walsingham dismissed Nathaniel to the suite of rooms on the second floor of the western wing that overlooked the tiltyard built by Henry for his jousting competitions.

As he stood at the window looking out over the smoky city, Nathaniel felt the tension of his long ride dissipate and a grey mood creep in in its place. The view was drenched in sun, yet he could see only shadows. The world had changed, or he had, and where there had been joy there was now only incipient threat – a sense that everything he knew was careering off-kilter. Fear hovered on the edge of his consciousness for no obvious reason.

The door closed quietly behind him. He started, turned, and there stood Grace. With relief, he rushed to her.

'Why, Nat,' she said, surprised. 'What is wrong?' She placed her hands on his cheeks to study his face, and became concerned by what she saw there. 'What troubles you? Is it Will?'

'No, he is well,' he dissembled. 'He recovers from a few injuries, but no worse than he has endured before.'

287

Grace wanted to hear more, but he persuaded her that he had been ordered to remain silent. She was relieved by his news, but her concern for him remained. 'There is a shadow over you. It is not good to keep such things locked away. Talk to me.'

Shaking his head, Nathaniel forced a smile. 'Another time. For now, I am happy to see you well.'

'And why would I not be?' She stepped away from him, before casting a suspicious glance back. 'What business occupies Will?' she asked, as if making polite conversation.

'You must ask that of him, when he is back in London.' He maintained a bright tone, not wanting her to realize she was in danger. But then the door opened and John Carpenter marched in. He nodded to Nat and waited.

'What is this?' Grace asked suspiciously.

'This is John Carpenter. He is an associate of Will's. You saw him in Alsatia.'

'Yes, I remember, but why is he here?'

'Sir Francis Walsingham has sent him. He is to keep you from harm.'

'Harm? I live and work in the Palace of Whitehall. Harm cannot reach me here. And who would ever seek to harm me?' Grace looked at Nathaniel with rising doubt.

Nathaniel's laugh eased her concerns. 'Why, no one, Grace! But Will—'

'Will! He would keep me locked away in a tower if he could,' she said with bitterness.

'Indulge him,' Nathaniel said quietly. 'You would not wish him to be consumed with worry.'

Knowing she had little choice, Grace glanced back at Carpenter and said acidly, 'I never tire of witty conversation with one of Sir Francis Walsingham's men.'

'Do not tease him,' Nathaniel whispered. 'His humour is not good.'

Quietly seething, Grace shook her head wearily and marched towards the door.

Once she had gone, Nathaniel exhaled in relief that she was in safe hands, but in the silence of the room his uneasy mood descended once more. He returned to the window to study the city. It was the heart of one of the greatest powers in the world, yet in the face of what he now feared existed beyond the walls, he wondered how secure it truly was.

# CHAPTER THIRTY

DESPITE FURIOUS PROTESTS, JOHN CARPENTER BUNDLED THE cloaked and hooded Grace into the back of a servants' wagon beneath a heap of filthy sacking that had been used for transporting grain and still swarmed with beetles. Carpenter was not a gentle man, and treated Grace as he would any person who was not important to him, woman or not. Clearly, whatever mission had been imposed upon him, he felt it beneath his dignity. He told Grace to remain silent for the duration of their journey or he would stop the wagon and leave her on the highway, where she would have to fend for herself against whatever brigands and cut-throats waited.

From anyone else Grace would not have accepted such treatment, but there was an increasing urgency to the proceedings that had started to concern her. She remembered the haunted expression on Nat's face, the look that said all was not well with the world, shocking in a man who always radiated a sunny optimism behind his sardonic exterior. What had happened, she wondered. What could turn a person to that degree? Something extreme, something terrible? As she had told Nat, Will was always over-protective, but this was beyond even his usual concerns. Will feared for her life, and he knew things that no one else did. She felt strangely queasy at the thought, and the wagon bouncing wildly along the rutted road didn't help her disposition.

Was it something to do with all the spiralling rumours of a Spanish invasion that had blazed through the country since the Scottish queen Mary's execution? There had been talk of a landing in Wales that had sent panic sweeping through the capital before it had proved false. And in the August past, word had circulated of two hundred Spanish ships in the Channel. These rumours had driven the occupants of the coastal towns inland in fear, and brought the rich to London for safety. England's Queen had even been forced to issue a proclamation demanding that they return to their homes. But what if all those rumours were about to come true? What if an invasion was imminent?

Obliquely, Grace realized she should have been more scared than she was, but ever since Jenny's disappearance – murder! she reminded herself – she had lived with the constant belief that tragedy was only a heartbeat away. Ironically, that had made her take more risks in her life.

*Reckless!* she thought bitterly.

Her mind drifted back to that night when everything changed and all her hopes for the future had slipped from her. She recalled the fragrance of the night-scented stock, and the moonlight on the cornfields, the soft breeze that made them stir as if some animal moved along the rows. The moon was so bright that the sky could not be called black. *Silver. The world glowed silver.*

She was still a child, though she considered herself a young lady and already well versed in the ways of the world. If only she had known what the world was truly like. The hounds still howled in the fields as the search for Jenny continued, and her mother and father were both still out.

She had found Will desperately rinsing his hands and face at the well. She was certain he had been crying, though she had dismissed it at the time as a trick of the moonlight. For some reason, he kept his hands from her view until he had finished his ablutions. He was barely a man himself, not long at Cambridge, but at that moment his face seemed much older. It was odd she remembered that; she hadn't thought of it before. She had never seen that expression before, or that openly registered emotion since. After Jenny, she always had to try to decipher his true feelings.

And then, when his hands were clean, Will had stepped forward and hugged her so tightly she could barely breathe. 'This is a hard world,' he had said to her with quiet passion, 'but you will not walk through it alone. I will be here to keep you safe. I vow it.'

Over the months and years that followed, Grace had turned those words over many times, and felt her own emotions solidify around them. Of all the reasons why she loved him, that was the first and the most potent. In that hard, hard world, he would keep her safe. He cared for her in a way that the other boys and men she had met never cared, could never care. They would love her, or promise her the world, but they would never vow to keep her safe.

She did love Will, even though she would never give voice to her feelings; even though he could never keep her safe. The wanting was enough.

And so she had been quick to uproot herself from her family and the quiet Warwickshire way of life, and Will had arranged for her to take up a position at the court, where he could keep an eye upon her, and guide her progress. And her father and mother had been more than happy to see her under Will's care.

Shortly after Grace's arrival at Whitehall, when she was still learning the twisting rules of that place, both written and unspoken, Will had taken her to one side and repeated his vow that he would discover the truth of Jenny's disappearance. His work, which she later found out was as one of Walsingham's men, would, he was convinced, provide him with clues and insight. He was passionate in this belief, but however much she questioned the hows and whys of this, he would give her no answer.

'Just know that all my days are directed towards discovering what happened to Jenny, and every action I take in my work will, in some way, illuminate the path to knowledge,' he once told her.

Finding the truth about Jenny. It was the bond that united them, on which her love for him had been built, and it was the thing that separated them both from the world. Her only fear, and it was one that nagged at her in the dark of the night, was that when the truth about Jenny was known, the truth that they both so desperately needed, it would destroy them. The bonds shattered. Hope for the future gone. Belief in life destroyed. Was that an overreaction? She always told herself it was, but in her heart she wondered.

With the afternoon sun beating down, it was hot and stifling under the stinking sacks. The wagon bounced along the road for an age, and every part of her ached. After a while the noise of the merchants approaching the city died away and she could only hear the sound of the birds. She was half tempted to peel away the coverings so she could look out, draw in some fresh air, but she was afraid of Carpenter's reaction.

After a while, the cough of deer echoed nearby, and Grace

heard the splash of oars. They must be near the river, to the west of London. The wagon eventually moved off the rutted road on to a more even surface, flagstones she guessed, and a short while later Carpenter brought the horse to a halt. As the sacks were pulled off her, she shielded her eyes against the glare of the late-afternoon sun.

When her vision cleared, Grace saw a grand red-brick façade, two towers flanking an imposing gatehouse, rows of mullioned windows and a hint of the great Italian style in the lines and symmetries of the building. All around there was rolling green land, and larks carolled high in the blue sky.

It was Hampton Court Palace, the old king Henry's greatest joy and source of pride.

'Grand enough for you?' Carpenter said drily and offered her a hand to help her from the back of the wagon. His tone remained gruff, but his features had softened a little, as though he had been considering her and her plight during the long journey.

Hampton Court was one of the world's most modern palaces. Sophisticated in intent and magnificent in design, it could still impress even the most jaded member of the court. Few understood why the Queen preferred to live in the heart of the smoky, foul-smelling city of London; but then few, as Grace knew, understood her desire to be at the heart of her government.

Elizabeth still visited regularly, when she wanted to escape the pressures of the city, or to stage her fabulous court masques, or the great dramatic presentations that had become the talk of London. Grace had been allowed to visit with her mistress for some of the festivities, but much of the palace had been off-limits to her. Yet at the entrance, Grace felt the familiar thrill as she was dwarfed by the vastness of the place, the extensive kitchens that were the pride of the nation, the enormous dining hall, the chapel, the pleasure gardens filled with perfumed flowers and herbs, the tennis courts and bowling alleys, all set against the expanse of the hunting park that sprawled for more than a thousand acres.

With the hood of her cape pulled over her face, Grace passed through the gatehouse into the courtyard with Carpenter. Servants seemed to go about their business in a leisurely manner with no monarch in residence to keep them on their toes. As Carpenter had anticipated, the two of them drew no attention.

'Nobody will know you are here. You are safe,' he said.

'But why did I not stay at the Palace of Whitehall?' Grace pressed him. 'If I am in danger, it is filled with guards and spies and all manner of defences to protect the Queen.'

Carpenter smiled tightly. 'If an enemy seeks you, why draw him to the home of our Queen and the greatest in the land?' His words hit home. Grace suddenly realized she was dispensable. They would keep her as safe as they could, but not at the expense of any of the other great and good of the land. It was something she knew instinctively, but was shocking to have confirmed so harshly.

Grace paused briefly before the great clock tower bearing the seal of Cardinal Wolsey, the man who had had his fine palace stolen from him by the King when he fell from favour. Everyone had their place, she recognized, and some people were worth more than others.

Carpenter looked up at the clock briefly with an odd expression of unease. The mechanism showed not only the time, but also the phases of the moon, the star sign, the month, the date, the position of the sun, and the season.

'What is it?' she asked.

Carpenter shivered and made no reply, instead urging her on into the palace.

She attempted to make small talk as he guided her to the quarters Walsingham had arranged to have set aside for her use, but she saw that his mind was elsewhere, and all she got were short, dismissive replies. She wasn't surprised when he refused to answer her questions about the threat she faced, and the rumours of the Spanish invasion, but she didn't like the way his voice grew harder when he spoke of Will. Something lay between them; if Grace were Will she would not want Carpenter at her back.

The walk through the palace was long, but at last they reached a small room overlooking the formal gardens. Grace suspected it was usually reserved for the servants of visiting dignitaries. It was plain but comfortable.

'I will be safe here?' From the window she examined the open outdoor spaces.

'We have sometimes found it is better to hide something in the open if it is in a place where no one is looking,' Carpenter replied. 'Only a handful of people know you have gone from Whitehall, and they can all be trusted. No one here knows who you are. Remain invisible, and calm, and let the background swallow you, and all will be well.'

'And you?' Grace grew uneasy as the reality of her situation slowly made itself felt.

'I will be near at hand.'

'How long do I stay here?'

'Until Sir Francis Walsingham grows tired of wasting a man, or your *friend* . . .' the word rang with contempt, 'decides the danger has passed.'

'No one will give me a good answer as to why I would be in danger.'

'There is no good answer.' Carpenter shrugged, and left her alone with her thoughts.

The hours passed slowly. Grace watched the gardeners at work, drawing the weeds. A man and woman from, she assumed, the kitchens, grabbing time away from the heat and the steam to court, walked together along the lavender path, hands behind their backs, heads down, voices lowered in quiet, intense conversation. It seemed to Grace to be a gentle love, slowly building upon pleasant foundations, one she didn't quite understand.

Food was brought to her, and left outside the door. It made her feel like one of the prisoners in the Tower. She paced the room, sat on the bed and dreamed, tried to make sense of the shifting patterns of her life and the world in which she existed. Then, as the shadows lengthened and merged into the encroaching grey, she returned to the window to watch the beauty of the silvery twilight drawing in.

At some point she fell asleep, but only for a short while, for though when she woke the moon was bright in the sky, it was still not yet wholly dark. Long shadows reached across the grey, quiet gardens. Nothing moved. She felt oddly out of sorts; she hadn't felt tired, or even noticed the encroachment of sleep, yet there she was, head on her arms on the small table by the window.

Stretching and yawning, she rose. She had decided she could not bear to be cooped up in the room any longer. The palace was quiet, the servants returned to their quarters. A few high-born people would be drinking in the withdrawing room, as they always did after dinner.

Opening the door cautiously, Grace checked for any sign of Carpenter. The corridor was empty and she stepped out with an odd tingle of excitement. The night air was chill and she stifled a giggle; it felt as if she was trespassing. Singing quietly to herself, she moved along the interconnecting corridors, treading lightly but secretly hoping she would encounter one of the servants so that she might have even a passing conversation. She could pretend to be someone else! The idea excited her even more.

But as she walked she met no one, and neither did she hear even the faintest of sounds rising from the furthest reaches of the vast building. She started to feel unsettled. It was as if everyone had abandoned the palace during her short nap.

As she passed through a deserted room, something caught her eye through a window overlooking the twilit countryside. There, amongst the row of black trees that lined the river's edge, she was sure a shadow had curled its way across the ground, like the smoke from a bonfire caught in a strong wind. It had gone now, but Grace peered out of the window to be sure. Suddenly, she jumped. There, in the trees, was a burst of flames, and another, and another. Torches igniting, she reasoned, but why? Something in those dancing fires made her unaccountably afraid. Hugging her arms around her, Grace watched the flames moving slowly, wondering who held them, why it mattered. Then, as quickly as they had burst into life, they winked out, one by one.

For a moment longer, she peered intently into the night, wondering if anyone would emerge from the treeline, but there was nothing. Were they watching her watching them, she wondered briefly, before dismissing the idea as ridiculous. No one could see her from that far away.

Yet for all her rationalizing, Grace felt a sudden urge to find Carpenter. Worried now by the lack of activity and the un-natural silence in the palace, she hastened on. Her heels beat out an insistent rhythm. She desperately wanted to call out, but was afraid of attracting attention to herself.

It was in a large room, where the Queen sometimes held a reception for foreign guests before one of the masques, that Grace came to a halt in front of a long ornate mirror. She didn't know why. For a while, she stared at herself, spectral in the half-light. She had the strangest feeling that she was looking at someone else, someone who shaped themself to resemble her, but couldn't hide the malign thoughts that lurked behind the features, in the hang of the mouth, or the narrowing of the eyes. It felt as if the glass wasn't there, that she could reach through the space only for the other Grace to grab her wrist and drag her in. Something about the mirror mesmerized Grace, was holding her fast, and she forced herself to move away from it, but not before she caught sight of a reflected shadow.

She turned, but the room was empty. She shivered. The shadow had been in the mirror after all, and not in the real world, and now it was gone. It must have been a trick of the moonlight, for there was no other explanation. As she hurriedly left the room, she decided that she didn't like mirrors at all.

Her uneasiness mounted, like the stem of a rose being drawn up the skin of her back. Where had everyone gone? Had the alarm for the invasion sounded and all fled to the security of London's walls? Could she really have missed such an alarm? Would Carpenter have forgotten to rouse her?

The guards' rooms were empty. No sound rose from the servants' quarters, from where she would have expected singing and laughter, and perhaps even a fiddle.

Suddenly terrified, Grace found herself at a window with a view of Henry's great clock, the colours a dull grey in the gloom. She knew something was wrong, but in her anxious state her thoughts were too wild to make sense of what she saw. Then it came to her: the clock was running backwards. She watched the gentle judder of the minute hand as it shifted anticlockwise, and she shivered, although she was not sure why.

*Its workings are wrong, that is all.*

But the season now showed winter, the month December.

Overcome with the compulsion to escape the palace and search the darkening countryside round about, she ran to another window overlooking the approach. At first all was still, but then – as before – came a brief burst of fire, closer than the last ones she had seen. Another flamed across to the right, but was gone almost in the blink of an eye.

The fires held her attention, and she waited for another while she considered what could possibly have caused them. As she looked on, grey shadows seemed to be bounding sinuously across the fields towards the palace, like foxes only larger. Grace tried to count them, but they moved too fast and were soon out of the moonlight and lost from view.

She stepped away from the window, her heart tap-tapping.

*The kitchens!* she thought suddenly. Of course! Everyone would be gathered there, telling stories, servants and gentlemen together, in the warmth of the ovens. That had to be the explanation. Focusing on the hope rather than the nagging feeling that such a thing could never be true, she hurried for the stairs that led down to the great kitchens underneath the palace.

Down the steps she went, and down again, leaving the quiet of the palace for the sumptuous underworld. She could hear the crackle of the fires under the ovens and the hiss of pots boiling above, the clank of lids lifted by the steam. She could smell the aromatic after-scent of the day's meal, oranges, sugar, mace, cloves, nutmeg and cinnamon, rich and powerful, intermingling with notes of strawberries, red wine and ginger.

Her senses were overwhelmed, so much so that she was oblivious of the absence of human voices. Only when she bounded excitedly from the final steps into the vast brick-vaulted room did she see it was empty. The only movement came from the candlelight that sent shadows rippling along the ceiling.

The remnants of the meal's preparation were still scattered across the great oak trestle that ran along the centre of the floor, juices dripping from the table edges on to the great stone flags. Cooking pots and utensils were piled high, yet to be washed.

Grace tensed and her skin prickled in spite of the heat. The kitchens should not be empty; indeed, they should be a hive of activity. The kitchen master would have his staff working hard to clear everything away so that all would be left clean and ready for the next morning.

She looked around. Jars were unstoppered. Cheeses lay un-covered. It was as if everyone in the palace had disappeared in the blink of an eye, their tasks left half finished, the ghost of their presence still haunting the place.

Grace moved tentatively across the vast room, feeling the blood pound in her head, trying to make sense of what she was seeing. The disappearance of so many people without a fuss? So quickly? And how?

The black, brackish waters of the fear she had managed to suppress for so long began to rise through her. The fires off in the dark. The grey shadows loping across the fields. What was happening? What was coming? She tried to laugh off her anxiety, but couldn't. She should run, hide. But where?

She stood by the largest oven. It seemed the fire inside it

was roaring out of control as if the flue had been jammed open. Grace could feel the flames burning higher, almost furnace-like, and the heat in the room rose accordingly. Spellbound, she realized that the heat was increasing faster than the oven could account for; the air had become dense and dry. Beads of sweat stood out on her forehead. It had become hotter than the hottest summer day.

Although Grace had heard nothing, she suddenly realized she was no longer alone. She whirled, her breath catching in her throat. Figures stood at the entrance to the kitchen, shimmering as if seen through a heat-haze. As still as statues, they were watching her.

'Who are you?' she gasped.

# CHAPTER THIRTY-ONE

BURSTING INTO THE BANQUETING HALL AT HAMPTON COURT Palace, Will hurled Carpenter against a wall before the man had even realized he was there. Mayhew and Launceston threw themselves forward to restrain Will, but the two of them struggled to contain him. His anger was like a storm, his face filled with lightning.

Blood dripped from Carpenter's mouth. Picking himself up, he wiped his face clean with the back of his hand and turned angrily on Will.

'Enough!' Walsingham strode into the room. His face remained as cold as ever, but there was a crack of simmering anger in his voice.

Will struggled against Launceston and Mayhew, but gradually calmed. As the fury drained from his face, he spat at Carpenter, 'You were supposed to protect her!'

'I did all I could,' Carpenter snarled.

'All you could? You ate and drank and idled your time away with the women in the kitchens!' Launceston and Mayhew were forced to renew their efforts as Will strained against their grip.

'I did the work with which I was charged!' Carpenter raged.

'I brought her here under cover, and secreted her in a room, and kept watch.'

'Then how did she disappear from under your very nose?' Will snapped. He ignored Walsingham, who waited at his side as if he were incapable of understanding the degree of emotion being shown. 'Or did you finally decide to act upon the grudge you hold against me?'

In his rage, it was Carpenter's turn to attack, only to find Launceston, knife drawn, standing in his path.

Knowing Launceston would use his weapon without a pause for thought, Carpenter stepped back and contained himself. 'You think I would sacrifice a woman to pay you back?' he snarled. 'I am not like you.'

'You were charged to watch over her.'

'And I did. Her food was brought to her room. She ate it. I remained in the room next to hers, with the door open at all times. No one came to her room. No one left. Yet when I looked in upon her an hour later, the room was empty.'

'You fell asleep!'

'No!' Carpenter's eyes blazed. Will tried to tell if the man was lying, but Carpenter was, as always, impossible to read.

'How did the Enemy know she was here?' Walsingham's quiet, steady voice cut through the angry atmosphere.

'I do not know,' Carpenter replied, dabbing at his mouth. 'No one here knew, nor anyone in Whitehall, beyond our trusted circle. And *his* assistant.'

Will halted his struggles as Carpenter's words settled on him. His head still pulsed with the beat of angry blood, but through it cut cold mistrust. When he looked around the group, they all met his eye.

*Never trust a spy*, that was the joke they shared when they were all in their cups. After Reidheid, Will was beginning to wonder if he could trust anyone.

'That is enough for now,' Walsingham commanded.

'No, it is not,' Will replied, ignoring the warning flicker in the spymaster's eyes. 'Grace is gone. The Enemy have her, I know it.'

'I share your concern,' Walsingham said insincerely, 'and I understand she was important to you. But there are more pressing matters. For now.' He gave Will a look that was supposed to be reassuring. 'We will not let her languish in the hands of the Enemy, of that you can be sure. No Englishman – or woman – will suffer at the hands of our foes while I exert influence over this office.'

Will understood the harsh reality of the situation. Grace was his personal priority, but she meant little against the great affairs of state. Deep inside him, the feelings he had kept locked down for so long threatened to well up, to tear him apart. He thought of Grace, and saw Jenny, and couldn't help but imagine what terrible things were happening to her now, what would happen in the days, months, years to come, unless he saved her.

Walsingham was speaking, but Will heard none of it. His head buzzed with the pulse of his blood, and thundered with his anger and self-loathing at his failure to protect Grace. But he would not give in to despair. His duty now was to balance the demands placed upon him by Walsingham and the task at hand with his need to find Grace before something monstrous took place. He recalled the cruelty in Cavillex's words in the Fairy House in Edinburgh. The Unseelie Court had embarked upon a path of torture. Their aim was to cause him pain and suffering, and to twist it and magnify it. The theft of Grace was only the beginning.

'Will?' Walsingham said. 'You are with us?'

'Of course.'

Carpenter still eyed Will murderously. Launceston's ghostly face remained a mask, but Mayhew held his head as if the world was spinning out from under his feet.

'The Spanish are preparing to invade?' Mayhew asked. 'We have heard that so many times. It is now true?'

'Their armada will sail upon England shortly.' As Walsingham clutched his hands behind his back, Will thought he could see a faint tremor in them.

Composing himself and shaking off Mayhew, Will said, 'Philip of Spain has attempted an invasion with his armada before, and failed. Badly.'

'We all know what happened,' Walsingham said, his tone dismissive. 'Two hundred ships amassed at Santander in 1575. After disease and incompetence, only thirty-eight finally sailed for Dunkirk. Five ran aground on shoals, three were driven back by storms, and the remainder were forced to shelter in the Solent before fleeing home.'

'After such a folly, then, why should we give his current plans any credence?' Will asked.

'And our ambassador in Paris,' Mayhew continued, 'Stafford – his despatches state very firmly that Spain is in no position to invade, that this armada is a flight of Philip's fancy.'

'Stafford is wrong – or worse,' Walsingham said.

'You suspect him?' Launceston enquired, raising an eyebrow in disbelief.

'Sir Edward likes his gold a great deal and he never has enough of it, by his account.'

'What other information do you have?' Will asked.

'The Dutch captured and interrogated the nephew of one of the papist cardinals who has had close dealings with Philip,'

306

Walsingham said. 'He revealed that, a year ago, the Vatican transferred a million ducats to a Spanish bank where it is held in escrow until the Pope receives notification that the invasion of England has begun.'

'So the King now has the funds he needs,' Will said thoughtfully. He rubbed his chin, watching the dust motes floating in a shaft of sunlight.

'The prisoner also spoke of the armada's destination and timetable.' Walsingham paused as he carefully considered his choice of words. 'Unfortunately, our Queen has chosen to believe Sir Edward's missives – he has always been one of her favourites – and so the necessary preparations to ensure that our defences are sufficient are not yet under way.'

'And the armada will sail soon?'

'Soon.' Walsingham was clearly not prepared to reveal all that he knew.

'We cannot conjure defences overnight,' Carpenter said. 'If the Spaniard truly has a great fleet, we would be stretched too thin once he reaches England's shores.'

Like a raven searching for carrion, Walsingham slowly paced the Banqueting Hall. 'Your analysis is correct. Time is fast running out.'

'And the Silver Skull must then be part of this invasion plot,' Will observed. 'The Enemy and the Spanish walk hand in hand. Each feels they use the other to achieve their stated aim – the conquest of England.'

'There will be little left for Spain if the Enemy get their way,' Carpenter noted bitterly. 'Can their King not see that?'

'Philip sees what he wants to see,' Walsingham replied. 'He believes God is on his side, and therefore all things will turn out well.'

'When God is clearly on our side,' Will said acidly.

Walsingham eyed him coldly, but did not respond to the barb. He folded his hands behind his back and proceeded to stare up at the vaulted ceiling.

'In Edinburgh, Don Alanzo de las Posadas said he was transporting the Silver Skull back to Cadiz,' Will continued. 'To keep the weapon safe until they were ready to use it, one would think. The Skull's powers could be unleashed anywhere from Norfolk to the south coast to Wales, and disease would rampage across the land. Once the armada has defeated our feeble fleet, and the plague has run its course, the Spanish will march into London with no opposition. They do not need the subtleties of the Shield for that. Let the Skull kill all.'

'And rule a land of the dead?' Carpenter asked incredulously, barely able to conceive of such a nightmare.

'They have no need of Englishmen,' Will said. 'They know that for the rest of their days they would be attempting to stifle revolt after revolt. Best to be rid of us for good.'

'Yet Philip is not an evil man,' Walsingham said, returning his attention to his spies. 'Merely misguided. He does what he does for his country and his religion, as do we. He would not want to see innocents suffer on a grand scale, Englishmen or not. No, I feel the Spanish will direct their attack along narrower lines.'

Will considered this for a moment. 'In London. If the Silver Skull is smuggled in, the Queen, the government, the entire court, could be wiped out. Our resistance would crumble.'

Launceston nodded. 'That makes sense. But other things do not: why travel from Edinburgh to Spain, when the Skull could have been brought directly to London and hidden away in the depths of the city until it was needed?'

'Because they know what we would do,' Carpenter said

firmly. 'Trawl every part of London until we found it. No, Spain is the safest place for the Skull until the time comes to unleash it.'

Will knew that a Spanish invasion weighed heavily on Walsingham's mind, but his own thoughts turned towards the Unseelie Court. Their aims were elusive, and constantly shifting. Their manipulations often appeared to point in one direction while the results lay in another, and they continually encircled the great events that were unfolding so it was hard to mark their place in them. They clearly needed the Silver Skull to strike a blow that would surmount Dee's defences, which had so far prevented them from crushing England in their fist. But why did they require the Shield to protect them so they could move through the disease-ravaged land?

'The Shield is well protected in the Lantern Tower,' Walsingham said. 'It is now beyond the Enemy's reach. Whatever they planned for, it need concern us no more.'

Will was not convinced, but he did not pursue the matter. His own immediate concern was where the Unseelie Court was holding Grace, and now he thought he knew.

'You want us to go to Spain, to kill or capture the Silver Skull,' he said, 'and to do whatever we can to undermine the plans for the invasion.'

A faint smile flickered across Walsingham's lips, quickly suppressed. Will had clearly divined his intentions.

'You want us to journey into the heart of our enemy's land?' Mayhew spluttered, incredulous. 'The Skull will surely be the most closely guarded prisoner in the whole of Spain, as closely guarded as Philip himself. How can we be expected to penetrate such protection, never mind survive such an enterprise?'

'We aren't,' Will responded, matter-of-factly, 'but if we

can destroy the Silver Skull in the process, our work will be done.'

Though he blanched a little, Mayhew nodded; he understood their responsibilities.

'You have only returned from Edinburgh this morn,' Walsingham said, looking at Will. 'The report I received from your assistant suggested the injuries inflicted on you by the Enemy were extreme.'

'Nat is prone to exaggeration,' Will replied. 'I heal well and am in good health. And fit to lead any mission into Spain.'

Walsingham studied Will for a moment, not wholly convinced. He had every right to be doubtful, Will knew; his wounds were still knitting, but the sea journey would give him plenty of time to make a full recovery, he considered. Walsingham clearly agreed, for he nodded and said, 'Then these fine men will accompany you. Arrangements have already been made. Your ship leaves today. But first you must visit Dee in Whitehall, for he has some new surprises for you. Make haste, and may God go with you.'

He gave a curt bow and strode out of the Banqueting Hall. Will could not help but admire the spymaster's cold focus upon his business, for he had essentially sent them all to their deaths, and dismissed them with nothing more than a nod.

'Well, then,' he said. 'There is barely time for drink and a visit to the doxy of your choice. Make the most of this time, gentlemen, for there will be few comforts in the days ahead.'

Will briefly caught Carpenter's baleful gaze as he walked from the room, and he wondered how much he could trust the man. Carpenter's grudge had festered for a year, and he was not someone who readily let go of his desire for revenge. The Enemy was expert at driving a spike into men's hearts through the flaws in their character. Had Carpenter betrayed Grace to them? Would he betray them all further? Will decided he must keep a close eye on his companion.

As he walked alone through the sunlit rooms of Hampton Court, his thoughts turned to Grace once more. In Edinburgh, Cavillex had made clear his intention to torture and kill Will in front of Grace. He surely knew Will would travel to Spain in search of the Skull, so logic dictated that Grace would also be held there in anticipation of Will's capture. He had no doubt that the Enemy would be waiting for him, but Grace would be waiting for him too, and the thought comforted him. Nat would say he was ready for a trip to Bedlam to so knowingly walk into the Unseelie Court's fiendish web, but Will hoped that knowing his foe as he did would be enough to protect him.

He spotted Walsingham ahead, deep in contemplation as he looked out of an open window across the fields that ran down to the slow-moving Thames. Whatever was on Walsingham's mind, it clearly troubled him. There was a mournful cast to his expression. The spymaster started when Will appeared at his side, and seemed inexplicably angry at being disturbed. Will knew from experience he had but a moment to ask his question.

'In Edinburgh, I was questioned at length by the Enemy. I gave nothing away—'

'As I would expect.'

'—but my interrogator was under the mistaken belief that I was kept informed of all that happens in England. He asked me what I knew of Dartmoor.' Will paused. 'What did he mean?'

He scrutinized Walsingham's face for any sign that he knew more of the subject than he might be about to reveal, but the Principal Secretary's face remained a clean slate, but for a faint knot of puzzlement in his brow.

'All I know of Dartmoor is that it is a bleak, inhospitable

place,' he grunted. 'I will discuss this matter with Dr Dee. He may bring some sense to it, though I doubt it. Dartmoor?' He shook his head slowly, and then continued on his way.

For all Walsingham's apparent ignorance, Will knew that Dartmoor was important to the Enemy. He resolved to make further enquiries.

Outside, he found Nathaniel and Kit Marlowe waiting in the sun by the carriage. Will had left them there on his arrival. Nathaniel appeared close to tears.

'Is it true?' he asked.

Will nodded. 'I am sorry, Nat, it is. Grace is gone.'

'How could the Spaniards have stolen her from under our noses within our very own palace?' he cried.

'They have their ways,' Will replied flatly, 'and nowhere is truly safe.' Marlowe caught his eye, and nodded knowingly.

'It seems the Enemy wish to cause you pain, in return for the suffering you have visited upon them,' he said. 'I have not heard of the struggle being made so personal before.'

'It must show that what I do is working, Kit.' Will held open the carriage door for them to clamber inside.

'That does not help poor Grace.' Nathaniel wrung his hands.

'Then it is a good job I have a plan to rescue her,' Will grunted as he climbed in after them. 'Do you think I would leave her to the pains of the Enemy? I would go to the very gates of Hell to bring her back.'

'I understand your affection for Grace,' Marlowe began hesitantly, 'but would this plan be a wise one?'

'I have decided to sail rapidly away from the shores of wisdom into the vast, heaving oceans of foolhardiness. Do not worry about me, Kit. Save your condolences for the Enemy.' Will kept the mood light, but he could not prevent an edge creeping into his voice, and he knew they both heard it. 'Bankside,' he called to the driver as the carriage moved off. 'I need succour before a visit to Dr Dee.'

'How can you even think of dallying with doxies and drunkenness when Grace is gone?' Nathaniel asked, his voice breaking. He gave Will a brief, fractured look of betrayal.

What could Will tell him? That it was the only way he could numb the pain he felt, and the fears of what might be happening to Grace at that very moment? He knew Nathaniel deserved better.

'There is always time for drink and women, Nat,' he said. The younger man wouldn't look at him for the rest of the journey.

Marlowe too was filled with questions about the Enemy, but could not raise any of them while Nathaniel was with them. But what concerned Will most was the odd look on Nathaniel's face. He had seen it many times before: the ghost of doubt, the spectre of fear, the dawning recognition that the world was not the way it appeared. Soon, he knew, he would be faced with a dilemma: to break his vow and send Nathaniel away, into the dangers that his father always feared, or to risk introducing him to a fate that mirrored Miller's, once the infection of the Unseelie Court finally took hold.

Will knew he was responsible for the change that had come over his assistant, and that he had a decision to make accordingly. They were nearing Bankside when he spoke. 'I must go away for a while on the business of Sir Francis Walsingham,' he said, trying to make light of what lay ahead. 'While I am gone, there is still much to be done here.' As the carriage jolted to a halt at Liz Longshanks's, Will paused and looked into Nathaniel's face, unsure if he should continue. Finally, his mind made up, he said, 'I have work for you both.'

# CHAPTER THIRTY-TWO

PROPELLED BY A SOUTH-WESTERLY, THEIR SHIP HAD ROUNDED the Cape of St Vincent early that morning. Passing along the Spanish coast past salt marshes, they had finally arrived at the rocky spit that protected the harbour of Cadiz, the second most important port in all Spain.

The sun was low on the horizon and a scarlet path flowed across the white-plumed waves. As the night began to press in, the lights of Cadiz flickered along the harbour, outside the taverns and in the squares, in the convent windows and the castle.

With sails billowing, the *Tempest* ploughed across the swell towards the town. A legend among seafaring men, the vessel was considered by some to be a harbinger of doom.

Captain John Courtenay stood on the forecastle, unfeasibly tall and powerfully built, tanned from the sun and the salt, his brown hair and beard wild, in denial of the urbane, sophisticated style of the day. His untamed appearance was emphasized by two ragged scars that marked his face in an X from temple to jaw, the result of torture at the hands of the Spanish in the New World. Beside him, England's greatest spy looked out at the nearing city lights.

'You have recovered well, Master Swyfte. You have a powerful constitution.' Courtenay understood exactly what Will Swyfte had endured in Edinburgh.

'A few scratches. We put these things behind us.'

Courtenay nodded thoughtfully. 'Aye. We would be poor men if we shed tears over every pinprick.'

Although the wounds of Will's torture had healed, the memory had not. Every time he stared down into the roiling green waves, he recalled that horrific sensation of drowning. He kept it close to him, a stoked furnace providing the heat that drove him on. With every new blow struck, the Unseelie Court raised the price they would have to pay sooner or later.

Courtenay trawled the deck, inspecting his crew at work with a sharp eye and a salty tongue, readying them for what was to come. He had been inducted into Walsingham's band of spies only a few months earlier when he had been given the captaincy of the *Tempest*, a galleon set aside for the affairs of England's secret service. Omitted from all official records and secure within its own well-shielded mooring at Tilbury, the ship was quickly credited with supernatural prowess, and stories began to circulate which were only encouraged by Walsingham, who knew that fear was a powerful weapon.

In truth, the *Tempest* was England's most advanced warship, a race-built galleon of the new design developed by John Hawkins, longer and with a reduced forecastle and poop deck that made it faster and more stable than any other at sea. Three-masted, with an advanced rigging system, it could easily be navigated by only a minimal crew.

And Courtenay was the perfect captain for such a vessel. He had been at Drake's side on his expedition against the Spanish in the New World, and had helped claim Nova Albion for the Crown. When war broke out between Spain and England in 1585, Courtenay had once again accompanied Sir Francis across the Atlantic, to sack the ports of Cartagena and Santo Domingo, and then to capture the fort of San Augustin in Spanish Florida. It was there that Bloody John earned his nickname. It was said he tore out the throat of a Spanish soldier with his own teeth and that his wild beard was stained red with blood for days after. Or so Will had heard tell, and he now dyed his beard red as an affectation whenever he sailed into battle.

Will watched the captain as he prowled the deck barking at his men. Though everyone on board had an air of calm detachment, beneath the surface tension grew.

It was 17 April. A fierce storm sweeping out of the Bay of Biscay had delayed their progress, but they had still reached their destination in little over two weeks out of Gravesend, at a good speed of seven knots once the high winds had passed. Under the billowing black clouds, Will had a premonition of what lay ahead. It didn't deter him. Somewhere there, across the sun-baked Spanish countryside, Grace was being held captive, he was sure of it; the lure designed to draw him in. For him the war had become personal.

At his back, the people of England relied upon him. Since Mary of Scotland's execution, it had felt as if the clock at Hampton Court Palace was moving inexorably towards midnight, an apocalypse of invasion and disease and death drawing steadily closer, and there was nothing anyone could do about it. The forces at play, shifting just beyond their perception, were too big for one man to confront, perhaps even for a nation. He knew that in the midst of all that his own troubles must appear minor, but that did not ease the pain.

As he watched the fading sunlight on the waves, one fear stayed with him: that he would be forced to sacrifice Grace in order to save England; and then he would truly be as damned as he had always imagined.

Now Courtenay strode back to Will with a broad grin. 'Get your mates ready, Master Swyfte,' he boomed. 'Time is drawing short.'

'A direct assault on Cadiz is a brave strategy, Captain. Are you sure this is the wisest course?'

'You stick to your devilish games on dry land. I know my business on the waves.' Courtenay's rolling laughter made Will doubt that his sanity was entirely intact. 'Any opportunity to lay some fire across the Spanish is a good one,' the man guffawed.

'Is not the port protected by shore batteries?'

'It is, but we can be in and out before the Spanish devils find their bearings. There is much in our favour, Master Swyfte. With the armada waiting to sail, the Spanish will expect England to be occupied with thoughts of invasion. No captain in his right mind would consider such an assault at this time.' He laughed again, too loud, too long. 'Even when they sighted us passing the Pillars of Hercules, we were but a lone ship. One solitary vessel sailing into Spain's great port! Rest assured, the nobles and the commoners will sit in the main square, they will drink and gamble and watch the strolling players, and they will give us not a second thought, if indeed a first.'

'Then I will be guided by your wisdom, Captain. You are a veteran of these matters, after all.'

'Ha, ha! We tore those Spaniards in two that day!' the mariner roared as he cast his mind back. 'Drake said we singed the beard of the King of Spain and he was right. April, it was, as now, but hot. We sailed our fleet straight into the harbours, here and at Corunna, occupied both and laid waste to thirty-seven naval and merchant vessels. Set the invasion back by a year! They had their ships and men here, too; they could have fought, if they had found the wherewithal. Now they are all at sea. So, by my calculation, one good English ship will suffice for a little mischief.'

'That sounds finer sport than my men landing silently under cover of darkness, but we too will sign our names in fire and iron.'

'I like your spirit, Master Swyfte. Now, I must be off to attend to my beard.' And the boisterous man marched away, singing a shanty as he directed his men with points and gestures.

The voyage had been a tedious one and Will was ready to act. Going below deck, he found Launceston, Mayhew and Carpenter playing cards. Their mood was sullen and it spoke of boredom. They abandoned their game at his nod, and sought out their rapiers and daggers without a word.

Carpenter glanced briefly at him, making no attempt to hide his disdain. Will suspected there would be a problem with the man at some point; his resentment and bitterness seethed, and seemed to be growing stronger with each imagined slight. Too much was at stake for Will to allow any such behaviour to compromise the mission, and he was afraid he might soon have to make a difficult choice.

Back on deck, the crew hurried about the ship as it eased towards the harbour, singing loudly of skulls piling high and the women who waited for them at home when their death-dealing ways were done. Salty spray misted the still-warm evening air.

Cadiz had grown up on a narrow spit of land hemmed in by the sea, and the ocean had shaped its history. Christopher Columbus had sailed from Cadiz to the New World, first linking Spain with its future source of riches, Will knew. And when Cadiz later became the home of the Spanish treasure fleet, the city had become a target for all Spain's enemies. Barely a year passed without the Barbary Corsairs launching a raid. And now England was once more testing its defences.

Hearing a conversation behind him, Will turned. His beard now a flaming red, Courtenay strode across the *Tempest*'s heaving deck as if he was on dry land. His eyes were on fire with a mad passion for what was to come. 'Spain embarks on an invasion of England, but first let England invade Spain – with four men!' He laughed out loud at the insanity of a mission that dwarfed even his own mad schemes.

'Ah, but what men,' Will responded wryly.

Courtenay looked at Will and the others and nodded his approval. 'I think you will provide a test for those Spanish dogs.' He peered across the water towards the city. Taking a deep breath of the sea air, he closed his eyes for a moment as if in prayer, and then roared, 'Break out the colours!'

As the English flag – a red cross on a white background – ran up the mast, he signalled to the quarterdeck and the trumpet blared out the call to arms, followed by the three sharp bursts Will had specified. In the harbour, what men had remained behind to defend Cadiz would now be racing for the galleys, but Courtenay didn't give them a chance. At his command, English cannon fire thundered against the city.

Cries, shouts and screams echoed across the waves as the shockwave of gunfire subsided, and the alarms rang out. Will could imagine the townsfolk fleeing in terror, seeking refuge in the castle of Matagorda that rose above Cadiz, where the commandant and his men surely waited to close the gates.

'One English ship!' Courtenay raged at the lights in the gathering gloom.

A galley began to make its way towards them, but a broadside from the *Tempest* disabled it before it got close enough to use its own guns. Courtenay ordered his trumpeter to play a mocking blast as the galley's crew swam back to shore.

Will knew that panic would be spreading through the merchant ships anchored beyond the promontory of Puntales. Some had been waiting for a change in the wind, others were en route to Northern Europe or the Indies, and more loaded with wine from Jerez, wood, wool and cochineal for trade across the Mediterranean. He watched their lights as several set sail, narrowly avoiding collisions as they fled to shallower water where the warship would not venture. They clearly feared the *Tempest* was part of a wider English attack.

A galley was not so fortunate. Bellowing orders, Courtenay sent a boarding party to seize it and, once the crew had abandoned ship, set it alight. The furiously burning vessel was then cast adrift. The currents carried it towards the harbour, where the flames spread to several small boats and another galley. The panic among the merchants watching the chaos added to the tumult ringing out through the night.

Then a broadside from the marauding galleon hit a gunpowder store on the harbour, and it went up in a burst of gold and crimson that set adjoining buildings alight. The thick, acrid smoke drifted across Cadiz, momentarily obscuring the twinkling lights. On board the *Tempest*, the crew cheered loudly, and Courtenay gave a proud nod. He signalled for anchor to be dropped and turned to Will, his eyes ablaze. 'I think that will end any resistance for now. The papists will be distracted by the fire and trying to halt its spread across the city, or they will be cowering in their homes or the castle, afraid we are going to ransack their riches. No one will notice four rats slipping into the alleys.'

Forcefully, he shook each of their hands in turn, and wished them good fortune, before returning to the matter of his ship and his men.

It was Will's turn to speak. 'Whatever lies ahead, know this: I have been proud to serve beside you.' He held out his hand and Mayhew, Launceston and Carpenter each took it, held it for a second, then shook free.

'Now,' Will said, 'let us take this war further into Spain . . . and to the Unseelie Court.' Bounding on to the rail, he slid down a rope into the rowing boat that waited for them. The others followed without a second thought.

Night cloaked the waves and they struck out towards the city, confident they would not be seen. Courtenay's plan was perfect: all eyes would be on the *Tempest* to see what it did next, and the townsfolk would be manning the defences or putting out the fires which now burned fiercely along the waterfront.

From the old fort and the battery on the harbour, the cannon continued to pump out an intermittent barrage, but the *Tempest* was out of range, and it was little trouble for Will and the others to keep out of the line of fire. They also kept far away from the Puental, the small, rocky landing area outside the city walls, which was under heavy guard as the only likely place for the English to set down their raiding parties.

On the harbour-front, it was a hellish scene. Boats blazed, the flames dancing across the black water and clouds of inky smoke billowing back over the city. Tubs of pitch used for caulking and repairs had been set alight, and most of the buildings near the gunpowder store were now on fire. The white walls of the town glowed red.

Rowing through the choking smoke and burning refuse to the edge of the harbour wall, Will pointed to a rope dangling down into the water. Cautiously, he hauled his way up and crouched behind a pile of filled sacks that were waiting to be loaded on to one of the merchant ships. The others soon joined him, peering over the top of their hiding place at the abject confusion that stretched along the entire length of the harbour.

Men ran with leaking buckets of water as they feebly attempted to put out the conflagration further along the harbour's edge. Foot-soldiers armed with pikes, helmets glinting in the firelight, raced to oversee the Puental and to keep guard in case the *Tempest* sent landing parties. Watchmen peered and pointed into the dark in case more galleons were on their way. The sound of merchants bellowing their concerns in a babble of conflicting foreign tongues added to the cacophony and the chaos.

'Look at it – it is madness,' Mayhew said approvingly, his face flushed.

Will nodded. 'We asked Captain Courtenay for cover to mask our arrival in Cadiz. I think he served us proud.' He scanned the hectic mass. 'Now, where is our contact?'

In the shadows of one of the many alleys that led down to the harbour stood a man wearing a wide-brimmed hat pulled low over his face. The glare of the flames revealed the lower half was clean-shaven, and he carried a walking stick which he waved slowly from side to side.

'There,' Will whispered. 'Stay here. I will make the introductions in case there is a problem.' Edging out from behind their sanctuary, he wove in and out of the panicking citizens before darting into the alleyway. 'De Groot?'

Looking Will up and down, the man nodded. 'You found the rope?' He spoke English with a strong Dutch inflection.

'You did well.'

'I ran here as soon as I heard the trumpet signal that had been agreed.' He glanced back up the alley. 'This way. We must move away from here. There are men of many nations in Cadiz, but Englishmen will not fail to attract attention.'

Both men flinched as another broadside from the *Tempest* crashed against the other end of the harbour, followed by a futile return of fire from the Spanish battery. In the confusion that followed, Will beckoned to Launceston, Mayhew and Carpenter. But as they sprinted towards the alley, a cry rang out from one of the watchmen.

'Quickly,' de Groot urged from the depths of the alley. 'I must not be seen or my use here will be over,' and he ran off into the dark.

Cursing, Will looked back and saw four foot-soldiers start in pursuit as he, Carpenter, Mayhew and Launceston darted into the alley. The path was steep and wound round so tightly it was impossible to see more than ten paces ahead or behind. As they moved away from the harbour, the sound of cannon became muffled, replaced by the crack of their boots on the cobbles and the persistent tolling of the fortress bell signalling the alarm.

Turning a corner, Will paused and made a chopping motion with his left hand, and the others melted quickly into doorways on either side. Clutching his dagger in his right hand, Will ducked behind a water barrel. Urgent voices echoed off the walls of the houses pressing tightly on either side, and the sound of running feet became a steady drumbeat, drawing nearer. Will waited. He looked to the shadowed doorways, but Carpenter, Mayhew and Launceston were invisible.

Out of the dark appeared helmets and breastplates glinting in the moonlight. Breath rasping from their exertion, the Spanish pursuers lumbered up the steep incline. Crimson scarves were tied and bowed just above their knees. Will saw the soldiers were all hampered by their pikes, which would be near useless in the constrained space of the alley. Holding his breath, he gripped his dagger tightly.

As the first soldier passed him, he lunged up with his knife and thrust it straight into the soldier's groin. Blood gushed on to the cobbles. The man pitched forward, screaming, and the other soldiers cried out in alarm. Their pikes clattered against the walls and each other as they tried to turn. Leaping to his feet, Will drove his dagger into the back of one pikeman's neck. Mayhew and Carpenter took on the third soldier and Launceston in a silent, fluid movement slit the throat of the last. The soldiers were poorly trained and overweight and didn't stand a chance against the Englishmen. By the time Will had wiped his blade clean, the four were dead.

De Groot returned to guide them back to a house on the Plaza de San Francisco beside the San Francisco church and convent. Ensconced around a flickering candle on a trestle that filled most of a small back room, Will, Launceston, Mayhew and Carpenter scrutinized their contact. After Reidheid, Will was not going to trust anyone easily. De Groot returned their attention with heavy-lidded eyes that showed no warmth.

'You are a merchant?' Will asked.

'I ply my trade between Flanders and Spain.' De Groot's tone was dour. He laid salt fish, cheese and bread on the table, and a jug of beer. 'Though I have provided information and assistance to your Sir Francis Walsingham these last three years.'

'As we were told,' Mayhew sniffed.

'You may use this house while you are in Cadiz. There is food and drink here, and clothes in the local fashions so you can go about your business without drawing attention to yourselves.' De Groot took out a clay pipe and began to stuff tobacco into the cup. 'But if you are caught, do not look to me for aid.'

Carpenter poured himself a flask of beer. 'Agreed,' he grunted.

'What news do you have?' Will asked. He cut a chunk of salted fish with his knife.

'There is jubilation across all Spain at the moment,' de Groot told them as they ate. 'Word has spread far and wide of the size of the armada and the martial power it wields. The common man believes England to be already as good as defeated.'

'They may be correct,' Mayhew muttered between mouthfuls before Carpenter silenced him with a contemptuous glare.

'Our job here is to make sure the Spanish are thwarted,' Will said, pushing himself back on his stool, a flask of beer in hand. 'We can do nothing about the armada, but we may still upset their wider plans.'

'And what are those wider plans?' de Groot asked, as he refilled Mayhew's flask. But he caught Will's eye and nodded. 'I see. Questions for another time.'

'We seek information on a ship that we believe would have dropped anchor here in Cadiz within the last few days,' Will said. 'Among its passengers would be a Spanish nobleman, Don Alanzo de las Posadas?'

'Yes, yes, there was such a ship.' De Groot nodded. 'There was talk of it in the taverns along the harbour. It dropped anchor in the morning, but no boat was sent ashore until night had fallen. I am sure one of those on board was indeed Don Alanzo. He spent some time trying to procure a number of carriages to take him to Seville.'

'Then that is our destination,' Will said, knocking back the last of the beer.

'One other thing that may or may not be of importance,' de Groot continued, raising a finger to his lips. 'He was very insistent that before he left he should call both at the convent and at the cathedral.'

Carpenter snorted. 'Saying his prayers to clear the stain upon his soul.'

'The cathedral perhaps, but at a convent?' Will wandered to the window, and peered out at the jumble of buildings falling down the slope towards the harbour. The clamour had died down, but he could make out the *Tempest* in the light of the burning debris in the water. Now he had seen his cargo safely ashore, Captain Courtenay had ended his attack and was heading out to open water. Will tried not to think of Grace and what he feared she could be enduring, but the thoughts fell unbidden across him like a shadow.

He returned to the room with a smile. 'We must not let small matters pass us by, for perhaps greater things may lie behind them,' he declared. 'But even if there is nothing more to it, then a man's religion in this world may well be a weakness we can exploit and put to our own use.'

# CHAPTER THIRTY-THREE

IT WAS A BRIGHT, GLASSY MORNING, SHORTLY AFTER DAWN, already warm, and likely to get a great deal hotter. The smell of smoke still hung in the air, but across the convent grounds all was peaceful. Keeping low, Will crept along the top of the white-washed wall like a cat, stalking the nun who hummed a lilting melody as she took her daily walk in the orchard. Dappled by the sunlight through the leaves, her head was bowed in reflection, her white cloak caught by the cooling breeze. A glance back to the convent revealed she was alone.

Dropping silently to the grass, Will darted through the trees, keeping enough cover between him and the nun to conceal him in case she looked back.

De Groot had worked wonders while the English spies rested. The Dutchman admitted that he worked for gold and nothing more, not love of England, nor hatred of Spain. Walsingham paid him an annual stipend, and it seemed that every year he threatened to go over to the Spanish, only to be bought back to the cause. It was a game, and one that all sides understood. Will had agreed to his demands, and in the early hours de Groot had sent a local girl who cleaned for him to the convent under the pretence of arranging a donation from the Dutch merchant. After the nuns had finished their morning prayers, just before first light, the girl spent a little while talking to them until she had gathered the information Will required.

The nun never heard him until his hand was clamped across her mouth and he was bundling her to the rear wall of the orchard. Her eyes wide with fear, she struggled and tried to cry out, but he was too strong.

'Sister Adelita, forgive me, I have no wish to harm you. All I ask of you is your help,' he whispered in fluent Spanish. He felt a sharp pang of regret that he had laid hands upon her, but he couldn't risk her raising the alarm before he had discovered what he needed to know.

On hearing her name, she calmed a little, but still resisted his grip. Her eyes were large and dark as they searched his face, but Will saw a steely defiance within them. He also saw that she was beautiful, possessing the delicate bone structure of a noblewoman and honey-coloured skin.

'I am about to remove my hand,' he continued. 'Please do not call out. I do not want to overpower you.' The hint of a threat laced the last words.

Slowly he moved his hand. She narrowed her eyes. 'How dare you trespass on this sacred land? We allow no men in this convent,' she hissed, venom lacing her words.

'My apologies, Sister Adelita. I was told you walked here at this hour each day. If I could have approached you in any other way, I would have done so. But time is short, and the matter urgent.'

'You are English,' she spat. 'Your people were responsible for the murderous treachery inflicted on this city last night?'

Ignoring her, he said, 'Sister, I must ask you about a nobleman who visited your convent within the past few days. His name is Don Alanzo de las Posadas.'

'My brother?'

Now it was Will's turn to be surprised, but he didn't show it. 'It was you he visited?'

Sister Adelita nodded, her thoughts racing. 'What do you, an Englishman, want with my brother?'

'I would know of what you spoke.'

'No!' she replied, her indignation rising. 'Those are private matters between brother and sister. Who are you to ask?' She grew suspicious. 'I will tell you nothing. You only wish to harm him.'

Will sighed. 'In fact, the very opposite is true. I once saved your brother's life, and he mine. We are divided by war, but rest assured I have only respect for him.'

'Then what do you want of him?' Sister Adelita held Will's gaze. He looked away.

'A friend of mine is in great danger, someone I have sworn to protect. A girl who was seized by evil men who claim to be allies of your brother, but whom I believe to be as much of a threat to him. I want to save her, and return her home. If Don Alanzo said anything of her to you – anything at all – please tell me.' Will wondered how far he would be able to go to get the information he needed if she did not answer of her own accord.

Sister Adelita searched Will's face. What she saw there appeared to appease her a little. 'She is the woman you love?' A half-smile ghosted her lips.

'No. She is the sister of the woman I loved,' he said, with an honesty that seemed to take her aback. 'There is little enough room for love in this world, Sister. It is a hard place, filled with duplicity, and violence, and loss, and we must seize our moments for comfort when we can, for they are surely stolen from us when our guard is down. The man you see before you was forged by the loss of his love, and I will not see others go easily down that path. This woman I speak of . . .' he paused, 'she is young and filled with hope and all the opportunities for joy that still lie ahead. I will do all I can to ensure her life does not follow the miserable path of my own.'

'Even though you might come to harm in the process?'

'My moment for love is gone. I am, to all intents and purposes, dead to the world. I have nothing left to lose.'

'I do not believe that,' she said.

''Tis true.'

He could see his words had touched her, but still she continued to probe. 'And you believe this is the path God has chosen for you? A selfless duty to protect others on the hard, dark road?'

'I wish I had your faith, Sister. I do what I do.'

She smiled tightly. 'And there is no benefit in this for England?'

Will looked up at her, unblinking. 'I have spoken truly.'

'I am sure that is correct . . . of the words you have spoken. But there are many more unspoken, are there not? I know the ways of spies. Yes, I see that is what you are. I lived with my brother long enough to understand that the voids between words can be more important than the words themselves.' Her eyes flashed and her voice hardened. 'I understand that deceit is set in the very fibre of your nature, and in the lies you tell yourselves to do your job. I could not trust my brother and I will not trust you, even with your gentle talk of love, and yearning hearts.' She stared deep into his face and added, 'However true that may be.'

'Sister—'

'No, leave here now and this matter will be forgotten. But if you persist I will raise the alarm, the authorities will find you, and you will pay the price faced by all English spies found on Spanish soil.' Turning without waiting for an answer, she walked back through the trees towards the convent.

For a moment, Will wondered if he should force the information out of her. A part of him was, he knew, capable of anything he needed to do to save Grace; another part knew that he died a little more with each step he took down that path. 'Sister, I go now to the cathedral,' he called after her. 'If you change your mind, you will find me there.'

She didn't look back.

Had he just lost his best chance to understand the plans of Don Alanzo and the Enemy? Conflicted, he scrambled back over the wall.

The bitter smell of last night's attack hung over Cadiz. In every face he passed, Will saw the ravages the plague might cause; every woman reminded him of Grace and what she might be suffering. He was consumed by a desperate sense of time slipping through his fingers like sand.

He spied Launceston, Mayhew and Carpenter waiting for him in the shade of a large tree in the centre of the plaza. Now dressed in the smart but well-worn clothes de Groot had provided, they looked like merchants debating a deal before the start of the day's business.

'There is nothing for us here,' Will said, his voice low.

Launceston read Will's expression. 'So, she did not talk. Then we should return to her and offer her some encouragement.'

'Torture her? Very good. Shall we then burn down the convent? Just to teach her a lesson?'

Launceston was unmoved. With a shrug, he said, 'She is Spanish.'

'You inhabit a simple and soothing world. I am faintly

jealous.' Will surreptitiously eyed the few townsfolk who were hurrying across the plaza. A couple of merchants, he guessed, a woman off to the market, perhaps to buy food for one of the large houses. After the *Tempest*'s attack, there was a jittery anxiety in their flashed glances, but life went on. 'We should not stay in the open too long. The cathedral, and then to Seville.' Heads down and voices lowered, they moved away.

'Why waste time at the cathedral?' Mayhew sounded as if he was in his cups. Eyeing the man, Will wondered if the corrosive despair of the Unseelie Court was worming its way ever more deeply into him. Of course he felt for Mayhew, but the loss of hope could make him a liability.

'A man such as Don Alanzo would not break his mission to visit the cathedral unless it signified something of importance. I do not see him as someone who is ruled by his religion.'

'Show me a devout spy and I will show you a man about to slit a priest's throat.' Carpenter's laugh held no humour.

'But where does that damned Spaniard plan to take the Silver Skull?' Mayhew continued, his words slurred. 'What does the Enemy have planned? And why are the Spanish—' Panic welled in him, and the words caught in his throat.

Carpenter clutched his arm roughly and hissed, 'Contain yourself.'

'We should turn back,' Mayhew said, his voice rising. 'What can we accomplish here, apart from our own deaths? Even if we find the answers to those questions, we will never get near to the Silver Skull. All is lost here. We must find other tactics—'

Carpenter drew his knife and, keeping it hidden in the folds of his shirt, leaned close to Mayhew with the point against the other man's chest. 'Your weakness endangers us all. Any more and I will be done with you,' he whispered.

'Leave him be,' Will interjected. 'He needs a little time to recover from the strain of travelling, perhaps. Take him back to de Groot's house. But keep him away from the wine. I will go to the cathedral alone.'

Mayhew's face fell at Will's intervention, but he left between Launceston and Carpenter without another word, shoulders slumped in a pale reflection of the arrogant man who had survived the Unseelie Court's assault on the Tower. Will was annoyed with himself for not noticing the decline earlier.

His attention was drawn by a gleam further along the street. It was sunlight glinting off the polished helmets and breastplates of eight Spanish soldiers making their way in his direction. Before they caught sight of his pale skin, he slipped into an alley and walked quickly away from the tramp of their feet.

When he was sure he had not been followed, he slowed his pace and attempted to adopt the nonchalant air of the locals without meeting the eye of anyone he passed. His unease at being alone in enemy territory was emphasized by the unfamiliarity of the place – buildings from the days of the Moor, the exotic scents of spices and unfamiliar blooms. But Cadiz was a hub for the trade routes, with a stew of nationalities bubbling within its walls, and that made it easier for Will to pass unnoticed.

The alley brought him to a bustling market filled with the sounds of competing voices haggling over fish and vegetables. Beautiful women enjoyed the appreciative gazes of the traders while pretending not to notice the stir they created in their wake. Aromatic smoke drifted from the stalls of the street-side food-sellers, heating their charcoal to cook the seafood fresh from the harbour. Everywhere Will looked he saw evidence of the riches brought back from the New World.

Skirting the edge of the market, he kept to quiet, shaded streets until he came to a large cobbled plaza, cooled by the sea breeze. On the far side of the square, a huge edifice of brilliant white stone soared up against the blue sky. Ablaze in the morning sun, La Catedral de Cadiz dwarfed the houses clustering around it. Statues of saints stared down from niches along the painted walls, and the stained glass windows glittered like jewels.

Shielding his eyes against the glare, Will scanned the plaza. At that early hour, only a few people had reason to be in the square, but two soldiers were deep in conversation near the cathedral's large wooden doors.

Conscious of drawing attention to himself, Will retreated to the winding alleys that made the town feel like a warren of rat-runs, though they were much cleaner than the streets of his home, and sweeter-smelling. He had not gone far when he heard footsteps behind him. Three or four pairs of feet. Will's scalp prickled in the quiet that surrounded the cathedral. The sudden activity struck a false note.

Alert now, Will ducked into a small alley. Pausing, he heard one pair of footsteps follow. And now more feet drawing nearer, ahead of him this time. At the junction with the next alley, he slowed, hand on the hilt of his sword, and peered round the corner. Two pikemen were searching every doorway and open window.

Cursing, Will doubled back and darted up another alley, only to find more foot-soldiers coming towards him. It seemed a net had been cast and was being closed.

He knew he had been betrayed. Sister Adelita must have gone to the authorities and informed them he was on his way to the cathedral. He'd been a fool. He had looked into her eyes and convinced himself he could trust her, but it had been a stupid, naive mistake that may well cost him his life, and England its survival. He grimaced. Nathaniel had always told him he allowed women to make a fool of him.

The search party drew closer on every side, methodically closing off his escape routes. Will tested doors to his left and right, but they were all locked.

He drew his sword. He'd give a good account of himself, but knew that he would eventually be overpowered. In desperation now, he searched for an escape route he might have missed. A figure suddenly stepped out in front of him.

Will raised his rapier instinctively, ready to strike. It was Sister Adelita, and his sword-point hovered a hair's breadth from her neck. She swallowed, realizing how very close to death she was. 'If you wish to keep your freedom, you must follow me,' she said.

'So you can betray me again?' Will's sword arm didn't waver.

'If I had betrayed you once, I would not be here.' Her eyes flashed.

Accepting the logic of her statement, he nodded and lowered his blade. 'Lead on.'

Moving swiftly, Sister Adelita led him back down the alley towards the sound of approaching feet. Will again wondered if he was a fool to trust her, but then she pushed open a rickety wooden door and led the Englishman into a small, well-kept courtyard where herbs grew in stone troughs surrounded by alabaster statues. A suntanned old man sat on some steps and flashed Sister Adelita a toothless smile as she and Will passed.

'The almshouses,' she whispered, 'provided by our convent for the sick and the needy.'

Still unsure that he was not being led into a trap, Will was on his guard as they moved through the neat dwelling. Reaching the front entrance, Sister Adelita waited until all the armed foot-soldiers had moved on before leading Will out beyond the edge of the closing net.

'I should not be seen talking to you,' she said. 'After your attack last night, the commandant's men are everywhere in Cadiz.'

'I agree. Come with me – I have a safe haven, a house. The owner is unaware of our presence,' Will lied.

Back at de Groot's, Will entered first and waved the Dutchman out of the back of the house so he would not be identified. Clearly not certain she was doing the right thing, Sister Adelita clutched her rosary so hard her knuckles showed white.

She started when she encountered Launceston, who was keeping watch through the window. 'How many of you are there?' she exclaimed in alarm.

'Only four,' Will replied, trying to calm her. 'We are no threat.' He turned to Launceston and said in Spanish for the nun's benefit, 'This is Sister Adelita. A friend.'

Launceston bowed and greeted the nun in her own language. Softening at the Earl's polite display, she bowed in return.

'Where are the others?' Will asked.

'Mayhew has lost his mind. He began to curse and cry, then threw us off and ran into the alleys. Carpenter has given pursuit.'

Will paused in reflection. Sister Adelita clearly had not alerted the men who had hunted him near the cathedral. Could it have been Carpenter? He cast a suspicious eye towards the Earl. Launceston also had been left alone with the opportunity for betrayal. Could he trust either of them?

'I must speak to Sister Adelita,' he said. 'If there is any sign of those Spanish soldiers drawing near, inform me immediately.'

He took Sister Adelita to the small back room where they could have some privacy. 'I would thank you for coming to my aid,' he said. 'What made you change your mind?'

She gave him a look filled with such pain that he was taken aback.

'I can see you are a good man, if misguided.' She swallowed, trying to damp down the emotion that was close to the surface. 'It seems we are all misguided at some time.'

'I wish no harm personally to your brother, or to you,' Will said, his voice gentle, 'but there are bigger things at play, matters that dwarf us all.'

She nodded slowly and pointed at her habit. 'This is not the life I would have chosen for myself. But someone had to make amends.' She searched his face for a moment as she weighed her next words, and then kneaded her hands with an edge of desperation. 'You know of the night-visitors. I see it.'

'Night-visitors?'

'Do not toy with me! I am no simple country girl!' Her eyes flashed with renewed passion, and she stepped so close only a hand's width separated them. 'The ones who watch from the dark fields. The meddlers, the invisible hand that continually steers us on to the rocks, the tempters and the tormenters. The Fair Folk,' she added with bitter irony.

'The Unseelie Court,' Will said. In the grip of her emotion, Sister Adelita had moved so close she was almost brushing against him. He was caught by her beauty, and felt a brief pang of guilt at the unbidden feelings. 'They are our Enemy,' he continued. 'It is my life's work to oppose them. A secret war has been fought between England and these damnable predators for a great many years, and now it is on the brink of becoming an open battle.'

'You fight them!' Large eyes glistening, Sister Adelita

appeared to become aware of her closeness to Will, but she did not step away. As she searched his face, her features softened and her breath caught in her throat. 'My brother has forged an unholy alliance with them. Or rather Spain has, sanctioned by the King. We have grown fat on the riches from the New World, and comfortable in the power we now wield. His Majesty is determined to maintain our influence. But the ends do not justify the means!'

The small, windowless room was hot and dark, the only light coming from the guttering stub of a candle on the beer-stained trestle. Sister Adelita's eyes never left Will's, and in their depths he thought he could see a stew of conflicting emotions – loneliness, perhaps, yearning and guilt. It was as if she had fought to contain her feelings for so long that the slightest weakness had brought all of them rushing to the surface.

'I fear for my brother,' she said softly. 'He is fiercely loyal to the King, and will do whatever he is instructed in the pursuit of his business. All must be sacrificed for the future of Spain! But God is greater than our country, and the King, and men, and God would not wish us to deal with these devils – whether to keep us in gold and silver, or even to bring the one true religion back to England.'

Will watched her full lips form the words. She saw him looking at her mouth and in the flickering candlelight her cheeks appeared to flush, but she still did not look away. Will felt another touch of guilt at the realization that he was enjoying her attention. As politely as he could, he stepped away from her and busied himself searching for another candle in a small cupboard in one corner of the room. Finding one, he lit it from the flame of the one that was about to go out, and set it in a drizzle of molten wax on the trestle. 'You have discussed this with Don Alanzo?' he asked, not meeting her eyes.

'We have argued, and fought, but he would never see reason.' At first there was a note of disappointment in her voice, but she hid it quickly. 'Our father disappeared when we were young, and since then he has grown hard, and driven.'

In that moment Will understood Don Alanzo a little more. Had the Unseelie Court taken their father? Was Don Alanzo now allying himself with the Enemy in order to get his father back?

'I was going to be wed,' Sister Adelita continued, 'and on the day before my marriage I told my brother he must break off all dealings with those vile things or I would be forced to do penance for the sake of my family. He refused, and so I set aside my love and my heart and came here to the convent. And still my brother continued along his path to damnation.' She stifled a sob. 'Does he think so little of me?'

Will wanted to comfort her, but he knew he had to distance himself. 'Men like us are pulled by greater currents,' he replied in a gentle voice. 'Our lives, and our desires, our hopes and dreams, become as nothing to the demands and responsibilities placed upon us. I am sure your brother cares for you deeply. I am equally sure he feels he has no choice over the course that he follows.'

Reassured by Will's words, Sister Adelita nodded in acceptance. 'When he came to me the other day, he seemed changed . . . hopeful. He told me he may soon have good news for me.'

*The destruction of England*, Will thought.

'And he said he hoped my penance at the convent would soon come to an end.'

'You would break your vows?'

'I . . . I do not know. I believe . . . I have given my life to God. I never expected, or hoped for, anything to change.' She looked briefly into his face, and then kissed him, softly at first, but then with increasing passion.

Heartbeats passed and Will pulled away, though she fought to keep him in an embrace. Gently, he prised her arms from him, holding her hands in his and looking into her eyes. 'I am a man of easy morals, and you would regret this if we continued,' he said. 'I would not wish that upon you.'

She bowed her head in shame, but he raised her chin, smiled and added, 'Sister, there is no shame in honest emotion. This business makes us into people we are not. It ruins lives, and forces us to battle with ourselves along the road to misery. We deserve better, all of us. Do not think badly of yourself, Sister Adelita.'

She allowed herself a slight smile, but her breath was still short with passion. 'One day let us hope we can all be who we truly are.'

Will nodded in agreement without really believing it. This war would never end, he was sure of that. There would be battles and bloodshed and death, but it would continue as long as men and the Unseelie Court were led on by their own weaknesses. To fight without hope of victory, to fight without truly knowing the reason for that fight, was the very definition of madness, but as long as it was a shared madness there would be no end to it.

'Did your brother give you any reason for his hope? Any information that might help me?' Time was passing, he knew. Time they could ill afford.

'He sought my aid. There is a priest here in Cadiz, Father Celino, who is known for his struggles with the Devil. He undertook the rite of exorcism for the soul of a young girl in Arcos de la Frontera, and, they say, cast out several demons. He is knowledgeable in such matters and is often petitioned by the local people, but many of their requests are frivolous and he will only consider matters on recommendation.'

'And your brother asked you to recommend him to this priest?'

Sister Adelita nodded. 'He met him at the cathedral. I do not know what they discussed, but later that night my brother left for Seville in a great hurry.'

Will dwelled momentarily on the implications of what she had said. 'I would wish to meet this Father Celino.'

Her face fell, and Will recognized the risks she was taking to help him.

He guided her back to where Launceston still watched the street just as the door burst open. Carpenter entered, dragging Mayhew with him, who shrugged himself free and stalked to the corner of the room.

'Do not accuse me!' Mayhew jabbed his finger at each of them in turn. 'I needed air and some time to gather my thoughts!'

Carpenter toyed with his knife, his eyes flickering between Will and Launceston, whose hand rested ready on his dagger.

'We simply need to know you will not drag us down to Hell, Master Mayhew,' Will said calmly. 'Your absolute support is required in this work. We cannot afford any personal weakness to lead us to disaster.'

'Or what? What will you do?' Mayhew raged. 'Kill me? Do it! Nothing can be worse than this life!' His despair was palpable.

Without hesitation, Sister Adelita stepped past Will and took Mayhew's hand in her own. He was surprised and thrown by her touch, his anger dying in his throat. 'You have troubles,' she said in faltering English, but her tone was sympathetic. 'I have spoken to your friend here, and I understand what you

341

do. It is God's work, and that is never easy, but the rewards are shared by all.'

Tears sprang to Mayhew's eyes, and he blinked them away quickly before the others could see. 'But I do not do God's work,' he replied, his voice barely a whisper. 'I am weak.'

Sister Adelita looked to Will and said in Spanish, 'Let me speak to him alone while you make your arrangements. If you wish me to recommend you to Father Celino, I will.'

Will nodded his agreement, but he had already started to formulate a plan. Once Mayhew had been led away, Carpenter said vehemently, 'He will be the death of us, I tell you now.'

'Then let him stand in line. There are more pressing matters that could lead us to the grave,' Will said.

'But how long are you going to keep protecting him?' Carpenter snapped.

'Till I am certain that he is truly a danger to us. I am not so quick in taking the life of a fellow Englishman as you, Master Carpenter.'

'No, but you are quick to abandon them.' Carpenter's reply was quick and pointed.

'You know I thought you dead.' Will's voice was heavy.

Bristling, Carpenter would have confronted Will had not Launceston, silent for so long, stepped between them. 'Is this how it will be? That we do the work of the Enemy and the Spaniards ourselves?'

'Listen to the voice of reason, Master Carpenter,' Will said.

'Besides, I can slit Mayhew's throat in an instant if he truly becomes a problem,' Launceston continued, a deadly smile on his lips.

Will sighed. 'Enough talk of slitting and cutting and killing the people we know. Let us direct our attention to the matter at hand.'

Silence fell between them until Sister Adelita emerged with Mayhew. Whatever she had said to him, it had calmed him considerably and he was full of contrition. Offering his apologies, he promised not to give in to his weaknesses. 'It was a momentary lapse,' he said.

Will went to ask de Groot – who was still outside, out of sight of the house – to make arrangements for their departure from Cadiz. On his return, they gathered their cloaks, caps and rapiers, and stepped out into the hot sun. Glancing around, Sister Adelita guided them into a tiny alley, and then along a circuitous route of narrow, steep streets, stopping every now and then to duck into empty courtyards out of sight of passers-by.

'At this hour, Father Celino will be in the vestry preparing to go out to minister to the sick,' she said. 'We have only a short time.' Eventually, they found themselves at a small door at the rear of the cathedral. Sister Adelita ushered them inside.

The hushed church was cool after the heat of the day. Soon, Will knew, it would be bustling with merchants discussing business, and local people at their devotions or lighting candles for loved ones at sea, but for now all was still and quiet. The stained glass windows cast jewels of light across the flagstones, and the great vaulted roof high overhead caught and magnified every sound. Holding a finger to his lips, Will silently cautioned the others to move as quietly as they could.

Mayhew, Carpenter and Launceston hid behind pillars along the nave, while Will waited in a small chapel close to the high altar. Nodding to Will, Sister Adelita hurried to the vestry door and summoned Father Celino. He emerged with a lazy gait, a tall man with a Roman nose, heavily tanned, with jet-black hair despite being in his fifties.

'Sister Adelita. Is there a problem?' he asked with a note of concern. 'I did not expect to see you here.'

'Yes, Father. It is about my brother,' she replied, her head bowed.

'Don Alanzo? Is he well?'

'I am worried about him, Father. I have not heard from him and I would know where he is so I can seek him out. I would know that he is well.'

'Your brother is in Seville, Sister,' Celino said, his voice arrogant and aloof. 'As always, he is engaged in important matters. He would not wish to have his affairs intruded upon, even by his own flesh and blood.'

'Then you cannot tell me who he sees?'

'Of course not!' Celino snapped.

Will signalled to Launceston, who waited like a spectre in the shadows behind his stone column, and nodded. Instantly, Carpenter, Mayhew and Launceston darted from their hiding places and grabbed Sister Adelita, who screamed as she attempted to fight them off.

'What is this?' Celino raged. 'Leave her alone! Help! Help us now!'

Unnoticed, knife in hand, Will glided silently to the priest's side and whispered, 'Be silent, Father, or it will not only be her blood that stains these hallowed flags.'

The priest stopped shouting. 'Who are you?' he asked quietly.

'English cut-throats who think nothing of spilling Spanish blood.'

Celino blanched.

'Kill her,' Will said.

'No!' Celino cried, but Launceston and Carpenter were already dragging Sister Adelita into one of the chapels. Her screams rang off the walls, until a moment later there was only silence.

'Lock the doors,' Will instructed Mayhew, 'and guard them, so we are not disturbed.' Then, grabbing Celino roughly by his cassock, he threw him across the altar. The priest's head hit the top and his eyes grew wide with fear as he began to intone a prayer.

'Do not waste your breath, Father,' Will said. 'No higher power will save you, and none on earth either.' Blood thundered in his temples as he stared into the other man's face. All his repressed fears about Grace, his rage at the suffering heaped on an innocent person, and his frustration that he could not move faster to find her, raged within him.

'You would dare harm a servant of God in His very house?' the priest stammered.

'There is a woman under my protection whose life is at risk. I would dare anything, Father.'

'What about your eternal soul?'

'Oh, believe me, my soul was lost long ago.'

'But God—'

'What do I care for God!' Will snapped, his knife-point dangerously close to the priest's face. 'The things I have seen . . . the pain that has been heaped on the people I know . . . If there was a God, would He allow such things to exist? Religion tears us apart when we should be coming together to fight greater threats.'

'The word of the Lord brings comfort—'

'—and pain and suffering to many who have suffered the whip of the papists, or the persecutions of King Henry's Church. This world will be consumed by the flames of Hell and still you will be arguing over whose Bible is stronger.'

Celino saw something in Will's face that made him even

more terrified. He began to recite another prayer until Will cuffed him forcefully across the face.

'I have questions, Father, and I am not in the mood to be resisted.' Will moved the tip of his knife slowly across Celino's cheek to touch his lower eyelid. The priest's breath caught in his throat. 'If the answers I receive are not to my liking, then I will cut out this eye,' Will continued. 'And if you continue to live out your fantasy of being a martyr, I will remove your other eye. And then I will whittle you down little by little until there is nothing left. We shall see whose will is stronger.'

Celino began to whimper and struggle in the panic that consumed him. Slipping the tip of his knife into the priest's nostril, Will ripped up through the soft flesh. Celino howled as blood flowed across his cassock and on to the altar.

'Pay heed to that pain,' Will whispered into the priest's ear. 'It is nothing compared to what is to come. Are you ready to answer my questions?'

Trembling, the priest nodded.

'Don Alanzo de las Posadas visited you here at the cathedral this very week. What did he want?'

Celino swallowed, his eyes darting between the chapel where Sister Adelita had been killed and the bloodied tip of the English spy's blade.

'Yes, we forced her to ask you about her brother's business. You could have saved her life if you told her what we needed to know,' Will said. 'Her death is on your conscience. Now . . . what did Don Alanzo want?'

Blinking away tears, Celino trembled his reply. 'To find the most knowledgeable man in all Spain on matters of the occult, and ancient mysteries, and the secrets of the past.'

'And you helped him?'

'Yes. There is such a man in Seville, a great philosopher and alchemist, who knows the languages of the Greeks and the Moors and the Arabs, and has a great library of volumes on the occult. His reputation is known only to a few, but I have consulted him on more than one occasion.' The priest's hand dabbed ineffectively at his ruined nose.

*Why would Don Alanzo want to contact such a man so urgently?* Will wondered. The Spanish had all they needed to use the Silver Skull, if not the Shield that provided protection. 'Who is he and where do I find him?' Will pressed the tip of his knife into the top of the man's cheek. A bead of blood appeared.

Trembling uncontrollably, the priest could barely form words. 'He . . . he is of mixed Moorish descent and has taken the name of Abd al Rahman, after the Emir and Caliph of Cordoba, a prince of the Ummayad dynasty during the Moorish occupation of our land. His true name is not known.' Celino tried to swallow, but his throat was too dry. 'He plies his trade in the Barrio de Santa Cruz, the Jewish quarter, on Susona Street, just north of Real Alcazar, the royal palace,' he croaked.

Will removed the knife, and Celino was convulsed by a shudder of relief. 'Very good, Father. Thank you. You live to pray another day.'

At his command, Launceston and Carpenter emerged from the chapel, dragging Sister Adelita. They threw her on to the flags before the altar. Spluttering in shock and disbelief, Celino stumbled down to throw his arms around her.

'They held a hand over my mouth so I would not call out,' she gasped. 'I wanted to, Father. Oh, I did . . .'

Sister Adelita was a good actress.

'You are the Devil himself,' Celino growled at Will, blood bubbling on his lips.

Shrugging, Will returned his knife to its sheath.

'Do you think four Englishmen can attack the heart of Spain with impunity?' the priest continued angrily, courage returning to him. 'We are the most powerful nation in this world and you . . . you are nothing but dogs.'

'My invasion of Spain is built on more solid foundations than your attack upon England,' Will replied, 'and I will not be turned away by prayers or curses or all the swords you can muster.'

Will gave the signal and Launceston and Carpenter manhandled Father Celino back to the vestry. Will and Mayhew accompanied Sister Adelita. As they walked, she kept her eyes ahead and her chin raised as if in defiance, but she secretly felt for Will's hand and gave it a brief squeeze of support. Her hand felt warm in his.

Once Celino and Sister Adelita were together in the room, Will inserted the large iron key into the lock. Looking at the two captives, he said, 'Take heed, Father. No lives have been lost here this day, and you will soon be found. But if you raise the alarm before we leave Cadiz, I will make it my last act on this earth to return here and slay you both.'

As he closed the door, the last thing he saw was the face of Sister Adelita, pale in the growing gloom, and filled with a look of such yearning it took him by surprise. He held her gaze for a moment before closing the door and turning the key.

Leading the others out through the rear door through which they had entered, Will said, 'We must make haste. Celino will be discovered in no time, and he will have the authorities on our heels before the sun has started to set. We must to Seville and out in a flash. Are you ready for the flight, and the fight, of your lives?' He looked at his companions, and they nodded their assent. 'Then let us depart!'

# CHAPTER THIRTY-FOUR

QUEEN ELIZABETH'S INCANDESCENT FURY TERRIFIED THE GREY-ing men gathered around the meeting chamber. 'One man!' the Queen raged in disbelief. 'All our futures are dependent upon one man!'

All eyes looked down. The Queen turned her powdered face from one to the other of her circle of closest advisers, waiting for a response.

Walsingham understood their reluctance. Elizabeth was like a storm at sea, quick to turn from coquettish flirtation to volcanic anger without the slightest warning. But who would tell her that her own indecisiveness had led the country to the desperate straits in which it now found itself?

'Will Swyfte is—' the spymaster began.

'Yes, yes! I know all about Master Swyfte's abilities!' she roared. 'Now where are the bearers of good news?' The whip-crack in Her Majesty's voice kept all heads bowed. 'Sir Francis Walsingham. You still say the armada will sail shortly?'

'That is the information I have, Your Majesty. There are conflicting reports – some say five hundred ships, some fewer, carrying a good eighty thousand men, perhaps less – but ships and men there are, in Lisbon, ready for the off.'

Walsingham saw the blood drain from the faces around him at the numbers he had presented. A fleet so large would surely destroy the English navy.

'Why can you not get good intelligence?' Lord Burghley, the Queen's principal adviser, snapped. Though a master of statecraft, he was a grey man in both appearance and manner. Too weak by far, Walsingham felt.

'Good intelligence costs money,' Walsingham replied sharply. He didn't need to mention that the Treasury was drained after years of the slow-burning war of attrition with Spain. 'How go the peace negotiations?'

'Your sarcasm is unwarranted.'

Lord Howard, a fierce but thoughtful man, commanded the English navy. His eyes flickered briefly towards Walsingham before he spoke. 'When we received reports last month of Santa Cruz's death, Your Majesty made the wise decision not to put our fleet to sea,' he began.

*Liar*, Walsingham thought.

'But now Philip of Spain will have filled Santa Cruz's boots and the armada will have direction again,' Howard went on. 'More urgency is required in the defence of the realm, I feel.'

Walsingham could see his Queen evaluating the potential cost.

'Drake calls for the fleet to be based at Plymouth,' Howard continued. 'From there, it will be better able to guard the full length of the south coast and to prevent any Spanish landing. And he argues most strongly for us to attack the Spanish first. He is a great strategist, as you know, Your Majesty, and he feels this is the best defence.'

After a moment's thought, Elizabeth said, 'Let us wait for more intelligence.' She looked around the chamber, her piercing eyes challenging anyone to voice dissent, however mild. In the silence that followed, her fingers tapped out a rhythm on the arm of her chair.

Walsingham steeled himself, then began cautiously, 'If the Duke of Parma lands his experienced troops upon England's shores, the battle is lost. We have no army save for the garrison at Berwick and the Yeoman of the Guard. Our fighting men are mainly raw and will be crushed by Parma's forces. And those of ours who have been hardened by battle can scarcely be trusted. Many are Catholics, many Irish.'

Elizabeth's anger drained away at his words. She knew the truth. Her gaze flickered to the tapestries on the walls, each one depicting her father – hunting, at the Field of Cloth of Gold, at a feast – and for a moment her defiance faded to reveal the doubts that haunted her.

'We lack weaponry and gunpowder is in short supply,' Walsingham continued, gathering force. 'Our coastal defences are rudimentary, and in some places construction has not even begun. Once the Spanish invasion begins, there is a danger the Catholics within this island will rise up in force. In the north, King James, who lives in mortal fear of the Enemy, will invade from Scotland to gain control of Dee's defences. These are our most desperate times.'

'And you work to rally good Englishmen behind us?' the Queen demanded.

'Of course, Your Majesty. The pamphleteers publish the stories we require – that the Spanish ships are filled with instruments of torture to inflict upon all good people, and pox-ridden doxies to be loosed upon our men and kill them with disease. That Philip has ordered his men to put children to the pike and crush the brains of babies. Others will be branded on the face so they know they have been conquered. Indeed, the

English people will have the fear of God in them if the Spanish land, but that will not be enough.'

'So we must rely upon our warships,' Elizabeth said quietly, 'and they may not be enough either.' She paused, as if gathering her thoughts, before asking, 'And the part the Enemy will play with this Silver Skull?'

A chill fell across the chamber. The silence was only broken by the cooing of the doves outside the window behind the Queen. All eyes turned to the spymaster, waiting for his answer.

'Their plans are still lost in the fog that they draw around them so well.' Walsingham was careful not to allow Elizabeth to contemplate despair; it would not help the cause. Bad enough the Spanish had an overwhelming force, but that they also had a weapon that could unleash plague across the land? That was too crushing to consider. 'Will Swyfte leads three of my best men. They will not shirk from the task ahead of them.'

'And if they are caught?' Burghley enquired. 'They will give Philip the reason he needs to invade.'

*He needs no reason!* Walsingham wanted to shout, but he kept a calm face. 'If William Swyfte is captured, we will deny all knowledge of his mission. He has been driven half mad by grief over the loss of his close friend Grace Seldon, and holds a personal grudge against Spain.'

'You will abandon him?' Burghley said. 'He will be tortured and executed.'

'That is the price we must pay.'

'And if Swyfte does not reclaim the Skull, all is truly lost!' Elizabeth raged. For all his caution, Walsingham could see she understood the true situation. 'He cannot fail. He must not!'

Without another word, the Queen strode from the chamber so her senior advisers could not see her tears of fear. Burghley started to take up the Queen's words, but Walsingham cut him short. 'William Swyfte will do whatever is necessary to retrieve the Skull, even at the cost of his own life,' he said, and quickly left the room before Burghley could question him further. The less the man knew, the less he could bend it to underpin his own feeble prevarication when advising the Queen.

Outside the chamber, Dee waited, his hood pulled up to hide his identity from hostile eyes.

'Any news?' Walsingham asked, as the two men made their way through the palace.

Dee shook his head. 'The Enemy's true plans remain hidden. They move pieces here and there to distract us, but I can find no guiding principle.'

'Except our destruction.'

'Except that.'

'You have heard all the prophecies circulating in Europe?'

'Of course. Things do not look well for any of us.' Dee took a deep breath. Walsingham could see the strain in his features. 'I have cast Elizabeth's horoscope,' the astrologer continued. 'The second eclipse of the moon this year arrives when her ruling sign is in the ascendant, twelve days before her birthday. That is a powerful portent. Momentous events lie ahead, and all that stands is at risk. The Enemy may finally destroy our defences and achieve their goal.'

'Do not tell Her Majesty this.'

'Why, I planned to tell her this moment,' Dee said tartly. 'I cannot wait to have my head on a pole above the gates of London Bridge for such high treason. So we put our faith in Swyfte?'

'We do. Unless you have another plan?'

Dee said nothing.

The wise man left to study his astrological charts and

Walsingham made his way to the palace gardens to dwell on his thoughts. Stepping out on to a path, he noticed Nathaniel and Marlowe deep in conversation on the bench beside the lavender. Walsingham saw the concern etched in the face of Will's young assistant and recognized the cause immediately. He wasn't an emotional man, but the sight brought back a rush of memories and feelings still raw after all the years.

His mother telling him the circumstances of his father's death. 'They haunted him until his heart failed him. They had noticed him, you see.'

His dreams of following his father into the legal profession when he enrolled as a student at Gray's Inn dashed by the thing that sat in the corner of his room and told him cruelly that his mother would be next.

At her graveside nearly thirty years ago, watching the figures hiding among the yews, sensing their jubilation at his mother's final suffering, at his own suffering. *We have long memories, and our punishment reaches down the years, down the generations.*

His mounting sense of injustice, tempered always by the hope that soon the misery would stop. His wedding to Anne. Her funeral just two years later. The coils of the Enemy drawing tighter and tighter around him.

His two stepsons, dying in a conflagration when a barrel of gunpowder blew up in the gatehouse where he had sent them to be safe.

So many deaths, so many tears, and all because of an act committed before he was even born. His father's crime? To help a young boy the Enemy were tormenting.

Over the years, through all the pain, they had driven him to be the man he was. And they would pay the price.

Queen Elizabeth's spymaster shook his head and called to Marlowe. At Walsingham's curt summons, the playwright came over hesitantly. Walsingham would have preferred him to stay out of sight – the man had too many weaknesses, too many cracks for the Enemy to prise open – but more important matters pressed.

'He has been touched by the Enemy?' Walsingham said, nodding towards Nathaniel.

'Yes, but lightly.' Marlowe nodded, pleased that Walsingham did not have stern words for him. 'He still has many doubts, and searches for ways to dismiss what his heart knows to be the truth.'

'Then help him in that task. Do not let him on to the path we walk. He deserves a better life.'

Marlowe was somewhat taken aback by Walsingham's concern. 'I will lead him down a garden path, filled with sunshine and flowers.'

'Good. We must never forget why we fight.' He fixed an eye on Marlowe. 'And now, tell me why you are here.'

'Will has charged us both with keeping watch upon the Lantern Tower. The Enemy have shown how desperately they require the Shield, and he fears they will attempt to steal it.'

'The Lantern Tower has many, many defences – some obvious, others hidden. But still . . . you do good work.'

Marlowe beamed. It was a small act of generosity, but Walsingham was pleased that he had done it; he was allowed little opportunity to be kind these days.

But as he moved away, a shadow fell over him quickly. Every way he turned, he could see the Enemy's hand. No one was wholly trusted, not even those closest to him. He had made so many sacrifices, and it was all at the point of being for naught. On any given day, Will Swyfte was the best man he had, but Walsingham was afraid the Enemy had found Will's weakness – the girl, Grace – and would use it to destroy him.

# CHAPTER THIRTY-FIVE

IN THE GARB OF A LEVANTINE SAILOR, WILL SWYFTE LED HIS three companions away from the crack of rope and the slap of billowing sails at Seville's harbour. De Groot's carriage had dropped them off at the waterside after the two-day journey across the dusty tracks of Andalusia, in the shade of undulating hills awash with olive trees and vines. They quickly merged with the crowd milling along the dockside, merchants haggling over prices, swarthy workers unloading bales and urns, sailors lounging in the shade, drinking and playing cards.

'How long do we have?' Mayhew whispered, furtively looking around to be sure they could not be overheard. He appeared to have regained much of his equilibrium since they had left Cadiz, although his face still showed the stress of surviving in the heart of enemy territory.

'An hour. Perhaps two,' Will replied.

'That does not give us much time,' Carpenter growled.

'Time enough to cut off the Spaniard's ears if he is still here, and to encourage him to tell us the whereabouts of the Silver Skull and the girl,' Launceston mused with apparent relish.

'Any more talk of the removal of body parts and I will start

356

to think you consider it more as entertainment than encouragement,' Will murmured.

Leaving the slow-moving Rio Guadalquivir, where the ships backed up for miles with their produce bought by New World riches, the English spies looked about them as they made their way through the city's streets. Beneath an azure sky, Seville carried its age with great dignity and sophistication. Everywhere they saw gleaming white walls and spicy Moorish domes of orange and brown and gold. Under the swaying palms, people moved at a lazy pace, their faces betraying the heritage of two thousand years of invaders.

It was a city where anything could be found: silver and gold from the Spanish Main, silk and spices from the distant east, rare books and telescopes from Constantinople, secrets from the four corners of the Earth and the answers to age-old mysteries.

They headed east through the sweltering stores and clattering shipyards of El Arenal towards their destination. Beyond the great cathedral dominated by its Moorish bell-tower, they found the solid walls of the Barrio de Santa Cruz. Passing through the arched gates into the warren of white-washed alleys and patios, they saw the houses here had a different flavour, with tiny grilled windows on tall, plain fronts.

In the barrio the streets were quieter, and they could move faster. Following the directions of Father Celino, they skirted the Real Alcazar palace with its lush rows of palms, terraces, fountains and pavilions in search of the home of Abd al Rahman.

Avoiding the guards at the palace gates, they headed north until they found Susona Street, a narrow route between larger thoroughfares with tiny, dark shops like caves, merchandise piled high on awning-shaded tables – gleaming brassware, pots and pans, fruit and spices – and an inn where old men with long white moustaches and snowy beards drank wine and talked quietly about the old days.

Their destination stood out from the other shops and stalls, having a simple painted sign of yellow stars and a crescent moon on a deep blue background. Through the open door Will glimpsed chalices, swords, and other items of dubious use but clear ritual intent. The sweet scent of incense drifted out.

Ordering Launceston to remain outside and keep watch, Will slipped inside with the others. Carpenter and Mayhew remained near the door while Will pushed his way into the gloomy interior through a series of heavy curtains. The only light came from occasional candles. As he moved, he noticed an extraordinary array of objects – balls of crystal, scrying mirrors, a human skull, obsidian-handled knives, jewels, wall coverings marked with arcane symbols and leather-bound books so big they looked impossible to lift. Shadows flickered in the candlelight so that the jumble of treasures appeared to move of their own accord. A gentle draught shifted hanging columns of colourful beads and stirred wind chimes. Will thought the whole was arranged in order to stimulate the senses and distract the mind.

Then suddenly he caught an unmistakable whiff of sweat beneath the incense. Whirling, he saw a pair of white eyes glowing in the corner next to the curtains through which he had entered; he had passed within a foot of the watcher without even knowing he was there.

'You are Abd al Rahman?' he asked in Spanish.

A North African man stepped into the candlelight. His shaven head was covered in swirling tattoos. One tooth was missing and his fingernails were excessively long and filed to mimic a beast's claws.

'I am Abd al Rahman,' he replied in English, noting Will's slight accent and adding with a faint sibilance, 'You search for something in particular?' He was a big man, strong and muscular. One hand rested on a curved knife at his belt.

'I hear you are a wise man, and knowledgeable in the ways of the ancients.'

Al Rahman brought his hands together slowly and gave a faint bow, although he showed no pleasure. 'You honour me.'

'I am surprised the Christian leaders of Seville allow a practitioner of the Devil's arts in their midst.'

'They drive out only those who are not useful to them.'

'You help them?'

'I help all, for the right fee,' the alchemist replied, his smile flashing white.

'Then you may come to my aid, for I am a weary traveller in search of information. And I can provide the gold you require.'

Al Rahman indicated a table where Will should place his payment, but his manner suggested he knew Will had no gold.

Will shrugged. 'Perhaps I can offer another inducement.'

Smiling faintly, al Rahman partially drew the knife at his belt.

With a weary shake of his head, Will said, 'One day things will go as smoothly as I imagine they might before I open my mouth.' He snapped his fingers.

Carpenter and Mayhew burst through the curtains. Each caught an arm, and with his free hand Carpenter brought his knife to al Rahman's throat.

Will leaned back against a table and folded his arms. 'Sadly, we are desperate men. Who knows to what depths we will stoop?'

'Do not think to threaten me,' al Rahman replied. 'I make a dangerous enemy.'

'Then we are evenly matched. I seek a Spanish nobleman – Don Alanzo de las Posadas. You know him?'

His eyes heavy-lidded, his features impassive, al Rahman shook his head.

'He has not been here?'

Again al Rahman shook his head.

'My assistant Nathaniel always says I am too trusting, but in this instance I believe you are not wholly conversant with the truth. Don Alanzo left Cadiz in search of you several days ago. It is inconceivable that he has not yet called at these premises.'

Al Rahman's eyes darted from side to side. Before Will could alert the others, the alchemist tore himself free, plucked a handful of powder from a pouch at his belt and threw it into the air. As the white powder swirled into Carpenter's and Mayhew's faces, they couldn't help but inhale, and a second later they were writhing in pain and starting to vomit uncontrollably.

Will pressed the cloth from his headdress across his mouth and nose, but he'd already inhaled some of the powder. His vision swam and his gorge rose. Through watering eyes, he saw al Rahman lunge with his knife, and threw himself to one side, upending a table piled high with bones and crystals. They clattered noisily across the floor and brought more artefacts crashing down. Will tried to reach his hidden knife, but al Rahman wielded his wicked curved blade in a blur of slashes back and forth, drawing closer to Will with each arc.

Glass exploded at the back of al Rahman's head with a loud crash and he pitched forward across Will. Launceston stood over them with a broken bottle.

'Quickly,' the ghost-faced Earl urged. 'A carriage approaches. I believe it must be Don Alanzo.'

'Go,' Will gasped, pushing the unconscious alchemist off him. 'Take the others.'

Launceston looked disdainfully at the still-retching Carpenter and Mayhew. 'You?'

Casting about him, Will replied, 'I will find somewhere to hide so I can observe events. I will meet you later at the arranged place. And if I do not join you, you know what to do next.'

Launceston cast him a brief look of understanding before fleeing the room, followed by Carpenter and Mayhew. Will stumbled to the back of the shop, where a purple hanging covered a door to a flight of stone steps. Behind him, al Rahman stirred. Will staggered up the steps and found himself in a large room that took up the entire storey of the house, with brick pillars supporting the ceiling where internal walls had been removed. Stars and crescents, and writing in a language Will didn't recognize, were painted on to the floor inside a large circle, and all across the walls, which were the dark blue of the night sky. Incongruously, in one corner stood a massive, three-faced, hinged mirror with a gilt-covered iron frame.

Trusting that the others had made good their escape, Will silently slipped back down the steps and listened at the hanging. Peering through the gap, he saw Don Alanzo enter, accompanied by a man in a thick cloak and hood, his face in darkness. The Silver Skull, Will suspected.

Don Alanzo helped al Rahman to his feet. 'I saw men running from this place.'

'Englishmen. They were looking for you.' Shaking his head, al Rahman recovered quickly. 'I told them nothing.'

'They are gone now. I will alert my men and they will track

361

the spies down, but the other matter is more pressing. Have you all you need?'

'I have both items. But I warn you: the red dust is in short supply. It comes from the high land near my home, brought by ship today. If we fail, there will be no other opportunity.'

'Then we do not fail!' Don Alanzo said vehemently. 'Make sure you succeed, or as God is my witness . . .' He caught himself. Will was curious to witness his edgy, darker mood; even in the danger of the bear pit, the Spaniard had retained his composure. 'When do we begin?'

'This business can only be conducted under cover of the night.'

'Thank God, there will finally be an end to it.' The Spaniard crossed himself. The note of desperation in his voice was palpable. He turned to the cloaked and hooded figure and said in a more measured tone, 'Do you hear – an end to it?'

The dark cave of the cowl was turned to Don Alanzo, but the Silver Skull's posture gave no sign that he had heard, or even cared. Will thought of him, first a prisoner inside his mask, then a prisoner in the Tower, and now a prisoner of the Spanish. He wondered if the Skull could bring himself to care about anything any more.

They were interrupted by one of Don Alanzo's men: word had arrived from Cadiz that an English spy was en route to see al Rahman, as late as Will had hoped. The Spaniard sent an order to mount a guard at both ends of Susona Street until his business was done, and that a messenger should be sent to the Real Alcazar – a city-wide search must be mounted for the English spies.

Once the man had departed, al Rahman intoned, 'The preparations will take some time and you must both be involved.'

'Upstairs?' Don Alanzo asked.

Al Rahman nodded. 'The space has been prepared.'

Will turned and quietly mounted the steps, then squeezed behind the giant mirror. He had no time to wonder if it was the wrong decision; there was no way out.

On the dusty floor, he stilled his breathing and tried to get comfortable as he listened to al Rahman and Don Alanzo beginning their preparations for whatever it was they were planning. There was the sound of scraping across the floor as objects were dragged into position. Flints were struck, and candles lit. The smell of tallow smoke and sickly-sweet incense reached his nostrils. A brazier ignited, bitterly sulphurous, and he heard the loud exhalation of bellows.

It seemed Don Alanzo and al Rahman barely spoke, and when they did it was only to proffer or request instructions. Will was sure there was no love lost between them; a relationship based on need and gold.

In his constricted hiding space, cut off from the world, the background noise became a hypnotic susurration, lulling Will into a state where his thoughts roamed free. Time passed without his knowing it, interrupted only by new aromas, subtly different sounds, the murmur of voices rising and falling. From his restricted vantage point, he watched the shadows grow and the gloom fold around him as the evening drew in.

From the open window, the sounds of the streets, the shouts of workers, the dense conversations passing beneath, the bang and rattle from the shipyards, the back-and-forth crackle of merchant and buyer, slowly died away. For a short while all was still. Then came the music. Drifting from different windows, the sound of fiddle and voice and harpsichord, rhythmic songs from Africa and the Orient, and the noise rising from the inns, voices raised in celebration of another hard day passed, in work and in love. It felt hot and muggy; the cooling breeze was long gone. To Will, it felt as if a storm was coming.

Back in the room, the mood had grown tense. Don Alanzo and al Rahman's exchanges were clipped. Objects clattered with barely restrained vehemence.

Just as Will's thoughts were turning to Grace, a low chant broke out from al Rahman. Although Will didn't recognize the language, there was something in the cadence or the rhythm of the words that made him uneasy.

In the distance, thunder rumbled.

The alchemist's voice grew louder. He held on to certain syllables in unnatural ways, punctuating each volley of noise with a click at the back of his throat. Will felt the pressure of ancient days begin to build in the room. He was sick of it all – the Unseelie Court, the things al Rahman practised, the world they represented. The comfort and stability of his childhood seemed like a solitary light on a distant horizon.

*What are they planning?* 'Thank God, there will finally be an end to it,' Don Alanzo said. *An end to what?*

Al Rahman's chant reached a climax. In its odd intonation, it sounded to Will like a supplication; or, perhaps, a summoning. Confident he would not be seen in the dark, he endeavoured to get closer by squeezing in between the mirror and the wall, but all he could see were the shadows of three people swaying in the smoke and candlelight.

One of the shadows ducked down and appeared to plunge a hand into a container on the floor, emerging with a writhing shape. The pathetic mewling of a cat echoed around the room. A shadow-knife darted, a gush of liquid cascaded before the cries stopped. The shadow of al Rahman tossed the now still form away. The body hit the wall and came to rest on the floor, glassy dead eyes staring directly at Will.

'Can this work?' he heard Don Alanzo whisper.

Al Rahman did not reply at first. Then he hissed, 'You must be prepared for what is to come, both of you. These matters are not easy for the untutored.'

'I am ready.' Don Alanzo attempted to deliver the words forcefully, but there was a waver which revealed his true feelings.

The shadow-al Rahman picked up what seemed like a small pot and held it on the palm of his hand.

'The red dust?' Don Alanzo asked, his words tinged with awe.

'So rare,' al Rahman replied. 'You have paid a great deal for it.'

'It will be worth it.'

'Again I stress, the ritual must be completed or there will not be another opportunity. The Silver Skull will remain fastened to his head for all time.'

Will flinched, suddenly aware: Don Alanzo sought to remove the awful mask from the man who wore it. What purpose would that serve?

The thunder rolled quickly towards Seville. The wind blew heavily now, rattling the window shutters. Lightning flashed. Will couldn't shake off the uneasy feeling that the approaching storm was in some vile way connected to al Rahman's ritual.

'The time approaches,' al Rahman said. 'And I ask you one more time: are you ready? Once this act is done, there is no going back.'

Don Alanzo hesitated. 'There is no other way?'

'This is the only way to break what binds the mask.'

Silence for a long moment, and then Will saw the shadow-Don Alanzo give a slow nod.

The storm boomed overhead. Rain lashed against the building in gusts, and lightning lit up the city.

Al Rahman began chanting again, his voice ringing off the walls as he attempted to be heard above the thunder. The words set Will's teeth on edge and made the pit of his stomach turn, he knew not why. The mirror rattled in the blustering wind tearing through the window, so much so that Will was momentarily worried that it would tip over.

'Now!' al Rahman cried. 'Raise him now!'

The candles began to wink out one by one in a rhythmic manner that could not be natural. The shadows on the wall became distorted, but Will made out a shape being lifted by Don Alanzo, larger than the cat but one he could easily hold in two hands.

*Raise him now.*

Will grew cold. A faint, dreamy whimper rolled out in a lull between the thunderclaps and the gusting wind, setting the hairs on the back of his neck on end.

If he intervened now Will knew he risked losing the Skull, the chance of finding the path to Grace, and his own life, but his indecision lasted only a fleeting moment. As another whimper echoed, he pushed his way out from behind the mirror and drew his rapier.

The final candle sputtered and went out.

The darkness was blasted away by a flash of lightning. Its brief glare captured a horrific tableau: al Rahman, hands held high, holding a knife with a curved blade, the cat's blood glistening on his face and bare chest; Don Alanzo, his face frozen in an expression of self-loathing and despair, the bundle in his arms his entry to Hell; and the Silver Skull, cowl thrown back, head aglow, standing rigid behind them. All eyes were fixed on Will.

The dark swept back into the room.

Al Rahman barked an angry warning, and Don Alanzo shouted something behind it that Will couldn't understand. He moved quickly from where he'd been standing before they could attack.

A flare of red light painted the room in a hellish glow. Al Rahman had thrown his mysterious red dust on to the brazier; Will wrinkled his nose at the foul odour, like the smell of burning flesh that permeated the torture chambers beneath the Tower.

'Stay back!' Don Alanzo raged at him, his sword drawn. The bundle was now held by al Rahman. 'Disrupt the ritual and I will kill you!' the Spaniard warned, anguish playing out on his features.

'Harsh words for an old friend,' Will replied and moved again.

The flare from the hissing brazier began to die down. As he circled, Will glimpsed something in the mirror in the dying light that chilled him to the core: the glass did not reflect the scene within the room, but appeared to show another place, wherein stood a woman, beautiful and terrible, and it was at him that she looked. He dismissed it as a hallucination, but when the dark had descended he could still feel the weight of her burning gaze upon him.

Don Alanzo kept pace with Will, watching for an opening. Al Rahman continued to chant loudly. An odd pressure began to build in the room. One shutter tore free and crashed back and forth in the ferocious wind.

Another flash of lightning.

The white glare caught al Rahman poised with his knife held high once more, the soft, small bundle crooked in his other arm. Sword raised, Don Alanzo stood between the tattooed Moor and Will. Tears were now streaming down his face. Will could not reach al Rahman to prevent him from bringing the knife down, but, suspecting what was hidden in the bundle, he knew he could not allow the blade to fall. Making an instant calculation, he darted to the right of Don Alanzo as the dark returned, and was ready when the lightning flashed again. Before al Rahman completed his sacrifice, Will drove his sword towards the Silver Skull.

'No!' Don Alanzo cried.

Will thrust straight into the Silver Skull's heart. As the figure crumpled to its knees, Will had the odd impression that he had opened his arms wider, as if to embrace Will's blade; as if he wanted to die. Blood ran from beneath the mask as Will withdrew his sword and the Skull pitched forward, dead.

Now there was no need for al Rahman to plunge his blade into that small bundle in his arms.

A terrible, broken expression burned into Don Alanzo's features. 'Father!' The Spaniard's devastated cry tore out of him.

One word, and Will understood everything. Sister Adelita had told him their father had disappeared when they were young. Away in the New World, he must have stumbled upon the Silver Skull and chosen to wear it, or had it thrust upon him, thus sealing his fate. Then he had been spirited away to England and locked in the Tower. Don Alanzo must have negotiated this one chance to free his father from the mask before the Skull was used in the invasion, knowing it could be worn by another victim.

Will knew how the mysterious disappearance of a loved one could turn a life on its axis and keep it locked in a frozen world of not-knowing and wishing. And then Don Alanzo had been given hope, as had Will too, only to see it snatched away; only to see everything he had hoped for since childhood destroyed. By Will.

Seeing the sheer, bloody hatred in Don Alanzo's face, Will recognized he had made the deadliest of enemies, one driven by a passion that went beyond the cold mistrust of national rivals. Don Alanzo would never rest until he had avenged his father's death.

His face contorted in an inhuman fury, the Spaniard threw himself at Will, slashing with his sword in such an uncontrolled manner that it was easy to sidestep the attack. 'Truly, I am sorry,' Will said plainly, before bringing the hilt of his sword sharply into Don Alanzo's temple. The man fell, unconscious.

Sheathing his blade, al Rahman threw down his burden and darted from the room, making good his escape. Will picked up the bundle and, peeling back the swaddling cloth, revealed a baby boy, eyes wide but drugged and dreamy. Stolen, Will guessed, from the ghetto that morning.

'You will be back with your mother and father soon, little one,' he whispered. He laid the child gently on the floor and turned to the Silver Skull. He knew the alarm would soon be raised, and he had little hope of making an escape with the body on his back.

After a futile attempt to prise the mask free, he accepted his only course of action. Plucking up al Rahman's curved knife, he braced himself and began to sever the head from the corpse. The blade was razor sharp and it proved disturbingly easy. Before he had embarked on his life as one of Walsingham's band of spies, the act would have sickened him. Now he was only numb. Blood stained his hands red as he sawed through sinew and ligament, hacking when he met resistance at the top of the spine. With a wrench and a final slash, the head came free.

Don Alanzo's father had given no sign of being a true Enemy – indeed his last act had suggested he had been as much a victim of the war as anyone – and Will wished he could treat his remains with more respect, but he told himself he had no choice.

Once the grisly task was complete, he put the masked head to one side and went to the still-unconscious Don Alanzo. Stumbling under his weight, Will carried the Spaniard down to the front of the Moor's premises, where he would easily be found. Then, ripping down the purple hanging and bundling it under his arm as he went, he returned to the upstairs room. Once he'd reclaimed the swaddled child and wrapped the head in a sack, he dropped a hot coal from the brazier on to the heap of cloth he had left in the centre of the floor. It would be easy to extinguish the fire before it spread to the neighbouring houses. As the smoke rose, he tucked the child into the crook of one arm, grasped the dripping sack in his other hand, and slipped out into the raging storm.

In a doorway opposite, Will waited until the smoke began to billow out of the windows and then shouted the alarm. It was soon taken up from the other houses along the street. Pressing himself back into the shadows, he watched Spanish soldiers run up to the Moor's house and find the unconscious Don Alanzo. Unseen, he melted away into the gathering crowd while the men dragged Don Alanzo free and attempted to put out the blaze.

But as Will moved through the deserted, rain-lashed streets, he began to notice grey shapes flitting behind him, caught from time to time in the brilliant glare of lightning. They appeared amorphous, insubstantial, but he knew what they were, just as he now knew for certain what he had glimpsed in the mirror in al Rahman's house.

Will knew too that nothing good lay ahead, and he feared for the safety of the child in his care. His instinct was to flee the deserted streets for a busy, bustling part of the city where he could lose himself in the crowds and the Unseelie Court would be less effective. But if they caught him before he reached his destination, they would show no mercy for an innocent child. Frustration turned quickly to anger.

At a crossroads, lightning revealed more grey figures racing from both sides. They were herding him away from the city's heart and towards the lonely streets behind the Real Alcazar. Wet and exhausted, he ran on, driven by his determination to take the child to safety and to bring Grace back alive.

Blinking away the rain, Will saw the best hope for his charge silhouetted against the roiling black clouds. 'Not much farther, little one, and you will be warm and dry,' he whispered. He allowed his defiance to suppress the certain knowledge that in saving the child he would surely leave himself trapped.

He was ready.

A reassuring light glimmered through the stained glass windows of Seville Cathedral. At the main entrance, he shouldered open the great oak doors, and briefly placed his burdens down before drawing the iron bolts behind him. The nave was awash with a golden glow from row upon row of candles. Away from the booming storm, the cathedral felt safe and secure. Will knew it was a lie.

As he raced past the lavishly carved wooden screens around the choir, his footsteps echoed up to the vaulted roof high overhead. At the cascade of gold over the high altar, the Retablo Mayor, he stopped and called for help. The figures on the gilded relief panels around the stately figure of the cathedral's patron saint, Santa Maria de la Sede, appeared to mock him with their silence.

'Sanctuary!' he called out.

From the passage to the right of the altar came a priest, balding, bushy grey beard, eyes dark pools. Hesitating, he took in Will's appearance and the sack in his hand, leaking blood.

'Here, Father. Please take this boy – he was stolen from his parents.' Will thrust the now wriggling bundle towards the priest.

And then, from the far end of the church, came the low, grating sound of a bolt being drawn back. No one was near – it moved of its own accord.

The priest crossed himself and muttered, '*En el nombre de Dios.*'

'Take him!' Will shouted.

The priest grabbed the bundle and examined the child's face with a nod. 'You want sanctuary?'

'For the child – nothing can be done to save me.'

The priest shook his head forcefully. 'My son, the Church will protect you.'

The second bolt on the great door began to grind slowly back. Will glanced behind him. 'No, I am done. Protect the child and return him to his parents in the morning.'

Quickly, he looked round for a place to make his stand. The nave was too open. The priest realized what he was doing.

'I will hold them off while you make good your escape,' he said.

'No!' Will said firmly. 'The child is your only responsibility now. Go. I will lead them a merry chase before I arrive at my destination.'

The great oak doors blew open with a resounding crash.

Rain gusted up the nave. In the dark mouth, Will could see no movement, but he knew they could see him.

'Go!' he shouted to the priest before running towards the north door. He recognized the irony of his predicament after he had so abused the priest on the altar at Cadiz, and then he was out in the storm again, and aware of the overpowering aroma of orange blossom. In the white glare of lightning, he saw rows of orange trees in a large, rectangular orchard with a fountain where worshippers would wash their hands and feet before praying in the cathedral.

Will hoped the trees might hide his progress, but he'd barely crossed the edge of the square when another lightning flash revealed movement along the roofs of the low buildings that surrounded the orchard. Members of the Unseelie Court loped along the orange tiles, impervious to the violent wind and driving rain, moving in on him from all directions. Their appearance was as changeable as the weather, sometimes beautiful when they were luring unwary passers-by, sometimes mundane when they wished to blend in with the human throng. Now they were cadaverous, eyes lost to shadow, skin grey, hair lank, as if they had just clawed their way out of the grave.

Behind him, Will heard the door crash open.

He turned east and dashed to the cloister, his ultimate destination now within reach. Over his head, the tiles rattled and shattered, fragments raining down in his wake. Through the orchard, the grey ghosts moved relentlessly towards him.

Crashing back into the cathedral, Will hurried along the short corridor to the foot of the bell-tower. Slamming the bolts shut behind him, he bounded up the steps of the broad stairway.

As he spiralled breathlessly upwards, it felt to Will as if he was rising into the very eye of the storm. The wind and rain blasted through the unglazed windows, and the lightning flashes lit up the whole of Seville and the Andalusian countryside beyond. As the thunder boomed again, he barely heard the door at the foot of the bell-tower crash open.

*No way back.*

The minaret accounted for the first two thirds of the tower and then the stairs narrowed, leading up to the belfry, added by the Christian king only twenty years before to replace the Moorish designs that had originally topped the building. Again locking the door behind him, Will ran up the final set of steps.

At the very summit, he gripped the walls for support as the wind tore through the large arched windows so forcefully that it threatened to topple him on to the ground far below.

Drawing his sword, he prepared to fight to the last. It was a good, defendable position. The Enemy could only approach up the stairs from the belfry door, and he was determined to take as many with him as he could.

The gale whipped his hair into his face, and his cloak lashed around him. He was sodden, weary and cold, but he gripped his rapier with grim determination. Heart pounding, he waited.

But as he stood poised, he became aware of sounds rising up the outside of the bell-tower in the brief lulls when the thunder rolled away and the wind gusted in a different direction. Cautiously, he hung out of a window.

As his eyes adjusted to the world of white flashes and all-consuming dark, he saw grey figures steadily climbing up the outside of the bell-tower, like insects, clinging on to the carvings and ridges as they made their progress regardless of the storm. A deeper chill ran into Will's heart. Quickly, he checked all four windows and saw the same from each one. A disorienting buzz echoed through his head and drops of blood began to fall from his nose to the wet flags.

The door to the belfry flew open.

# CHAPTER THIRTY-SIX

*The cries of the hunting party echoed through the frozen forest, accompanied by the occasional crack of an arquebus that sent the birds shrieking through the black trees.*

*'They waste their shot and powder when they cannot see us,' Carpenter gasped, his breath clouding in the cold. Shivering uncontrollably, he pulled his thick woollen cloak around him, but could find no warmth.*

*'If fortune is with them, they can still hit us,' Will replied. In the pack across his back he carried the object Dee had coveted for so long, the thing that could only add to England's mounting power.*

*They struggled through the calf-deep snow in the face of the bitter wind, scrambling over fallen branches and plunging into hidden hollows where the brambles concealed beneath the white blanket tore through their clothes and skin and left spots of red in their wake. The wind was laced with snow and the grey clouds banking up overhead suggested another blizzard like the one that had disrupted their escape from Moscow.*

*'If we do not find our man soon we will freeze to death out here,' Carpenter said. He no longer attempted to hide his fear. The bravado he had exhibited shortly after Walsingham had brought him into the fold had dissipated in the heat of his very first undertaking. What he*

had seen in the snow-covered courtyards of the Kremlin fortress had changed his life for ever. There would be no peace for him again. It was a feeling Will knew only too well, and he regretted its being inflicted upon Carpenter, however inevitable.

'We must first lose our pursuers.' Will glanced back, but there was no sign of the Tsar's men in the half-light. 'We cannot lead them directly to our man or all will be lost.'

Then, from somewhere behind them, a ferocious roar rolled out through the forest.

The blood drained from Carpenter's face and he gripped Will's arm. 'What was that? A bear?'

'Nothing to concern us.' Will tried to urge his companion on, but Carpenter was rooted to the spot.

'It was with the Tsar's men. With them!'

'The Enemy has many weapons at its disposal, and employs many beasts to do its work. You know that,' Will said, trying to calm him. With concern, he watched the spiralling panic in Carpenter's eyes. The frost rimed his beard and eyebrows. From the outset, he had been afraid Carpenter had been sent on such an important mission too early, but as ever they were short of good men.

'Is that what killed Jack and Scarcliffe and Gedding?' The scene of slaughter in Kitai-gorod, the walled merchant town beside the fortress, still lay heavily on both of them. It had taken all Will's abilities to talk Carpenter through his devastation at the time.

Will took Carpenter's shoulders. The barks and howls of the hunting party's dogs were drawing closer. 'John, our lives mean nothing here. We do this not for personal reward, or acclaim, or the Queen's favour. We do this for our country, for the people of England.'

Carpenter stared at him, remembering only the blood-soaked bodies.

'John.' Will shook him, too hard. 'Though we both give up our lives here, we must see our burden delivered to London and to Dee.'

The safety of our country depends on us. We do not matter. Our lives are not important. Once you accept that fact, you are free. Do you understand?'

The other man nodded slowly, but Will was not sure he was convinced.

'If one of us falls, the other must make sure the package reaches our man so he can deliver it to the ship. That is the only thing that should concern us. You know the rules of our business: do not risk all we seek to achieve for the sake of one man. We are already dead. Repeat that.'

'We are already dead,' Carpenter said flatly. He blinked away a freezing tear.

Another roar, so loud it felt as if whatever vile creature had made the noise was but a few paces away. The hairs sprang erect on the back of Will's neck.

The noise jolted Carpenter out of his stupor and together the two English spies drove on into the forest, increasingly thankful for the whiteness of the snow as the light began to fade. Branches tore at their faces and objects hidden underfoot threatened to trip them, but they continued as fast as they could.

Another roar, close behind. The sounds of the hunting party had faded away, as if they had decided to leave the pursuit to a more effective hunter.

'If it has our scent, we will never lose it,' Carpenter gasped.

'There is a storm coming and that may provide cover for us and our tracks,' Will replied.

For what seemed like an eternity, they scrambled through the bitter Russian winter. They could no longer feel their feet. The heat drained from their limbs until they felt leaden and only the threat of what lay behind drove them on.

Finally, as night descended among the branches, a light appeared ahead: a lantern, gently swinging to draw them in.

'There!' Carpenter cried, exultation in his voice.

Will was distracted by a fleeting movement in the trees to his left. Afraid their pursuer had pulled ahead and was circling round them, he came to a halt and peered into the gloom. 'We may need to take a different path,' he said.

'What is it?'

'Whatever was at our backs could be lying in wait to attack us unawares.' He searched the trees, listening intently, but the snow muffled all sound. Another movement, closer this time, shimmered on the edge of his vision, a figure that was nowhere near as large as the roars of their pursuer had suggested.

'You see it?' Carpenter hissed.

And then Will did, and the cold that crushed the forest in its grip swept into every part of his being. Standing among the trees, almost swallowed by the encroaching dark, was a woman, her forget-me-not-blue dress whirling around her in the wind.

Jenny.

His Jenny.

The cold did not appear to touch her. Her arms and head were bare, her skin so pale. She looked exactly as she had done the last time he saw her, stepping through the cornfield to meet him, her eyes like the sun, her smile filled with love. Was she a ghost? A dream caused by the cold? Had she come to haunt him at the moment of his own death, as she had haunted him ever since she disappeared?

His heart soared, and suddenly he was running towards her, oblivious of everything else, dimly aware of Carpenter calling his name anxiously.

Then came the roaring, so loud it felt as if he was in the middle of a tempest. Whirling, Will saw a huge dark shape erupt from the trees and drive into Carpenter with such force that he was thrown through the air against a tree. The beast descended on him in a storm of fangs and rending claws. Will was fixed to the spot in the shock and horror of the moment as it ripped through the clothes on Carpenter's back. A mist of blood sprayed into the air. Carpenter's screams were painful to hear. Somehow he'd scrambled free and managed to draw his knife, but then the beast fell on him again.

It looked like a bear, but somehow more than a bear.

Will ran towards the bloody scene and came to a slow halt. Remembering Walsingham's rules, he knew there was nothing he could do to save Carpenter.

Spinning round, he searched the trees for Jenny, but only snow and wind danced where she had stood. He ran, calling her name, but there was no response, nothing to show she had ever been there.

Had she saved him from the beast's attack?

The ache in his heart was almost unbearable, but he pushed it down deep inside him, as he always had, and ran for the light in the distance, trying not to think about Carpenter and the awful sounds rising behind him.

Moments later, he was packed under heavy furs in the back of a sleigh that hurtled down a steep track through the trees. Whip-cracks echoed around him, and a voice promising that he would not rest until Will was at Archangel and safely on a ship chartered by the Muscovy Company. England beckoned.

Lulled by the motion, on the edge of sleep, despair came and went. Wherever Carpenter might now be, he hoped the man's ghost would forgive him, but the success of their task was paramount.

Obliquely, he recalled Walsingham telling him, 'There is no room for any emotions.' At the time he had believed he understood.

And he thought of Jenny, and however much he told himself it was a vision, he was sure something substantial was there, a hint, a hope, although he couldn't understand the whys of it.

Jenny was alive, he was sure. And he would not rest until he had discovered the truth.

# CHAPTER THIRTY-SEVEN

WILL CAME ROUND, NOT KNOWING HOW LONG HE HAD BEEN unconscious. Sensations flooded in: the fragrance of pine and the sweet scent of Spanish broom. Heat leavened by the occasional breeze of chill air. Dust on the back of his throat, and the rough rocking of a carriage. His wrists were manacled behind his back and his feet were shackled, and his body ached from being too long in one position. Underneath that was the dull throb of recent blows and new bruises.

Fragmentary memories of his stand at the top of the bell-tower in Seville returned, the lashing rain, unnatural figures climbing through the arched windows while others came up the steps from the belfry door, too many for him. A flash of light like the sun caught in a mirror, a sudden pain at the base of his skull and then nothing.

As he had expected, they hadn't hurt him too badly. They were saving him for the horrors to come, as Cavillex had promised.

He wasn't alone. A guard sat on the opposite seat next to the other door, casting glowering glances towards Will. Black-haired and bearded, the guard wore a brimmed hat, a red and gold cloak, and stuffed and slashed breeches tied above the knee. He was armed with a rapier.

Scanning the interior of the coach, Will saw no sign of the Skull. He wondered where it was now.

Through the window, he could see a mountain peak, the source of the chill air occasionally blowing through the carriage. The sky was a brilliant blue, and there was no sign of the storm that had swept Seville. The landscape around the road was dry and dusty, and beyond that it drifted into a bleak, depressing vista of rock piles and detritus from what Will assumed were old mine-workings scattered far and wide. Farther away still, a pine forest rose up the windswept slopes to the foot of the mountain.

'Why, if I did not know better I would say that was Mount Abantos,' Will said. The guard's eyes flickered towards him.

Eventually, the carriage slowed. Shimmering in the hot sun, a mountainous structure of grey–pink granite towered over the desolate landscape. Will was caught by the imposing sight that somehow was both inspiring and threatening.

'El Escorial,' he whispered to himself. 'I hear the King is more a monk than a man of the world,' he added aloud. 'He likes his prayers where others enjoy their tupping, and they bring him to a similar climax.'

Flinching, the guard went for his dagger until he realized the English spy was trying to goad him. He grunted and looked out of the other window.

Chafed by the shackles, his muscles burning, Will watched the village of San Lorenzo de El Escorial pass by in the shadow of Philip's gleaming monument, twenty-one years in the building and the centre of the Spanish empire. As they drew nearer, he craned his neck to admire the grand achievement of the construction. Nine towers reached for the sky above the vertiginous, plain walls that made it appear an unassailable cliff-face. Its appearance was as austere as the King was rumoured to be, yet in the proliferation of fountains and rows of exquisite statues, its glorious basilica and spires, and its sheer size, the palace appeared as much an illustration of the power of Philip and Spain as it did a monument to the glory of God.

As the carriage rolled up the sweeping driveway, several guards in helmets and breastplates and wielding halberds ran out to meet it. The door was thrown open and rough hands dragged Will out. Blinking in the brilliant Spanish sun, he found he couldn't stand from the cramps in his legs and fell to the stones. A guard grabbed each arm and dragged him into the forbidding palace's interior.

Philip's residence was laid out as a huge quadrangle with a series of intersecting corridors, courtyards and chambers. Will was hauled along at speed, cuffed each time he fell, and cuffed again when he gave a sardonic response. Finally, he was thrown into a large hall lined with dark portraits of severe faces and accusing eyes.

At the far end of the chamber, dressed in black, Don Alanzo knelt in prayer. The guards threw Will to the floor before him, and surrounded him with halberds levelled.

'You must think highly of me to believe so many fine men are necessary to keep me contained,' Will said.

'You are no threat,' Don Alanzo replied. 'You never were.'

Will's gaze was drawn to the corner of the hot room where a pool of icy darkness appeared to draw the light from the candles surrounding it. There, a plain black coffin rested on a trestle near the window. A smaller black box stood on top. A shadow fell over Will as he recalled the blood, and the sawing, and the final wrench that tore the head free.

'I am truly sorry for your father's death,' he said.

'Shut up!' Don Alanzo was suddenly raging. 'You are a devil! You defiled his body!' He struck Will across the face with the back of his hand. Will tasted blood.

Turning away so the guards would not see his emotion, Don Alanzo rested one hand upon the coffin. 'He was a great man, and an honourable one. He gave his life for Spain. That will not be forgotten. An English city will be renamed after him once we crush your country underfoot.'

Guilt consumed Will at the thought of Sister Adelita risking her life to aid him. And now he had paid her back by slaughtering her father. And he felt guilt too at the man's death, even though he had slain him to save the child. Will had killed many men in the course of the Queen's business, but all the deaths had been just. Not this one. Though a Spaniard, Don Alanzo's father was innocent of any crime against England.

'He was an honourable man,' Will agreed. 'He cannot have known of the destructive power of the infernal Silver Skull when he first affixed it to his head.'

'You know nothing of the circumstances,' Don Alanzo spat.

'And for all our bitter disputes, I know too you are an honourable man,' Will continued. 'Would you see such terrible disease inflicted on my countrymen? Is victory for Spain worth the deaths of innocents on a grand scale? Where is your God in all of this?'

'Enough,' Don Alanzo said in a low voice trembling with passion.

But Will wasn't to be silenced. 'Spain is our enemy, but never would I have thought your King would sanction such devastation. Victory at any cost? Where is just rule in that? It was not too long ago that my people fell under Philip's aegis during his marriage to Queen Mary—'

'I said enough!' Don Alanzo whirled, spittle flying. Will could see that those very doubts tormented the Spaniard. 'I would see all of your countrymen slaughtered for what *you* have done,' he hissed.

Shifting his weight to ease the ache from his bonds, Will hoped a calm voice could persuade Don Alanzo of the greater threat of the Unseelie Court. 'I do not believe it. I see the hand of others in this impending atrocity. The whispers in Philip's ears lead him down a dangerous path from which there is no return.'

Don Alanzo steadied himself before uttering in a cold, cruel voice, 'From the outside, El Escorial is a palace, and a monastery, and an impregnable fortress. From the inside, it is a prison from which you can never escape. More secure than your Tower in London, it is the most heavily guarded building in the whole of the empire. Do not harbour thoughts of escape. No one can get in. No one can get out. This will be your home in your final days. You will rot here. Take him away.'

The guards grabbed Will's arms and hauled him to his feet before levelling the points of their halberds an inch from his neck. As he left the room, he glanced back at Don Alanzo, a forlorn figure, head bowed in front of the dark coffin.

Outside, they beat Will until he lost consciousness.

He came round tied to a chair in a vast room, the walls of which were covered in frescoes depicting scenes from Spanish military victories.

'The Hall of Battles.' The voice was like a wind across snow. In the corner of the room, a woman stood, motionless, shoulders slightly hunched like an animal poised, ready to attack. Her hair hung lank around a bloodless face, her eyes were red-rimmed, unblinking. There was something of the grave about her. With excruciating slowness, she began to come towards him.

'You are one of the Unseelie Court,' he said, avoiding her gaze.

Her dark, hungry eyes never left his face. 'My brother told me that is what you call us. *Unholy.*'

As she inched forward, a suffocating dread closed about him, a visceral reaction to something beyond his five senses. With each step, the tension increased until his breath burned in his chest as he waited for her to lunge for him.

'I know you,' she intoned. That simple statement carried with it the weight of something terrifying.

Before Will could consider its implications, his vision swam. When it cleared, her appearance had shifted. It had an unearthly beauty. She was undoubtedly the same person, with that same hungry gaze, but now she radiated a deep, powerful sexuality that affected him despite himself.

She came to a halt before him. *Presenting herself*, he thought. Her posture accentuated every curve of her body, the heave of her breasts, her hard nipples protruding through the thin silk, her hips at an angle, crotch slightly pushed forward. She challenged him to admire what he saw.

Knowing what lay beneath sickened him. As he looked away defiantly, he realized her sexuality was more than just physical. Slowly, she drew his gaze back to her, and however much he fought he could not resist. Sweat beaded his brow, and he shook from the strain of fighting her. She was like a succubus and the heat rose in his groin.

She leaned forward until her luminous face was only a finger's breadth from his. He could smell the perfume of her skin, and her hair, and a muskier scent beneath it. 'You are mine now,' she whispered. Reaching down, she ran the tips of her fingers along his thigh.

'Your brother,' he said, desperately trying to ignore her tantalizing, 'is Cavillex?'

She nodded slowly. 'My name is Malantha.'

He craned his neck, looking around for the guards, but they were alone.

Malantha appeared to sense what he was thinking, for she said, 'I do not need protection.'

'If I were free—'

'Not even then. Cavillex presents a fearsome face to the world, but I am worse. Much worse.'

'I imagine Philip finds your wiles invigorating,' he said.

'Personal weaknesses exist in all humans. You can hide them away, pretend they do not exist or that God and prayer have expunged them, but they remain.'

'Until you work them loose.'

Her gaze held him fast.

'I have many weaknesses,' he continued. 'I must be easy game for one such as you.'

'You pretend to many weaknesses,' she replied. 'But there is only one that truly matters.'

'You see my weaknesses so clearly?' Will said in a dismissive tone.

'All people can see another's weakness if they open their eyes. But most of the time, you choose to ignore, or you pretend, or you lie to yourself. But they are there. What is writ in the heart is clear in the face.'

'You see them as weaknesses. But they can also be strengths, driving us on to achieve great things, to strive, to overcome pain and hardship.' Will's voice grew hard and defiant.

'Believe that if you wish,' she replied. Slowly, she began to circle him. As she disappeared from view, he could still feel her, like a fire burning at his back.

'Is your brother coming to oversee my torture again?' he asked.

'My *brothers* are engaged elsewhere in important affairs that demand their attention. Not just in Edinburgh, but in France, and Venice, and Moscow, and the New World.' Malantha paused directly behind Will. She lowered her icy voice, and it sounded as if she was smiling. 'We have been playing this game for a long time, by the way you measure it, and we move with the slow turn of the seasons, a slight push here, barely noticed, another shove there, unseen, guiding, steering, drawing strands across all your world until everything is in place. And then you will see the true design of the plan we have wrought.'

Will sensed Malantha draw near until he felt her warm breath on the nape of his neck. The hairs prickled erect, and a heat began to burn in his belly. Part of him thought she was going to tear at his exposed flesh with her teeth, like an animal; another, deeper part hoped he would feel the brush of her full lips. She repelled him, yet drew him in. He was sickened by the conflicting feelings.

When the anticipation became almost unbearable, she slowly moved her head round his until her breath caressed his left ear. Will waited for her to whisper cruel words. Instead, her tongue flicked out and licked his lobe, and he recoiled as if he had been burned. The sensation was erotic, but it also felt as if she had been tasting him.

'Cavillex trusts me to ensure that you pay the price for what you did. We have only contempt for your country and we will destroy it piece by piece without emotion. But you have gained our attention. You slew one of us.' She stepped back in front of him. And there, in the blaze of her eyes, Will saw clearly the monster that lurked beneath the seductive, alluring surface. 'This is now a personal matter. *Quid pro quo*. And,' she added, 'by the end, you will wish it was my brother here.'

'True. His own brand of torture already failed.'

'Torture is not a fair word for what I do. There is something of creation about it, it is a skill that makes the heavens sing, a drawing together of subtle themes, of resonances, a slow build of contrasting emotions, desires and agonies, until they fall into a glorious harmony, and then you will be crushed by the artfulness of it.' Her voice lost its honeyed tone and became gravelly. 'Your mind and soul will be destroyed long before your body falls apart.'

'And King Philip sanctions that?'

'Philip will do whatever I tell him.' She laughed, and it was a sound laced with poison. 'His only concern is that the armada succeeds and England falls. Failure could wreak untold damage on the Spanish empire and his own reputation. And if I tell him a dangerous English spy is a threat to his precious Enterprise of England – however ridiculous that might seem – he will do whatever he deems necessary.'

'With a little encouragement from yourself, perhaps, when he is enchanted by the comfort of your thighs.'

Malantha smiled, and Will felt his skin prickle. 'Men are men. It is their nature, and easily manipulated by any woman who knows.'

'But the Spanish king knows nothing of your true plans, of how you will use the Silver Skull to achieve your sly aims.'

'*You* know nothing of our true plans. You think you know, but you have been wrong at every turn. We are too subtle . . . too sly . . . that is why we win. We are the wind that moves the oceans when all your power could not achieve more than a few ripples.'

'My ripples ended the life of the last Silver Skull. You will now be looking for another candidate, I assume?'

She leaned in to him until he was lost in the dark, echoing depths of her eyes. His thoughts squirmed at the contact. 'A small victory, if that was even what it was. Now we will find one we can truly control.' She made a dismissive gesture. 'But that was always our plan.'

'And so you will destroy all of England's people.' It felt as if a weight was lying on Will's chest.

'In part. But if that were all 'twould be a sorry response to your crimes.' She caressed her lower lip with one slender finger.

'Our only crime is to defend ourselves. In your arrogance, you may think that is crime enough.' He tried to see, to uncover hints of what she schemed in her face, but it was a mask; Malantha was too clever to reveal anything she did not want him to know. 'Then what else do you plan?' he pressed.

'A message, delivered with accuracy, that shows we will never be opposed again.' She took a step back, and watched him over one shoulder, almost coyly, although he knew it was a pretence.

'More than the death of all Englishmen and women?'

'That is a cudgel blow. Our true message will be delivered with precision to amplify the pain and to underline that for every slight against us we will respond a hundredfold . . . a thousandfold.' Her eyes narrowed, glowing with hate. Will was left in no doubt of the intensity of the threat.

'And how soon do you plan to carry the Silver Skull to my home?' he enquired.

'Oh . . .' and she paused almost coquettishly, 'soon.'

'And where—'

'Enough questions!' A pointed, almost talon-like nail scraped up his neck to his cheek. 'It is time to prepare the way for your torment. You recall what my brother told you lay ahead?'

Will did not respond.

The doors behind him opened and someone walked slowly, softly, towards him. He strained to see, but the newcomer remained out of his frame of vision.

Malantha drank in every expression, every flicker of emotion, and when she was satisfied, she summoned the person to stand in front of the spy.

It was Grace. She was unharmed, though pale.

Will struggled to disguise his relief. Over the days, terrible thoughts had forced their way into his mind of the suffering she might have endured at the hands of the Unseelie Court. It was more than he could have hoped to see her alive.

'Grace . . . you are well?' he said, his face struggling to give nothing away that would give Malantha joy.

Grace responded with a pale smile. 'Yes. It is good to see you, Will.'

'They will pay for what they have done to you,' he said emotionlessly, adding so quietly Malantha could not hear: 'We will have you away from here in no time.'

Grace's brow furrowed. 'But . . . I do not want to leave.' Her voice had a lazy, honeyed tone, and she cocked her head on one side as if in a dream.

Her words were like a slap across his face. 'What can you mean?'

'This is our great chance, Will. These people . . . your enemies . . . they know what happened to Jenny. I see now why you do what you do. You knew they had knowledge of her disappearance.'

'No . . .'

'You know. Do not lie to me, Will. And they have promised me they will tell all about Jenny, and then I . . . we . . . will know the truth, and we can finally find peace.'

'You cannot trust them. Grace, she is lying,' Will said forcefully. 'She knows nothing. Jenny . . . Jenny is dead.' He couldn't bring himself to believe it even as he uttered the words.

'Is she?' Malantha said. 'Would you not like to know the truth once and for all, like your friend here?'

'Not in this manner. Your manipulation will not work.'

Standing behind Grace, a touch of the true Malantha showed in her features; she did not believe him.

Grace kneaded her hands uneasily. 'I cannot bear not knowing any more. I will do anything they ask of me to discover the truth. Anything. The only way to stop me is to kill me.'

# CHAPTER THIRTY-EIGHT

THERE WAS NO ESCAPE. WILL, NOW FREE OF HIS BONDS, LOOKED out of his cell window at the top of the tower, but the walls were sheer. Even if he found rope of sufficient length, the tower was in clear view of the army of guards that swarmed throughout the palace far below. Don Alanzo had been correct: El Escorial was the most secure building in all of the Spanish empire, a true fortress, the perfect prison.

From his window, he had a vista that at any other time would have been reserved for visiting monarchs, across the desolate waste surrounding El Escorial towards the lush green near Madrid. And his cell was filled with the finest furniture and works of art from across the empire. The irony was not lost on him.

Grace's appearance had disturbed him deeply, but his concerns were interrupted by the grinding of a key in the lock. The door swung open to reveal several guards – he was never left alone with fewer than five – whose captain stepped in to bark, 'Kneel, English dog, in the presence of the King.'

'I kneel only before those who are worthy of my respect,' Will said. For his insolence, the guards threw him to the floor and pressed pikes against the back of his neck so that he could not raise his head.

Lifting his eyes, he watched a pair of black velvet slippers walk slowly into the chamber and stop before him. He felt the pike points lift from him and only then was he allowed to look up. Dressed all in black with his hands clasped tightly behind his back, King Philip of Spain was an ascetic figure. Will was surprised to see in his eyes a gentleness not normally evident in monarchs.

'An English spy.' He looked Will up and down with disdain. 'And not just any spy. They tell me that you are England's greatest spy, William Swyfte. Is this correct?'

'Sire, we are all burdened by our reputations,' Will replied, 'but mine provides me with a parade of entertainment while yours, I am sure, does not.'

Looking about the room, Philip ignored the gibe. 'Tell me, what is the point of a spy when everyone knows his name?'

'You are not the first to ask that question.'

'Does not your whole business involve secrets, duplicity, deceit and shadows?'

'And you think I am not involved in those things?'

Philip gave a condescending nod. 'I understand. What you see is not always what is. You are not England's greatest spy. For if you were you would not be here.'

'I would rather be perceived as victorious than great.'

'You shall be neither. Your execution is forthcoming—'

'After my torture.'

Philip winced and looked away as if he had glimpsed something distasteful. 'And your country's days are numbered,' he continued. 'The armada is due to sail soon.'

'Your armada has floundered before.'

'Not this time,' Philip said sharply. In that instant, Will

394

could see the strain the King was under: victory would cement Spain's reputation and empire for all time; defeat would deal a blow from which he might not recover. Realizing he had revealed too much, the Spanish king sniffed and said, 'I simply wished to see what kind of man England thought was the best it could offer in opposition to my plans. I am not impressed. If you are the best, then this business is already concluded.'

Philip turned on his heel and marched to the door. He slowed when Will said, 'You pray to God, but a devil whispers in your ear.'

The King turned and fixed a warning eye on Will.

'Do her kisses ease your conscience?' Will pressed. 'Do her warm caresses blind you to the choices you make?'

'Beat him,' Philip said to the guards. 'Severely.'

'You fail to understand,' Will continued. 'You think you have taken me prisoner. But I am exactly where I wish to be.'

A shadow crossed Philip's face when he saw Will's expression and he hurried from the room.

# CHAPTER THIRTY-NINE

IN THE LEE OF A HEAP OF ANCIENT MINE-WORKINGS ON THE edge of the spoiled land around El Escorial, Launceston, Carpenter and Mayhew waited. Every now and then one of them would scramble over the blackened rocks to peer through the yellowing grass and weeds at the massive stone fortress. The sky was aflame with the end of the day, scarlet and gold and orange.

'Do you think Will still lives?' Mayhew had a feverish air that had intensified as they made their way to the plateau from the Madrid road. His nails had been chewed to the quick.

Playing with his throwing knife, Carpenter did all he could to show he really didn't care what the answer was. 'Perhaps,' he said.

'Then why should we risk our own lives?' Mayhew added, desperation in his voice.

'Because it is what we do.' Launceston was studying the guards at the great palace's gates, and those patrolling its walls. More came and went on the road winding around the small village that was dwarfed by the vast edifice. He could see no obvious way through the defences.

Mayhew rested his head on his knees with a resigned sigh.

They were exhausted after tracking the carriage which had brought Will from Seville to El Escorial. But Will's plan had worked so far. As they had agreed on the journey from Cadiz, sooner or later Will would allow the Enemy to take him. The Unseelie Court wanted him punished, and slowly and cruelly, as Cavillex had said. Will had calculated he would be taken to the centre of their operations in Spain for his punishment, somewhere the Enemy could linger over their torture. And there, he hoped, he would also find Grace.

Hidden by the storm, Launceston had kept watch on al Rahman's home, and had followed Will and his pursuers to the cathedral. And he and the others were waiting when the unconscious Will was brought out.

'He took a great risk. They could have killed him the moment they captured him,' Mayhew observed.

'Will knows the Enemy well,' Launceston replied without taking his gaze off the palace. 'Simple death does not provide enough revenge for them. Pain in the heart and head is their preferred response to an act of aggression against them. Remember, Will told us that devil Cavillex insisted that Master Swyfte would be brought to his friend Grace, to watch her suffer at his own slow torture and death. They would not walk away from such an exquisite response.'

'Exquisite?' Mayhew repeated, unsettled.

'Swyfte is a gambler. Risks coloured his plan, as they always have done, and it is others who pay the price,' Carpenter said bitterly. 'While gaining his friend, we may have lost the battle – and the war.'

'He knew what he was doing,' Launceston said distractedly. 'The girl would have been held at the centre of the Enemy's plans. And where else would the mask have gone before it was used?'

'They could already have tortured him,' Mayhew continued. 'Cut bits off him. He could be useless to us. He may not even be able to walk.'

'Then we leave him and finish the important business – the girl and the Skull,' Carpenter said.

'Do you hate him so much?' Mayhew asked, mopping the sweat from his brow. The final hours of daylight were hot. Fat flies droned in lazy paths, and the air was thick with the stink of the palace's waste.

'He left me for dead.' The edge in Carpenter's voice revealed his raw emotions, even after so much time had passed. 'The Tsar's soldiers found me, and their allies . . .' he spat, 'and they called off the beast that was tearing me apart. If Swyfte had waited, he could have rescued me and I would not have had to suffer all those months of . . . of . . .' He swallowed, waved the remainder of the sentence away with the back of his hand.

'You are a child,' Launceston said baldly.

Carpenter was so taken aback by the insult, he could only gape.

'Or a dog,' Launceston continued, not caring what Carpenter's response might be. 'You whine and whine. "Poor me, I have been so mistreated." But you live, do you not? You survived. You are the stronger for it.'

'You do not know what deprivations I suffered at the hands of the Tsar's torturers,' Carpenter snapped.

'Whine and whine,' Launceston continued. 'You think you are the only one to suffer? To experience pain in the line of our work?'

Carpenter thrust his knife at Launceston, the blade trembling, but the Earl only gave it the merest pale, aristocratic glance before returning his attention to the guards swarming around the palace. 'Master Swyfte remained true to his work. He completed his business, as directed, and England is better for it.'

'Is it?' Carpenter growled. 'I have seen no sign of the object we retrieved since the day Swyfte brought it back. And I paid for it with my suffering!'

Launceston shrugged. 'He was not distracted or weakened by his emotions. There are bigger things here than your petty feelings. Child.'

Shaking with anger, Carpenter could barely hold the knife still, but Launceston no longer gave it, or the other man, even a cursory glance. Carpenter slumped back against the rocks and ran his still shaking hands through his hair, casting murderous glances towards Launceston.

'You trouble me, Carpenter,' Launceston continued. 'If you surrender to your emotions so, it makes me wonder how far you might go to gain revenge to soothe your poor, hurt feelings.'

'Exactly what are you saying?' Carpenter snapped, eyes full of hate.

'Perhaps you would even go so far as to ally with the Enemy to see Master Swyfte paid back in full.'

Barely had Carpenter begun the lunge with his knife than Launceston's own blade was at his throat.

'Stop it! Stop now!' Mayhew interjected, glancing around to see if the argument had been overheard. 'If we cannot trust each other, we will forfeit our own lives when we are in the thick of it. We must protect each other's backs.'

Slowly, Carpenter relented, although his anger barely subsided, and Launceston moved his dagger away.

'You have never given in to your emotions?' Mayhew said to Launceston.

'No.' The Earl's face became more ghastly as the shadows lengthened.

Mayhew eyed him curiously. 'You speak little about your past. We have all been touched by misery, or by the hand of the Enemy. Why have you given yourself to this business?'

'Sport,' Launceston replied.

'Sport?'

'Yes. I like to kill our enemies.'

They sat in silence until night fell.

It was then that Launceston prised himself away from the top of the spoil-heap and said simply, 'It is time.'

Hoods pulled down to hide their faces, they moved across the desolate landscape. As they neared El Escorial, Launceston motioned for them to be extra vigilant. The guards watched the approach to the palace and continued to patrol the perimeter. Others were stationed in the vast formal gardens.

'Impregnable, they say,' Launceston mused, his voice a whisper.

'I do not know who I fear for the most,' Mayhew said. 'Us trying to get in, or Master Swyfte trying to get out.'

Launceston levelled his blade at the guards. 'I fear for them.'

# CHAPTER FORTY

STILL RAW FROM HIS BEATING EARLIER, WILL WAS DRAGGED through the palace by the guards. From a courtyard open to the moonless sky, and under one of several porticos, he eventually arrived at the statues of David and Solomon that flanked the entrance to the basilica. There, Philip of Spain waited for him, and motioned for the guards to take him in.

'A fine place for torture.' Will admired the huge dome overhead and the simplicity of the basilica's interior. They seemed to reflect Philip's character perfectly. Bruises shaded Will's cheekbones and there was dried blood on his lips and nostrils, yet he kept his head high, and grinned.

On the edge of the shadows, Don Alanzo levelled a cold, baleful stare at Will. He was dressed in mourning black, but his features showed only hatred. Beside him, Grace waited. She met Will's eyes once, then looked away.

'There will be no torture here,' Philip said.

'No physical torture,' Don Alanzo added, before bowing apologetically when the King glared at him.

Philip waved a hand to dismiss the guards. They checked Will's bonds one more time, whispering threats in his ear before departing.

Once the door to the basilica was closed, Malantha appeared from behind one of the columns. Will glimpsed chalky skin and that implacable gaze before she unveiled her potent sexuality, at odds with the sanctified surroundings. Refusing to acknowledge her presence, Don Alanzo looked away, but Grace didn't seem to notice Malantha was there.

'I am starting to believe you are a guilty secret,' Will said. As she fixed her icy, unblinking stare on him, Will had the impression she was imagining slowly cutting open his body.

Shifting uncomfortably, the King quickly changed the subject. 'Today saw the funeral of Don Alanzo's father. A great man, brought low by a dog.'

Will glanced over at Don Alanzo, whose hateful glare never wandered from the Englishman's face. 'You will not believe me, but again I offer my condolences, in good faith,' he said.

'My sister blames me for our father's death,' Don Alanzo said. 'She will have nothing more to do with me, and has ensured I will be refused entry to her convent. Now you have taken two people from me. You will pay for both of them.' He gave a slight bow to Malantha, who gave a brief, dismissive nod in return. 'Our allies . . . your Enemy . . . are correct. Sometimes death is not enough to right a wrong. Pain must be inflicted in the heart, and the mind, and on the soul.'

Will looked to Grace. 'Our captors have turned cruelty into an art, Grace. Do not trust them.'

Striding forward, Don Alanzo struck Will forcefully across the face with his leather gauntlet. Blood bloomed on his lip.

'Please do not hurt him,' Grace begged. 'I will do anything.'

'Of course you will,' Malantha said.

'I have brought you here, under the eyes of God, so you will know there is no treachery in my words when I make this offer: help us and we will spare your friend's life,' Philip said to Grace in English.

'No!' Will shouted. 'Do not believe them!'

Don Alanzo struck him again.

'You vow, before God?' Grace said.

'I so vow.'

'Grace, go no further with this. The Unseelie Court will not allow it,' Will spat. 'He is so deep under their spell that even the threat of damnation will not deter him.'

This time Don Alanzo knocked Will to the floor.

'Please,' Grace sobbed, wringing her hands.

'I so vow!' Philip said firmly.

'I will do anything you ask. But, please . . . please . . . do not hurt him any more.'

The Spanish king nodded to Don Alanzo, who guided Grace to the door as Will struggled to his feet. By the time he was standing, Grace had gone.

'And so the torture begins,' Malantha said.

'And you save my life?' Will sneered, spitting a mouthful of blood.

'Once she has done her duty, we will allow you to live,' Malantha replied, 'although you will be in no state to enjoy it. We will ensure your friend gets to see how you work. Inside. And in your mind, when you scream and cry and beg for us to take her life instead. And then we will allow her to live on with the knowledge of what she saw, and it will never leave her.' She raised her arms in a flamboyant request for applause. 'My brother proposed your death, I know, but he lacks my assured touch in these matters.'

'An honourable man,' Will accused Philip, who was about to leave. 'Wait, Your Majesty. You have an aspiration to higher wisdom.'

'What do you mean?' Philip asked suspiciously.

'The design of this building, your great monument, is based upon the Temple of Solomon, as described by Flavius Josephus.'

'A spy who deals in death and deceit, and yet you are an educated man?'

'I am a man of contradictions, like all men, Your Majesty,' Will replied. 'My point is that you would not have chosen this design, nor selected the statue outside that door, if you did not aspire to the Jewish king's great wisdom. Then rise to it, I beg you. There is still time to walk away from the path you have chosen.' His deferential tone was laced with urgency.

'The war I fight is a just one.' The King raised a lace handkerchief and dabbed at his lips. 'I have the support of the Pope himself. God, Master Swyfte, is on my side.'

'If God is on any side, it is certainly not the Devil's.'

A tremor crossed Philip's face as he was forced to confront the true nature of his secret love. Quickly, Malantha stepped behind him, her hand rising to caress his neck out of sight of Don Alanzo. But she kept her icy eyes on Will the whole time, flaunting her power.

Philip's face hardened. 'This world will be a better place when England is crushed.'

'Our differences are clear, but what we share is much stronger,' Will pressed. 'I ask Your Majesty one final time. Not as Protestant to Catholic, nor as Englishman to Spaniard, but as a man to another man, as members of the great brotherhood of men, I ask you again, turn away from the path you have chosen. Or else you must suffer the consequences.'

Philip gave a weak, boyish laugh. 'You stand before me in chains . . . on the brink of humiliation, and pain, and death . . . and you give *me* an ultimatum?'

Will saw in the King's eyes that he would not be swayed. 'You should kill me now, sire. It is the only way you will be safe.'

Laughing again, almost nervously this time, Philip walked to the door near the altar that led to his private quarters. Before he left, he turned to Malantha and said, 'You will come to me tonight?'

'Of course,' she said, and smiled her cruel smile. The King hurried out, closing the door behind him.

'Now the children have left, you can be about your adult business,' Will said.

'We have no need to sully our hands with your blood at this point,' Malantha replied archly. 'For now, only one thing remains to be done.'

Barely able to stop himself from shaking with emotion, Don Alanzo loomed over Will. 'The time for talk has passed. The Enterprise of England starts tonight, and the end of our business is in sight. And your end too. I leave with your friend Grace, within the hour, to join our armada and go on to England.'

'What do you plan?'

Don Alanzo's face showed no sign of triumphalism or cruelty, just a cold hatred. Will looked from the Spaniard to Malantha. There was cruelty enough in her features. She nodded slowly, relishing the thought of what was to come.

'We will affix the Silver Skull to your friend's head, and when she is delivered to England she must choose between her country and the man she loves,' Malantha intoned. She pressed her hands together in a mockery of prayer. 'Release the power of the Skull, or see you torn apart as we discussed.'

'You will do that anyway,' Will spat.

'We will,' Malantha said, her eyes ablaze.

'Grace will choose England.'

'You truly believe that?' Malantha nodded when she saw the response in Will's eyes. 'And so, in this way we will destroy everything.'

# CHAPTER FORTY-ONE

RISING UP LIKE A SPECTRE FROM THE DARK LANDSCAPE, Launceston slit the guard's throat in one swift movement, holding the head back by the hair so the gush of arterial blood did not stain the red and gold cloak. Once the man's convulsions had ended, the Earl stripped off the Spaniard's cloak, breeches and hose and wrapped them in his own black cloak.

Emerging from behind one of the piles of detritus from El Escorial's construction that still scattered the land, Carpenter and Mayhew discarded the remainder of the stones they had used to lure the lone sentry to his death. In the shadow of the monolithic palace, they studied the manoeuvres of the guards once again.

Carpenter's throwing knife drove deep into a second sentry's neck. Catching the unfortunate man before he fell, Carpenter dragged him back into the shadows, away from the torch under which he had stood.

Mayhew's chosen victim was a young guard who had broken off from the patrol to urinate on the edge of the wasteland, but Mayhew's clumsy approach dislodged a shower of rocks down a slope to splash in a muddy pool. Whirling round, the

Spaniard saw Mayhew stumbling towards him, and struggled to lower his pike with one hand.

Desperately, Mayhew threw himself forward, and the pike-head ripped a gash across his cheek. His pained cry shocked the guard so much he dropped both his weapons. Terrified that the noise would alert the other sentries, the English spy flailed into his victim. As they thrashed together on the ground, he eventually managed to clamp his hands round his opponent's neck. Spitting and gasping and clawing at Mayhew's face, the guard continued to struggle while Mayhew increased the pressure.

He was still choking the man long after he had stopped moving. Carpenter and Launceston finally dragged him off and shook him roughly.

'Steady yourself!' Carpenter hissed. 'You are going to be the death of all of us!'

As Mayhew calmed, Launceston rested his hands on his companion's shoulders and said, as if offering friendly advice, 'At even the first sign that you are again allowing your emotions to run free, I will cut your throat. Do you understand?'

Mayhew gulped and nodded.

Carpenter continued to flash murderous glares at Mayhew as they took the final Spaniard's clothes and wrapped them securely before dumping all three bodies behind a pile of rubble.

'What if he does not come?' Mayhew asked.

'This is the hour, this is the night. If he is able, he will be ready for us,' Launceston replied. 'And if he is already dead or disabled, then we look to the Silver Skull, and then the girl.'

'And leave him here?' Carpenter pressed.

Launceston nodded. 'Are we ready?'

Crossing the wasteland in the dark, they were all acutely

aware of how little time they had before the sentries were missed and the alarm was raised. Further down the slope towards the village, they found their location by nose alone. Like Hampton Court Palace, El Escorial had been built according to the latest methods. Water was piped in, and waste taken out.

The sewer tunnel emptied out on to the slope away from the palace, ensuring the stench never reached the walls. Lined with granite, the sewer was big enough for a grown man to crawl along, but it was as black as pitch and its choking stink left them all gagging as they stood at the opening. Tying kerchiefs across their mouths and noses, they fixed their cloak bundles on their backs, and exchanged a brief glance as they decided who should go first.

With a shake of his head, Launceston dropped to his knees and eased his way into the sewer. Carpenter roughly thrust Mayhew in next, then followed. Within moments all three men were coughing and spluttering, swearing profusely, yet thankful too, as the vile smell distracted them from the oppressive claustrophobia of the dark, stifling space.

Progress was agonizingly slow. 'This is our lives in essence,' Mayhew spat. 'Crawling through shit and piss towards an uncertain future.'

'At least on this occasion you can keep your head above the surface,' Launceston replied, his words muffled. 'We should be thankful for that.'

A little further on, he came up hard against an obstruction. Feeling around in the dark, he realized it was an iron grille. Just as he turned to inform the others, there was a loud click and another grille slid into place behind Carpenter, trapping them. Mayhew whimpered, what lightheartedness he'd acquired suddenly vanishing.

'I dare you to panic,' Carpenter growled.

'A cage . . .' Mayhew began, fighting to calm himself. His breath came in short gasps.

Calmly, Launceston defined the shape of the grille with his hands. 'We knew we would not be allowed free access to the palace. The Spanish may be the spawn of Hell, but they are not fools.'

Mayhew's ragged over-breathing echoed in the confined space, but he knew better than to speak. Fumbling around in the dark, Launceston finally located one of Dee's sachets of powder in his waterproof pouch. Resting the sachet on the point where the grille was bolted into the stone, he delved back into the pouch and removed a stoppered vial made from hide. 'This is not as potent as the mixture Will carries, but it should suffice,' he said. 'Press back and cover your faces. This will not be pleasant.'

Fumbling to unfold the sachet, he took the hide vial and dripped a small amount of liquid on the powder. He had a scant moment to throw his arm across his face before a blast threw him back against the rear grille, his head ringing and his face burning. When they had recovered, the front grille hung loose and it took only a little heaving from Launceston's shoulder to push it free.

'Dee is a foul black magician,' Carpenter muttered, 'but I am glad he is our black magician.'

Scrambling along the remainder of the tunnel, they eventually emerged into a large pit. Overhead, light gleamed through a series of holes in the seat of the privy.

'Heaven,' Carpenter gasped.

'At least Heaven is not obscured by an arse,' Mayhew grunted.

Iron rungs had been fixed into the walls lining the pit, presumably for workers to climb down to wash out the excrement when it backed up. At the top of the rungs, Launceston listened for a moment and then cautiously led the way into a small chamber. On a trestle there was water for washing.

'Hurry,' Launceston whispered, 'or they will smell us long before they see us.'

Stripping off their foul-smelling garments, they washed themselves as best they could before dressing in the guards' clothes. A larger, empty chamber lay beyond, and then a quiet corridor running along the western edge of the palace. Launceston led the way with Carpenter again at the rear. They were poised to change direction at any moment if they heard approaching feet.

Eventually they located the large kitchens, almost empty now the evening meal had been prepared and served and most of the cleaning up had been completed. From just beyond the door, they watched as bowls and plates were put away, and spice and pickle jars returned to shelves. Carpenter spotted a young scullery maid lazily mopping up a spillage not far from the door. Indicating to Launceston and Mayhew that they should stay out of sight, he pulled his hair over the scars on his face and strode confidently into the kitchen. After a cursory look around, he went over to the scullery girl. Fearing admonishment, she lowered her eyes and pretended not to see him.

In fluent Spanish, Carpenter said to her, 'Please. Will you help me?'

The girl glanced across the cavernous room to where her superior was overseeing the selection of ingredients for the following day's meal.

'A moment of your time,' Carpenter pressed.

As he had expected, the scullery girl eyed him suspiciously.

He drew out the crucifix he had taken from the dead sentry and, looking around again, whispered dolefully, 'My mother died this day. I would say a prayer for her, but I cannot be seen to be avoiding my duties. Is there a quiet place hereabouts? For only a moment?'

At the sight of the crucifix, the girl softened. Smiling shyly, she led him to a storeroom half covered in a dusting of white flour.

'Thank you,' he whispered. As she turned to go, he asked, 'What is your name?'

'Chelo.'

'You are a kind and beautiful girl, Chelo.'

She blushed.

'My name is Eduardo. I am new to the palace. I would have worked here sooner if I had known you were in the King's employ.'

She blushed again, but didn't resist when he took her hand. 'Perhaps you would find time to walk with me one day?'

As she looked deep into his eyes her pupils expanded, and he knew he had her.

'Where are you from?' she asked. 'Your accent . . .'

'My mother is French. I grew up in the New World.'

Her eyes widened with excitement. 'Is it as they say? Dragons in the sea, and silver on the streets . . . and a city of gold . . .'

'All of that and more.' He sealed the connection by kissing her hand. 'But I hear there are wonders here too.'

'Here?'

'An English spy held prisoner? You have heard of that?'

She sighed as if this were the most boring thing in the world. 'Of course.'

Carpenter restrained a triumphant grin. 'And where is he being held?'

# CHAPTER FORTY-TWO

LOOSENING HIS BELT, WILL CRACKED THE STAY OF THE BUCKLE. It was hollow inside and stopped with a small blob of wax. He placed this to one side, and then tore off the cuff of his shirt, which he wrapped around the door handle of the chamber. He had seen the demonstration by Dee before they had left for Spain, but he still could not grasp how the combination of powder embedded in the cuff and the liquid in the buckle could have such an effect. Typically, Dee had dismissed all his questions with irritation.

Removing the wax stopper, he turned his head away, covered his eyes, poured the foul-smelling liquid on to the cuff, and then threw himself across the chamber.

The subsequent explosion left his ears ringing. Looking round, he was confronted by a thick pall of grey smoke that smelled as bad as the liquid. The door was in ruins.

Out in the corridor, three guards lay unconscious, another attempted to stem blood from a terrible wound on his leg, and the fifth staggered around in a daze. Deciding the dazed guard was the worst threat, Will put one arm round his head and twisted hard. With an audible crack, the neck snapped.

The wounded Spaniard made a pitiful attempt to stop Will,

but the blood jetted from between his fingers. He was about to shout an alarm when Will slammed the heel of his hand under the guard's chin, throwing the head back to deadly effect. Before he had even hit the floor, Will had claimed the man's rapier and dagger.

From the window, he scanned the desolate landscape, but it was too dark to see anything. He trusted Launceston, Mayhew and Carpenter would have followed him from Seville – they were good at what they did – but were they good enough to get inside such a well-guarded palace-fortress? He had to presume he was on his own.

All he had done since Grace's abduction was allow his emotion to get the better of him. Launceston and the others had tolerated it out of loyalty, but he knew they would all be wondering why he hadn't taken the Silver Skull when he had it, why he'd not forsaken the child and his plan to be kidnapped in order to find Grace.

And now he was in danger of losing both Grace and the Skull. Will cursed himself, cursed the Unseelie Court, and then cursed himself again.

As he knew it would, the explosion had drawn attention. Cries of alarm reverberated through the entire wing; the sound of running feet clattered on the tower's spiral steps. Will had hoped he would at least have time to reach the bottom of the tower so he could lose himself in the maze of corridors and courtyards. Now he would have to fight his way out.

The blood in his temple beat out a steady rhythm that matched the words in his head: no one would stop him.

Free at last, he met the guards climbing the stairs head-on without slowing his step. His heart swelled and the blood pumped through him. Nothing would deflect him, no one could harm him. In the Spaniards' eyes he saw fear light, as if they too felt that the Devil was beside him. Dazzling, his rapier slashed back and forth, into the neck of the first, across the face of the second. With a leap, he ploughed into the massed guards, and then rolled across the top of them. Bodies crashed against stone. An arm shattered. A spine broke. Skulls cracked. The dagger flashed in his other hand, and blood sprayed. By the time he had passed the last guard, all were dead.

How many soldiers were in the palace? How many would he have to kill before he reached his objective?

At the foot of the tower, three more guards were on their way up, two with pikes, the third, a captain, carrying a sword. Instantly, he took Will on, parrying with some skill. He attempted to return Will's attack, but England's greatest spy had learned from the best swordsmen in Europe. And he had the advantage of height. There was no time for niceties. As the captain struggled to strike upwards, Will kicked his blade to one side and thrust his sword through the man's neck. The captain fell backwards, frantically trying to stem the bubbling blood.

Something in Will's face scared the remaining pikemen – he could see uncertainty and then fear flare in their eyes when they locked gazes with him. It was enough that they faltered in their attack. Will slashed his sword across the wrist of one so that he dropped his weapon, which Will deftly kicked towards the other. As the second guard struggled to bat the pike away, Will impaled him on his sword. He finished off the first with his knife for good measure.

With a bound, he was over the flailing, bleeding bodies and out into the corridor beyond. Cries rang out here and there, but in the confusion it seemed no one was really sure where the explosion had originated, or what it indicated.

Once out of the confines of the tower, stealth became the

key. All around, Will could hear cries of alarm and guards charging around, searching for him. Torches burned intermittently along the corridors, but in that austere place the gloom was never far away. Will kept to the shadows, moving from doorway to pillar, courtyard tree to arch, emerging in a flash of steel every now and then to slit a throat or run through any guard who got too near.

In room after room, he set small fires of tapestries and furniture with the torches and lanterns he found. The smoke sweeping through the complex and the loud crackle of the flames would cause confusion. He had no regrets — he had given King Philip ample opportunity to prevent this destruction.

And he killed everyone he encountered. At first he attempted to hide the bodies, but soon he realized there were too many and it was slowing him down; they would be found soon enough. The corpses trailed behind him, too many to count. No longer a man, but a supernatural being born of blood and death, he progressed relentlessly towards the front of the palace where he presumed a carriage would be waiting to take Grace and the Silver Skull away from El Escorial.

At some point, the stream of deaths became dream-like. He saw only sprays from opened arteries, bones revealed to the air, blown pupils; he smelled only iron blood and bowels released in the throes of death; he heard only desperate pleadings and final moans. And still he moved on.

Malantha and the Unseelie Court loomed darkly in his mind and he thought: *You have driven me to this. You have made me wound my own soul with each life I take. You will pay in full.*

Yet a part of him wondered if it was all inside him to begin with. Had the Unseelie Court, with their deft, unnatural skill, only brought this aspect of him to the surface? Was this what he was really like? A brutal killer, as contemptuous of human life as he believed them to be.

As the Englishman swept through the final courtyard, fortune began to turn against him and even his skills were not enough. The entire palace was roused as body after body was discovered, one long, furious alarm demanding his death. Boots thundered on stone, coming from several directions at once. Within moments, Will saw his way ahead blocked by at least twenty men charging towards him with pikes and swords.

Cursing, he darted to his left into another corridor, no longer knowing where he was going. Concerned palace workers shrieked and withdrew when they saw him run by, drenched in the blood of others.

But his random trail had confused his pursuers, who were now unable to cut him off and forced to follow in his wake. All Will was aware of was impressions of grand rooms, the echoes of his boots on flagstone floors, and the sound of a storm at his back.

Finally he was confronted by a knot of seven guards racing towards him down a corridor. Unable to get past them, Will was forced to back against a wall. This, he suddenly realized, might be the end.

'Come, then!' he roared. 'Who dies first?'

The guards hesitated until they saw that mere weight of numbers must crush the lone, insane Englishman. But as they advanced, one at the back suddenly pitched forward, coughing blood. A blade protruded from his throat.

As he fell to the ground, Carpenter slowly removed his knife and flashed a contemptuous glance at Will. Mayhew and Launceston stood with him.

Together, they fell upon the disoriented guards, slashing and stabbing and thrusting until none was left alive.

417

'Better late than never,' Will said to Carpenter. The others stared at him in silence for a moment, and Will realized how he must look to them – a blood-drenched, demonic apparition. 'Come. Back the other way.'

'You have led us a merry chase,' Mayhew said. 'If you had only stayed in the tower we might have saved you.'

'Instead of bringing the entire hordes of Spain upon our heads,' Carpenter snapped.

'There was no time to lose,' Will said. 'Don Alanzo is to take Grace away from here this very night.'

The sound of more guards approaching echoed from all directions. 'The only end will be ours,' Mayhew muttered. 'We will never be able to fight our way out against all the King's men.'

Will feared he was right. As they hesitated, unsure which way to go, he fumbled for the handle of a door.

'Not there,' Carpenter cautioned, too late. As the door swung open, Will saw an array of bodies scattered around. Three were guards, but there were at least ten of the palace's workers, including a young woman.

'Who did this?' Will asked. Even after all his slaughter, the blood-letting of those who posed no threat was shocking to him.

'I fear I lost control, a little.' A feverish gleam lit Launceston's eyes.

'Are we no better than the ones we fight?' Will said with quiet intensity, his anger growing. 'We kill, yes, but we do not murder innocents.' The sound of pursuit shook him back to the present, and he continued, 'This is a matter for later. For now, hide beneath the bodies. Do not show your faces, but smear the blood upon you. If luck is on our side, it will buy us a little time.'

Leaving the door ajar, Will ran to the far side of the chamber. Lying down, he pulled the body of a guard across his midriff and the girl's arm over his face. The limb was still warm. As the running feet neared, the others scrambled into place, their stolen uniforms helping to disguise them. Mayhew was the last to settle, a second before the door was flung wide. Will heard the outraged cries, the prayers and calls for revenge, but as he had expected their pursuers did not investigate and quickly went on with their search.

When he was sure they were gone, Will pushed the bodies away from him, and hissed at the others. Mayhew was obviously shaken, his face haunted, but both Carpenter and Launceston seemed calm. 'The carriage might be leaving at any moment. We cannot afford to delay.'

'And what strategy have you dreamed up that will get us out of this mess?' Carpenter asked. 'Or have you finally completed the process of killing me that you started in the Muscovy snow?'

'A bold strategy,' Will said. 'Did you expect any less?'

It was bold, it was dangerous, it had the potential to bring down upon his shoulders the wrath of Walsingham, Burghley and the Queen herself, and it would probably see him consigned to the Tower with an appointment with the block. Yet as the cries of the guards rang out through El Escorial, he knew he had little choice. 'To the basilica,' he said.

Their ploy among the dead had bought them a little time. The guards that had passed the door must have been the last wave and the passages beyond appeared silent. Flitting through the dark of the final courtyard, they reached the still sanctity of the basilica. But in the glow of scores of candles, they were quickly spotted by three guards who waited near the altar. Two carried halberds, the third a rapier. Walsingham would have hesitated at violating the sanctity of a church, Will knew. But he had little choice, and cared less.

One guard shouted an alarm and hammered on the door beside the altar, while the other two approached, halberds levelled at the ready. Carpenter took one down with his throwing knife, while Will and Mayhew despatched the second. So swift he was barely seen, Launceston slid his knife across the throat of the man guarding the door.

'What lies behind there?' Mayhew asked.

Without responding, Will tried the door. It was locked. He motioned to Carpenter and Mayhew to use a heavy pew as a battering ram. Within moments the door had been torn from its hinges.

On his knees, head down in prayer, King Philip of Spain did not deign to acknowledge them. Will could see he was preparing to meet his Maker – to become a martyr to his faith. Noticing his thin, pale forearms protruding from the sleeves of his black gown, and the hollowness of his cheeks as his thin lips whispered to his God, Will thought how frail the King looked at that moment.

''Tis the King,' Carpenter said incredulously.

Launceston caught Will's arm and whispered, 'It is one thing to beard the Spanish on their home ground, but another altogether to threaten the life of a monarch. You are but an ordinary man. To challenge a king in such a manner goes against the established order. You could bring all of Europe down on England's head. The Queen will not take this lightly.'

'If I had another path I would take it.' Will strode over to the kneeling monarch and said, 'Your Majesty, you must come with us.'

Philip did not look up from his devotions. Will nodded to

Carpenter and Mayhew, who, after a moment's hesitation, took Philip's arms and gently helped him to his feet.

'I fear, sire, you are our passage out of here,' Will said. 'You have my word you will not be harmed.'

Philip seemed unmoved and unafraid, confident the English spies would not get far, surrounded as they were by a fortress filled with fighting men. 'England will burn for this,' he said. Holding his head at an aloof, disinterested angle, he refused to meet Will's eye.

Will searched the connecting chambers, but there was no sign of Malantha. 'Where is that witch who has your ear?' he demanded, but the King would not answer. 'Her strength lies in her subtle manipulations from the shadows,' Will spat. 'Confrontation is not her way. But this is not the end of it. I vow this now!' He called the last words loudly, sure that wherever Malantha was, she could hear him.

Containing his desire for revenge, Will led the way out of the King's quarters, through the basilica and into the court-yard, where fifty or more of the King's men were brought up short, the blood draining from their faces at the sight of their King in the hands of their enemies.

Drawing his dagger, Will pressed the point to Philip's throat. 'Safe passage,' he called out, 'or the King's death will be on your conscience.'

Swords drawn against the murmuring, uncertain Spanish, Launceston, Carpenter and Mayhew huddled around Will and Philip.

With a snarl, one of the soldiers raised his pike, but an officer quickly thrust an arm across his chest.

'Safe passage and your King will not be harmed,' Will said.

Slowly, the ranks parted and the little group moved steadily through, eyes flashing for any sign of an attack. Will knew they could not risk the King's death; the repercussions would be terrible if any harm came to the monarch. Would he – could he – go that far, if he had to?

The Spanish soldiers closed around the English and their captive until they were an island in a sea of steel armour, threatened from every side by pikes and swords. Step by step, they advanced, Will's knife never leaving Philip's throat, the entire courtyard enveloped in an anxious silence. The tension cried out for release, but each man knew that that would only result in slaughter.

*Hold steady*, Will thought. He cast an eye towards Mayhew, the most likely to crack and bring everything falling down, and then to Launceston, who still had the gleam of bloodlust in his eyes.

As they came to the portico leading out of the courtyard, Will ordered Carpenter to collect two pikes. They moved through the first set of doors, and Launceston slammed them shut. An eruption of anger blasted from the other side as the soldiers threw themselves against the doors as one, but Carpenter had already rammed one of the pikes through the iron ring-handles; the doors bowed, but the pike held. Not for long, though, Will knew.

With the clamour ringing at their backs, they hurried through the palace, dragging the Spanish king along with them.

Emerging into the warm night, they saw a carriage waiting in the courtyard. Beside it stood Don Alanzo and Grace. Holding the Silver Skull, opened like a vile instrument of torture, the Don was about to fix it on Grace's head.

His gently persuasive voice floated through the still air. 'Place this 'pon your head. You must do what I say. We will release you from it when your task is complete.' Yet Will could see that the Spaniard was reticent, unsure about what he had been instructed to do.

'Grace, do not!' he called.

Whipping round, Don Alanzo tossed the mask through the open carriage door and went for his sword. Grace cried out and would have run to Will, but the Don held her back with one arm.

'In case your eyes have failed you, señor, we have the King here,' Will shouted.

'And that will be added to the list of crimes for which you will pay,' was Don Alanzo's reply. With a flourish, he brought his sword-tip close to Grace's breast. 'Let us see where your loyalties truly lie.'

Blood throbbed in Will's temple. He could feel the eyes of Launceston, Carpenter and Mayhew upon him. And from somewhere unseen, he could feel too the terrible regard of Malantha, teasing, taunting, urging.

'Well?' Don Alanzo mocked. 'Release the King or the girl dies.'

'Give me the Skull or the King dies,' Will responded.

'Then let us see whose life you consider more valuable.' Don Alanzo pressed the sword-tip against Grace.

'So be it . . . kill the King,' Will ordered. He couldn't bear to see the look of horror that flared in Grace's face.

Don Alanzo laughed, but it caught and died when he understood that Will was not bluffing. Hesitantly, Carpenter drew his knife.

His eyes fixed on Don Alanzo as he weighed up whether he could save Grace before the killing blow, Will heard frantic activity at his back.

Carpenter's blade clattered across the flags. Carpenter himself was on the ground, his lips and nose bloody. Half turning,

Will saw Philip fleeing across the courtyard in the direction of the palace. He was about to give chase when he was struck so heavily across the temple it drove him to his knees, dazed.

Muffled voices penetrated the haze in his head, and as he staggered to his feet he saw Mayhew running to Don Alanzo with Launceston in pursuit.

*Mayhew. Traitor.*

His head spinning, Will was powerless as Don Alanzo thrust a screaming Grace into the carriage, and bounded in after her.

Mayhew cried out, but the carriage began to move away. At the last moment, he flung himself on to the step, clutching on to the open window. Turning, he planted one boot into Launceston's chest and sent him sprawling.

The carriage built up speed, rattling out of the gates and away across the dark Spanish countryside.

# CHAPTER FORTY-THREE

'LEAVE ME ALONE!' MAYHEW SHOOK HIS FIST AT GRACE IN A rage. Her tear-stained face was filled only with contempt.

As the carriage raced away from the palace, Don Alanzo leapt forward and knocked Mayhew back into his seat, eyes blazing. 'You do not speak to her like that!' he snarled. 'You have no right to speak to anyone . . . traitor.'

Mayhew felt as if his heart would burst. The strain of keeping his treachery hidden for so long had led him to the point of nearly ending his own life. And now a corrosive guilt had been added to the potent mix. He held his head in his hands and tried not to think about what he had lost – his life in England, his countrymen, his Queen, his country itself – and he wondered how he would ever live with himself.

'But . . . I helped you.' Mayhew's voice was a confused whine. Even he could hear the pathetic note. Why was the Spaniard treating him so badly? Surely he had brought victory to Spain.

Don Alanzo studied him for several long moments, and Mayhew couldn't meet the intensity of his gaze. Then the Spaniard said: 'You are no Spanish spy or I would know.'

'No. I . . .' Mayhew's shoulders sagged, and he could barely force out the words. 'I help the Enemy. The . . . the Unseelie Court.'

Contempt dripped from Don Alanzo's words. 'You sold your soul for what easy gain?'

It was a question he could not easily answer. 'If only you knew,' he said, his voice breaking.

Don Alanzo looked at Grace, who was watching Mayhew with disdain. 'She does not need to hear these things.'

Mayhew nodded. 'Agreed.'

'Then there is some humanity in you after all,' Don Alanzo sniffed. He turned his attention away as if Mayhew was beneath his notice.

And the Spaniard was right, Mayhew accepted. He was a traitor, a despicable human being. He deserved the loathing that would be heaped upon him. Memories rose like spectres from his mind where he had kept them locked away for so long.

*The funeral of his father on a cold November day at their parish church in the village outside Hastings. The bitter air salty with the scent of the sea. Stark trees black against the grey clouds. Crows cawing their desolate chorus. At the graveside, he slipped his arm round his mother, whispering that he would look after her, provide her with a regular stipend from his new work under Sir Francis Walsingham at the Palace of Whitehall. He had privately agreed to work for the secret service, but it was three days before his induction into the true mysteries of existence. A time when he had still thought there was hope in the world . . .*

*Eight weeks later, and the snow was heavy on the roofs of the village, and the ground as hard as his heart had grown. The crows were still thick in the trees, but now he viewed them in a different light. A visit home after his assignment to the guard at the Tower; at the* time he had thought it a short-term posting, filled with long periods of boredom. As he stepped over the threshold, he thought how thin and pale his mother looked. Her skin was parchment yellow, and when he hugged her he could feel her bones like hoes and trowels. 'You are working too hard. You must rest more,' he told her. She smiled weakly, was wiser than he was . . .

Two months passed, and he had missed three visits home because of the demands of his work. When he arrived at the cottage after dark, the parson waited, like one of the crows that never appeared to leave the surrounding trees. His mother was very ill, the parson said. He feared her time was short. She lay in her bed, delirious, calling out for his father, her own father and mother. She looked barely more than bones with skin draped over them. The rapid decline in such a short period shocked him, and he cursed himself, and the world, and wished for more and bargained with God. But she did not improve.

Under special petition from Sir Francis Walsingham, he was given time away from his post to care for her in her final days. They were long, the nights longer, filled with tears, and anger, and her anguished cries as the pain gripped her. But she did not die within the week, as the parson had forecast, nor within two weeks, and by the end she was screaming in agony day and night. He had clutched his ears, buried his head in his hands, and wept until he was sure he was being driven mad by her unending suffering.

The desire to help her drove him on, but he could do nothing to relieve her agony, and finally his failure consumed him. He could bear to see her in pain no longer. And then, after praying for her to live for so long, he prayed for her to die, soon, that moment, so her torment would be ended along with her awful cries, and that destroyed him even more; he had asked God for the death of his own mother.

But she did not die. And for a while he did go mad. He never left the house, and he did not eat for days, cursing and yelling.

Then one night, when the moon was full, he saw that the field beside the cottage was filled with statues, grey and wrapped in shadow. They seemed to be watching, as the crows had. He ran to his mother, and prayed over her, but he was drawn back to the window time and again. The statues disappeared, but the shadows remained, flitting back and forth in the moonlight across the field.

The knock at the door came soon after. In the days that followed he could never remember the face, although at the time it burned into his mind, and he knew he would feel its eyes upon him for the rest of his days. But he recalled what passed between them. His mother would never die. She would remain in that purgatory of agony, and he would be with her for the rest of his days, never escaping her screams, cursed to watch her unending suffering.

He could not bear it, and he threw himself to the floor, and tore at his flesh, and for a while knew nothing.

When he had recovered a little, the honeyed voice told him there was hope; and he pleaded to know what it was. Anything, he would do anything, and the voice said that was good. He would work for them, just for a while, and do the little things they asked, inconsequential things, and in return they would give his mother balm, and when his time of service was done, they would ease her suffering into death.

For a while the requests were inconsequential, but then, gradually they grew in import. But he had already set off along the road, and so each new thing was just one tiny step. When he discovered knowledge of the Palace of Whitehall and what was there, and then passed it on, it was nothing; there were no consequences. And when he revealed what he knew of the Tower, it was worse, but not much. But then he was helping them to overcome the defences that Dee had put in place. Then he had helped release the chain of misery and death that still had not come to an end.

The carriage jolted over a rut and Mayhew stirred sharply from his reverie. As his eyes opened, he was startled to see Don

Alanzo looming in front of him, the Silver Skull open and gleaming in his hands.

'What—' Mayhew began, but his question was cut short as Don Alanzo pressed the mask against his face and closed it with a clang. Panic rose in him, and his head swam with frightening images, things he had never seen and could never possibly have known. The sensation of movement across his mind unsettled him, until he felt a thousand points of agony as if insects were burrowing into him, through the skin, and the bone, and into his brain. He wanted to scream, but could not utter a sound.

Somewhere in the distance, he heard Don Alanzo saying, 'Do as you are ordered and the mask will be removed. Resist us and be damned for ever.'

And Mayhew wondered if he was cursed to be a slave to others for all time, and if his suffering would never end.

# CHAPTER FORTY-FOUR

CRASHING ON HORSEBACK THROUGH THE DENSE FOREST encroaching upon Lisbon on three sides, Will crested a ridge to look down on a scene that was at once breathtaking and chilling. In the bay on the estuary, edged in the silvery light of the moon amid pools of stark shadows, were some one hundred and thirty ships – only a few warships, galleons, galleys and galleasses, the rest armed carracks, hulks and a few lighter vessels. The formidable fleet was so dense it was like another city floating beside Lisbon, lantern light glimmering here and there aboard each ship, banners fluttering gently in the warm night breeze.

The armada.

Will knew that somewhere in the teeming city, Don Alanzo would be meeting the armada's commander, the Duke of Medina Sidonia, in order to secure a place for him and Grace on one of the ships. Will had to find them before the fleet sailed.

Weariness sapped him of any response beyond a dull relief that he had finally reached his destination after constant riding along dusty, deserted back roads, foraging for food, lying low, stealing a new horse whenever his mount tired.

It was 8 May, and more than a week had passed since he and Carpenter and Launceston had escaped from El Escorial in pursuit of Don Alanzo's carriage. At their backs, the still night had been shattered by the outcry as the King's men flooded from the palace to scour the surrounding countryside for the escaped English spies. The three companions had moved carefully across the desolate terrain, using the spoil-heaps and the thickets for cover until they reached the village nearby. There they purchased three old nags and made their escape. Once they were sure they had left their pursuers behind, Will had instructed Carpenter and Launceston to proceed to where they had agreed to rendezvous with the *Tempest*: their orders, to carry the news of what had happened to whatever forces waited to confront the armada. England's future hung by a thread and they all had a part to play.

Will took a moment to study the array of ships before wearily guiding his equally exhausted horse down the road that wound around the hillside. Below, Lisbon nestled within its walls, an ancient city whose narrow streets wound in confusion away from the quay. Like Cadiz and Seville, Will noted, the city bore the influence of the Moors who had been expelled by the Crusaders more than four hundred years earlier.

For eight years now, Lisbon had been under Spanish rule. Philip knew the city was crucial to his plans for his empire's dominance of Europe and the New World, as gateway for trade with Africa, the Far East, India and the Spanish colonies in the Americas. But now the vast harbour in the estuary of the River Tagus played an even more crucial role. It was home to Philip's armada.

As Will passed through the city's walls he left the fragrant pine-scented air behind and plunged into a place where the smell of excrement and urine fought with rot for dominion in the dark streets. Instantly he felt something was wrong. Though it was evening, Lisbon was busy with sailors carousing and fighting and whoring.

An oppressive sense of decay hung everywhere. The narrow streets of the Alfama area were crowded with beggars calling to him, and reaching out for his boots, sometimes clamouring so tightly around his horse he could barely continue forward. Shops along the way were empty and closed, some boarded up. The area swarmed with prostitutes, far from their stews, competing for trade in shrill voices that often led to violence. In the even darker alleys reaching from the main thoroughfares, Will glimpsed sudden movements and flashes of steel, heard cries cut suddenly short. He passed a rotting corpse on the side of the street, unclaimed.

He could not shake from his mind the memory of Grace's look of betrayal when he ordered the King to be killed. She knew that he understood that Don Alanzo would respond in kind and kill her. It was as if all her hopes had been shattered in one moment. The decision had almost broken him, but there was no way he could go back on it; what was done was done, and he would have to live with the consequences of his actions.

He channelled his feelings into a slow-burning hatred for Mayhew. He and he alone was responsible for Grace's suffering. There would be a reckoning.

Rather than head for the port, Will made his way towards the slopes leading up to the Castle of Sao Jorge above the city. Once the royal residence, it still overlooked the homes of the city's wealthier inhabitants that clustered close to its protection. Here the streets were quieter. Will eventually located the house he was looking for in a long white terrace of well-kept merchants' homes, far enough away from the rich and important residents to avoid attention. Looking about him, Will dismounted and tethered his horse.

A gentle knock was answered by a man in his late twenties, strong, clean-shaven and tanned, black hair framing an intelligent face. He matched the description that Will had been given back in England.

'You are Luis Inacio dos Santos?' Will kept one hand on the pommel of his rapier.

'I am,' the man said in heavily accented English. For a moment, the two men eyed each other, watching for hints of betrayal, danger, an attack. Then the Portuguese gave a formal bow, admitting Will to the gloomy interior. Santos possessed the strength and posture of a soldier, but his face had the sensitivity of an artist. Both impressions were accurate. Will knew he had been an acclaimed painter of portraits in Lisbon until the Spanish invasion, when he had joined the resistance. The Portuguese had capitulated in the face of Philip of Spain's overwhelming force, but resentment simmered in the shadowy streets, and Santos was an easy turn for Walsingham's men. He hated Spain, and the Spanish king, in a more visceral manner than any Englishman.

The room was small and dark with a low, beamed ceiling. One stubby candle guttered on a small trestle. The furniture was sparse, one chair near the hearth, two stools and a bench, but the floor was scattered with fresh rushes. Resting against one wall was a half-completed portrait of a beautiful, raven-haired woman, dusty as though it had not been touched in many months.

Will stripped off his cloak and draped it over the bench. Santos gestured for him to take the high-backed chair. After days in the saddle, Will was surprised how good it felt to sit.

'You have a ship moored off the coast,' Santos said. 'Word

433

came through this morning to prepare for the possible arrival of an English agent. Though,' he added, 'such rumours have been flying back and forth for months now. I sent missive after missive about the build-up of the armada. Why was I ignored?'

'The Queen has her favourites,' Will replied, 'and she does not always heed the most trustworthy voice.'

'You must be exhausted after your journey. I can offer you food.'

'A bite and perhaps some wine, but matters are pressing and I cannot rest.' He explained to Santos about Don Alanzo and Grace. The Portuguese man listened intently, stroking his chin and nodding.

'That makes sense. This afternoon word reached me of a Spanish nobleman in the city, but I have no knowledge of where he stays or which ship he will be joining. This past hour also saw the arrival of a messenger from Philip's palace at El Escorial. He is believed to be carrying orders for Medina Sidonia to prepare the armada to sail, but that will not be possible until tomorrow at the earliest. The Duke has already waited two weeks for the order. Another day will matter little. You can afford at least a few hours' rest.'

Will wondered if the attack on El Escorial had prompted the Spanish king – and Malantha – to move with haste. If preparations were not wholly complete, that could work in England's favour. 'I thank you for your concern, but I cannot rest. If it is not possible to locate Don Alanzo in the city quickly, I must get aboard one of the ships,' Will said, as if talking to himself. 'Such arrangements take time, if it is even possible. Even though I speak the tongue of Philip, or could pass as a mercenary Frenchman, the chances of discovery are high.'

Laughing, Santos held up a hand to slow Will's anxious

words. 'These matters are in hand. Rest. The world will not end before dawn.'

Although Will knew that Santos spoke the truth, he could not shake off an oppressive feeling of mounting doom, that secret plans were coming together in the darkness. Yet after days with only a snatched hour of sleep here and there, his eyes drooped quickly and he fell into a deep, dreamless sleep. He was woken by Santos later, when the room was filled with the warming aromas of food. His stomach signalled its approval.

Santos indicated a fine spread. 'Red mullet from Setubal and mussels from Cabo da Roca. Goat cheese from Sobral de Monte Agraco, zimbros from Sesimbra and pastries from Malveira. Cheesecakes and nuts, and for your pleasure, a bottle of Muscatel, also from Setubal. The best of Portugal, still, despite the Spanish occupation. Please . . .' He gestured again. 'Eat and drink your fill.'

Santos's hospitality was as much a mark of his pride in his country and his defiance of Spanish rule. Whatever the message, Will was thankful. He ate hungrily, and when he was done, was ready with the questions that weighed upon him.

'What has happened to Lisbon?' he asked, clutching a cup of wine. 'As I rode through, it was worse than the worst parts of London, filthy, seemingly poor. Where are the riches?'

'Another thing for which we must thank the Spanish,' Santos said bitterly. 'The armada has brought more than thirty thousand men to Lisbon, all of them whoring, fighting and thieving while the ships sit uselessly off our harbour for week upon week. They consume our food faster than we can replenish our stores. Everything is in short supply, and what is available is beyond the cost of the common man. The people starve by the day.' He gestured to the remnants of the meal.

'As you can see, I am more fortunate. I have my own suppliers in the countryside.'

*The Portuguese resistance is well looked after.* Will took a sip of his wine, even more grateful for what he had eaten and drunk.

'The Spanish run riot through our city, and the Portuguese have locked themselves behind their shutters, but even then there is no escape,' Santos growled. 'In their filth and degradation, the Spanish sailors and soldiers grow diseased and ill. They desert by the score, and good Portuguese men are pressed to fill their spaces. Lisbon can take no more. The sooner we are rid of this damned armada the better.'

'Do not wish it upon England,' Will said, 'but I understand why you are keen to help.'

'And help you I shall, to the best of my ability. A spy within the fleet itself may do little alone to turn the tide of battle, but still you may cause some damage in the thick of it. And if the worst happens, and the force lands on England's shores, you will have valuable information that may aid any resistance.'

'If the Spanish set foot in England, the hour will be dire indeed,' Will agreed. 'But how might I best disguise myself effectively among Spanish sailors for such a long sea voyage?'

Sitting back in his chair, Santos folded his hands together and smiled. 'You will not be among Spanish sailors.'

'Who, then?' Will was puzzled.

'Among your own kind. Englishmen.'

Will eyed Santos incredulously.

'It seems not all your countrymen have the same pure motives as yourself. Believe it or not, there are some two hundred Englishmen here among the Spanish crews. Mercenaries, or those driven by the passion of Our Lord who believe this a crusade to return the one true religion to your land, some priests who plan to become rich converting heretics, and exiles keen to reclaim their fortunes and their estates once rightful order has returned.'

'A shipful of traitors, then.' Though unsurprised, Will was still alarmed that there were so many eager to betray the land of their birth.

'Ships,' Santos corrected, 'for they are scattered among the fleet. I know for certain that eight are aboard the *Nuestra Señora del Rosario*. And there is rumoured to be an Englishman of great status aboard Medina Sidonia's flagship, the *San Martin*.'

'The flagship? There is an Englishman in the command?'

'They call him Don William.'

'Sir William Stanley,' Will noted coldly. 'That treacherous dog. I had heard he was in Dunkirk marshalling another part of Parma's invasion force. Stanley cares for naught but himself. He betrayed the entire city of Deventer in the Netherlands to the Duke of Parma. If he is here, then he feels success in his blood.' Will looked across at Santos. 'But how did you find this information? And how might I gain the necessary paperwork to find a berth? I would prefer not to be press-ganged and end up at the oars of one of Medina Sidonia's galleys.'

Raising a lamp to guide his way, Santos indicated that Will should follow him. As they climbed the flights of creaking stairs, he said, 'It may be that your woman will be aboard the *Santiago*. *La urca de las mujeres* is the name by which it is more commonly known.'

'The ship of the women?' Will was, for once, at a loss.

'It carries the wives of many of the married officers, the only women permitted to sail with the fleet. No whores to distract the men. Though I have heard tell that one officer smuggled his wife on board disguised as a man, to provide him with comfort on the long nights at sea. Medina Sidonia does not want his men's fighting edge blunted by nights of carnal pleasure.' He smiled, then frowned. 'But the *Santiago* is one of the most heavily guarded ships in the armada. I fear you will not get aboard it.'

Will stored the information away as Santos led him up a final, short set of stairs to an attic room. The stench of blood and urine hit him the moment the door was opened. The dark swept away from Santos's lamp, revealing a bare floor and a steeply sloping ceiling. Chained to the far wall on a bed of straw was a man. His head hung down so it was impossible to tell if he was alive or dead. As they walked in, the emaciated captive stirred and grunted. He was barely conscious and Will could see he had been beaten.

'Who is he?' he asked.

'An English mercenary who goes by the name of William Prowd. I found him drunk in a bar and lured him back here on the pretext of more wine.' The Portuguese man studied his hands intently. 'He told me all I need to know, and I have his papers, signed by Medina Sidonia's recruitment officer, so you will be able to slip on board his ship, the *Rosario*.' Santos collected the wine-stained papers from a stool and handed them to Will.

'Unless he has friends aboard.'

'He tells me he travelled alone, as his regular acquaintances feared England's firepower, even against a fleet of this size.'

Lifting the man's battered and bruised head, Will studied him for a moment while he thought. The captive's left eye had closed up, and there was a patchwork of purple bruises and broken veins across his features. His lip had been split and one tooth was missing. 'There will be risks aplenty, but this will at least give me an opportunity. I thank you. Now I must disguise my appearance as much as possible, for I have unfortunately been the subject of several pamphlets published in London detailing my adventures, each of which came with an engraving, which, although it failed to capture my true heroic nature,' he added with sarcasm, 'could make me recognizable.'

Santos guided Will out of the room, but did not close the door. 'I will find you a razor, some shears and dye. Now: have you all you need to bring misery to the hated Spanish?'

'What you offer and my own wit is all I need.'

Santos's polite bow only just hid years of mounting hatred. 'Then I must tidy up here. I will meet you downstairs shortly.' He drew a knife from his belt and prepared to step back into the attic room. Before he did so, he turned back briefly, his face looking haunted in the lamplight. 'These times make monsters of all of us,' he said. 'I wonder sometimes where is the simple man who took joy from the art he created in the hills around Lisbon. I fear he is lost for ever.'

Santos stepped into the attic room and closed the door behind him.

# CHAPTER FORTY-FIVE

'TAKE ONE MORE STEP AND I WILL CUT OFF YOUR EARS AND your nose!' the Spanish officer barked in faltering English. One hand lay on the hilt of his knife, and he looked as if he wished to mutilate Will whether he complied or not.

Will stopped at the top of the rope ladder, on the brink of stepping on to the deck of the *Nuestra Señora del Rosario*, according to Santos one of the most heavily armed ships in the Spanish fleet.

'Papers!' the officer demanded. Snatching them from Will's fingers, he cast one eye over the stolen documents while keeping the other on Will's face. The cursory glance came to a sharp halt, and he read one section in detail, his brow knitting, before staring closely at Will. He drew his knife and Will was sure he had been discovered, and was about to go for the secret blade given him by Dee. But then the officer jabbed his weapon in the direction of a clutch of three men further along the deck, and thrust the papers back into Will's hand with a contemptuous expression.

Playing his part, Will relaxed, gave a sullen nod and climbed up on board. Clean-shaven, with trimmed hair dyed to dark brown, he was now one William Prowd, a mercenary fighting man fresh from the campaign in the Netherlands. As such, he would not be expected to be a seasoned sailor and could easily disguise his ignorance of the backbreaking work on deck. And with a supply of dye to keep his hair brown, he hoped he could survive for weeks, if necessary. By judgement or chance, Santos had done his work well.

But Will was now trapped on a ship full of England's avowed enemies who would take his life in a moment, amid a vast fleet filled with thousands more cut-throats all en route to what promised to be the fiercest battle the world had known. He would not be able to rest for a second.

Dawn had broken, clear and golden, and with it came a light wind off the Atlantic. The sticky scent of pine from the forested hills mingled with the tang of salt and the rich aroma of fish from the small boats unloading their catch on the quayside. Amid the discordant screech of seagulls, Will had made his way to the ship early to avoid unnecessary scrutiny.

The *Nuestra Señora del Rosario* was moored on the far side of what the locals called the floating forest. It was a carrack, with a soaring forecastle that would prove a terrifying prospect for any would-be boarders. It was also the Spanish pay-ship, carrying the wages of every man sailing with the armada, and as such Will knew it would be a prime target for England's pirates. The last thing he wanted was to be slain by his own countrymen within sight of home, if he survived that long.

The three men eyed Will suspiciously as he drew near. They were all English. Two were mercenaries like Prowd, happy to sell themselves to the highest bidder. Henry Barrett was a barrel of a man with enormous muscular arms, a big belly, and a shaven head. Jerome Stanbury was slight next to his associate but still muscular, with a hooked nose and lank grey-black hair hanging down to his shoulders. The third, Walter Hakebourne, was a coastal pilot. It was he who would guide the Spanish ship to safe harbour once they arrived in England. A small man, he appeared permanently anxious and on edge, as if he expected an attack at any moment.

'Have ye heard the news?' Stanbury said. 'King Philip has sent the order to sail. This day, May the ninth, is one to remember, eh, friend? We will make good money out of this, for even when we reach England the Spanish will require much fighting and peace-keeping.'

'How long till we are ready to depart?' Will asked.

'*We* can be ready in hours, for this is a well-run ship. It is under the command of Don Pedro de Valdes, one of the armada's best admirals,' Hakebourne stuttered. 'But the rest of 'em? I would say two days,' and he hawked his disgust over the rail.

As the day warmed, they continued to speak about little of import in the curt manner of men who trusted no one: the poor quality of the food, their doubts about the provisions purchased for the voyage, the inadequacy of many of the Spanish sailors. Guiding the conversation in an oblique manner, Will attempted to discover more information about Medina Sidonia's plans for the armada, but it quickly became clear that the men knew little of real value.

Then a buzz began to spread across the other ships in the harbour, voices raised cheerily in shouts and song, as the news of the arrival of the King's orders and the certain knowledge that the crews' long wait would soon be over moved through the mighty fleet. Such was the irony of their work that whenever they were at sea they craved the comforts of port, but when on dry land they could not wait to return to sea.

'This will be over in no time,' Barrett grunted. 'The Spanish officers told Hawksworth that Elizabeth still persists with peace negotiations with Parma, when Philip has no intention of seeing them concluded. There is no time for England to get her defences in place. We will stride right up to the door of the Queen's bedchamber, knock politely and ask for entry!'

They all laughed, but Will's mind was racing. 'Hawksworth?' he asked, feigning ignorance.

Uneasily, they exchanged brief glances as Stanbury said, 'Sir Richard Hawksworth. You have heard tell of him?'

Will had. Hawksworth had spent his time in the shadow of the treacherous Sir William Stanley, but his reputation for deceit and cruelty was, if anything, even greater. In the Netherlands, while helping Stanley complete his betrayal of the city of Deventer to the Duke of Parma for a substantial purse of gold, Hawksworth was rumoured to have sent his own brother to his death for money. In a stew of traitors, cut-throats and liars, Hawksworth would be the most venal and the least trustworthy. But what concerned Will was that Hawksworth had spent a great deal of time at Elizabeth's court, and while he and Will had never met face to face, he would know of his reputation, and perhaps other telling details too.

The mention of his name had troubled the others as well, for they had grown bad-tempered and fractious. But there was still one thing Will needed to know before they sloped off below deck. It was not an easy question to ask.

'I have heard tell,' he said, leaning in conspiratorially, 'of strange things occurring around this fleet. Portents . . . and apparitions. I would not sail with a fleet that is cursed.'

Will knew that sailors and fighting men were superstitious, no doubt a response to the closeness of death in their daily lives, but even so he was surprised by the reaction to his words. Barrett, Stanbury and Hakebourne crossed themselves and looked down at the deck. Hakebourne muttered a prayer, while Stanbury pulled out a rabbit's foot, which he gripped as if his life depended on it.

'I myself saw, two nights gone, mysterious lights under the waves after dark had fallen, moving from the shore to ship . . . several ships,' Hakebourne whispered.

'And the beer turned to vinegar at an inn on the quayside after a drunken Spaniard cursed the Fair Folk.' Barrett looked over his shoulder as if he expected someone to be standing on the ship's rail at his back.

'Spectres,' Stanbury muttered. 'Glimpsed in the evening mist, stalking the forests around Lisbon.' He pointed an accusing finger at Will. 'Do not mention them again.'

Will didn't need to – he already had the answer he required: the Unseelie Court was accompanying the armada to England. He was in the midst of more enemies than he had feared.

His question had cast a pall over the conversation, but as they prepared to break up so Will could find his berth for the night they were hailed loudly by a tall, flamboyantly dressed man with a pockmarked face. Will noticed he rarely blinked, so that he resembled one of the lizards Will had seen basking in the sun on the rocks on his journey from El Escorial.

'Watch your back,' Stanbury muttered quietly. ''Tis Hawksworth.'

The man's heavy-lidded gaze flickered across those present before alighting on Will. Hawksworth's brow knitted briefly before he spoke, and his gaze kept returning to Will for unsettling periods. 'I have just returned from a council of war on the flagship,' he pronounced. Will knew Hawksworth was not one of the inner circle, however much he pretended, so he could only have been on the ship as an associate of Stanley, and was unlikely to be privy to anything of importance. 'You will have heard the order to sail has arrived, yes? But the King also sent another missive, warning that English spies may attempt to sneak into the fleet. We must be on our guard at all times. You all have correct papers, yes?' He spoke to the group at large, but his eyes suggested he was only addressing Will.

Will showed him Prowd's papers, and that appeared to satisfy him, although as he swaggered away from the group he cast one final, curious glance at Will.

Will was put to work in the hold, securing siege guns for the land war, which would be put to good use against vulnerable English towns along the south coast once the Spanish broke through the sea defences.

The crew was worked hard, but the sense of anticipation was high. The boredom of waiting had started to prove self-destructive, and everyone was eager to put to sea, however much danger lay ahead. As they laboured, Barrett and Stanbury bantered with a gallows humour, only falling silent whenever Hawksworth passed by. He appeared to do no work himself, and spent most of his time attempting to ingratiate himself with the Spanish officers, who showed little interest, indeed, appeared to be irritated by him.

As night fell, Will found a cramped sleeping space in the gloomy, noisy below-deck. The crew would sleep on the bare boards with only one coarse dogswain blanket for comfort and a folded jerkin for a pillow. It was impossible to move without jostling another crew member, and the air was heavy with the vinegar-sour reek of sweat, urine, and vomit from those who had consumed too much drink. After they'd eaten a meal of fresh mullet, the men turned to raucous singalongs or played cards, or told tales of their time at sea across the globe.

Much later, when he was sure his absence would not be noticed, Will crept on deck, and looked out at the lights flickering across the floating city, mirroring the stars above.

He considered swimming among the ships to try to find Grace and the Silver Skull, to steal them away before they put to sea, but the chances of his being discovered were high, whereas those of his locating the ship of the women were low.

Medina Sidonia's flagship, the *San Martin*, was moored close by. Throughout the day Will had been surreptitiously watching the comings and goings on board for any sign of Don Alanzo, without any luck. Now, as he stood at the rail studying the ship, a chill fell upon him. Grey shapes flitted across the deck, insubstantial in the dark. Others might have thought them moon shadows, but Will knew better.

He watched the Enemy, trying to make sense of what they were doing on board, wondering how much the Spanish knew of the danger in their midst; for he knew the Unseelie Court would easily turn on their current allies once England was destroyed. Suddenly he became aware that one of the indistinct figures had come to a halt and was standing at the rail.

*Looking at him?*

With a shudder, Will ducked and moved quickly away from his vantage point. Had he been seen? Worse, had he been recognized?

Returning to the seething activity below deck, he tried to lose himself among the mass of the crew.

The night was hot and uncomfortable in the crowded, confined quarters. Will bedded down with his knife in his hand, but the only disturbances came from sailors stumbling over him in the dark, and the subsequent curses and kicks.

The next day passed with a sense of mounting anticipation as the fleet readied itself for war, and on 11 May, Medina Sidonia was ready to take advantage of a light easterly wind. After the crack of a cannon and a puff of white smoke, there was a tumult of beating drums, loud cheers and raucous singing.

Anchors were raised and the first galleon pulled out of the port. The harbour-front was crowded with people watching the spectacle, though Will knew many were only there to see the back of the hated fleet.

Gradually, the armada set sail downstream. But the long string of ships had barely begun to clear the mouth of the Tagus when the wind turned and blew directly at them, and they were forced to drop anchor and wait. Storms raged up and down the coastline, and as Will watched the churning black clouds he couldn't help but wonder if Dee had something to do with it. Rumours of his conjuring abilities had circulated around the court for decades. Will had no idea whether they were true, or if he was simply a very clever and skilful man. Still, as lightning flickered and the crew grew irritated at the delay so early in their campaign, he wondered.

The wait dragged from hours into days and then weeks, the tension slowly escalating. Tormented by thoughts of what was happening to Grace, Will tried to distract himself as much as he could. Whenever he was able, he took the opportunity to watch the constant stream of boats plying their way back and forth from Medina Sidonia's *San Martin*. He knew what they contained: intelligence reports from Philip of Spain's network of spies detailing the readiness – or lack of it – of the English forces. And still the wind blew, lashing occasional bouts of stinging rain, and rolling the sea up into choppy waves of white-topped grey.

On 27 May Will was brought up short as he swabbed blood off the deck after a fight between a Spaniard and a press-ganged Portuguese sailor. A familiar black-garbed figure stood on the deck of the *San Martin* which was sailing ahead and to the starboard of the *Rosario*. It was Don Alanzo, cloak wrapped tightly around him against the elements, deep in conversation with Medina Sidonia himself. Suppressing his excitement, Will kept his head down, swabbing hard, so the Don would not see him. But when he looked back at the *San Martin*, he realized Hawksworth was watching him. He tried to pass off his attention as idle curiosity, pointing out the fluttering pennants and new gilding to a clearly uninterested Stanbury. When Will glanced back, Hawksworth was gone, but he knew he would have to be more careful.

That night, in the face of a yet another fierce gale, Will and a handful of other crew members were sent up on deck to supplement the seasoned crew. As the deck bucked and heaved under his feet, he fought to stay upright. After a while, the skin of his face burned from the lash of the rain and the spray and the bite of the wind. The officer barked orders in Spanish. Will had to feign ignorance, forcing him to attempt to give directions by pointing. After a while, he found it easier to leave Will alone and struggling to do what he could under the personal guidance of Hakebourne.

The other ships loomed like black castles in the dark on all sides, lamps glowing in their windows, as they fought their own battles with the gale. As Will gripped the rail in the face of one severe swell, he caught sight of a ship he had not seen before. It moved with a speed that belied the conditions, its strange grey sails billowing. Gooseflesh prickled along Will's arms.

As it neared, Will was surprised to see there was no activity on deck despite the cruel weather. The ship had an unsettling spectral quality, at times fading into the spray, at others seeming insubstantial even when the wind dropped. Will's heart began to beat faster as an inexplicable dread fell upon him. Flashes of greenish light came and went in the windows and on the forecastle, like the glows that burned over the marshes, luring travellers to their doom. Will searched for some identifying banner or name, but there was none.

'What is that vessel?' he called to Hakebourne above the howl of the gale, although he guessed the identity of the crew who sailed it.

Hakebourne kept his eyes down as he tied a knot, at ease with the roll of the deck. 'I see nothing,' he shouted back.

'There!' Will indicated. 'Astern!'

Hakebourne still did not look up. 'Nothing,' he replied, half turning his back on Will.

And then, as he watched, there *was* activity on deck, as though a veil had been drawn back to reveal the mystery behind it. Various figures walked upright effortlessly, or clambered up the rigging, but it was the one who stood on the forecastle, arms raised to the heavens, that drew Will's attention.

Flashes of lightning burst among the clouds overhead. No, not lightning, but colours – red and green and purple. The rest of his crew like Hakebourne continued to ignore them, but Will noticed their heads were bowed, and, where he could see them, their faces strained. Their expressions only eased when the mysterious ship slipped away into the deep dark. It was not long afterwards that the gale dropped.

'It appears we are blessed, as the Spanish tell us,' Will commented to Hakebourne.

The other man only grunted in reply in a manner which seemed to suggest he thought they were more likely cursed.

And on 28 May the inclement weather finally cleared. One by one, anchors were raised, and the vast, floating city of the armada began to make its way out of the Tagus and into open waters. Each ship that passed Castle St Julian was marked by the celebratory thunder of cannon. And it was well past dawn the next day when the last of the fleet left the mouth of the river behind.

The string of ships stretched for miles, a formidable sight for any enemy, but it was forced to move at the pace of the slowest hulk and that made progress excruciatingly slow. Will was relieved that there was at least some movement, and he could see his mood reflected in the faces of the crew members around him. The waiting had made them irritable, and that had led to arguments and fights.

Shadows moved across the deck as the hours passed, but the scenery on the shore barely seemed to change. Two days later, the mighty armada was still south of the Rock of Lisbon, and it took thirteen more days just to travel along the coast to Finisterre.

As they rounded the cape late in the afternoon, an outcry below deck drew Will's attention. He found a knot of angry seamen gathered around the provisions store, with a raging Barrett in the forefront.

'What is wrong?' Will asked.

Barrett flipped the lid off a barrel to reveal mouldy ship's biscuit heaving with maggots and worms. 'The rice is the same,' Barrett thundered. 'And here.' He opened another barrel, and Will recoiled from the foul stink. 'Beef. Gone bad. All of it. And the fish too.' Barrett threw the barrel lid down so that it shattered into pieces.

'All the provisions?' Will asked.

'Half of them. These damn Spaniards are like children. I should never have trusted them to mount an efficient campaign. They will poison us all long before we engage in battle.'

Will pulled a green biscuit from the barrel. It broke apart in his fingers, and a fat white maggot dropped to the deck. 'These have been here a while?'

'Since the autumn,' Barrett snapped. 'All the delays to the armada, and they sat upon their provisions. What were they thinking? There are already twenty men below, vomiting and fouling their quarters after eating this filth. The wine too has gone sour, and the water is undrinkable. I will have none of it.'

'Come, lads,' Will called to the grumbling crew members who had gathered around Barrett. 'Will we let them treat us this way?'

He was pleased when he heard an angry response from the English sailors, and soon the Spanish and Portuguese had joined in, shouting complaints and cursing.

'We should take this matter to Valdes!' Will shouted. As the men stormed to the forecastle in search of the commander, Will held back, happy with the disruption he had caused. The more disgruntled the crew, the worse they would perform when battle was joined. But as he waited, a hand caught his forearm. It was Hawksworth.

'Do I know you?' he asked. 'Your face plays upon my mind. It would be ill-mannered of me if we have fought beside each other in some campaign or other, or been in our cups in a tavern, and I did not recognize you.'

'No, sir, I do not believe we have ever met.' Hiding his concern with a duck of his head, Will tried to go, but Hawksworth would not let him.

'That accent. Do I hear a hint of Warwickshire?'

'Sir, I have family in the Midlands, but I have not been home in many a year.'

Hawksworth studied Will for a moment, and then asked, 'And what campaigns have you been on?' His brown beard had grown bushier during his time with the fleet, and he tugged at it as he mused.

Barrett hurried up, shaking his fist in triumph. 'Valdes has agreed to hear our complaints,' he called. 'Come on, Prowd. Listen to what he has to say.'

Will was grateful for the interruption and hurried away with Barrett, but he could feel Hawksworth's eyes upon his back.

As more and more provisions were found to be rotten, the fierce complaints spread like wildfire from ship to ship, and Will did all he could to spread discontent. Medina Sidonia sent for more supplies, from Spain, from anywhere in Portugal. Men were falling ill with the flux, fouling their living spaces and bringing down the violent ire of those who slept near them. Will stood back, watching the chaos, as barrel upon barrel of stinking food was tossed overboard. His confidence grew that the armada was sailing to disaster, and he turned his attention to searching for an opportunity to reach Grace on the ship of the women.

For four days, the fleet waited off Finisterre for victuals and fresh water to arrive, but there was never enough. In the end Medina Sidonia called a council of war. Although initial orders demanded that no ship return to Spain under any circumstances, it was decided to put into Corunna to resupply.

Seeing his opportunity, Will volunteered for the shore crew who would oversee the collection and distribution of provisions across the fleet. It was a prime job, but to Will's frustration Hawksworth, Barrett and Stanbury were also assigned to the large team.

Eager to get ashore, he watched the rugged expanse of sheer cliffs and the waves crashing against the sharp-toothed black rocks along the north-west Spanish coast. Eventually the fleet sailed into a pleasant crescent bay with the ragged spur of the Pyrenees rising up, purple and cloud-capped, in the distance. Perched over the bay, a stout castle and a fort, where a battery pointed seaward guarded the walled city of Corunna. Red, blue and yellow roof-tiles on the private houses glinted amid the gleaming white marble of the palace and public buildings, so the city appeared to be studded with jewels in the morning sun. Along the sea front, peasants wound their way with laden donkeys towards the market.

For most of the day, the lead ships settled into the harbour and dropped anchor, but when dusk fell nearly half the fleet – more than fifty ships – still waited at sea for daylight.

On the quayside, among the other crew members from the *Rosario*, Will waited for an opportunity to slip away, but Hawksworth seemed to be watching his every movement. Will felt angry and frustrated. What was the traitor thinking? Every word Hawksworth said and every move he made reeked of suspicion, and Will began to fear the alarm would be raised and he would be hauled off to the flagship and publicly executed. The strain of having to be constantly alert was beginning to tell, and he found himself sleeping fitfully, woken repeatedly by every slight noise in the filthy, stifling, overcrowded quarters.

His ruminations were disrupted by the sight of a storm sweeping in from the ocean. Lightning crackled in furious jagged bursts along the horizon, and as the wind gusted into the harbour the ships bucked and rolled on the swell. The lanterns hanging outside the taverns swung wildly, the leaping shadows distorting the faces of those who waited with the shore party. When the rain began to lash in horizontally, they fled into one of the taverns for shelter.

While the rest of the men availed themselves of the local wine, Will stood at the window and watched the storm grow in intensity. The flashes of lightning revealed the ships at anchor rising up on mountains before disappearing beneath a roll of black.

Then other lights appeared in the sky, painting the roiling clouds in the same colours that Will had witnessed over the ship with the grey sails. Was the Unseelie Court attempting to protect the fleet from nature's fury?

'So Philip has sent his armada against England knowing that his enemy is much stronger and refusing all the entreaties of his advisers.' Will was startled by Hawksworth's appearance at his shoulder. His breath reeking of wine, the traitor looked out across the harbour to the eerie wash of light. 'Everyone told the King not to send the armada at this time,' he continued, 'but still he persevered. He stated his belief that God is on the side of the Spanish, and wherever weaknesses arise, God will help the Spanish overcome them. *The confident hope of a miracle*, he calls it. But consider this, Master Prowd. What if the Spanish king does not put his faith in God after all? What if our sly Philip knows more than he says?'

Will watched the lights slowly die away until only darkness remained.

'What if, instead, Philip had made a pact with the Devil, and England's sea forces face an infernal surprise that will destroy them? Out there, hidden among the fleet, is something beyond belief, waiting to be used.'

'You know of these things for certain?' Will asked. Could Malantha have given the armada some secret weapon?

Hawksworth leaned in close so his hot breath warmed Will's ear. 'Mark me, Prowd, Death waits ahead, and no one will be able to hide from his touch.'

# CHAPTER FORTY-SIX

CLAMBERING ON TO THE DECK OF THE *SANTIAGO*, THE SHIP OF the women, Will knew he had little time to find Grace before the guards came hunting for him. His heart pounded, and he could barely believe he was there. Weeks had passed since they had dropped anchor in Corunna, and only now had this opportunity arisen. On the gentle swell of the water below, the other men of the reprovisioning team, red-faced and sweating in the heat of the day, struggled to prepare the barrels to be hauled up from the rowboat.

He was taking a tremendous risk. If he was found among the women he was likely to be flogged or even killed by an officer, but it had taken some planning to get assigned to the work group delivering provisions to the *Santiago* and it was unlikely he would get another chance.

At the rail, both sentries paid him scant attention, preferring to argue quietly over Medina Sidonia's decision to continue with the invasion despite the damage wreaked on the fleet by the storm. Will sensed they were both on the brink of desertion.

Easing out of their line of vision, he slipped quietly away. He tried to appear insignificant, to blend in, but there were eyes everywhere. Medina Sidonia had posted troops along the entire quay and throughout the city to prevent any more desertions.

The mood across the fleet had been increasingly desperate since the storm all those weeks ago. That night, the ships left at sea had been forced to run in the face of the tempest. Some suffered shattered mainmasts and lost rudders, and while others had limped to shelter further along the coast, thirty ships, including several galleons, had been missing for weeks.

Four days after the storm, Medina Sidonia had called another council of war. Following a receipt of a missive from the King, the Duke and his commanders felt they had no choice but to wait in Corunna until the missing ships had been found, repairs had been carried out, and the entire fleet had been reprovisioned. The last ship hadn't returned until 15 July.

For Will, the long wait had been interminable. The Spanish commanders kept the men working hard under the hot sun, but his thoughts turned continually to Grace, the shadow that was falling across England, and the brooding threat of the Unseelie Court working their mysterious schemes just out of sight. Time and again he had been despatched into the dusty countryside as one of a team searching out wood for new barrels for provisions, until he thought he would go mad with the boredom.

At least the frantic repairs and reprovisioning provided some cover in the cluttered harbour. Everyone was even busier now the order to sail had been issued. When he saw an opportunity to search the *Santiago*, he took it with relief.

At the top of the steps leading below deck, Will glanced around quickly. No one watched. He moved swiftly into the stifling dark.

The *Santiago* was the oldest ship in the fleet, a six-hundred-ton hulk, flat-bottomed with a spacious hold but clumsy at sea and one of the vessels that slowed the armada's speed and efficiency. Will had earlier glimpsed the women moving about on deck. They looked like ravens as they took the sea air in their black dresses and caps, but they had been ordered below lest they tempt sailors who had been starved of comfort for so long. Yet still Will had not caught sight of Grace. Was she even there? The thought left him deeply worried.

Below deck, the women had attempted to bring some comfort to their meagre quarters. Sheets had been strung from ropes across the hold to provide a modicum of privacy and bunches of dried lavender and muslin bags of rose petals offered some relief from the rank smell.

As Will appeared at the foot of the creaking steps, the curtains shifted as suspicious eyes inspected him. Puzzled mutterings rolled around the dark space and for a moment he was afraid the alarm would be raised, but from the looks he received from some of the younger women, he guessed they had felt as deprived of company as the men. They flashed quick, nervous smiles and held his gaze a moment too long. Even the older women occasionally let their gaze linger, for all their disapproving expressions and mutterings about his presence in their midst.

The sound of barrels banging up the side of the ship reminded Will that time was running out and he took the risk of asking one of the young women if she knew of an English woman on board. Shyly, the girl pointed to the back of the living quarters where an area had been curtained off with sailcloth.

Will pushed through the heavy, rough material, and there, hugging her knees, a chain fastened to one ankle and affixed to the hull, was Grace. And she did not wear the Silver Skull.

His relief palpable, he squatted before her, fighting the

457

urge to hold her tightly. Her shock gave way to a rush of silent emotion, but after a moment she pulled back, her eyes blazing. She jabbed a finger towards him and fumed, '"Kill the King"?'

'Grace . . .' Waving his hand, he urged her to be quieter.

Reluctantly, she lowered her voice, but still seething said, 'Have you come to finish the job? Where is your dagger?' She thrust her chest towards him and framed her heart. 'There. Does that make it easier?'

'Grace . . .' He saw how dishevelled she looked, her dress stained with food, her hair unbrushed.

'"Oh, yes, I will protect you, Grace. Until it comes to a hard choice and then I will blithely toss you to the wolves."'

'You are alive, are you not?' he snapped.

'No thanks to you.' She looked him up and down, taking in his disguise.

'Months apart and your first instinct is to scold me like a child? You are the most infuriating woman I know.'

'I can give you your due reward once we are away from here. How will you free me from this chain?' With frustration, she gave it a yank then let it clatter to the boards.

'This is not the time,' he began hesitantly.

She gave a sarcastic sigh. 'Of course not.'

'We are in the midst of the enemy fleet. There is no chance of escaping with our lives at the moment.'

'Then how did you get here?' She offered her hand so Will could help her to her feet.

'I am now William Prowd, a mercenary in the employ of Philip of Spain. Trust me, Grace. When the time is right—'

'Oh, yes, I trust you. Of course. When the time is right. In the meantime, I will continue to enjoy the indignities heaped upon me.'

458

Will took a breath to steady himself. 'Have you been ill-treated?' he said, pronouncing every word carefully.

'I confess, apart from chaining me like a dog, Don Alanzo has treated me well,' she sniffed.

Will took her face in his hands and examined her eyes. They were still dreamy, carrying a hint of whatever subtle control Malantha had exerted over her at El Escorial. He knew that although she was not in the Unseelie Court's thrall at that moment, they still planned to use her in their plot, and then her life would be forfeit.

'What has happened to the Silver Skull?' he asked tentatively. 'Don Alanzo intended to make you its bearer.'

It was then that she told him that Don Alanzo had fixed the mask to Mayhew on the carriage ride from El Escorial.

Though Will hated Mayhew for the suffering he had set in motion, he couldn't help feeling pity for the next victim of the damnable mask. 'Then perhaps there is still some honour within the Spaniard,' Will said. 'Now, I have little time here before I am discovered. You must tell me what you have learned during your time with Don Alanzo. He speaks to you?'

'He occasionally visits me to enquire after my well-being and if I have any needs, and we pass the time, if not as friends then as people who share a bond.' Her face darkened and she looked away. 'A bond of suffering.'

'Do you know where Mayhew is? Is he hidden on the flag-ship?'

She shook her head. 'I only know he was taken aboard a ship with grey sails. It appeared deserted. And I . . . I have not seen its kind before.'

'Then I must board that grey-sailed ship and see for myself,' Will said, knowing exactly what that might entail. 'Mayhew is the architect of much of the misery we have experienced. He will pay dearly for his crimes.'

The clattering of the barrels continued, accompanied by a bout of shouting and cursing. Soon, he knew, they would come looking for him.

'Don Alanzo did not tell me his plans,' Grace continued, 'but he was unguarded in some of his comments. He does not see me as a threat, and he knows there is nothing I can do until the Spanish plot comes to fruition. There is some hidden weapon—'

'The Silver Skull?'

'No, another. Something that will be used when the Spanish fleet encounters our English ships. Don Alanzo appeared troubled when he realized he had mentioned it to me. It seemed to me that this was a secret even the Spanish commanders did not know . . . something of which only Don Alanzo and a few others were aware.'

'Spies are privy to many secrets denied the common man. That is our benefit and our burden. He said no more? What it was? Where it is held?'

She shook her head.

'Any more of the Spanish invasion plans?'

'No.' After a brief pause, she added, 'But Will . . . I asked him about my sister. I asked him about Jenny.'

Will flinched. 'Why would you question Don Alanzo about her?'

Grace paused again, seeing the pain in his face. 'I know your work is in some way connected to Jenny's disappearance, or so you think. If she was taken by Spanish spies, you would not tell me, for fear I would rush to Walsingham, or the Queen herself, and demand all that we can do to gain her return, even if it be war.'

'And what did Don Alanzo say?' he asked.

'He sat down, here, and listened carefully to all my pleadings. He knew something, or he would not have listened.'

'He knows nothing. Don Alanzo understands the world in which we operate, that is all.' Will didn't mean to sound so cold or bitter.

'He told me he would make enquiries as to her well-being.' Tears stung her eyes, and in them Will sensed a hint of an accusation that he had not done enough.

The clattering outside ended and something akin to silence descended on the ship. 'Grace, I must go. We shall talk of this later,' he said.

'And when will that be?' she asked tartly. 'I would plan my swooning.'

'Soon.'

'I heard the order to put back to sea. Do you wait until we make land, which means England will have fallen, and our lives will amount to nothing? Or do we go down at sea under the weight of English cannon?'

'Trust me. I will do everything in my power to help you.'

Relenting, she gave an exasperated nod. He held her hands and an uneasy moment passed between them, before he stepped past the sailcloth and hurried back through the living quarters.

Back on deck, one of his fellows, a gruff Spaniard, angrily accused him of slacking. A fight was brewing until the guards stepped in and urged the Spanish seaman over the rail and down to the rowboat.

As Will waited to follow, a shadow loomed over him. It was Hawksworth. He must have been elsewhere on deck, and must have arrived after Will.

*How much did he see?*

His answer came when Hawksworth leaned in and whispered, 'I know who you are,' before sweeping away across the deck.

# CHAPTER FORTY-SEVEN

THE SHORE PARTY WERE SILENT ON THE BOAT BACK FROM THE *Santiago*. Will watched the quayside for guards gathering to arrest him, but every man was occupied with the frantic reprovisioning of the fleet. Why hadn't Hawksworth revealed Will's identity there and then on the ship of the women? Why had he simply whispered to Will in the certain knowledge that Will could have slit his throat and attempted to make good his escape?

Once their boat was moored, Will uneasily joined the throng hauling barrels out of the warehouses while he worked on a course of action. It was easy to lose himself in the bustle of noisy activity. New barrels were still being built amid a clatter of hammers before they were filled and lowered with grunts and curses into every available rowboat.

Still no one came for him. It made no sense, unless Hawksworth had a grander scheme in mind. But what could that be?

For the rest of the day, Will remained alert, scanning his surroundings – the groups of stone-faced soldiers, even the dark interiors of taverns and stores. But there was not a hint that anyone was any the wiser about his true identity, and it made him nervous.

He was torn, but he knew there was too much at stake to flee. Finally he decided to continue as planned in the hope that he could deny any allegation Hawksworth made. Back on board the *Rosario*, he acted as normally as possible, exchanging lewd banter with Barrett and Stanbury as he went about his allotted tasks. Occasionally, he glimpsed Hawksworth, but the traitor gave no sign that anything had passed between them. That puzzled Will even more.

Twilight brought a cooling breeze that eased the heat of the day. Will sat with the others on deck while the officers discussed Medina Sidonia's orders at the forecastle. After so long in Corunna, there was an eagerness to get back to sea, although it was tempered by apprehension at what might lie ahead.

The gun to make ready finally sounded at midnight. Will dozed fitfully, in case Hawksworth made his move during the night, and at dawn every crew member was up with the crack of the cannon ordering them to sea. It was another very hot day, and it took until mid-afternoon for the fleet to assemble, but by the following dawn they were finally out of sight of Spain.

Will glimpsed Hawksworth regularly, talking to the officers or overseeing some mundane task, but the man continued to give no indication that anything had passed between them. As each day progressed, the tense atmosphere magnified until Will longed for something to happen to end the unbearable waiting. But before his identity came to light he had to board the grey-sailed ship.

Like the shadow of death, the vessel of the Unseelie Court loomed regularly out of the night, its grey sails reminding Will of a shroud, its empty deck a grave. It paused alongside the *Rosario*, as well as the flagship and other warships, for a short period each night. Moving with unnatural speed, it appeared to mark out a predetermined route through the fleet, as though following a ritual path.

Will knew he had little time to board the ship, find the Silver Skull and make good his escape, but he made his preparations. In the hold amongst the carpenters' tools, he had found the grapnels used by boarding parties and had secreted one on deck.

On the chosen night, as most slept, he crept barefoot up into the salty night air, ready to begin his vigil for the grey-sailed ship. The armada was sailing under a bank of low cloud, and with poor visibility and a choppy sea the night watch was preoccupied. Drizzle made the deck slippery, and moisture dripped from the sails. The lamps of the other ships in the fleet flickered and glinted across the water.

Huddled against the elements, Will waited. Finally, he caught sight of the silhouette of a lightless galleon ploughing across the waves on a slanting path between the other vessels. By its speed he knew it must be the grey-sailed ship.

As he searched for the grapnel, he caught sight of someone emerging from below deck. Ducking down at the rail, Will watched, stock-still, as the figure searched slowly while trying to keep out of view. At the foot of the steps to the poop deck, the swinging lantern revealed the profile of Hawksworth, sword drawn, but held low at his side.

'Prowd?' he hissed.

Cursing under his breath, Will peered over the rail. The grey-sailed ship had now moved alongside, keeping an exact pace with the *Rosario*. Although it was dark, Will could see there was no movement on deck, no one on the poop deck or forecastle, no lookout. To the casual eye, it could have been abandoned and drifting with the current, if not for the purposeful way it had been steered alongside. An illusion, Will was certain, like the Fairy House in Edinburgh, which always appeared empty from the street.

The cursed ship was now close enough to reach with the grapnel, but Will couldn't risk moving with Hawksworth searching for him. Nor could he risk a fight on deck.

After a moment's thought, he left the hook where he had hidden it and pulled himself on to the rail. Fleet-footed, he clambered up the rigging, the damp, oily rope slick beneath his fingers and toes. Away from the shelter of the deck, the wind tore at him and the rain lashed as the ship rolled on the swell. Hooking his arm through the rigging, he waited in the knowledge that Hawksworth would not think to look up.

His frustration mounting, he accepted the moment had passed for the night. As he watched the grey-sailed ship, the hairs on his neck tingled as if someone was looking up at him. He wondered who or what really stood on that seemingly empty deck.

Below him, Hawksworth continued to prowl, rapier ready to repel any attack, with all the balance and poise of a master swordsman. It appeared he had decided to eliminate Will himself, rather than hand him over to the Spanish. Will couldn't understand Hawksworth's thinking. The capture of a spy who could be tortured to provide vital information was a prize that warranted a high reward. A dead body was proof of nothing.

Will drew his knife and waited.

Hawksworth moved warily around in the drizzle, clearly puzzled that Will had vanished. He'd obviously seen Will leave his sleeping space, and had decided either that he was up to no good, or that it was the best time to despatch him unnoticed.

Fingers cramping in the cold, Will held on in the face of the harsh wind. When Hawksworth was beneath him, he dropped. The traitor's cry was lost to the gale as Will smashed him to the deck, and before he could recover Will propelled him into the rail, winding him. Lunging with his knife just at the moment when the ship bucked over a large wave, Will skidded on the wet deck, and he half went down, one hand keeping his balance.

Eyes blazing, Hawksworth brought up his sword with a skill that surprised Will. 'Prowd,' he snarled, 'or should I say Swyfte?'

Will couldn't wait for the man to raise the alarm. Using the momentum of the rolling ship, he threw himself forward and plunged his blade into Hawksworth's gut. His opponent's eyes bulged with shock as if he hadn't been expecting any attack. Dropping his rapier, he clutched at his stomach. Blood splattered from his mouth.

'No!' he gasped.

As the blood ran into the rain, the traitor slumped down against the rail, desperately trying to stem the flow, knowing it was already too late.

'You fool!' he whispered. 'I am a spy, like you!'

'Lies at the last?' Will knelt next to the dying man so they would not be seen, ready to use his knife again if Hawksworth attempted to call out.

'I worked both sides, but gave the last to Walsingham.' Hawksworth's clothes were now sodden with blood.

'He said nothing—'

'Walsingham never says anything!' He coughed and more blood ran from his mouth. 'The Spanish were close to uncovering me. My time was short, and I needed your aid.

467

Together, we could have made our escape when we engaged the English fleet. I have details of Parma's invasion force . . . locations . . . numbers . . .' He coughed again, growing weaker.

'You are the fool! Why did you not identify yourself?' Will demanded. His anger masked his painful regret.

'I had to be certain. And now it is too late!' Hawksworth gasped, eyes closing in agony. 'We spend so long pretending . . . we waste our life on lies . . . we are always brought down by our own deceit. All of us.'

Hawksworth's final breath rattled from his throat, and his chin slumped on to his chest. Briefly, Will bowed his head too, so that they resembled a mirror image of each other, one alive, one dead. His guilt quickly turned to anger at the stupidity of it all, the confusion, both of them hiding behind masks, each mistrusting the other.

When he was sure no one watched, he dragged Hawksworth to the rail and pushed him over into the sea. With the wind, and the crash of the waves against the hull, the splash was not audible. The body went under and was gone. He stared into the water as bitterness washed over him.

The grey-sailed ship still kept apace with the *Rosario*, but as he watched it gained speed and pulled ahead, sailing across the prow and away into the dark towards the *San Martin*. It had been a grim night. Will stifled his feelings of failure with the knowledge that he could return the following night to try again.

But as he carefully made his way towards the steps that led below deck, he thought he saw a dark shape waiting there, a shape that quickly disappeared down as he neared. Had someone seen him dump Hawksworth's body? Worse still, had someone overheard their exchange?

He hurried after the figure, but when he reached the sleeping quarters no one stirred. There were only the snores and murmurs of the crew, and the sound of the waves on the hull, a steady, deathly beat like a funeral drum.

# CHAPTER FORTY-EIGHT

'THE TIME OF RECKONING HAS COME,' LAUNCESTON SAID DIS-
passionately. It was as if he were preparing for a saunter along
the shore. Unnervingly motionless, he looked out to sea where
the ships waited.

Beside him on the quayside at Plymouth, the setting sun
warmed Carpenter's face, the brassy light blazing across the
jumbled rooftops where they tumbled down towards the sea.
'Call it what you will,' he replied, 'we are likely sailing to our
deaths, and death at sea is not like death on dry land, the brief,
honourable pain of a sword thrust or the creak of old age. It
is lungs bursting with water, and madness as breath is sucked
away, or roasting alive in hellish fires, or limbs left shattered by
cannonshot, your blood leaking into your shit and piss.'

'Death is death,' Launceston said.

Everywhere was unnaturally quiet at the end of the working
day. The doors of the warehouses had clattered shut, and the
merchants had bidden each other a quiet farewell, hurrying away
with the workers from the sail-lofts and the other businesses
that served the great ships. The delivery carts rolled off amid
the fruity aroma of horse dung. The taverns and stews around
the harbour were deserted; most of their regular drinkers were

now aboard the ships, while others hid away in their homes in case they were pressed into service.

'If these are our last days, Robert, we should live them to the full,' Carpenter mused. 'Be the men we want to be, or dream we are, or give voice to the whispers in our heart. What say you?'

Launceston considered this for a moment, and then nodded. 'You speak sense, but for some of us that is not such an easy task.'

Clouds of midges still danced in the lazy heat, and as the shadows lengthened the sounds of boots beating a steady pace over the cobbles drew towards them from the direction of the dark, labyrinthine streets falling down the steep hill to the dock. A confident, upright man emerged, striding purposefully, his hands clasped behind his back, his chest puffed out and his head held high as if he was being watched by everyone he passed. His brown moustache and beard were carefully trimmed for the occasion and his hair swept back from his forehead. His features would have been familiar to almost all Englishmen and women from the surfeit of pamphlets in circulation to mark the successes of their bravest adventurer, navigator and sea captain.

'Sir Francis Drake,' Launceston said. 'Does "vice-admiral" fit him better than "privateer" these days?'

'No one can doubt what he has done for England, whatever his title.'

Drake had dressed in his finest clothes: a new doublet in deep brown with gold stitching at the shoulders, a high white collar, and a black collarbone protector held by a gold chain. He walked up to them with a pronounced swagger and enquired, 'Walsingham's men?'

'Yes, sir,' Carpenter replied. 'We are to accompany you

471

on the *Revenge* in case the knowledge we have gained of the Enemy . . .' he corrected himself, 'the Spaniards may be of some use in the coming battle.'

'Very good,' Drake replied. 'Good men are always welcome aboard my ship.'

'It is true, then?' Carpenter enquired. 'The armada has been sighted?'

'Fifty Spanish ships, off the Scilly Islands this very dawn, seen from the lookout of the *Golden Hind*, assigned to patrol the western approaches to England. The captain, Thomas Fleming, raced to tell me himself. This day, July the twenty-ninth, will never be forgotten, for it is the day that the sleeping beast of England was woken.'

'As we had heard,' Launceston said, 'the Spanish race up the Channel to engage us at their leisure.'

With pride, Drake looked to his ship, the *Revenge*, resting elegantly on the sparkling sea amidst the other vessels. 'I have spent the afternoon on the Hoe, looking out for any change in the wind. I have said my goodbyes to my wife Elizabeth, and now I am ready.'

'Should there not be more haste?' Carpenter ventured.

'More haste?' Drake repeated superciliously. 'Nothing could be done until the tide had turned. Besides, these are Spaniards and we are Englishmen. I could put out tomorrow morning and still whip them like the dogs they are.'

News of Drake's arrival at Sutton Harbour had spread quickly along the narrow streets. Soon groups of onlookers had gathered to see the great man, shooing the clutches of excited children that raced along the harbour's edge.

Drake briefly moved among them, bragging about the natural prowess of an Englishman, and by the time he left they were all cheering and pumping his hand.

'He plays his part well,' Launceston noted, 'like Will.'

'I am not so sure it is a role with Drake,' Carpenter replied. 'He believes his own legend.'

A rowing boat took them out from the quay to the *Revenge* in the lee of St Nicholas's Island. Drake's eyes never left his ship as they neared. 'How can the Spaniards even hope to win this war?' he snorted. 'They circulated full details of the strength of their armada, hoping it would strike fear into us and encourage the powers of Europe to support them. All it did was give us a tactical advantage.' He waved his hand towards his ship. 'Thirteen years old, forty-three guns, firing shot of nine pounds to sixty pounds in weight. Fine firepower for an Englishman! Thanks to the Spanish, we know their most heavily armed vessel, the *San Lorenzo*, has but forty guns, and sixteen of those are sakers or minions firing only four or six pounds a shot.' He laughed, his eyes gleaming.

Carpenter watched him closely. He had heard the stories but had never encountered Drake before, and he wondered if the bravado rang true. Whether it did or not, Drake's confidence was infectious. The black mood that had gripped him since he had disembarked the *Tempest* lifted slightly.

A hundred feet long at the keel, but appearing even larger, the *Revenge* grew more imposing as they neared. It was weather-worn and its green and white chevrons had faded slightly, but that only served to give it the appearance of a seasoned war-horse. Carpenter could smell the cloying bitterness of the fresh tar that turned the keel a shining black.

On deck, the men waited in small groups to greet Drake. He never met their eyes, but Carpenter could see they were comforted by the vice-admiral's presence. As if in silent prayer, Drake glanced up the mainmast to where the sails were furled at the yards, gave an approving nod, and began his final inspection.

As the last glimmer of the setting sun lit the waters, the wind from the sea turned, and with the tide on the ebb, the signal gun fired. Slowly but steadily, the *Revenge* and the other English galleons began their journey down Plymouth Sound. Night fell.

Once they were in open water, the crew scaled the rigging like monkeys to unfurl the sails. Carpenter knew that this was a crucial time. The Spanish fleet could have been waiting to bear down on them, but the topmen had reported no ships ahead, although the danger would remain until first light. Drake gave the order for all lanterns to be extinguished, and they moved forward as part of the night.

Launceston stood at the rail on the poop deck, his deathly pallor unnerving some of the crew who bowed their heads and crossed themselves as they passed. Carpenter thought a strange mood had come upon him.

'Will they strike now, coming out of the dark before our journey has even begun, like the death we spoke of on the land?' the pale aristocrat mused.

Carpenter didn't know what to say, and left Launceston at the rail to accompany Drake as he strode proudly across the still-warm deck, the master of his world.

When dawn came, the seas were still empty and the tense mood lifted slightly. The fleet of fifty-four ships led by Lord Howard of Effingham sailed out into mist and squalls.

Later that day, an exuberant Drake summoned Carpenter to the poop deck. 'Would you like your first sight of our enemy?' he said gleefully.

Carpenter peered into the drizzle, but could see nothing, even when the rain cleared briefly. He eyed Drake to see if he was finding humour at the expense of a man who had not earned his sea legs. He was surprised to see the vice-admiral watching him deferentially.

'I, and all England, owe you a great deal,' he said. 'You have turned the tide of this war.'

Carpenter was lost for words. From behind his back, Drake handed him a long tube of shaped beechwood, bounded by brass hoops. A second tube slid in and out of it, and there was glass in the end.

'What is this?' Carpenter asked, still unsure if he was to be made the subject of a joke.

Drake pressed the tube to Carpenter's eye and positioned him. Spanish sails loomed up in Carpenter's vision, shocking him so much he almost dropped the device. He lowered it, and could no longer see the sails.

'They are far away,' he stuttered, 'beyond my natural sight. Yet this device lets me see them. Is this some of Dee's magic?'

'It is Dee's magic,' Drake laughed, 'but not in the way you mean. It is called a tele-scope. This arrangement of glass draws closer what is distant. No supernatural power there, only human ingenuity.'

Admiring the tele-scope, Carpenter said, 'I never knew we had such a thing. How is that?'

'No one knows. No one will know, for many years to come. It is a secret, and you would know about those things. There is plenty that never reaches the ears of the common man, am I correct?'

Carpenter nodded. 'But what has this to do with me?'

'As I heard it from Sir Francis Walsingham, Dee worked upon a type of this very device in years gone. He heard whispers and talk among his kind . . .' Drake smacked his lips in disapproval, 'that some Italian painter had drawn designs for this tele-scope a century past, and so he set about building one. He struggled to find the right glass, until word reached him of another similar design, being studied by the Tsar's magicians.'

Carpenter's brow furrowed. 'In Muscovy?'

'The Tsar's device did not work either, but he had a different part of the puzzle. And so two brave spies were sent to retrieve his invention—'

'This is what Will brought back!' Carpenter said, examining the simple tube. 'I thought it was some great weapon.'

'You do not understand its importance,' Drake said. 'Only a true seaman would. This tele-scope will turn the tide of battle. We can study the Spanish ships from afar, watch their preparations, their direction, and we can be upon them at the point of *our* choosing.'

Carpenter was too stunned to speak.

'I heard you paid a great price for the recovery of the item that led to this great thing Dee has made,' Drake continued. 'Know you, then, that every scar you bear marks a thousand . . . nay, ten thousand . . . English lives that will be saved this day. Saved by you, Master Carpenter. Your sacrifice will keep England free.'

Dumbfounded, Carpenter could barely respond to Drake's praise. He made his way down the steps from the poop deck, his mind struggling to reconcile the bitterness that had encysted his heart since Will had abandoned him with the new knowledge of what they had won.

As he gathered his thoughts, standing by the rail in the salty spray, he decided this new information had to be conveyed to Launceston, whom he had not seen since dawn had broken. He searched along the length of the deck, and then plunged into the stifling, near-deserted confines below, his puzzlement growing by the moment. Eventually, he had exhausted all possibilities apart from the section of the hold containing the sail stores, timber, carpenters' tools and other items necessary to keep the great ship afloat.

When he called out, his voice was lost beneath the symphony of sound that filled every ship, the constant boom of waves against the hull and the chorus of creaking as every board flexed to cope with the pressures upon it. His view obscured by canvas hanging like curtains amid piles of timber, he pushed through the obstacles, pulling back sheet after sheet.

As he drew back the final covering, he was convulsed with shock. Had he suddenly stepped into Hell? As red as the Devil, Launceston loomed over a sticky mess, his knife still dripping. When he looked at Carpenter, fires blazed in his eyes, and it took moments for him to focus. With a faint, dreamy smile, he said softly, 'What wonders to behold.'

It took several seconds for Carpenter to comprehend what lay before him. 'Is . . . is that the cabin boy?'

Launceston examined the mess, and appeared to see it for the first time himself. His smile now had the sheepish cast of a man caught out drunk before night had fallen. 'Do not judge me, John,' he said.

'Judge you?' Carpenter ran a hand through his hair as his thoughts reeled with all the possibilities that now lay ahead.

The knife slipped from Launceston's slick fingers and he stood up, his expression haunted. 'I have . . . unnatural desires, John. I know my shortcomings, and I fight every day to keep them under control, but what you said . . . about being who we are . . . in the shadow of death—'

'I did not mean *this*!' Head in his hands, Carpenter crashed on to a pile of timber. 'I must think. Damn you! This will destroy everything!'

'We are who we are. Our natures rule us, for better or

worse. What makes me like this makes me a valuable tool for England, and the Queen, and Walsingham.' He released a deep, juddering breath.

As Launceston's words settled on him, Carpenter glared. 'They know?'

The Earl did not respond directly. 'I do not wish to be this way. My life is filled with torments,' he said, his voice breaking. 'This business makes us monsters to deal with monsters. I wish only the peace of a summer afternoon, but this is my world now, and for always.' With disgust, he looked down at what lay at his feet. Tears sprang to his eyes and streamed down his cheeks. 'Help me, John,' he pleaded.

For a moment Carpenter fought to overcome his revulsion, and then he rested a hand upon the Earl's shoulder. 'We must dispose of all this before it is discovered. And get you cleaned up.'

'Thank you, thank you,' Launceston muttered pathetically.

'We are in this together,' Carpenter said with a sigh as he saw the magnitude of what lay ahead. 'Curse you, Robert. Damn you.'

# CHAPTER FORTY-NINE

CREEPING ON DECK WHEN THE SUN HAD SET, WILL FEARED IT was his last chance to board the grey-sailed ship. Since he had killed Hawksworth, every attempt had been thwarted by events beyond his control, and now, with battle looming, he knew he had to risk all.

Hawksworth had been missed the day after Will had disposed of the body, but it was presumed he had either thrown himself overboard in a fit of despair or had fallen; it was not an unusual occurrence. Will had spent the first few days brooding over the stupidity and confusion that had led to Hawksworth's death, but he knew it was one of the risks of his profession. Soon the dark thoughts were washed from him as he was sucked into the feverish preparations for the coming fight. Day after day the crew engaged in dry runs of the battle procedure under the urgent eyes of the clearly unsettled commanders. Fearful faces turned towards the grey horizon in every free moment, and rumours spread below deck like fire. Increasingly frustrated by the lack of opportunity to reach the Unseelie Court ship, Will could only wait. And then, that night, he seized his moment.

There was a substantial swell, but he had his sea legs and there was no more rain. Barefoot and keeping low, he moved to the starboard rail on the main deck and looked out across the resting fleet. The lamps had been extinguished, and all he could see were the silhouettes of the nearest galleon and hulks. Four bells sounded mournfully under the moaning of the wind in the rigging – the watch was half over.

Licking the salty spray off his lips, Will cast a glance towards the poop deck where the lookout stood, the sole member of the skeletal watch above deck. The few others still awake had been charged with minor tasks on the gun deck, ensuring the cannon, powder and shot were all ready for the battle to come. The rest of the crew grabbed fitful hours of sleep in preparation for what was likely to be an eventful day.

Will had noticed that whenever the grey-sailed ship came alongside, the lookouts always turned their backs to it, finding, he guessed, that it was easier to pretend nothing was there rather than face up to the existence of such an abomination. That made his task easier.

Collecting the grapnel from its hiding place, Will waited at the rail. Along the south coast of England, beacons blazed, calling the nation to war. It was Saturday, 30 July, and the armada was at anchor at Dodman Point in a state of heightened anxiety after sailing east along the Channel.

Earlier, Will had been convinced his final opportunity to find Mayhew and the Skull had slipped through his fingers. As the crew watched the beacons, an English pinnace had swept across their bows and fired a single shot. But it was more to mock than threaten and the little vessel disappeared as *La Rata Santa Maria Encoronada* returned fire to no avail. Then the English fleet was sighted, but they did not attack. Medina Sidonia and his commanders had made sure they had the weather gage, the best position in relation to the wind and coastline. They would wait out the night before battle commenced at dawn.

Will caught sight of the grey ship on its strange, circuitous journey round the fleet. It sailed with what appeared to be increasing urgency. As it came alongside, he clambered on to the rail, braced himself against the rigging and swung the grapnel before letting it fly. It fell short, splashing into the waves. Desperately, he hauled it in and adjusted his next throw. This time the hooks caught in the rigging of the ghostly vessel. Securing his end to the *Rosario*'s rigging, Will gripped the rope and then swung his legs up. Crossing his ankles over the tightening rope, he hung like one of the monkeys that performed in the market on Cheapside, he thought ruefully.

Will had left some slack, but his fear was that one or other of the ships would sail apart and rip the rope free, plunging him into the black waves. He had little time, he knew. Ignoring the blast of the wind, he eased himself along the rope. At the mid-point between the two rolling ships, the rope swung wildly and it took all his strength to hold on. Beneath him, the waves driven high by the furious confusion of battling currents grasped for his back but a hand's breadth beneath him. His clothes were soon soaked by the spray.

Gritting his teeth, he forced himself to keep moving towards the grey-sailed ship, shifting one hand at a time, his fingers sliding on the slick rope, his heart beating madly.

By the time Will reached the rail of the Enemy galleon, his limbs were shaking from the cold and the strain. With a final effort, he hauled himself over the rail and on to the deck. The roll of the ship made him land harder and more noisily than he intended, and he rushed to hide in the lee of the quarter-deck.

The stillness on board was unsettling. And a strange odour hovered over everything, sickly-sweet but with a florid bitterness beneath, like the mould on an apple in the autumn orchard. Then he heard the tramp of boots that paused above his head and then moved towards the steps.

Drawing his knife, Will waited in the shadows beneath the stairway as the ship pitched and yawed. When a figure loomed at the foot of the steps, Will made his move. He brought his knife up and across the Enemy's throat. He caught a glimpse of long brown hair and blazing eyes, and then, as the hands went to the ruined throat, Will spun his opponent round and pitched him over the rail into the sea. Without the element of surprise, the kill would not have been so easy, he knew.

Without further delay, Will headed below deck. Here, the constant roar of the sea had retreated, but the sickly orchard smell was stronger. He could hear nothing beneath him apart from the steady heartbeat of the bilge pumps keeping out the seawater. The crew would be in the berth, resting among the cannon, and he did not want to risk disturbing them and so bringing every one of the Enemy down upon him.

Where was Mayhew being held, he wondered. As he carefully made his way through the ship, distorted sounds faded in and out of the unnatural silence, reminding him once again of the Fairy House – voices chanting in an incomprehensible language, mournful pipe music.

The door to the officers' quarters was ajar. Peeping through the thin gap, Will saw a group of the Enemy seated round a table, heads bowed, their faces hidden in the half-light. Faint nods and hand gestures suggested they were communicating with each other, but all was quiet.

Slipping by, he continued until he found the captain's cabin. The door here was also partly open. Flickering lanterns cast shifting shadows as a male figure swayed soundlessly around the room in what appeared to be some kind of ritual. He was tall and slender with iron-grey hair and beard, wearing a long black gown with silver diamond-pane embroidery. His face had a ghastly pallor, and his sunken eyes were dark pools of shadow so that his face resembled a skull. His movement reminded Will of the pattern the ship defined on the sea.

*A dance of death.*

A bitter aroma filled the air, incense or burned herbs, and near the captain's feet gleamed a chalice and a knife with a cruelly curved blade.

Creeping along the creaking boards, Will continued to search the galleon, dreading that at any moment he would be discovered. Amid the sour stink rising from below the water level, he heard a high-pitched sound coming from behind a closed door. He listened for a moment, and then eased the door open.

A slow-pulsing white light forced the shadows back, and held them briefly before they swooped back in. It came from a glass globe just large enough to be contained in two hands, resting on a small table. Inside the globe was another that opened and closed like the pupil of an eye, releasing the steady beat of light. It was an object of such a unique appearance, it had to be of some importance, but Will could not guess its use. Three more of the globes stood on plinths on the boards beneath the table, oddly unmoved by the rocking of the ship, but no light emanated from them.

Wary of some magical defence, Will studied the room before taking a step. There, in the glare beyond the globe, a figure lay on a mat on the boards, asleep or drugged. A glint of silver told him it must be Mayhew. Beside the door was an open-topped barrel. From the salty smell, it appeared to contain only seawater, but when he cautiously reached towards the surface to test the liquid an eel-like creature about as thick as his arm burst from the depths, snapping for his fingers. He withdrew his hand just in time. He had glimpsed teeth like needles and had never seen the like before.

Time was short. Will intended to kill Mayhew and dump him and the Silver Skull into the sea to be lost for all time. Steeling himself, he stepped towards the prone figure, only to find himself facing the door. What was this?

The disconnection left him reeling. Again he tried to approach Mayhew. Again, the same thing happened. He felt cold fingers on his spine. What *was* this? His head swam and pinpricks of pain ran along his arms and legs after each attempt, but it seemed he was not able to get near to Mayhew, nor reach the globe to destroy it. Unease gave way to angry frustration. A spell of protection, he decided, perhaps caused by the pulsing globe.

Will was determined not to leave the ship in failure. If he couldn't retrieve the vile mask, perhaps he could strike a blow at the Unseelie Court's capability to influence the coming battle. Retracing his route to the steps, he grabbed one of the lanterns that illuminated the corridor. The sounds in the ship seemed to him more clear now, as if the longer he spent on board, the more attuned he became to its peculiar qualities. A carpet of rats scurried away from his feet as he descended to the lowest level, the orlop deck. Here were stored the spare sails, rigging, timber and carpenters' tools and magazine. Amid the foul smell of bilge in the damp and the dark, he swayed across the rolling deck to where the grey sails hung. He knew he could not have much more time. The ship would soon start to weave away and he would be trapped.

Stacking the timber to create a pit, he used the lantern to set fire to one of the sails within it, and then heaped on rope and wooden tools. Flame caught and the deck began to fill with thick smoke.

If fortune were with him, the fire would send the cursed ship down to the bottom of the Channel, and Mayhew and the Unseelie Court with it. At worst, he hoped it would at least cause enough damage to cripple the galleon and make it worthless to the fleet.

As he darted silently up the steps, rapid activity erupted in the berth. He only just made it past the door before it was thrown open and figures rushed out on the trail of the rising smoke.

Will came up into the salt spray and the wind, the deck rolling beneath his bare feet. As he ran to the rail, his heart began to thunder – the ships had begun to part. The grapnel rope connecting the two vessels was growing taut and in no time would be torn free.

Throwing caution to the wind, Will leapt from the rail. His grasping hands caught on the spray-slick rope, but his exhausted fingers began to slide off. Below, the churning waves reached hungrily for his feet.

Kicking wildly, Will clasped again in desperation and this time his hands held. His muscles burning, he strengthened his grip and then swung his tired legs up to hook his feet over the line. It thrummed beneath his fingers as the two great vessels moved apart.

He hauled himself along the rope hand over hand, buffeted from side to side by the wind and the rocking of the ships. The *Rosario* drew near, but he was moving too slowly. The rope was about to tear free. Dropping his legs, Will used his arms alone to power him on. With his last reserves exhausted, he swung on to the *Rosario*'s rigging, and with relief released the grapnel rope into the churning water.

And there he hung for a moment, exhausted, sodden, hands burning, his chest heaving from the exertion. But then a smile crept across his wind-lashed face as he saw the grey galleon come to a halt. The smoke swirled from below and climbed in the wind. With satisfaction that he had struck a decisive blow, Will lowered himself to the deck to watch the mounting conflagration. A second later he heard movement at his back. Barrett, Stanbury, and several others were closing in on him.

'Spy!' Barrett snarled. Before Will had time to react, he felt a fist slam into his head.

Will came round to the silver of a new day. His wrists were bound behind him, his head was still ringing, and a light breeze was caressing his bruised face. As his vision cleared, he saw he was on a ship's forecastle, not his own, looking down at a crew gathered in a crescent. They stared back at him with eyes full of hate. And in front of them stood Medina Sidonia and several of the other Spanish commanders. Will guessed he had been transported from the *Rosario* to the flagship, the *San Martin*. Looking about him, he was pleased to see the grey-sailed ship listed alongside, although the extent of the fire damage wasn't visible from his vantage point. He guessed he had been under observation since he had killed Hawksworth, and his boarding of the Enemy ship had been the final condemning evidence against him.

Don Alanzo stepped before Will, hands clasped behind his back. The Spaniard looked the English spy up and down slowly, and then nodded, pleased. Though he attempted to remain aloof, a deep hatred burned in his eyes. 'You are like a disease, infecting the very heart of our glorious empire,' he said quietly, his voice trembling. 'But we have a cure.'

'Your empire is already black and corrupted. Your sister knew the truth, Don Alanzo.' Will's head throbbed as he spoke, and pain stabbed through his limbs. He could taste blood.

In a blaze of anger, Don Alanzo moved as if to strike the Englishman, but caught himself. 'Your part in this business is now done.' He paused. 'By business, I mean life.'

'So, an execution at sea. Do I not have the right to be heard?'

'A spy has no rights.'

'I hope you feel the same if you are ever captured on English soil.' Will nodded towards the grey galleon. 'Should you ever reach England. Without your dogs, you are a toothless opponent.'

The Spaniard's eyes blazed. 'Our allies are already at work repairing their vessel. You have caused a delay, not an end.'

'With England's ships so close, a delay may be more than enough.'

Don Alanzo held Will's gaze. 'I know the inner workings that drive you.' A shadow crossed his face, and for a moment Will understood him too: the murder of his father still haunted him. 'You have no regard for your life, and there is little I can do that will cause pain,' he continued. 'But you must know punishment for your crimes before you die . . . your crimes against Spain, and against my family. Against me.'

'There is nothing you can do—' Will was cut short by a disturbance in the crowd. Barrett and Stanbury dragged Grace to the front. Her frightened eyes looked up at him in desperation. Will struggled against his bonds.

'Leave her!' he snapped.

'I had no wish to harm her. You did this. You brought her to misery. Let that stain your conscience as you die.'

'There is much of the Unseelie Court in your cruelty,' Will said.

Don Alanzo winced, but there was still some joy in his eyes at the pain he was causing Will.

'Do not kill her,' Will pleaded. He looked to Grace who stood silently by.

'I will not. She is vital to the plans of our allies, and therefore to our plans. But I can protect her no longer. I allowed her to sail on *la urca de las mujeres* to keep her safe from harm. You have forfeited that right. She will be taken from here to that ship . . .' he indicated the grey-sailed ship, 'and she will travel with our allies.'

'No!' Will yelled. He wrenched at his bonds furiously. 'No man or woman can abide being among them for any period. Their very presence is corrupting. She could be driven mad, or worse. You know this, Don Alanzo!'

'On your head,' the Spaniard said quietly.

Grace cried out as Barrett and Stanbury roughly dragged her towards the rail to transport her to the grey-sailed ship. In fury, Will renewed his efforts to reach Don Alanzo and felt the pommel of the guard's sword crash against the back of his head.

When he came to, Grace was nowhere to be seen. His hands still tied, he leaned against the rail, a rope wrapped around him and stretching across the deck, the other end trailing over the side into the water. The crew and several Spanish soldiers gathered in a crescent around him.

'With battle close, we have no time to waste here, or I would relish inflicting suffering on you,' Don Alanzo said. 'Your death will be quick, but your suffering no less for haste.'

'Do it, then.' Will's head was hazy from the punishment of two blows. 'I have damaged your plans. My life is a fair price if it brings you to your knees.'

Don Alanzo ignored Will's taunting. He appeared calmer now that he could see Will's end was close. 'You are not a seafaring man. Nor am I. Punishment at sea has its own particular flavour, I am told. According to the mercenaries aboard, what you are about to undergo has proved effective in the Dutch navy.'

Will's gaze followed the trailing rope. 'Keelhauling,' he said.

Don Alanzo nodded. 'Pulled tight, the rope will drag you down, under the water and along the keel. Barnacles affixed there will slice through clothes, and tear off skin, and the bloody prisoner that emerges on the other side of the ship is thereby made repentant. Pulled slack and slow, the prisoner hangs beneath the keel, and drowns. Either way, Will Swyfte, you will not survive this ordeal.'

Unbidden, the terrible, bursting sensation of drowning Will had experienced in the Fairy House flashed across his mind. 'Come, then. I would not delay your encounter with my countrymen. Your own reckoning awaits.' He glanced towards the grey-sailed ship, and tried not to think of Grace.

At Don Alanzo's nod, two men lifted Will on to the rail, and then steadied the rope trailing from his back. On the other side of the deck, four sailors prepared to drag him under.

'And so the debt to my father is paid,' Don Alanzo began. 'This day—'

'Do not torture me with prattle.' Will flashed Don Alanzo a defiant grin, and leapt from the rail. He took pleasure in the men's angry cries as the rope burned through their hands, and then he hit the water. The cold shocked the last of the wool from his head, the turmoil of the water turning him this way and that. His lungful of air would not last long. The two teams of sailors pulled the rope taut and were dragging him directly beneath the ship. Salt stung his wounds and the muffled sounds of his struggling throbbed in his head. His body crashed against the barnacle-encrusted hull and he was held tight.

The air burned in his lungs, and however much he tried, he could not escape the haunting memories of Edinburgh.

With a tremendous effort, he ignored the panic flecking his thoughts of what would happen the moment he exhausted his breath, of the water rushing into his lungs, of the feeling of being trapped. By will alone, he calmed himself.

Numb from the cold, he wrenched at his bonds until they eased enough for him to tear his hands free. Then, pressing his left arm against the keel, he released the trigger on the blade hidden in the leather harness under his shirt. He prayed he would have the opportunity to thank Dee for his ingenuity.

Twisting, he desperately rubbed his restraining rope against the blade. Strand by strand it frayed – agonizingly slowly, it seemed to Will – and then it broke under the sharp edge. Lungs bursting, he drifted down from the keel, towards the dark depths.

He knew he could not last much longer without air. On deck, they would realize the rope had broken and would be watching out for him. Kicking out for the stern, he struggled to swim. He was exhausted and his clothes dragged him down. Just beyond the rudder, Will surfaced before his lungs burst and sucked in a huge, racking gulp of air. Shivering from the strain and the cold, he fought to tread water. They would not be able to see him from above, but one of the other ships might spy him if he waited too long. From above came the calls of his enemies as they hung over the rails, searching the water.

Gulping air, he continued underwater beneath the next ship. The rest of the fleet was visible all around, but they would be too distracted preparing for the battle to see him in the water. After a brief rest, he carried on, surfacing for air at every ship, until he reached open water.

He was free, but adrift in the middle of the English Channel. How long could he survive before exhaustion dragged him down to his death?

# CHAPTER FIFTY

'GOD'S TEETH, THE SPANISH ARE SLOW-WITTED RABBIT-SUCKERS.'
On the forecastle of the *Revenge*, Drake watched the armada in
the first light of dawn through his tele-scope. 'We are at war.
Did they expect us to sit back and wait for them to attack?'

'What could have distracted them?' Carpenter mused.

'Ha!' Drake laughed. 'Their topmen have finally seen
us. Now there will be a commotion aboard their ships, and
Medina Sidonia's prayers will amount to naught!'

Closing the tele-scope with a snap, Drake set about ordering
his men to prepare for battle, boosting their spirits with loud
bragging and comical contemptuous comments about their
enemy.

The evidence of his own eyes had now convinced Carpenter
of Drake's legendary skills. During the night, Drake, Howard
and the other commanders had left five ships floating in easy
sight of the armada. It had fooled the Spanish into thinking the
entire fleet was steady, while eighty ships were taken upwind to
claim the weather gage. The English now had the advantage.

Nearby, Launceston waited calmly by the rail, as though the
horrors of the previous day had never happened. But Carpenter
saw the Earl's eyes flicker towards him; a bond had been forged,

however much Carpenter was repulsed by it. If Drake guessed what had happened, he showed no sign of it; word had gone out that the cabin boy must have fallen overboard during the dark sail out of Plymouth harbour.

'If they had had Drake's tele-scope they might have got an early warning in the grey light,' Launceston said. 'We should give thanks that Walsingham and Dee see a greater picture than you or I.'

'I will give thanks if we survive this damnable thing,' Carpenter growled. 'I am not meant to feel the world rolling beneath my feet. Dry land for me, and soon!'

'Look. It begins.' Launceston raised his arm and pointed to a squadron of eleven English ships streaming west and then tacking between the armada and the Eddystone rocks at a speed that must have startled the slow-moving Spanish ships.

'Our race-built galleons,' Launceston noted approvingly. 'None faster.'

'Stop speaking some foreign language,' Carpenter snapped. 'Race-built? Is this some salty-haired sailor's argot?'

Launceston allowed himself a faint smile.

A signal flag went up on the mizzenmast of the lead ship, and barked orders rolled out across the waves. Gunports snapped open in response, and a moment later it was as if the gates of Hell had been flung open. Flames flashed across the water, accompanied by a thunderous noise as the cannon on each ship in turn blasted the Spanish. Plumes of white smoke rolled out and the smell of powder was caught in the wind. Carpenter was gripped by terror and excitement at the spectacle. After one broadside the squadron raced back to the fleet, untouched.

It was then that Carpenter and Launceston both noticed a curious sight and leaned across the rail to get a better look. Seemingly against the wind and the currents, a grey-sailed ship was limping away from the Spanish fleet. Its starboard side looked as if it had been blackened by fire. It was soon lost behind a wall of vessels, and before Launceston and Carpenter could question what they had seen, the armada responded to Drake's opening attack.

As Medina Sidonia fired his signal gun, the Spanish fleet sailed into their prearranged battle order: a crescent stretching several miles across with a short spike in the centre. To an uneducated eye, this vast floating city looked imposing, a mass of white canvas sails painted with the red cross of the crusades, the water barely visible between them.

But Launceston waved a lazy hand towards the mass and said, 'See – they create an illusion. The warships are all on the outer edge of the formation, but inside . . . useless hulks, transport ships . . . Their number is much less than it appears.'

'Nevertheless,' Carpenter said, 'it only needs one piece of shot to take me apart.'

The *Disdain*, the personal pinnace of Lord Howard, sailed out to fire at the Spanish: a challenge; in response Medina Sidonia raised Spain's royal standard, ordering his fleet to battle.

'Is Swyfte out there, somewhere on those enemy ships, I wonder?' Carpenter said as he watched the dense fleet begin to attack. 'What irony to be blown to pieces by your own countrymen after risking so much.' He struggled with his conflicted emotions and then said, 'Let us go below deck. Until we are needed, it will be safer there.'

'Are you sure?' Launceston asked with an odd tone.

Flushed, his eyes blazing, Drake marched up, consumed by the moment. As the *Revenge* raced towards the fray, it seemed to Carpenter that the fleet's vice-admiral was overcome by an almost religious fervour.

On the gun deck, Carpenter saw the master gunner wait, poised, as the vessel clipped across the swell. Ahead, the Spanish galleons loomed up out of the drifting smoke. His hand held high, the man waited, and then dropped it with a bellow.

Carpenter reeled in shock from the devastating noise. Gunfire rolled in continuous thunder from the bow chasers to the broadside cannon to the stern chasers and finally to the windward guns, flash of red flame after flash, acrid black smoke rolling out of the gunports. He staggered back, clutching his ears.

Into the gun deck's stifling world of smoke and fire came the shriek of the shot tearing towards the Spanish fleet, the sound of the splash where it fell short, or the thunderous boom and crack of disintegrating wood where it met its target. There were screams too, louder and more shocking than the destructive boom of the cannon fire.

As each gun fired, it was hauled back in and prepared for the next shot. With all the ships in the fleet now firing at will, the noise never stopped. On the *Revenge*'s gun deck, it seemed to Carpenter that there was mad confusion as men ran back and forth with shot and stoking powder, cursing as they burned themselves on cannons, diving out of the way of the recoil.

He ducked to avoid flying splinters. 'Come, this is Hell,' he choked. His ears still ringing as he wondered if he would be permanently deaf, he motioned for Launceston to follow him out. Staggering to the rail, they saw the Spanish return fire, but their response was leaden – one shot for every three that came from English ships.

Launceston indicated movement among some of the Spanish galleons. 'They are fleeing downwind,' he said, but as those vessels broke ranks, they caused confusion among the others.

Carpenter noticed Drake's excitement as he saw his moment.

With a barked order, the adventurer sent the *Revenge* to fire at the wing where the Spanish squadron's flagship was now unsupported. Another English ship, the *Triumph*, sailed to join her. 'Frobisher,' Launceston said with a nod.

The Spanish flagship faced the attack alone and saw its rigging and forestays and part of the foremast disintegrate under Drake's broadside. As the Spanish galleon continued to hold its ground, Drake marched by and announced loudly, 'It tries to draw us in. It is a trap, but we Englishmen are too clever for that!'

'He acts as if he takes the air along Plymouth harbour,' Carpenter bellowed above the roar of another broadside. 'Does this madness not trouble him in the slightest?'

Leaning on the rail, Launceston studied the bodies floating in the water, some so blackened and torn they could barely be identified as human. In one area of the sea, near the Spanish ships, they were so thick it seemed as if it would be possible to walk across them without getting wet feet.

For the next three hours, the English taunted and baited the Spanish, ducking into an attack then sailing out of reach of the Spanish guns, before both fleets continued eastward. The slow speed of the armada, barely more than that of a rowing boat on the Thames, was a source of amazement to Carpenter, until Launceston pointed out that the fleet had to move at the speed of the slowest ship to keep the formation intact.

Beside them, tele-scope held to his eye, Drake commented, 'They appear to be protecting a curious grey-sailed ship. Why is that so important they would risk the loss of so many other vessels?'

'Surely that ship, in some way, must be vital to their strategy?' Launceston replied.

Drake mulled over this puzzle for a moment before pacing

the deck to check on his crew, but Launceston and Carpenter both remained focused on the mystery of the grey-sailed ship, and in their hearts they knew who sailed aboard.

'That ship may have sustained some damage,' Launceston said, 'but if the Spanish continue to protect it, then its threat remains. What is it they plan? And when will they strike?'

# CHAPTER FIFTY-ONE

EXHAUSTED AND COLD, WILL STRUGGLED TO STAY AFLOAT AS the world erupted in fire and thunder around him. Fragments of shattered hulls and broken masts had been his support for hours as he was caught up in the fleeing ships, but his legs had grown numb with the cold and his fingers could barely grip. Dark, acrid smoke drifted continuously across the water so it was impossible to tell the time of day, with flashes of flame seen dully here and there through the dense bank.

In that twilit place, his existence was reduced to surviving from one moment to the next. Hulls cleaved out of the smoke as currents pulled him under, dragging him along in their wake, and so he kept pace with the armada. Red-hot English cannonballs crashed into the water all around him with a hiss and a cloud of steam. Broken bodies bumped past him, shattered limbs, a head, boots and hats, and once he saw what he imagined to be a letter to loved ones, never to be read. That he still lived was beyond Will's ken.

After he spied the grey-sailed ship limping away, his concern for Grace had kept him going in the maelstrom that began the moment the battle started. The English shore was tantalizingly close – sometimes he even imagined he could see the people of Devon lined along the cliffs, watching the battle – but each time he struck out the ferocity of the fight drove him back. And so he had been sucked into the churning heart of the conflict.

Nearby he saw the *Revenge* and the *Triumph* attack the stricken flagship of the Spanish squadron on the wing of the armada's formation. Through the heavy smoke generated by the English guns, a carrack swept towards Will en route to aid the stricken Spanish flagship. For a second, he remained frozen by the familiar outline: it was the *Rosario*, bearing down on him like death.

Exhausted, he searched for the reserves of energy to swim out of its path, but at the last he faltered and the prow struck him a glancing blow. Dazed, he went down, swallowing water, and for a moment he was back in Edinburgh, slowly drowning.

As the cold dark reached up for him, Will somehow found enough strength to push up for the surface. Gulping air, he clawed on to some flotsam, his head still dull, his mind drifting from the blow. The thunder of the gunfire receded, became muffled, disappeared, and there was only the sound of his ragged breathing and the blood roaring in his head. Half-seen images faded in and out of the smoke.

In the confusion that followed Drake's attack, the Spanish vessels careered recklessly. The *Rosario* collided with another ship, shattering her crossyard and spritsail. Losing all control, the carrack slammed against another, destroying her bowsprit, halyards and forecourse.

Then a tremendous explosion shocked Will out of his stupor. On the *San Salvador*, a ship Will had helped reprovision, the stern powder store had exploded upwards through the poop deck and the two decks of the sterncastle. Amidst the plume of smoke, timbers had been hurled up to the height of the mast-tops before cascading down on the closest ships.

As the wreckage rained all around, Will dived down. Streaming trails of white bubbles plunged within inches of him where the timber shards and splinters fell.

Surfacing with a gasp, he saw bodies raining down too, limbless, blackened. The *San Salvador* blazed like the sun before thick black smoke turned the day into night. On the shattered deck, men on fire dived into the sea. Will wondered which was worse: drowning, or being burned alive.

In the midst of the confusion, a sudden squall hit the flailing *Rosario*, shattering her foremast. Sailors with axes ran to cut it loose from the rigging, but it was too late: the carrack was crippled.

In the chaos of the listing vessel, men plunged overboard, fighting to stay afloat in a sea full of bodies and burning wreckage. Clinging on to his own frail raft of timber, Will watched many drown.

One sailor struck out strongly for a section of broken crossyard. Another reached it first, but as he struggled to climb across it, the other man dragged him off and held him under until he drowned. It seemed the act of brutality came as naturally to the survivor as breathing, and when he turned his head Will recognized the heavy-lidded, lizard expression of Barrett. Shock flared briefly as he spotted Will, but then a sly look told Will all he needed to know as the swell brought the two enemies towards each other.

With chaos around them and the black smoke heavy on the water, it seemed it was to be just the two of them, locked on a course of destruction. With a grin, Barrett drew his knife and clamped it between his teeth. He knew Will's own blade had been taken from him before the keelhauling.

In a surge of grey-green water, they clashed together like the waves breaking against the Eddystone rocks. Barrett stabbed wildly. His strength ebbing, Will avoided the first blow, and caught Barrett's wrist at the second. In their struggle, they were dragged off their respective makeshift rafts and splashed into the water. They went down quickly.

Cheeks and eyes bulging, Barrett's face was a mask of fury, but the water impeded his attempts to stab, and instead he went for Will's neck. The water grew black around the flailing men, the shimmering grey light far above.

Back and forth they rolled, sinking ever deeper, until Will's lungs burned and he knew his last moments must be upon him. But then a deep clarity – a calmness – descended. He thought of Grace, of his beloved Jenny, and knew he could not die there.

Pressing his forearm against Barrett's throat, he triggered the hidden blade. Blood gouted out in a black cloud. In a frenzy, Barrett gulped mouthfuls of seawater. The last thing Will saw as he struck out for the surface was Barrett's eyes rolling white as he sank down into the murky depths.

On the surface, Will filled his lungs and found the crossyard that Barrett had abandoned. His fingers slipped on the wet wood and he could barely hold on. He was aware that, around him, the sound of gunfire was gradually dimming. The battle must be coming to a close for the day. He knew that this was his one opportunity to seize the chance to escape the madness, or he would not survive the night.

Around him, the sea was thick with bodies and wreckage. His strength fading, he dragged some timber to him and fished some of the rigging out of the water. Looping the rope around, he made a makeshift raft of spars and barrels and crawled on top. With one arm trailing in the water, he paddled slowly away from the burning ship.

The urge to close his eyes and sleep was powerful. Barely conscious, he realized the Spanish admiral Medina Sidonia had given the signal to abandon the *Rosario*, and the armada sailed on, leaving Will's former shipmates to their fate, despairing that they had been abandoned so readily. Will understood why: compared to the grey-sailed ship, the rest of the fleet was dispensable. It was a brutal message to relay to the Spanish ships, and would be bad for morale. It also revealed the true extent to which the Unseelie Court had mesmerized the Spanish commanders: the Enemy were more valuable than the thousands of men under Medina Sidonia's command.

On the heaving seas, the armada eventually faded from Will's view. As the smoke gradually dispersed, he slipped in and out of consciousness. Night had fallen.

In the thin light of a crescent moon, it took Will a while to realize that once again he was surrounded by a fleet of ships, just silhouettes against the night sky. They appeared to be under battle conditions with no lights shining, but in the gloom he could just make out the pennants that festooned the vessels. There was the Cross of St George, dark against the white background.

*Home*, he thought.

He shouted out into the dark. His voice was frail at first, but eventually found strength. It was answered by a cry from near by, and when he responded in English and identified himself, there was rapid activity on deck.

That was all he remembered.

For a time he swam through darkness to an island where grey figures slowly drew towards him, whispering terrible things that filled him with dread. Then he awoke. Unable to recall any of the words, he remembered only the sickening way it made him feel.

'Ho! You have slept the sleep of the dead, Will Swyfte! Or the just! One or the other, I cannot be sure.' The booming voice filled the cabin and Will's eyes flickered open.

There was no mistaking the wild hair and fiery red beard. Captain John Courtenay strode around the cabin, passionate and intense. Will closed his eyes and smiled. He sensed he was the least important thing on the captain's mind.

'I am on the *Tempest*?'

'For two days now.'

'Two?' Will repeated incredulously.

'You were plucked from the water by the *Triumph* aboard a merry raft you had constructed, and Frobisher delivered you here.'

'Then, it is . . . August the second?' Will struggled to rise.

Courtenay eyed him askance and said, 'It might be well to rest a little longer after your ordeal.'

'There is no time to rest. I have much to tell, and there is much we must do. The Enemy plots—'

'As always.'

Almost falling backwards, Will steadied himself before taking a step. His legs felt like lead, his head light. 'And Spain's armada?'

'There have been victories, small perhaps, but each one adds to the pile. Not least the capture of the *Rosario* and all the riches it contains. We drove the Spanish fleet past Torbay, and yesterday held them off from Weymouth in a fight more vehement than ever has been seen at sea. The flagship of Medina Sidonia himself, the *San Martin*, was riddled with gunfire, the royal standard in tatters, and was only saved at the last by a line of Spanish galleons.'

502

Breathing deeply, Will reached the door. He was acutely aware of every ache and pain. 'And today?'

'Today is Wednesday.' Courtenay clapped his hands loudly. 'Today is the defence of the Isle of Wight and the Solent.'

'You are in the vanguard of the attack?'

'My orders were to stay away from engagements, unless our firepower was desperately needed. We have greater business than a few poor Spanish bastards. The Enemy have not yet shown their colours. But you and I know they will, and then we must be ready. But first, if you are insistent upon putting your feeble limbs to the test, come and meet old friends.'

Taking him gently by the arm, Courtenay led him out of the cabin and on to the deck. The morning sun was bright. On the blue sea all around, the English fleet was becalmed, coloured pennants and flags hanging limp, while trails of black smoke drifted high across the Isle of Wight and the Hampshire coast: beacons summoning the militia to the defence of the nation. And watching the activity at the foremast were Launceston and Carpenter.

Trying to disguise the weariness in his face, Will left Courtenay and lurched over towards his companions. Carpenter looked around and scowled when he saw Will, but then marched over to meet him. Will was surprised when Carpenter shook his hand, although the man's expression showed no warmth.

'We will never be friends, but I understand you more,' Carpenter said bluntly. 'I am glad you survived the damned Spanish. Hiding out among our bitter enemy is the kind of bravado that will surely carve your name into history.'

Will was puzzled by what might have led Carpenter to this change in attitude, but did not question it. 'I would wish

503

to thank Medina Sidonia personally for his hospitality some time.'

They joined Launceston. In his usual aloof manner, he nodded as if it had only been an hour since he saw Will last. 'This weather ensures there will be little more fighting this day. We drift slowly eastward.' And with a faint air of disappointment, he added, 'It is quieter here. On the *Revenge*, there was action aplenty. And death too.'

'And so why did you return to the *Tempest*?' Will asked.

'Courtenay may be mad, but he is a haven of sanity after the *Revenge*,' Carpenter growled. 'Any more of Drake's bragging and I would be heading for Bedlam, and locking the door myself.'

Will smiled and looked towards the eastern horizon. He was exhausted and had been close to despair, but now he enjoyed the simple thrill of being alive. 'Then the fighting begins again tomorrow,' he said. 'But our task is harder even than that faced by Howard's brave band. Somewhere in that sprawling fleet sails a grey ship which purports to be the architect of all our misery. The Enemy will be working hard to repair the damage I wrought, and soon it will be brought into play. The Spanish seek to hold out until it is ready, for they know it could mean victory for them and destruction for England.' He reached out and grabbed the forearms of his two fellow spies. 'Come, gentlemen, we must prepare ourselves, for this business is only going to get more dangerous.'

# CHAPTER FIFTY-TWO

IN A RED GLARE, THE LAST OF THE SETTING SUN ILLUMINATED the forest of masts of the Spanish ships at anchor just off Calais. The fleet was tightly packed into its defensive crescent formation. In the middle of that mass, there was no chance of Will identifying the grey-sailed ship, even with its distinctive outline, but he studied the enemy with Drake's tele-scope none the less.

'Why do you fear this ship so?' Drake asked. 'It is only more Spanish rabble, yes?'

'No. These allies of Spain have the wit and cunning of Dee, and the information I have gathered suggests they hold a great weapon.'

'Enough to threaten us?' Drake said with gently mocking disbelief. 'Time and again our tactics have shown the Spanish to be no more than children. We drove them away from England's coastline, which was their last chance for a bridgehead or a haven where they could replenish their diminishing supplies of food, water and munitions. Then we pursued them across the Channel, where they were at the mercy of the open seas, and now they wait for Parma's aid. If they had a great weapon, surely they would have used it by now.'

Drake's comment sounded a warning bell in Will's head – it was something he had considered himself several times. Why hadn't the Unseelie Court used whatever dark powers were at their disposal? But he knew the Enemy were expert at misdirection and subtle manipulation, and when they seemed least of a threat was when they were at their most dangerous. Knowing the plans Howard, Drake and the other commanders of the English fleet had concocted for that very night, he expected the sleeping beast to be woken.

'Well, if we do see that ship, it will be blown out of the water by good English cannon,' Drake sniffed as he reclaimed his prized tele-scope. It had proved an invaluable aid in marshalling his strategy over the last week.

Will didn't react, but his dilemma consumed him. Drake's suggestion was the correct one, but how could he stand by and watch Grace die, even if it meant victory? Ever since she had been taken, he had vacillated between the old Will – who had spent his days in study and good humour before the Unseelie Court had entered his life, who would put the survival of his friends above any abstract notion of loyalty to country – and the man he had become, corrupted by a world where there appeared to be no right or wrong, only survival in the face of unspeakable threats, and where terrible things had to be done for good ends.

It was Sunday, 7 August. The *Revenge* was at anchor at the head of a fleet that appeared to be sleeping. At the rear, the *Tempest* was ready for battle should the Unseelie Court show its hand, but Will, Carpenter and Launceston needed to be at the heart of what they expected to be a decisive night.

The English fleet lay upwind of the armada, with the floodtide in their favour. It was a strong position, but a little further along the coast, in Dunkirk, Parma had gathered his invasion force, and was ready to join the armada in barges sent from ports along the Flemish coast. No one on the English side knew the level of preparedness of Parma's army, nor their numbers, but it was clear they had been in regular contact with Medina Sidonia. Everything might have been different if Will had not killed Hawksworth. England's greatest spy had confessed, but Howard, Drake and his own companions knew the error was understandable in a business of hidden identities and deceit. Will was much harder on himself. If England fell for want of the information Hawksworth had, the spy knew he could never live with himself. For now, though, it was imperative to deal with the situation before them.

All was not yet lost. Dunkirk was blockaded by England's ally Justin of Nassau and his ragged but fierce Dutch Sea Beggars, but they would surely crumble if Medina Sidonia sent ships to drive them away. If the Spanish broke through the English fleet with Parma's army, England was only a few miles away. Will turned the options over in his mind. There were so many variables, and everything was crucial. And the Unseelie Court had yet to show its hand.

Drake turned his face to the last of the sun, and for the first time Will saw none of the braggart and only the devout man who was prepared to sacrifice everything for his God and his country. 'I must lead the men in prayer,' the vice-admiral said, 'and impress upon them what is at stake for their families and their country if we fail this night.'

After Drake had departed, Will joined Carpenter and Launceston on the main deck. They were both introspective as they prepared themselves for the night ahead, although Will noticed an edginess in Launceston, and a greater intensity in his eyes. Without conversation they toured the ship, watching the stern-faced Englishmen silently and pensively going about their business at their stations, stacking the shot and the powder on the gun deck, fetching the water to dampen any fires on board, checking the rigging and the sails on the main deck ready for the order to sail. In his cabin, the ship's surgeon had his knives and saws already laid out.

And then it was only a matter of waiting for the tide to turn.

From the rail, Carpenter studied the eight ships that had been selected. 'I do not know which is the worse death,' he mused. 'Frozen in the forests of Muscovy, or burned alive in an inferno. But there is one common factor in both.' He glared at Will.

'You say I am some pariah, leading you to mishap?' Will replied wryly.

'I say nothing. But if you see a connection, perhaps there is some truth in it.'

'Fire or ice, Heaven or Hell, we are always caught between two sides, John. The only one that truly concerns me is wine or beer, and we can decide that in the Bull when we are safely back in London.'

'Fair comment.' Carpenter shook Will and Launceston's hand in turn. 'For England, for the Queen.'

He left quickly, but Will thought he saw something of the Carpenter he knew before their experiences in Muscovy, and envied him the peace he appeared to have reached.

They were each transported to one of the three ships at the centre of the formation of eight. From their new commands they watched the tide turn and waited for midnight. By the time the moon glimmered silver on the water, the ships were pulling at their anchors in the strengthening tide. The creak of timbers drowned out any noise the skeleton crew made as they completed their final preparations.

When midnight came, Will looked to his left and right where Carpenter and Launceston waited. From all eight vessels came the dull thud of the crew chopping through the ropes that held them fast. Thus freed, the ships were caught in the tide and moving downwind in complete silence towards the armada.

Relieved that the waiting was over, Will moved quickly around the deck, where clutches of men waited for his orders. They were understandably apprehensive. Will nodded to each in turn, acknowledging their bravery, and then turned to the helmsman who had set the course for the heart of the armada and was busy lashing the vast rudder in place. Down in the ship's hold, more men waited, hands cupped around smouldering match. Here the smell was almost too much – pitch, brimstone, gunpowder and tar – and the men coughed and covered their faces with scarves.

'On my mark,' Will said loudly, counting a steady beat in his head, as he knew Carpenter and Launceston would be too. The ship picked up speed, hull pushing through the waves. The men turned their faces towards him as he raised his hand, their eyes white in the gloom.

'Now!' he bellowed.

In the hold, match was plunged into pitch and flints were struck. Sparks glowed like stars, flames flickered, caught, surged into life, and after a moment smoke quickly began to fill the dark space. Will waited until the last man had dashed to the steps and then followed on to the deck, where tiny pockets of fire were already being whipped up in the night wind.

Their faces lit orange, the men waited anxiously against the rail.

'Well done! Heroes all!' Will called. 'Your work here is over!'

Relieved, some of the men leapt directly into the sea as the fires caught, flaring up at their backs, while others swung on ropes to the dinghies that were being towed alongside.

Will turned to see an amazing sight: castles of fire growing larger by the moment as each of the eight ships caught alight, all at full sail. Red and gold danced across the black water, and the glow surrounding each ship made it impossible to see what was happening away in the dark. Now deafened by the roar of the fire rushing along the ship from stern to prow and licking up the rigging towards the sailcloth, Will could not hear the cries of alarm from the lookouts on board the Spanish fleet. Heat seared his back and neck, but still he was determined to wait until the very last. He was scanning the waters ahead.

As expected, the more manoeuvrable pinnaces moved out from the armada at speed towards the eight English fireships. Hurling grapnels, the Spanish sailors struggled to defeat the flames. Will knew they would be terrified that the burning boats were packed with gunpowder and stone as the Dutch Hellburners had been at Antwerp three years earlier. They wouldn't know that the English did not have the resources to duplicate that feat.

As the Spanish fought to direct the two outer ships towards the beach, Will saw Carpenter and Launceston both dive into the water, satisfied that the main body of the fireships would reach the Spanish fleet. But just as he was about to follow suit, a Spanish pinnace reached the fireship alongside his own. On board, he saw the crew part to make way for a figure wearing a cloak and hood. He seemed to be clutching a bag against his chest. Swinging on to the grapnel rope, he began to make his way towards the burning ship.

Will's own ship became an inferno around him, but he was oblivious of the danger. As the flames licked ever closer, his attention was caught by the mysterious figure. Who was it? What could he possibly hope to do alone?

The man crossed the gulf between the two ships. On the burning deck, he pulled from his bag an object which Will recognized with a growing sense of dread: the shimmering globe from the cabin of the grey-sailed ship. With the flames only paces away from him, Will could barely breathe without searing his lungs, but still he watched as the figure knelt on the deck and hunched over the globe amid the raging fires.

Here, Will was sure, was an unforeseen danger. Picking up a grapnel that one of his men had used to lower himself into the dinghy, he hurled it across the water, where it caught in the sail of the Spanish pinnace. Without another thought, he swung across the gulf.

Relieved to feel the cool night wind after the blazing heat of the fireship, he heard the rip of the sail before he landed heavily on the pinnace's deck. The four Spanish sailors were taken by surprise. Two were thrown overboard before the remaining two rounded on him. Will drew his rapier, but rather than face him the frightened sailors both chose to abandon ship.

Reclaiming the grapnel, Will threw it on to the rail of the fireship. As he swung out against the hull and began to climb, he had the strangest sensation that the vessel was starting to slow. Glancing back, he saw he was right. The pinnace and the other fireships were now slightly ahead of him.

The heat was like a blacksmith's furnace as he pulled himself over the rail and on to the deck. A sheet of flame roared up the rigging of a mast and ignited the sails. Burning ribbons of sailcloth fell to the deck. It appeared to be snowing fire. Pitch blazed across the deck while flames licked out of the door to the officers' quarters.

Will glimpsed the face hidden in the hood of the figure hunched over the globe. It was Don Alanzo.

The Spanish spy's cloak had obviously been soaked in seawater, for steam rose off him. Acutely aware he had no such protection, Will advanced quickly before he was seen.

The globe now throbbed with that slow-pulsing white light. Don Alanzo must have sensed movement because he spun round, drawing his sword. When he saw it was Will, shock quickly gave way to malice.

'Are you charmed? What does it take to stop your foul heart beating?' he snarled.

'More than you have at your disposal,' Will replied, brandishing his rapier. The blade glinted red.

Suddenly, the ship came to a juddering halt, almost throwing Will off his feet. Don Alanzo laughed at Will's puzzlement, and then nodded as Will's eyes fell upon the globe, which now pulsed with even greater intensity. Slowly, inexorably, the fireship began to move back towards the unsuspecting English fleet.

'And so the world turns on its head. What was a threat to us now becomes a spear driven into the heart of our hated enemy. With allies like ours, nothing can ever be as it seems,' Don Alanzo mocked.

'Indeed, you think you are on the road to Heaven when you are sliding down to the pits of Hell.'

It was then that Will made his move and lunged with his sword, but Don Alanzo was quick and parried easily. The ship gathered speed as it moved towards the English fleet. The wind of their movement drove sheets of flames at Will and

512

his opponent. It was a nightmarish arena for two such master swordsmen. The raging heat seared Will's face and hands; smoke brought stinging tears to his eyes so his vision blurred as he attacked a second time. With his left arm thrown across his face to shield him from the heat, Don Alanzo was pushed off balance, each thrust a fraction awry.

Ducking and thrusting, Will tried to get to the glowing globe, but the Spaniard continually threw himself in the space between. Whatever the vile nature of the object, Will could see it was no longer operating as it had in the cabin. Neither he nor Don Alanzo were affected by the globe; its power was seemingly directed into the ship itself, forcing it ever backwards.

The intense heat was sapping Will's energy. Blazing splinters of wood fell from the yardarm, flames raced across the deck from the burning pitch. He was left with little room to manoeuvre.

A roaring wall of flame now encircled them. Even if the English ships had their lanterns alight, Will would not have been able to see them. If the fireship crashed into the fleet, all would be lost. The ships were so tightly packed that the blaze would spread like wildfire from one to another.

Thick smoke snaked around both swordsmen. The air was now so hot it burned their throats and lungs, and the fumes from the brimstone made their heads spin.

Bounding back and forth within the fire, Will and Don Alanzo performed an intricate, deadly ballet. Despite the conflagration drawing ever closer, he could see in the Don's fierce eyes that he would not desert his post. His hatred for Will, the murderer of his father, burned as brightly as the flames. Will was convinced he was prepared to go to his death as long as he took Will with him.

The fire forced them into closer combat so every sword-stroke became even more difficult to direct. Will's blade tore through Don Alanzo's steaming cloak; the Don's missed Will's cheek by a hair's breadth. But whatever thrusts and feints he executed, Will could get no closer to the globe.

Smoke rose from their clothes, now singed by the fire. Their skin reddened, their breath shortened, but still they fought on.

For a brief, shocking moment, Will thought that he was in Hell, that all his life had prepared him for this moment, and that fire would be all he saw for ever more.

And then the air was torn by a resounding crack that sounded as if the ship itself was splitting in two. The mainmast, cracked near the base, now fell towards them in a cascade of flaming sail, rigging and yards. Throwing himself to one side, Don Alanzo slammed hard on to the smoking deck.

As the mast crashed towards him, Will propelled himself beneath the falling fire. His boot crashed hard against the globe and it shattered in an explosion of light with a sound like a child's cry. Will continued his motion in a tumble that took him mere inches away from the mast's thunderous impact. Flames soared up into the night sky with a *whoosh* and the deck crumbled beneath it. Kicking out, the Englishman launched himself towards the rail as the boards fell away beneath him.

Behind him there was only flame. Don Alanzo had either been consumed by the fire or fallen into the gaping, blazing hold.

Will's own clothes were alight, fire licking up his back. Placing one foot on the rail, he dived. A trail of flame followed him into the black water.

After the heat, the cold almost stunned him. Striking back to the surface, he saw the fireship now heading back towards the armada, where the others were already causing chaos among the Spanish fleet. Upwind, the sound of the signal cannon set the English galleons in motion.

The battle had begun.

# CHAPTER FIFTY-THREE

ADRIFT IN THE HIGH SWELL OF THE NIGHT TIDE, WILL STRUCK out towards the distant shores of Calais, but the current was too strong. The blazing beacons of the fireships cast a ruddy glare across the water, and for a while he thought it was the last sight he would see.

'Swyfte! Swyfte!'

He heard his name barked out over the surging sea and the wind, but whoever called was hidden by the rolling swell.

'Here!' he yelled back.

Tossed violently by the waves, he fought to stay afloat in his sodden clothes. A moment later a dinghy crested the swell. Carpenter was leaning over the prow searching the water, Launceston and a seaman rowing behind. Carpenter caught sight of Will, and directed his oarsmen with urgent shouts. Each time Will struck out for the dinghy, he was washed back, but Launceston and the seaman battled against the swell to bring the boat alongside him. Will felt rough hands grab his arms and drag him up and over the side of the dinghy. Chest burning from his ordeal, he rolled on to his back and looked up into the scarred face of Carpenter.

'We saw you dive from the fireship,' Carpenter said.

Coughing up seawater, Will gasped, 'You came back for me, John.'

He waited for Carpenter to claim his moral superiority, but Carpenter wouldn't meet his eyes and only said acidly, 'Could we leave England's greatest hero to drown?'

'You have my thanks, John, and you, Robert.' Scorched and near-drowned, Will took a moment to gather himself. Then he turned and glanced towards the soaring flames. 'Together we led the start of the battle here, but there is much more to do. Let us head back to the *Tempest*, for I suspect those grey sails will soon heave into view.'

A series of tremendous blasts tore through the night. Near the armada, the cannon of one of the fireships had exploded, blasting hot metal and burning wood into the scattering pinnaces and small boats. Columns of fire rose from the water, reminding Will of the Templar chamber in Edinburgh.

*The fires of Heaven and Hell.*

One by one the cannon of the fireships exploded. Burning fragments rained on the nearest line of the armada. Confusion already rife, the Spanish ships raced haphazardly to escape the coming inferno. As the panic escalated, there were collisions, torn riggings, shattered yards. Their defensive formation quickly fell apart, yet still the armada survived.

'Damn them!' Carpenter raged. 'The Spanish have the luck of the Devil.'

Enemy vessels avoided the path of the fireships by the smallest of margins, but none of the Spanish fleet caught ablaze. Still blazing, the remnants of the fireships settled into the water in succession along the shore.

Will shrugged. 'A bonfire of Philip's ambitions would have been a good sight, but the confusion itself is enough. We have increased our advantage.'

They rowed the dinghy back to the English fleet. In the darkness they could hear the jubilation rising up from every deck. After the long fight along the Channel, they had finally broken the armada's formation. The Spanish fleet was scattered to the four winds.

Back on board the *Tempest*, Courtenay roamed the deck, singing his bawdy shanties at the top of his voice. The English sailors cheered. Launceston looked faintly baffled by the attention and Carpenter embarrassed, but Will leapt on to the ship's rail and looked across the crew. Courtenay quietened and silence descended upon the deck.

'This night we have struck a blow against the forces that wish to stop every Englishman living free, but it is only the start,' he announced to the assembled company. 'A battle like no other awaits us, and we must not rest until every Spaniard is sent fleeing back to his homeland with the fear of all Hell in his heart. No one asks you to lay down your lives. We ask only for the steel in your arms and the fire in your heart, that you stand proud and fight hard for your families, for all who wait in their homes praying you will keep them safe.' Will gestured towards where the fireships now smouldered. 'The flames we ignite this night will burn on through history. Let them be a beacon to all who are oppressed, a promise of hope to those who live in fear and shed tears of despair. For right! For England!'

The crew joined in the rallying cry. When he jumped back to the deck, they mobbed him and slapped his back as he pushed his way through to Courtenay.

'England's greatest spy,' Carpenter noted archly as he passed.

'And he plays his part well,' Launceston added.

Will flashed them a grin. 'We all play parts, friends. Mine simply has greater purpose than most.'

Courtenay stood at the forecastle watching the dying fires on the shore. Soon only embers would be left of the eight ships.

'Tell your topmen to look out for grey sails,' Will told him. 'That cursed vessel may be hiding because repairs are still under way, or it may be biding its time to emerge with the greatest impact. We must not be blinded by the illusion of this small victory. The darkest times lie ahead.'

They snatched a few hours' sleep, and at first light they were awoken by the blare of trumpets and the boom of Howard's signal gun. Anchors broke water next to all of the hundred and fifty ships in the English feet, sails unfurled into the morning wind, and within the hour they were away in pursuit of the enemy. Word went from ship to ship that as a mark of Drake's brilliant campaign he would be allowed to lead the attack on the Spanish.

Desperate to bring his armada back together, Medina Sidonia led the ships still left at Calais in pursuit of the vessels that had been scattered along the coast. As dawn broke, and with a south-westerly propelling them at speed, the English gave chase through the straits and into the North Sea.

Will never took his gaze from the horizon. But rather than the grey-sailed ship, the first vessels he saw were Spanish, seven miles off Gravelines, a small port in Flanders under Spanish control. At the rear was Medina Sidonia's *San Martin*. Will knew the Spanish commander would realize he had few options. Fleeing would condemn his fleet to the sandbanks and shoals that lay hidden along the coast. All he could do was turn and fight.

Courtenay clapped his hands in eager anticipation. 'What a day for blood!' he bellowed. With the Spanish now in such disarray, the English were not afraid to confront them at close quarters. The *Revenge* closed on the *San Martin*, and within seconds the air was thick with cannon smoke from both fleets, and the sound of the sea was lost beneath the rolling thunder of guns that never seemed to fall silent.

Drake held his fire until his opponent was barely more than a galleon's length away. Then the bow guns cracked, followed by the thunder of his broadsides. Medina Sidonia responded in kind, and the shot tore holes in both ships. Out of the cacophony came the screams of the wounded and the dying.

'Sea warfare is madness,' Carpenter hissed to Will. 'Give me a knife in a dark room and that is enough. Two swords at most, but definitely on land.'

'Drake is not mad.' Will watched as furious battle was joined. 'He has his flaws, but he is a brave man. He has thrown himself into the forefront to take the Spanish guns.'

The Spanish flagship came off worse. Unlike their English counterparts, the Spanish crews were not trained to reload their cannon rapidly, and as increasing damage was inflicted on the *San Martin*, so the Spaniards' ability to respond diminished. English chain ripped through rigging and sail. The planking just above the waterline shattered under Drake's heavier guns.

After his initial attack had weakened the flagship, Drake pulled the *Revenge* away, leading his squadron in pursuit of the other Spanish warships and leaving Frobisher and the *Triumph* to continue the slow destruction of the *San Martin*. Bellowing his orders as he strode the deck, Courtenay on the *Tempest* set off behind the *Revenge*.

Their flagship in a desperate state, other armada ships moved to protect it, managing to re-form their defensive crescent. The smaller, more agile English fleet swept in to pound the wings relentlessly. The *Revenge* fired continuously into the dense mass of Spanish ships, the barrage so intense the smoke from the guns blocked out the sun. The air was filled with a constant whining rain of exploding, splintering wood. The gunfire was so loud that every order, every conversation was bellowed, but still the cries of the dying and wounded rose above it. Will could see its chilling effect upon all on board the *Tempest*; though they were the enemy, the suffering of the Spanish left no one untouched.

The *Tempest* sailed into the thick of the battle where there was little room for manoeuvre, the way ahead obscured by dense smoke, the ships so closely packed in the ferocity of their combat that it was possible to see the awful death-throes of the enemy.

Grimly, Will witnessed hundreds of slaves chained to the oars in the Spanish galleasses fall where they sat, under fire from arquebusiers or shot from the English galleons. On one warship, he saw the Spanish commander's head explode in a mist of blood and bone from a random shot. Another's hand was taken, a third lost his leg at the knee. Some resembled pincushions from the deadly splinters rammed into their bodies after the cannonshot blasted apart their ships. Sickened, Will watched them stagger back and forth across the deck, all sense lost. Blood sluiced across the boards as thickly as seawater at the height of a storm.

Wincing at each cacophonous explosion, Carpenter was increasingly appalled by the intensity of the battle. 'Every fight I have seen on the waves since I joined the fleet has been worse than the previous one,' he shouted at Will, his voice laced with horror. 'This is slaughter not fit for animals.'

'And they would do the same to us if they had the opportunity,' Will yelled back, ducking as a Spanish cannonball screamed overhead. 'We do what we have to, to survive. There will be shouts of glory for whoever wins this day, but we here, on both sides, know there is none in it.'

For nearly the whole day the battle raged, while the *Tempest* roamed the outer limit of the mass of Spanish ships searching for the true Enemy, but the smoke was so thick that even the topmen could not see far ahead. Launceston had seemed entranced by the parade of atrocities and the sickening skein of blood, but in the sudden shift of smoke caused by the explosion of a ship's magazine a movement caught his eye. 'There!' he yelled and pointed beyond the immediate carnage.

Heaving into view through the drifting smoke, beyond the infernal chaos around them, were grey sails.

'Captain Courtenay!' Will shouted. 'The chase is on!'

Bloody John ordered the helmsman to change direction as the crew scrambled about the deck. The *Tempest* shifted course in pursuit of the grey-sailed ship, already vanishing into the smoke.

The Spanish ships were too preoccupied with basic survival to give the English galleon any attention. Through the collapsing enemy formation, past tightly contained dramas of death and destruction where ships fought one-sided duels, it swept.

Making haste to the forecastle, Will, Carpenter and Launceston searched the drifting acrid clouds for another sign of their quarry. Finally, they broke through to a clear stretch of sea and there the grey-sailed ship surged ahead with near-supernatural speed and manoeuvrability.

Will could just make out that repairs were still under way on the fire-blackened starboard side of the ship. New timbers had been fitted, but he noted with satisfaction that there was a faint list to the vessel, like a wounded beast limping to its lair to recover. Whatever damage he had caused, it had prevented the grey-sailed ship from following its ritual protective route among the fleet, and perhaps, he wondered, stopped it using whatever weapon it carried on board. He pondered how different things might have been had it been able to take part in the fight off the Isle of Wight, and then near Calais.

'Your requirements, Master Swyfte?' Courtenay asked, interrupting Will's thoughts.

'First, try to contain it against the other ships, and then shall we see how it withstands a broadside or two.'

'And then prepare to board?' The captain's tone was eager.

Will hesitated, not wanting to bring the toxic contact with the Unseelie Court down upon the *Tempest*'s crew. 'There is nothing worth plundering on board that foul vessel, Captain.'

'Then we should send it straight to the bottom,' Carpenter nodded. 'Silver Skull and all.'

Will couldn't argue with him, but the thought of Grace on board left him chilled. 'Let us choose our options as the situation unfolds, Captain,' he said, not knowing what he would do if he was forced to make that awful choice.

Nodding his agreement, Courtenay called for the master gunner to ready his men. The *Tempest* ploughed through the swell, but the grey-sailed ship easily remained ahead, making for where the English fleet was attacking the south-eastern wing of the armada formation.

'Why now?' Will mused. 'They have held their cover in the most desperate circumstances and not used their weapon.' The answer struck him the moment he had finished speaking. 'Unless their repairs have only now ensured they have enough speed to escape whatever carnage their weapon wreaks.'

As he spoke, he glimpsed movement on board the grey ship. Something small and writhing had been passed over the rail and dropped into the sea. In the water, a shadow grew as whatever had been dumped there increased in size at a phenomenal rate. Within moments, what looked like a black tube was barrelling towards them, a furrow of white surf breaking the surface.

'In the name of God, what is that?' Carpenter breathed.

An anxious cry to the helmsman echoed behind them. They turned to see Courtenay, his face white and strained, hanging over the *Tempest*'s rail to peer into the sea. Leaning hard on the wheel, the helmsman began a barely perceptible shift in the *Tempest*'s course, but it was just enough to miss whatever was thrusting beneath the waves. There was a crash as it skimmed the edge of the keel, and the *Tempest* lurched over at an alarming angle, throwing everyone on deck off their feet. Catching Carpenter's sleeve, Will prevented him from going over the rail; others held on to stays and rigging for dear life.

As the wake passed, the *Tempest* righted itself with a crash that sent seawater washing across the deck.

'What was that?' Carpenter raged.

From the drawn expression on Courtenay's face, Will could tell he must know the answer. But before he could reach the captain, the truth revealed itself before his eyes. The mysterious shape surged on from the *Tempest* towards another English galleon. With collision imminent, a black, serpentine creature erupted from the water on the vessel's starboard side.

'Sea serpent!' Will gasped, horrified by the thing's vast size and power. Glistening like an eel, it was a man's size across and as long as two galleons.

Needle-teeth snapped with a sound like the clashing of a hundred swords. Will was transfixed as the crew's faces turned up, and up, and a shadow loomed across them. Rooted in horror, the men crossed themselves.

Arcing over the vessel, the serpent smashed through the

foremast and pulled it down into the sea on the other side. Sailors scrambled across the boards to hack at the rigging before the ship could be dragged down to the depths.

Will knew it was the creature he had seen in the barrel on the grey-sailed ship, now grown unbelievably large.

Joining them, Courtenay's gaze never left the white wake tearing into the thick smoke. 'I have encountered their kind before, out in the stormy Atlantic returning from the New World. The damnable beast almost took me, and my command, down to the bottom. Nothing can stop them. They tear ships into matchwood and consume every good man as they swim through the drink.'

'This is the Enemy's weapon,' Will said. 'Stalking silently beneath the waves to destroy our ships.'

From deep in the smoke, they heard another crash, the sound of splintering wood, cries that rose above the thunderous guns.

'Engrossed in the noise and fury of battle, no one will know it is there until too late,' Carpenter said. 'This monstrosity will turn the tide of the battle.'

'Then we must stop it,' Will said, turning to face the others.

'How?' Carpenter said. 'What weapons have we that could strike dead a thing like that? Even if we could catch it. Musket and arquebus fire are too small. The big guns would never land a shot 'pon it at the speed it moves.'

Will quickly turned over the options and then said, 'You are right, but I have a notion. Leave it to me.' To Courtenay he said, 'Captain, can you get us close enough to attack the beast?'

'Close enough is too close,' Courtenay replied. 'But then no man ever gained glory with faint heart. Aye, we'll do our damnedest.'

Will looked out to sea, searching for the grey-sailed ship, but it had already disappeared into the fog of battle. Launceston read his mind. 'If we lose the Enemy ship, misery may lie ahead. They still have the Silver Skull.'

'If the serpent destroys our fleet, the Spanish will regroup, collect Parma's army and England will fall. Come, let's after it.'

As the *Tempest* sailed on, they encountered a broken galleon rapidly taking on water. The hull was torn in two, shattered masts trailing in the water like oars. Men clung to the wreckage. Several were dead, chunks of them torn away.

Amid the boom and crack of gunfire came the sound of another vessel being wrecked. The sea serpent had settled on the fringes of the armada's south-easterly wing, where several English ships were harassing the Spanish fleet. More wreckage, another badly damaged galleon, drifting directionless.

Finally they emerged from the smoke. The serpent's wake was clear on the swell, a large V flecked with foam near the point. They watched helplessly as it prepared to attack another vessel, its head breaking the water. The circular mouth flexed. A short distance from its target it submerged and then erupted from the sea in a cascade of white, crashing through the rigging and stays and bringing down the mainmast as the terrified crew fled the deck. Splashing into the swell on the far side, the wake continued forwards before beginning a wide turn for another attack.

'Is it . . . growing larger?' Carpenter asked. 'Soon it will be able to ensnare an entire ship in its coils.'

'Draw its attention!' Will shouted to Courtenay. 'We must deflect it!'

Courtenay ordered the helmsman to set a course that would put the *Tempest* between the serpent and the damaged galleon. The north-westerly filled the sails and sped them on. With the captain's approval, Will called together four sailors and instructed them to fetch some items from the stores and magazine.

'You are sure this is the correct course?' Launceston asked, his blithe manner hiding the doubt he obviously felt. The same doubt could be seen in the faces of the crew, who flashed unsettled glances Will's way.

'I thought you would thank me for easing the boredom of a sea journey,' Will replied. One foot on the rail, he smiled to himself, his confident gaze searching the water ahead.

The four sailors scrambled up on deck with the barrel of pitch and the powder Will had requested. 'Mix the preparation, then hold tight till we are ready to use it,' Will shouted to them.

'Brace yourselves!' Courtenay barked.

Gripping the rail and the rigging, the crew steadied themselves as the *Tempest* plunged into the path of the serpent. At the last, it submerged, but the wake threw the galleon's prow towards the sky, the stern almost plunging beneath the waves.

Muscles straining, Will held tight. A sailor with a pock-marked face lost his hold on the rail and with a cry flew backwards. He missed Will by a hand's breadth and slammed into the cabin door with bone-breaking force.

For a second, it felt as if the vessel was going over. Silence gripped all those who clung on, eyes screwed shut as they waited for the momentum to continue. But then the *Tempest* crashed back, swamping them with water.

'She is the sturdiest ship in the fleet, but we cannot maintain this punishment,' Courtenay yelled.

'Then pray we do not have to,' Will shouted back. He eyed the sailors working on the preparation and received a curt nod in return. 'Get us near to the beast, Captain. We must draw it out of the water to attack us.'

'Now we are all to be sacrificed to your mad scheme?' Carpenter asked.

'All schemes are mad until they succeed, John. Think of the stories you will be able to tell once we are back in Bankside.'

Carpenter's derisive snort followed Will as he ran for the rail. With Courtenay's bellowed directions from the forecastle, the helmsman's manoeuvres kept the vile serpent within view. Each time they tried to divert the beast, the encounter brought them close to disaster. Will could see the crew growing increasingly rebellious.

Finally, the wake turned towards them. 'There, my pretty, now we have you,' Will muttered. He ordered his team to ready themselves.

Expressions fixed and grim, the eyes of everyone on board turned towards the furrow in the water surging towards them. No one moved, not a word was uttered.

Moments before the serpent broke water, Will yelled, 'Get ready!'

The barrel of pitch and powder was lofted high by two sailors. Another stood by with a flint.

The beast erupted from the water, mouth wrenched wide, teeth gleaming. Cries of terror echoed across the *Tempest* and men threw themselves on to the deck. Staring deep into the creature's maw, Will stood his ground.

'Now!' he ordered.

The flint was struck, the barrel ignited. With a roar, the two sailors flung the burning barrel into the serpent's yawning mouth. Will threw an arm across his face as his flaming, make-shift weapon burst, and sticky, blazing liquid flooded out.

The monstrous creature thrashed wildly, its upper body afire. The lashing tail slammed against the *Tempest*'s hull, throwing Will and the others off their feet. Scrabbling on his hands and knees, Courtenay hauled himself up to the rail, and gave a shout of relief when he saw no serious damage had been done to his vessel.

Will leapt to the captain's shoulder, and they were joined by the still-fearful crew, their faces drawn and pale. A moment of silence gripped every man as they peered over the side.

In the water, the serpent's thrashing began to slow, and eventually it grew still until it floated, dead. An acrid smell akin to burned leather rose from the still-smouldering corpse of the fantastical beast. The crew cheered, but Will quickly silenced them.

'Celebrate our victory, but this is no time to rest. We must return to the hunt for the grey-sailed ship!' he called.

Emboldened by the serpent's death, the crew returned to their posts with gusto. The helmsman guided the *Tempest* back towards the fray, but they could all see that as the evening drew on the worst was over.

The Spanish continued to fight, though the English assault had whittled away their capabilities, their ships and their men. Even with their guns silenced, some sailed bravely to try to aid their fellows in more immediate danger. At times it seemed as if the water was no longer visible amid the wreckage, the bodies and the frothing crimson blood.

The south-westerly drove the English ships on and pinned the Spanish back. The defensive formation of Philip's fleet had collapsed, their powder and shot mostly gone, only arquebus and musket fire being returned. Some carracks and hulks were reduced to chaotic piles of floating timber that echoed their former shape. Many crew had abandoned ship and now attempted to escape in small boats.

'We have won,' Carpenter said, the relief evident in his voice. 'Now it is just a matter of clearing up the dregs.'

'Yet we will never win until the Unseelie Court is destroyed,' Will replied, his voice hushed and distant. Searching the dying embers of the battle for any sign of grey sails, Will's thoughts turned once more to Grace: what would the Enemy do with her now the Spanish had been defeated? Would they simply spirit her away, never to be seen again?

*Like Jenny.*

Launceston, whose attention had rarely left the carnage, indicated a pattern of shifting lights visible through the pall of smoke. Will recognized the colours he had seen over the grey-sailed ship. As he turned to search for the outcome of the Enemy's conjuring, the *Tempest* was buffeted by a strong wind. Black clouds churned in the south-west, rushing towards them.

'What—' Carpenter began.

'Unnatural,' Will replied. He was turning to Courtenay, but the captain had already seen the approaching squall and cast out the order to trim the sails. The rain hit them soon after, so intense they could barely see beyond the ship. As the gale battered the English ship and the crew fought to hold her steady, the surviving Spanish vessels attempted to use the weather to flee their destruction.

For half an hour, the squall continued in full force, but Courtenay's expertise kept the *Tempest* clear of any collisions.

Then, as the clouds cleared, they saw the remains of the armada sailing north away from the battle, struggling to resume their crescent formation. Everyone knew the Spaniards were out of ammunition and sailing into dangerous waters, but the

English sailors' hearts fell when they saw how many enemy vessels had survived. The English fleet began the pursuit to finish the work they had started.

In the light of the setting sun, the *Tempest*'s topmen caught sight of their quarry. Their hail drew Will's attention to grey sails heading west.

'They have abandoned the armada?' Carpenter said. 'What, they flee now?'

As Will weighed what he knew of the tactics of the Unseelie Court, he considered their possible course of action, until a chilling realization dawned upon him. 'They sail for England,' he said, voicing his thoughts to himself. 'With the Silver Skull still aboard.'

'The ghost has been given up?' Carpenter suggested. He gripped the rail and peered after the disappearing vessel.

'No. No!' Will became animated as he finally understood the Unseelie Court's hidden plan. He grabbed Carpenter's shoulder and shook him, waving one hand towards the grey ship. 'Consider this: the English fleet is now being drawn away from our waters. The militia line the south coast in anticipation of Parma's invasion force. A force will protect the Queen, but London's defences are now wide open. We have been distracted from their true objective.'

'Do you mean to say that the armada . . . the entire might of Spain's empire . . . was merely a distraction?' Carpenter said incredulously.

'They have sacrificed the Spanish on the rocks of their vanity. The empire . . . all the lives lost . . . mean nothing to them. It simply served to draw our might, and our attention, away from where it was most needed.'

'London?' Carpenter looked to the ship disappearing towards the horizon.

'The seat of our nation. The core of our defences against them. And the Queen.'

'All a manipulation.' Carpenter's voice was filled with disbelief. He couldn't grasp the extent of the deceit, but gradually the magnitude of the repercussions was written clear on his face. In silence, the three of them stood at the rail as the *Tempest* gave pursuit, but the grey-sailed ship was faster, and soon it had disappeared from view.

# CHAPTER FIFTY-FOUR

IN THE HOUR BEFORE DAWN, A SEPULCHRAL SILENCE LAY ACROSS the Palace of Whitehall. Up past midnight discussing the fleet's fortunes against the armada and the strategy for the coming days with Walsingham, Burghley and her other advisers, the Queen had finally retired to her chambers. In a display of confidence at the success of her forces, she had already made plans to spend the next day hunting in Epping Forest, while waiting for news of the battle off Gravelines, but to those around her it was clear that she remained uneasy.

Nathaniel and Marlowe had spent the early evening drinking in the Traveller's Rest in the shadow of the palace walls. For most of the night, Marlowe had to no avail tried to cajole the owner to stage a play he had been writing. Nathaniel had paid little notice, his attention drawn to the nervousness that blanketed the other drinkers. The mood was subdued, the conversation barely rising above a murmur. No entertainment had been planned for the inn yard, and trade was sparse, though Nathaniel had heard things were more brisk in the church across the street. The gossip raced back and forth: the armada had been defeated; the English fleet had been destroyed; the

Spanish were at that very moment landing on the south coast; death and destruction drew near.

The same air of apprehension hung over the entire palace, from the kitchen staff to the Queen's maids, from the gardeners to Walsingham himself. Marlowe had questioned the spymaster on more than one occasion as the evening drew on, but Nathaniel was not privy to the conversations; whatever the response, it did not improve Marlowe's mood. It was as if he had received a portent of his own death; Nathaniel wondered if it was just the way of writers.

'We are like children, wrapped in a mother's skirts,' Nathaniel complained as they wandered through the formal gardens filled with the rich perfume of night-scented stock. Moonlight glimmered off the diamond-pane windows of the row of buildings where the gallery looked over the courtyard in front of the Queen's residence. From beyond the jumble of buildings to the west came the dank, florid smell of the summer river, the cries of the watermen long since having ceased for the night.

'Do not yearn for conflict and danger, Nat. Relish these moments of peace, for they are few and far between.'

'But men are putting their lives at risk in the defence of England even as we speak. In defence of our lives, Kit, yours and mine, and we do nothing but wander through the gardens at night out of boredom. Does that not irk you to the very heart of your being?'

'We keep watch. We are ready if needed . . .'

Shaking his head, Nathaniel tried to allow his anger to suppress his fears for his master, and for Grace. The more he learned about the world Will inhabited, the less he understood, and he felt powerless. There were more dark shadows than he had ever been aware of, and though he feared he knew what lurked within them, he was not sure he wanted to know the truth. He had trouble sleeping, his nights were haunted by grey figures flitting through the dark, and things that should not exist under the eyes of God.

He paused and cocked his head. Gentle pipe music, lilting and entrancing, drifted over the peaceful palace grounds. A smile leapt to his mouth unbidden. 'Do you hear that? Such beautiful music. Who would play at this hour?'

Marlowe shrugged. 'I hear nothing.' And he continued to trudge along the path beside the low box hedge.

'At least you have some purpose here. A spy. What can I offer, apart from keeping you company?'

'I am not a swordsman like Will,' Marlowe said. 'My strength lies in getting in my cups with cut-throats and gambling with rogues. Petty thievery and low deception.' The note of bitterness in his voice was potent. 'Choose a writer to live in a world of lies! Walsingham knows men well.'

Nathaniel slowed as he heard the music again. Faint and caught on the wind, it came and went in a strange manner. Its melody was enchanting, but he now heard a more disturbing note beneath.

Catching it for the first time, Marlowe paused too. A troubled expression crossed his face, and that alarmed the younger man. 'What is it?' Nathaniel asked.

Marlowe waved a hand as if it were nothing, but Nathaniel could see it was important to him. As his companion lifted his head to sniff the air, Nathaniel was aware that he too could smell a rich perfume, slightly sickly, drifting across the gardens.

'Come,' Marlowe whispered. He broke into a run until he reached the passageway that led into the courtyard in front of the banqueting house. The square was bright in the light of the moon. All was still. From the shadow of the passageway, Marlowe studied the courtyard intently, taking in the chapel in the far corner and the haphazard collection of buildings to his right where an arch led through to the palace's private wharf on the river.

'It is empty,' Nathaniel began, but Marlowe silenced him with a quick wave of his hand.

Ahead of them was the Lantern Tower where the Shield had been stored, and all but a chosen few were denied access. At the top of the tower, a green light pulsed. It was so faint it would have been easy to miss, but now Nathaniel had seen it, he found it impossible to take his eyes off it.

He had no idea what could cause such an odd hue, but it had the look of a beacon, though whatever it was calling, or warning, he was not sure.

Marlowe turned to him and hissed, 'Something is amiss. I see no signs yet, but I feel it in my gut. There is danger nearby.'

Nathaniel let his gaze wander over the empty square. He realized he too could feel something akin to whatever was troubling Marlowe.

An expression of sympathy crossed Marlowe's face. 'Nat, it would be better if you stayed away from here—'

'No!' Nathaniel interjected. 'You would send me away at the very moment when I may actually prove I have some use in this world beyond fetching and carrying for my master?'

'There are things that you should not see, or know exist. Once in your head, they can never be put out, and this life goes from being a joy to a burden that you would be rid of soon. That is the nature of our business.' The playwright searched Nathaniel's face and grew sad. 'I can see you will not be deterred. You are a brave man, Nat. But take my advice: whatever you see, put it out of your head the moment your eyes fall upon it. Ask no questions, of yourself or of me. Simply accept, and move on.' Marlowe delivered his speech even though it was clear he didn't believe it was possible. 'Do you understand?'

Nathaniel nodded, not understanding at all.

'Good. Then no more talk.' The playwright drew his knife and turned to watch.

After a moment, a solitary figure wandered into the centre of the courtyard and looked around with an air of confusion. Nathaniel was startled to see it was Grace.

Marlowe tried to silence him as he called her name quietly, but he was too late. Nathaniel was so relieved to see her he darted out into the moonlit square. She appeared stiff and unyielding, and when he looked into her face he saw a blankness that reminded him of a child's doll.

Quickly, he pulled her into the shadows and said quietly, 'Grace? What ails you?'

She continued to stare blankly. Then a tremor crossed her face and she blinked once, twice, lazily. When she looked at him, her eyes had a dreamy, faraway look like someone deep in their cups, or on the edge of sleep.

'Nat,' she breathed. 'Oh, it is so good to see you. It has been . . . how long has it been?' Her brow furrowed in puzzlement, quickly gone, and then the lazy smile returned. 'I have had the strangest dream, Nat. Of life aboard a magical ship, of great adventures across a sparkling sea beneath the light of the moon. Of friends, whispering comfort in my ear, and joy. Oh, Nat! The kind of joy you never experience once you are grown.' Closing her eyes, she continued to smile at her memories.

'How did you get here, Grace? Where have you been?' Nathaniel probed gently. He could see she was not herself, and wondered if she had taken one of the potions that the cutpurses sometimes used to dull the senses of their victims in the stews on Bankside.

Ignoring him, she wrapped her arms around herself and swayed gently in the breeze.

From the passage entrance, Marlowe beckoned furiously. Nathaniel tried to guide Grace towards him, but she resisted.

'No, Nat. I have work to do. For my friends,' she hummed. 'I led them to the guards so they could come in . . .' Her brow furrowed again, as though at an unpleasant memory, but nothing dark would stay with her. 'And now I must show them through the maze of the palace. They need me, Nat. I cannot deny my friends.'

'That is not a good idea, Grace,' he began, but he could see she was not listening to him. Gradually, she pulled away and drifted across the courtyard, his presence already forgotten.

Nathaniel ran back to Marlowe and said, 'She has helped her captors to enter the palace.'

'We must alert the guards, then. To the gatehouse.'

Marlowe suddenly grabbed Nathaniel and dragged him back into the passage. Pressed against the wall, they saw grey shadows shimmer from the arch that led to the gate, following in the wake of Grace towards the buildings on the other side of the courtyard.

Blinking to clear his eyes, Nathaniel thought he must be seeing moon-shadows, so insubstantial did the shapes appear. Then his attention was diverted by a cloaked and hooded figure walking slowly, its head and shoulders bowed as if it was consumed with despair. More shadows followed, slightly more substantial this time; Nathaniel felt his eyes were clearing, although he could not explain the strange effect.

Once the courtyard was empty, Marlowe motioned for

them to leave their hiding place. They skirted the edge of the courtyard, hesitating every now and then in case more of the intruders appeared. As they edged through the archway to the gatehouse that lay next to the river entrance, they were suddenly overwhelmed by a smell of rot.

The gates hung wide so they could see the path that led to the warehouses along the river, and the wharf. Two guards lay on the cobbles in the entrance, the moon illuminating skin that was blackened and suppurating. A vile stink rolled off the bodies. Nathaniel retched. As he edged closer, he saw that large boils had risen up around the unfortunate men's necks. A thick white foam covered their lips.

'Plague!' he gasped, throwing himself back against the wall of the arch. 'But . . . but the guards were well earlier. I saw them. And plague does not strike one dead so quickly!'

Marlowe led him away several paces and whispered, 'Steady yourself, Nat. This plague is not natural. It comes from a weapon which the Enemy have under their control—'

'The Spanish have a weapon that can bring disease?' Nathaniel asked, disbelief colouring his voice.

Marlowe didn't reply. And then Nathaniel knew his worst fears were true: that there was another enemy, beyond the Spanish, and he knew instinctively what it was, what they were. Marlowe was struggling to find the right words so Nathaniel interjected, 'What kind of weapon does this, Kit? I have not heard the like of this anywhere.'

'I told you – no questions. We will talk of these things later, but now we must raise the alarm.' Nathaniel followed him into the gatehouse, but they'd barely taken three steps over the threshold before the foul smell told them all they needed to know. 'Damn them!' Marlowe cried, his voice hoarse with anger.

'They are slaying every man they encounter. Is there no protection from this vile weapon?'

'Dee searches for some defence, but as yet has found none. If used gently, without the protection of the Shield, I am told it has a range – like an arquebus. Stay beyond that range and you will be unharmed.'

Nathaniel nodded his approval. 'Good. That we can do.' He hesitated as a thought struck him, and then said, 'The Queen! If these guards are dead, the others may be taken by surprise. We must protect her!'

'We are also charged with protecting what is held in the Lantern Tower. That will be the Enemy's first port of call.'

They ran from the gatehouse back across the courtyard and into the buildings that led to the banqueting rooms. Through the windows, they could see the maze of buildings that surrounded the Queen's residence – the Black Gallery and the Tryst Rooms on the far side, and in the foreground, the row of stone houses next to the Lantern Tower. Nothing seemed to be moving in the immediate vicinity.

As they made their way down the corridor, they heard the sound of a guard's challenge ahead. They came to a corner, stopped and peered round cautiously. At the far end of the Great Hall, a guard in a helmet and breastplate levelled his halberd at the hooded intruder and demanded to know his business.

The figure did not respond. For a moment he hesitated, until the guard prodded him with the halberd, and then he held out his hand, palm upwards. Dropping the halberd, the guard cried out, a gurgling sound escaping from his throat. Nathaniel watched in horror as boils burst from the man's neck, the skin blackening and mouth foaming white. His eyes rolled and he fell to the ground, convulsing a little until he stilled. The whole process was over in a flash.

'So quick,' Nathaniel whispered.

The guard dead, Nathaniel then became aware of figures on the other side of the hall. It was as if they had just stepped out from behind some unseen curtain. Were they the shadows he had glimpsed earlier? They now had more corporeal substance, though he could see none of their faces. They appeared to swathe themselves in shadows that were cast by no obvious source of light.

And Grace was among them. Two of the shadowy figures guided her towards the door on the far side of the hall, the others loping behind. There wasn't a sound; it was as though the hall was filled with ghosts.

Peering through the window, Nathaniel saw more of the intruders fanning out across the palace complex. 'Kit, they are everywhere. We cannot confront them all. What do we do?'

'Stealth, Nat,' Marlowe whispered. 'There is nothing to gain by revealing ourselves yet. An opportunity will present itself.' He did not sound convinced. Nathaniel could see the anxiety on his face as he searched desperately for an answer. Hissing for Nathaniel to follow, he slipped quickly and silently across the Great Hall to the open door.

'It is just you and me now, Nat,' he said grimly. 'The two of us, to save England and the Queen.'

# CHAPTER FIFTY-FIVE

THE DESPERATE RHYTHM OF POUNDING HOOVES MATCHED THE
pulse of the blood in Will's head. Under the light of the moon,
he urged his horse along the sun-baked lanes, over the marsh-
land where lights burned ominously and past the peaceful
fields where the corn waved in the night breeze. Carpenter
and Launceston kept pace alongside.

During the long hours that the *Tempest* pursued the grey-
sailed ship, the three of them had remained in constant counsel.
There was no doubt in their minds that the Unseelie Court
would head directly for the palace at Whitehall, to seize the
Shield in order that they could unleash whatever plan they
had nurtured since the Silver Skull had been taken from the
Tower.

As they sailed into the Thames estuary, Will instructed
Courtenay to put them ashore before they reached Tilbury. He
guessed that the grey-sailed ship would take the most direct
route, slowing to navigate the upper reaches of the river to
London Bridge, before the Enemy moved to smaller boats to
reach the palace. Horses would be faster.

Parched by the dust, they finally reached the city walls just
before dawn. Admitted by the night watch, they galloped west

through the deserted streets to where the palace sprawled hard along the river. As they neared, Will's attention was caught by the inexplicable and troubling faint green halo around the Lantern Tower.

Dead guards littered the eastern gateway, their features ravaged by disease. Without slowing to examine the bodies, the three spies continued to the yard next to the Black Gallery.

'No sound of resistance,' Will whispered as he dismounted. 'Has no alarm been raised?'

Carpenter pointed through the arch to figures making their way among the adjoining buildings. 'Our arrival was noticed,' he said. 'The palace is overrun. Are we too late?'

'Courtenay will soon be here to raise the alarm and seal off the palace, as ordered.' Drawing his rapier, Will directed his two companions towards the Black Gallery. 'Till then we must do what we can.'

At the stairs to the Tryst Rooms, they stopped and Will said, 'We must go our separate ways. I will attend to the Lantern Tower. The Unseelie Court will surely attempt to break through the defences Dee has put in place. You must protect the Queen at all costs.'

Carpenter and Launceston raced on up the stairs. The catch on the door to the Black Gallery turned with a clank and Will hurried into the map room, pulling the door closed and locking it behind him. He moved on through Dee's library and his workshops – all empty – and then out into the warm summer night.

Using the palace's maze of passageways, courtyards, gardens and buildings to hide his progress, Will made his way to the Lantern Tower.

The glow around its summit troubled him. He had, of course, heard the rumours of unearthly noises emanating from there at night, but he had assumed that that was a result of a widespread suspicion of Dee and his work.

Carpenter had been correct: the palace was overrun. Will only got the vaguest impression of the shadowy figures prowling through the quiet buildings or searching the open spaces: of staring, malignant eyes and hollow cheeks, of tall, thin bodies and grasping hands. The servants and the members of the court still slept, so silent had the invasion been, but the Enemy culled all armed men as soon as they came upon them.

Will was sickened when he saw a good man's throat slit, a nightwatchman run through, before the victim had even seen his opponent. He tried to estimate the numbers, but they were constantly and rapidly moving. Of the Silver Skull there was no sign.

On more than one occasion, he had to double back through the deserted kitchens or into the banqueting house to approach from a different direction. Once he had to take refuge in a store filled with an odd mix of carpenters' materials and unwanted items from one of the ships moored at the palace wharf – fishing nets, grapnels, sailcloth and barrels of pitch. He hid behind a pile of dirty rope while footsteps paused briefly at the door before moving on.

It was as he cautiously stalked along a dark gallery, alert for every footfall, that Will was suddenly overcome with an unwavering conviction that he was being watched. The hairs on his neck prickled erect, and his breath caught in his throat. Someone was in the gallery with him, he was sure. Heart pounding, he darted among the furniture and searched behind the tapestries, but there was no one. Yet the eerie sensation only became more intense.

Eyes darting into every shadowy corner, he hurried to the

end of the gallery. And there, in passing, he glanced into a mirror. Malantha stared back.

Lashing out, he smashed the glass with his sword-hilt, but even in the glittering shards he could see her hate-filled gaze multiplied a hundred times. He raced out before the disturbance brought the Enemy to him, but the unsettling sensation remained with him.

Reaching a window overlooking the Lantern Tower court-yard, he glanced down and saw a disturbing sight. Before the door at the foot of the tower where the Shield was held, three insubstantial figures watched a fourth who knelt over another of the pulsing glass globes. This one glowed with a dull, ruddy light like a blacksmith's forge.

*Will Dee's defences hold?* Will's knuckles whitened as he gripped his rapier.

Four more figures entered the courtyard from the direction of the river. At the forefront, Cavillex strode purposefully towards the tower, a barely restrained look of triumph on his face. Will recalled Edinburgh, and the cruelty and brutality of Malantha's brother. Golden hair flowing behind him, Cavillex appeared lithe and strong and filled with vitality, unlike his cadaverous companions. He came to a halt by the door, and a smile crossed his icy features.

The globe flared brighter. The door opened.

# CHAPTER FIFTY-SIX

AS WILL MADE HIS WAY TO THE LANTERN TOWER, CARPENTER and Launceston crept along the empty, echoing corridors of the upper floors as they wound their way towards the Queen's rooms. From the windows, they watched helplessly as the Unseelie Court despatched guards with brutal efficiency, peering into rooms, darting through doorways, moving steadily towards the royal apartments.

'Hold,' Launceston insisted as they sneaked into the Blue Gallery. He beckoned Carpenter to a view over the lawns and paths. There was Grace, her head bowed slightly, a dreamy smile on her lips, pointing to the Queen's chambers. Beside her stood Mayhew, his hood now removed so that the deadly Skull gleamed in the moonlight.

'She is entranced,' Carpenter murmured. 'She cannot help herself.'

'Still, she guides them – she knows the palace better than Mayhew. If the opportunity arises, we must show no mercy . . .'

'Save your bloodlust for Mayhew, Robert. That damned traitor deserves to be carved like a side of beef.' Carpenter glared at the Silver Skull for a moment, all his anger now directed towards his former ally.

Moments later, the two men arrived at the Queen's chambers. No guards waited at the door. And there were no bodies. The door itself was slightly ajar.

Fearing the worst, Carpenter drew his rapier and pushed the door open. The windowless antechamber was dark and empty. They waited a heartbeat until their eyes adjusted to the gloom, and then entered. No sound came from the bedchamber beyond. At the doorway, they hesitated, fearing the consequences of breaking into the Queen's chamber at night, for all the seriousness of the occasion. Finally, throwing caution aside, Launceston pushed the door open.

A flickering candle on a side table illuminated another empty room. Carpenter and Launceston exchanged an uneasy glance when they saw the bedlinen appeared to have been torn back hurriedly.

'We are too late,' Carpenter said. 'They have her.'

Acting as if he had not heard, Launceston was deep in reflection.

'The Unseelie Court is on its way. We must leave or they will trap us here!' Carpenter urged him.

'Wait. If the Enemy had already been here, the guards would be dead at the door. No, they left to investigate the attack. Perhaps they were directed by . . . someone.'

'But then where is the Queen?' Anxiously, Carpenter looked back towards the antechamber. He already imagined he heard the footsteps of the Enemy drawing nearer.

Closing the door, Launceston turned slowly; his attention was drawn to the candle. Its flame bent in a draught, and yet the windows were shut and heavy curtains drawn across them.

Striding to the candle, he traced the source of the draught to the old oaken panelling marked with the Queen's initials. Along one edge was a dark vertical line. With his fingertips, he eased open a hidden door.

'A secret passageway,' he said. 'Not sealed tight amid a hasty exit.'

'Enough talk.' Carpenter pushed Launceston into the secret passage and, following him, closed the door behind them with a soft click.

The passage was dry and dusty. Rats scurried ahead of them. They continued in the dark for a little way, wishing they had brought the candle with them, until a soft glow appeared ahead. Hands on sword hilts, at the ready, they edged forwards.

Out of the dark loomed a silent figure. A sword flashed towards Launceston. Reacting instantly, the Earl threw himself against the wall. The blade missed him by a hair's breadth. Drawing his own rapier, Launceston engaged the attacker, and drove him back until the half-light washed over him.

'Marlowe!' Carpenter exclaimed, and Launceston ceased his attack.

Relief flooded Marlowe's face and he lowered his blade. 'Thank all the powers there are,' he sighed. 'I am more dangerous with a quill than a sword. I thought this was the end of me.'

The playwright led them to what turned out to be a series of windowless rooms. In the first, Nathaniel waited with Walsingham and Dee, their faces drawn. Through the half-open door to the adjoining room, they could see the Queen, seated on a chair, her head in her hands, her face as white as Launceston's in the gloom. Without her red wig, grey stubble on her head, she seemed aged and impotent – far removed from the regal figure they all had seen at court.

'She would not have you see her like this,' Walsingham said quietly, and pulled the door to a little more, but there was only one light and he did not want to plunge her into darkness.

'Is it as bad as we fear?' Dee asked, his eyes blazing. He wore a black gown embroidered with a pattern of gold circles.

'Worse. The Enemy has the run of the palace,' Carpenter replied.

Walsingham hung his head. After a moment, he said, 'The Queen would already be lost if Master Marlowe and Master Colt had not raised the alarm. There is still hope—'

He was interrupted by a loud crash echoing down to them from the Queen's bedchamber. Then more. The sound of furniture being thrown around.

'Trapped,' Launceston said. 'How long before they find this hidden passage?'

# CHAPTER FIFTY-SEVEN

SCRAMBLING OUT OF THE WINDOW OVERLOOKING THE LANTERN Tower, Will pulled himself up on to the roof. The lichen-crusted tiles threatened to crumble beneath his boots and pitch him to the courtyard far below. The door to the Lantern Tower hung open. Cavillex had ventured inside, but Will knew it was the place Dee mysteriously treasured above all else and he would have ensured an array of protective doors and defences.

The tower was one of the newest buildings in the palace. It had been erected not long after the beginning of Elizabeth's reign by her decree and under Dee's strict design and jurisdiction. Around the top, beneath the conical tiled roof with its weathervane, ran decorative battlements which lent it a semblance of power. Will simply hoped the stone was secure enough to take his weight.

A golden dawn dispelled the gloom that would have made his task impossible. Weighing a grapnel he had recovered from the store of ships' items in which he had hidden, he braced himself, and then whirled it round his head before loosing it. His first attempt didn't even reach the tower. The second time the grapnel bounced off the stone wall with a resounding clang that he feared might draw attention. The third attempt failed too, and the fourth. A quarter of the way up the tower, visible through a window, the supernatural globe's glare had now turned ruddy again.

On the fifth attempt, the hook caught, slipped a little, and then held tight on the battlements. Wrapping the oily rope around his wrists, Will tested the line. His recent wounds burned, and it seemed that every muscle in him ached – could he hold on? Putting all doubts out of his mind, he launched himself off the roof.

The hook and the masonry held. Bracing against the impact, he thudded into the tower wall, then steadied himself and began to climb rapidly. One floor below the top, he pushed out and swung in an arc to crash through one of the arched windows. Jagged glass tore the skin on his hands and arms, and caught in his hair and doublet, and he tumbled into a bone-jarring landing on the stone steps. Scrambling to his feet, he ignored the cuts and drew his rapier. At the top of the steps, the way was barred by a heavy oak door marked with a series of Dee's sigils. From beneath it pulsed the familiar green light, so like the illumination from the Unseelie Court's ghostly globe.

The stairs spiralled down to another floor, and from somewhere below that he could hear Cavillex talking in a language he didn't recognize. As he prepared to descend, an odd feeling seized him: his thoughts twisted like the eels they hauled from the reaches of the Thames, and his stomach knotted and heaved. Blood began to drip from his nose.

*Cavillex*, he thought. But that did not seem right. There was a mystery here, he was sure.

A door crashed open below. Dee's defences were slowly falling. With no time to waste, Will bounded down the steps, ignoring the pain from his wounds. He reached a room that covered the entire floor of the tower. The dark was just giving way to first light and he could make out that the chamber was empty apart from a trestle in the centre.

Whispery voices and echoing footsteps grew louder as the Enemy ascended the steps towards him.

On the trestle, Will found the silver amulet inscribed with mysterious words and symbols: the Shield. He wondered how something that looked so insignificant could be so important.

As he moved to take the artefact, a door burst open. A feeling of dread rushed into the space. As Will's senses skewed, shadows flew, accompanied by a harsh, distorted noise that reminded him of crows in a winter sky. The dank, decaying, underground smell of loam settled on the chamber. He knew what was coming. And however much Dee had prepared him to face the disorienting qualities of the Unseelie Court, he was never ready.

Whispers rustled on the edge of his hearing, an icy wind blew, and they were there. As silent as the grave, grey figures with hate-filled, red-rimmed eyes surged around him. Their haunted faces had the ghastly pallor of dead flesh, their hair hung lankly, and their cloaks and jerkins and doublets were worn and silvered with mildew as if they had lain too long in the ground. Deep in Will's head, the whispers continued in the language he didn't understand, but seemed to be urging him towards despair. In the half-light, the Unseelie Court appeared misty and insubstantial, spectres rather than flesh and blood, but Will knew it was an illusion, and they were solid enough to feel the bite of cold steel.

Resisting their subtle manipulations, he levelled his rapier at them. 'Come, then,' the spy said. 'If you have not been in a grave this night, you will be in one tomorrow.'

Drawing their swords, the Enemy attacked.

Will lost all sense of who or what was in the room with him. All he could do was slash and lunge with his sword. Some blows were parried, others found their mark. One of the Enemy fell at his feet. Another thrust a blade that nearly tore open Will's neck. The Enemy were faster than most men, their stamina greater, and though Will's sword skill was more refined, the fight was unequal.

In the chaos, Will glimpsed Cavillex, red-rimmed eyes flaring, his contempt too strong to contain. It felt as if the dark was closing in on every side, yet somehow he managed to keep himself between his opponents and the Shield.

Like ghosts at twilight, three of the Unseelie Court moved around him. Will despatched one with a thrust through the heart, but the other two surged forward from opposite sides. Parrying the first, Will stepped deftly to one side and hammered the hilt of his sword into the jaw of the second. Bone shattered. As the other cadaverous swordsman sprawled over the falling body, Will followed through with two thrusts to the hearts of each to end their lives.

Disbelief turning to cold fury, Cavillex looked around him at the Unseelie dead and dying, and then to Will, now dripping with blood. He raised one hand to halt the attack. 'How honourably you kill.' The voice, like stones dropped on a coffin, echoed from all parts of the room.

'There is no honour in any of this,' Will replied, turning to face his Enemy. 'Only survival.' He kept one eye on the Shield, which was tantalizingly just beyond the reach of his fingers.

As Cavillex stalked forward, Will levelled his sword and said with a calmness that masked his burning emotions, 'We have business, you and I.'

'Why, we have been in business for a long while,' Cavillex said enigmatically. He raised a slender hand which had the pale waxiness of a corpse, and pointed towards the Shield. 'You transported that to the very place where we desired it to be.'

Will laughed, but the oppressive presence of Cavillex sucked any humour from his voice. 'You try to make a cake out of crumbs.'

'I make the truth out of shadows . . . shadows to you. What safer place for the Shield than here? If we had kept it in Edinburgh, you would not have let us rest. With it here, we could go about our work untroubled, knowing the item we valued most was ready for us when the time was right.' The red eyes burned into Will.

*Another manipulation. Was he truly that easy to direct?*

'Yes, you always do our bidding,' Cavillex said, as if reading Will's thoughts. 'You, your fellows. We know what makes your hearts beat faster. We understand your fears and sadnesses. We see the crack in a man's door, ready to be pushed wide open.' The weight of his attention became unbearable.

Keeping his sword trained on Cavillex, Will took a step back and fumbled blindly behind him until his fingers closed on the Shield. 'You could set the Silver Skull loose, destroy all of London, perhaps all of England. But why do you need the Shield?' he asked, wiping the blood from his nose.

'Because we do not wish to destroy all.' Cavillex's presence seemed to be drawing all light from the room. Will felt as if he was standing in the deepest dungeon. 'Dartmoor looms large in the minds of my people. And there are greater punishments than death, as you well know.' An icy smile, challenging Will to deny it.

A clatter rose from the stairs behind him. Cavillex didn't look, but his smile grew broader as if he knew exactly who was coming. Without taking his eyes off Will, he gave a languorous summons with the fingers of his left hand, and the Silver Skull entered.

'Mayhew. You traitorous bastard—' Will began, feeling the anger begin to bubble up inside him. But he was interrupted by the sight of another figure behind the Skull.

'Grace!' He looked to Cavillex as Grace came to stand beside her cruel manipulator. 'If you have harmed her—' His voice was cold steel.

'She has not been harmed. See?' Pale fingers caressed Grace's chin and lifted her head. She blinked dreamily, her gaze finally alighting on Will.

'Will . . . it is so good to see you,' she said.

'Our taking of the palace would have been so much more difficult without her help,' Cavillex smiled.

Other members of the Unseelie Court surged into the room, surrounding Grace until she was lost behind a wall of pale faces and black, malicious eyes. It was impossible for Will to get to her. Backing away until his heel was on the first step of the flight he had descended, Will moved his sword back and forth, ready for the first attack, but he knew the numbers were not in his favour.

'We shall go from this room, and take your Queen and infect her with a disease that will eat away her skin, her bone, her senses, yet keep her alive,' Cavillex said. 'She will suffer unimaginable agony, without respite.'

Will thought he saw Mayhew flinch.

'And once we have her, we will release a plague across all London,' Cavillex continued. 'An entire city will die. With the Shield, we will be untouched by the foul infestation unleashed by the Silver Skull, and we will walk through it, and your Queen will accompany us so she can see the corpses of her people rotting in the street. And then we will return home, taking her with us to live on with the memory, and the pain.'

Will was stunned by the cruelty of Cavillex's scheme; the unnecessary death and suffering. Could this be purely because their supremacy had been challenged?

'Your nation will be crushed by the magnitude of the blow struck against it,' Cavillex added. 'And that will only be the beginning of England's agonies.'

Will examined the Shield in his hand. 'So, without this,' he showed Cavillex the amulet, 'you cannot unleash the full fury of the Skull and survive. You would be corrupted too, here at the heart of the whirlwind.' He took another step back up the stairs. 'It seems to me that the cost of this item is high,' he said, holding the Shield up again so Cavillex could see it. 'How many of your lives will buy it?'

'You are a lesser creature and you have already taken too many of our lives,' Cavillex growled. He reached for Grace's arm and gently led her forward. 'As you seem to value life so lightly, then your friend's death will be meaningless to you.'

Will hid his concern. 'If you wish to barter the girl's life for this trinket, think again. That route has already been tried. My loyalty lies with Queen and country . . . and my duty is to see the destruction of your kind.'

Raising Grace's arm, Cavillex stroked the palm of her left hand in a manner that made Will shudder. 'You misunderstand. No barter. We will take the Shield from you when we slaughter you. The girl's life is a punishment for your brutality. The sight of her dying, the consequence of your actions, will be the one you take with you to the grave.'

Cavillex's words struck Will with force. Barely able to contain his anger, he took a step forward, but the ghastly grey crew closed ranks around Grace once more.

Raising his right arm to point at Will, Cavillex continued with cold contempt, 'You English claim to be the injured party, but slaughter comes so very easily to you. You kill without regard, you murder your own, even, over squabbles about religion and politics. If morals do not guide you, how can you expect us to act any differently?'

Will found himself unexpectedly agreeing with his foe's words, but he didn't show it. 'You have forced us down to your level,' he snapped.

Cavillex's laughter was harsh and mocking.

'Again, this is about survival,' Will said. 'We cannot afford the luxury of morality or charity when we are being preyed upon by your kind.' Even as Will spoke, he could hear the hollow ring to his words.

Cavillex seemed to tire of Will suddenly. He turned to Mayhew and said, 'Enough of this. She is to die, now, in a way that will scar him for ever.'

The dawn light shimmered off the Silver Skull so it appeared the sun was rising within the chamber itself. Will saw Mayhew's head fall slightly, and his shoulders sag. He wouldn't meet Cavillex's commanding gaze.

In Mayhew's hesitation, Will saw a chink and acted quickly. 'Do not do it, Mayhew. Grace is innocent in all of this. Kill her and you will be damned for ever.'

'He is already damned,' Cavillex said lightly. 'That is the least of his concerns.'

'Mayhew,' Will pressed, holding out one hand to his former companion. 'Do not ally yourself with these monsters. Whatever rewards they have promised you, it cannot be enough to turn your back on your fellow man, or on your own humanity.'

'Do you think we bribed him with gold? You truly do not

understand us.' Cavillex laughed. 'We know every part of you. We understand your weaknesses, your flaws, and we play them as a musician plays his instrument. Your weakness makes you its mare, and it rides you hard, and you cannot throw it off, whatever you do. None of you are so strong. The only way he will be free of his torment . . . the only way he will be free of the mask, is to do my bidding.' He pointed a pale, slender finger at the Silver Skull and then directed it to Grace. 'Kill her. Now.'

Mayhew turned his face to Will as if offering his apologies, and then raised his hand to Grace's forehead.

'No, Matthew,' Will pleaded. 'Grace does not deserve this.'

Again, Mayhew hesitated, and Will sensed a flicker of humanity remaining behind the mask. Suddenly, Mayhew turned and planted his hand on the nearest grey figure. Caught off-guard, the Enemy was rooted for one brief moment and then chaos descended on the chamber. Will saw the startled Enemy warrior convulse at Mayhew's touch. Boils burst on blackening skin and eyes grew thick with pus. Mayhew turned to the next, and then another, both hands reaching out.

The inhuman shrieks were so loud Will thought his ears would burst. As the shadows whirled in panic and pain, he thought he saw Cavillex throwing himself away from Mayhew in the direction of the door, afraid of the fate that had been planned for Grace. The red-rimmed eyes would haunt him for ever.

'You do not know us as well as you think,' Will called after him, sensing victory. 'Our weaknesses do not define us.'

But as the Enemy fell around Mayhew, Cavillex had time for one final blow. Will caught the glint of a blade driving towards Grace. Instinctively, he lunged and hauled her out of its path. The knife buried itself in Mayhew's chest.

Cavillex's parting words set Will's teeth on edge. 'Some part of our account will be balanced this day,' he hissed. 'Your Queen will die.' And with that, he was gone.

Still in the thrall of the Unseelie Court enchantment, Grace stood dazed and seemingly oblivious as Mayhew lay beside her, the shining mask splattered with blood. 'Grace, take care of Matthew in his final moments,' Will called to her, unsure if it would have any effect. He knelt briefly beside Mayhew and whispered, 'At the last, you did right.' And then he was down the steps in pursuit of Cavillex. The prize – the life of the Queen.

# CHAPTER FIFTY-EIGHT

GLIDING SILENTLY THROUGH THE UNNATURAL STILLNESS OF THE dawn, Cavillex went in search of the Queen's quarters. Will was close behind.

Grey shadows of more of the Unseelie Court patrolled the palace grounds, seemingly oblivious of the drama that was unfolding around them. But Cavillex appeared so consumed by a furious rage at the deaths of his kind and the failure of his plan that he did not raise the alarm. His only thought was of revenge of the most brutal kind.

Rounding a corner, Will spotted him among three more of the Unseelie Court. Cold, cruel faces snapped towards him, black eyes devoid of all compassion; his mind reeled under their gaze. Doubling back, he raced upstairs.

As his quarry passed the foot of the flight, Will flung himself off the steps with no thought for the stone flags beneath. The element of surprise served him as well as it had on the grey-sailed ship. The force of the impact knocked Cavillex to the floor. Will was up in an instant, his rapier drawn, and he had struck two blows before his snarling foe had drawn his own weapon. Blood soaked through Cavillex's doublet, the patches quickly spreading, and for the first time Will saw a hint of panic in his Enemy's eyes.

It was fast replaced by the rage of a wounded animal. Roaring, Cavillex lunged, hacking and slashing with a fury that drove Will on to his back foot. Suddenly, he hurled himself past the English spy's defences and grappled Will to his knees. The rapiers clattered across the flagstones. Gripping Will's head in his hands, Cavillex pressed his face close. Will felt his breath upon him – it was like the stink of the grave – felt himself swim in deep shadow and those hideous red-rimmed eyes. They burned deep into Will's mind, turning over his thoughts, driving into his memories, abusing the most private part of him.

He felt a sickening change: his muscles knotted, every fibre and sinew strained, and he remembered the dead scarecrow in Alsatia that had once been a man.

With a tremendous effort, he fumbled for his knife and brought it up hard into the side of Cavillex's neck. The in-human scream burned through Will. Cavillex lurched to his feet, catching Will with a sharp backhand as he staggered away, clutching at his wound, blood seeping between pale fingers.

Dazed, Will lay sprawled across the flagstone floor, but he could already feel the pains deep in his body diminishing. By the time he could stand, Cavillex was gone, but blood betrayed his path. He picked up his rapier and ran in pursuit.

When Will reached the Queen's chambers, Cavillex was already ransacking the room with three others of the Unseelie Court. The latter rounded on the spy instantly, seemingly more animals then men. Will registered that Elizabeth was not there before he was caught up in a furious ballet of parrying and thrusting. Sword blades sang, blood flowed, a loud crash was heard, but Will dared not divert his attention. Driven back by the intensity of the Enemy's onslaught, he fought for his life, seeing only steel and cold eyes and fanged mouths that snapped and snarled like the beast that had attacked him in the frozen Russian forest so long ago.

But then one of the Enemy fell forwards, a blade protruding from his back, and another suddenly clutched futilely at his throat, across which a blade had been swiftly drawn. The third was so distracted by the sudden slaying of his associates that he was unprepared for Will's sword through his chest. He sank to the floor in an exhalation of blood.

Carpenter and Launceston stood over the bodies, and were already turning to confront Cavillex. He stood by an entrance to a hidden passageway behind the panelling. Drenched in blood, he could barely stand.

Then, snarling something in his unsettling language, Cavillex drew on the last of his reserves and slipped into the doorway.

'The Queen!' Carpenter exclaimed.

Will charged past him into the passage. Cavillex was already lost to the dark, but his urgent movements gave his whereabouts away. Careering into a room, Will took in Cavillex caught in a vicious struggle with Nathaniel while the Queen was pressed into a corner, shielded by Walsingham and Dee.

'Nat! Leave him!' Will barked, but he was too late.

Cavillex leaned in and whispered into Nathaniel's ear. Horror gripped Will as he recalled a similar moment with young Miller in the alleys of Alsatia. He saw Nathaniel's eyes became glassy, the blood drain from his face and an expression of dread fall across his face like a shadow. Swaying for a moment, Nathaniel slithered to the floor, his head in his hands.

Despite his terrible wound, Cavillex turned to Will, his eyes gleaming with triumph.

Despair became rage, and Will lunged forward, ready to run Cavillex through. Before the spy could inflict the killing blow, Carpenter grabbed him forcibly and pulled him away.

'Wait,' he said. 'There are worse things than death.' His words, unconsciously echoing Cavillex, brought Will up sharp. Carpenter pointed to Launceston, who was standing in the entrance to the passageway, ghastly in the gloom. 'Why not let Robert spend some time with him?'

'What? Why—'

'Trust me,' Carpenter whispered. 'I have never approved of our companion's . . . tastes . . . but perhaps there is a reason we are all the way we are. This is my gift to you, to draw a veil over our past disagreement. Launceston has a . . . specific touch. Let him use it.'

Not understanding, but his anger spent, Will allowed Carpenter to guide him away. He turned to Nathaniel, who lay broken on the floor, eyes fixed on a point far beyond the panelled walls of the room.

Will knelt next to him. 'Oh, Nat. What have I done?'

He was only vaguely aware of Launceston stepping past him, grabbing a barely conscious Cavillex and dragging him into another chamber. The door closed. And the lock turned.

Closing his eyes, Will tried to hide his grief. When he opened them again, he was surprised to see tenderness in Dee's face as he helped the Queen back to her bedchamber, remembering, perhaps, the young girl he had tutored so many years ago.

Stepping hesitantly up, Walsingham helped Will to his feet with equal tenderness. The stern features had softened a little, and Will thought he saw tears in the spymaster's eyes – of concern or relief, Will did not know. 'There is still time,' he said softly, taking Will's arm. 'We may be able to aid your assistant, if we act quickly. Leave him with me.'

'Thank you, sir,' Will said, barely daring to hope.

A shadow crossed Walsingham's face and his voice hardened. 'Now, go, and run these foul creatures from the palace. Kill as many as you find.'

Behind the spymaster's words, Will heard something that ran much deeper than the war between England and the Unseelie Court. It troubled him. He felt weary of all the death and misery, and Walsingham's tone suggested there would never be an end to it.

Reluctant to go, Will glanced back at Nathaniel and then made his way along the secret passage with Carpenter. He couldn't shake off the memory of Miller, hanging from the rafters, slain by a whispered word. As he stepped out into the Queen's chamber, he heard Cavillex's agonized cry. The sound seemed to continue unbroken until Will had left the rooms far behind.

They scoured the palace grounds, but could find no sign of the remainder of the Unseelie Court. It was as if Cavillex's invading force had vanished into air with the coming of the dawn.

The *Tempest* had docked, and while Carpenter went to find Courtenay and his men, who had sealed off the palace from the rest of London, Will made his way back to the Lantern Tower. His heart lifted a little when he found Grace, her eyes clearer, though still dreamy. She looked around the chamber, puzzled. 'Will? Where is this place?' She sounded as if she was ready to sleep. 'Whitehall? But . . . I was at Hampton Court?'

Had she really forgotten her time with the Unseelie Court?

Will dared not hope, but whispered to himself, 'Every fighting man needs luck.'

Confused, Grace was about to ask him what he meant, but then she shook her head, and gave him a lazy smile. In her brightening eyes, he saw her love for him. Though he'd always known of her affection, the depth of her yearning was laid bare by the hazy remnants of her enchantment, and it shocked him. This was the sister of the woman he loved – he couldn't return Grace's feelings. Yet he had sworn never to see her come to harm. Would he now break her heart? His thoughts in turmoil, he could only smile and turn away.

His attention was caught by poor, dead Mayhew. Kneeling beside the body, he saw the Key – the magical jewel used to release the mask's deadly power – was missing. Without it, the Skull and the Shield were useless. He felt oddly relieved that the weapon would not fall into Walsingham's hands, and the round of death continue without end.

Cavillex's words returned to him: if men could not act to some higher standard, they deserved to be destroyed, just as the Unseelie Court surely deserved it. His Enemy had spoken the truth, Will decided. He recalled joining Walsingham's crusade as a grief-stricken young man, then becoming bitter at his loss, and consumed with the need for revenge, and hatred for the Enemy. Now he wondered if things were as simple as he had once believed.

His reflections were interrupted by Grace pointing towards Mayhew's body. Her expression had grown uneasy. There, on the wall plaster, words had been written in drying blood. Mayhew had used the last moments of his life to leave a cryptic message.

'*Bury my mother*,' Grace read. 'What does that mean?'

# CHAPTER FIFTY-NINE

ACROSS LONDON, THE CHURCH BELLS WERE RINGING. IN THE dead August heat, Will waited in the shade of a soaring elm and tried to ignore the powerful stink of the slums that sprawled along the Thames to the east of the Tower. Majesty and vileness, side by side; that was London, that was his life.

Nearby, the Earl of Leicester strutted to and fro, revelling in the attention of the thousands of men waiting in ranks and on horseback. He was obviously playing the hero in his imagination, though he had not been called on to fight. On a ridge overlooking the river, the camp at West Tilbury was a splash of colour. Red, gold and blue pennants fluttered on the light breeze, flags flew proudly above the white pavilions erected to shield the nobility from the midday sun.

Eschewing the crowds that lined both banks of the river and hung from the windows of the houses with the best views, Will had opted for a period of quiet contemplation while he waited for the Queen to arrive. Indeed, there was much to consider.

Somewhere, far to the north, the Spanish were fighting devastating seas, their ships sunk and torn apart, soldiers and sailors drowning, men washed up on beaches, barely alive but sure to be slaughtered by the local people. The price that nation had paid – and would pay – for the poor judgement of their King and his commanders was great. But here at home, the English ships were returning to port, every man aboard a hero. It seemed a new day was dawning.

As the Queen's barge arrived to a fanfare of trumpets, this being the last point of its triumphant journey along the river from the Palace of Whitehall, the sense of anticipation mounted. Now, following the causeway across the foul-smelling marshes where clouds of flies buzzed, Elizabeth made her way to the camp on a white gelding. Cannon fire proclaimed her arrival.

The procession was led by the Earl of Ormonde, carrying the sword of state, and two pages dressed in white velvet. One carried her helmet on a cushion, the other led her horse as she dismounted and strode along the ranks. She dazzled all who saw her – a silver breastplate over a white velvet gown, her auburn wig a blaze of fire, sparkling with diamonds and pearls. The men cheered, and shouted their devotion to Elizabeth and to England.

And yet Will was not moved to join them. Whatever he saw, he knew there was always another, hidden face behind it. Walsingham had already told him something of the carefully rehearsed speech the Queen planned to deliver at Tilbury the following day.

'Let tyrants fear,' she would say. 'I have always so behaved myself that under God I have placed my chiefest strength and safeguard in the loyal hearts and goodwill of my subjects.'

Her words were clear, Will thought. They were as much for the ears of the Unseelie Court as for her own people, or Spain. The Enemy would be listening. They were always listening.

She would go on to say, 'I know I have the body of a weak

and feeble woman but I have the heart and stomach of a King, and of a King of England too, and think foul scorn that Parma or Spain or any Prince of Europe should dare to invade the borders of my realm; to which, rather than any dishonour shall grow by me, I myself will take up arms. I myself will be your general, judge and rewarder of every one of your virtues in the field.'

*Let tyrants fear.*

The Unseelie Court would never rest, but a gauntlet had been thrown down. England would meet them head on.

Will was joined by Walsingham, who had travelled as part of the Queen's entourage on the second barge. Out of place in his sombre black gown yet seemingly untouched by the oppressive heat, he stood beneath the elm next to his greatest spy, hands behind his back as he watched the Queen inspecting her loyal soldiers.

'I would say it went well,' he mused.

'Apart from the death and the suffering.' Will couldn't help the bitterness creeping into his voice.

Walsingham sniffed. 'There is always that.'

Easing, Will nodded. 'Yes, we won a great victory.'

'And you played a great part in that, Master Swyfte.'

'And the others: Carpenter, Launceston . . .' He paused as he remembered another young man who had been so proud to join Walsingham's band yet had encountered things he had never dreamed existed, things which stole his life from him. 'And Miller. They too should not be forgotten.'

'Oh, they will be. As will you.'

Will eyed Walsingham askance. The older man gazed out at the assembled company, his face unreadable.

'Your task, and that of those others like you, is to move behind the skin of history, not upon its surface.' Walsingham continued to follow the Queen's progress, giving an approving nod whenever the cheers rose up again. 'Your work is by design invisible, and it will remain that way. If it were to be made public, it would detract from the glory of the Queen and the true heroes of England.'

'I have a public face now,' Will retorted.

'Yes. We created the legendary William Swyfte to provide comfort for the people of England, so they knew they were cared for, protected in the many hardships that assail this world by someone greater than themselves. But that will only continue in stories told by the fireside or in the taverns, and soon those stories will die. There will be no public record of the part you played this day, you or any of your band.'

'The pamphlets—' Will protested.

'Will be destroyed, one by one, over time. When the accounts of these days are written in years yet to come, it will be a story of the heroism of honest Englishmen. However great the sacrifices made, it will not be a story of deceit and trickery. That would not do justice to the legend of England. It is your destiny to be forgotten. You must come to accept that.'

Will shrugged. 'I care little what happens when I am gone.'

'Of course, there will be rewards in this life, for you and your associates. Riches, women, drink. Enjoy it.'

'For ever unknown,' Will said reflectively. 'I find some comfort in that, oddly.' A thought that had troubled him for a while surfaced, and he asked, 'Tell me of Dartmoor and what happened there.'

Shaking his head slowly, Walsingham said, 'We keep our secrets dearly, Will, all of us.'

'And you will keep your secrets from me.' Will nodded, understanding the message in Walsingham's words – Will

Swyfte was merely an instrument of the Queen, sent out to kill, or to clean up the mess of plotters. The truth was meant for greater men than he.

Clasping his hands behind his back, Walsingham studiedly ignored Will's probing gaze. 'You must never speak of Dartmoor again,' he said in an aloof tone. Will turned away, hiding his mounting anger that something important was being hidden from him.

Leicester continued to strut in a bid to catch the Queen's eye, but her attention was clearly upon her new favourite, Robert Devereux, the Earl of Essex, who rode at her side. Even in the shadow of great affairs of state, the true, base motivations of humanity still held sway, Will saw.

'This day has seen the beginning of the end of the Spanish empire, and the ascendancy of our own,' Walsingham said.

'The world we inhabit is nothing but madness and brutality. And England's empire will be built upon it.'

'Then so be it. Better our madness and brutality than theirs.'

'The Unseelie Court has been pressed back, but they will not be defeated.'

'No, they will always challenge us. That is why we must always be vigilant. But as our power and influence grow across the globe, so will our ability to resist them, on every front, in every land. And here at home, Englishmen and women will finally find peace.'

As the old man turned his face to the sun for the first time, Will saw tears glistening in Walsingham's eyes, and the shift of deep, long-suppressed emotions in his face.

'Not an ending, then,' Will said softly.

'A beginning, of many things.' Taking a deep breath, Walsingham steadied himself, then continued with surprising sympathy, 'I have some troubling news. About your assistant.'

Before Walsingham had finished speaking, Will was hastening from the camp, making for the spot beyond the palisaded embankments where his horse was tethered.

London shimmered in the heat as Will raced through the rutted, dusty streets to Bishopsgate. The church spire was visible above the rooftops, but he could hear the screams long before he saw the old priory and its cobbled courtyard and the gardens beyond. The dusty, smeared windows were now obscured by bars, the stone worn, tiles missing from the roof, and grass sprouting among the cobbles. Two open sewers ran on either side, filling the air with the permanent stink of human excrement.

Will hammered on the door until the Keeper came. He was a big man with a large belly, long, grey-black hair and stubble on his chin. A large ring of iron keys hung at his belt. He eyed Will suspiciously until Will introduced himself, and then the Keeper clapped him on the shoulder and proclaimed the glory of England over Spain. His breath stank of sour wine.

Will had no time for niceties and demanded to be taken to Nathaniel. With a shrug, the Keeper complied. Screams rang from behind every door, and in the long, vaulted cellar the inmates of Bethlehem Hospital prowled in their own private worlds, clawing at the dank walls or kicking the filthy straw in a frenzy. Everywhere reeked of dirty clothes, urine, excrement and vomit.

'This is Bedlam. There is never quiet here,' the Keeper said.

They reached a quieter annexe and the man unlocked a door on to a windowless room. After Will's eyes adjusted to the dark, he fought back a wave of grief that made him want to cry out. Nathaniel squatted on the dirty straw, hugging his knees. His head lay on his shoulder and his face was blank, his eyes staring deep into the shadowy corner of his cell, but seeing nothing.

'The dark is good for those distraught from their wits,' the Keeper said, 'and they must be kept free from all distractions. It is best for him,' he added, seeing the murderous look cross Will's face.

'Has he spoken?'

'He says nothing. He eats if we feed him, but there is nothing left of him.' He shrugged. 'He will not recover.'

Turning, Will flung the man against the wall and pressed his face against him. 'Do not beat him,' he snarled.

'They must be beaten, for their own good.'

'Do not beat him, or I will return and deal to you tenfold whatever you deal to him.' Will could feel the anger boiling within him. He threw the Keeper from the cell in a rage, but he knew that anger should surely be directed at himself.

Pausing for a moment to control his churning emotions, he squatted in front of his assistant. 'Nat, it is Will,' he began quietly. 'Your master . . . Your friend.'

No reaction crossed Nat's face. And when he did not move, Will took his friend's head in his hands and looked deep into his face.

'I have failed you, Nat,' he continued. 'There are times I fear everyone close to me will be destroyed.' As he watched his friend, the weight inside Will grew until he felt it would crush him. 'I will not abandon you,' he whispered.

# CHAPTER SIXTY

STARK SLABS OF EXPOSED GRANITE SPARKLED SILVER UNDER THE full moon hanging over the uplands. Brackish streams trickled down through gorse and sedge, catching the light like jewels. It was a warm night, sweetly scented with the aromas of a country summer. Across the vast expanse of desolate grassland, not a light twinkled; it appeared as if all human life had been extinguished.

Dusty and tired from his long journey, Will let his rapid heartbeat subside, his breathing still, as he listened to the singing of the breeze in the grass. Turning slowly, he surveyed the empty Dartmoor landscape. Alone in the world. It seemed that from the moment Jenny had walked out of his life all those years ago, nothing had changed.

Long nights of agonizing had followed long days visiting Nathaniel in Bedlam, turning over in his mind all he knew, allowing unseen connections to rise slowly from his memories, until at last he made his decision.

Ahead of him, the standing stone towered against the starlit sky, almost twice his height. Beardown Man, the locals called it; a reminder of when giants walked the earth, some said, a warning from the Devil of the fate that awaited all sinners, others averred. Will thought the latter was probably closer to the truth, according to the legends that had grown up around Devil's Tor, where he stood: the ghostly sightings, the ethereal music playing on summer nights, the noises deep in the earth.

He had left his horse tethered at the foot of the tor, and had made the last part of his journey with only his thoughts for company. Now he stood on a rock with a commanding view of the lonely moor. 'Here I am, then,' he announced. 'Come to me!'

Only the sighing of the wind answered him.

He continued to wait, and then made his way to a lichen-covered boulder where he sat patiently. He knew they would come in their own time, when they had shown it was not at his bidding.

Time passed slowly. Thin strands of pearly mist drifted across the grassland. Then, for no reason that he could discern, the skin on his arms became gooseflesh.

When the mist had passed, figures stood like statues here and there across the tor, their faces turned towards him, all detail lost to shadow. None moved; none spoke.

After a moment, activity caught his eye. Striding towards him through the grass and past the threatening sentries came a tall and slender individual. He wore grey-green robes decorated with a strange design in gold filigree, like the symbols of an unknown language, faintly visible whenever the moon caught them. His age was indiscernible. His cheeks were hollow and dark rings lay under his pale eyes, but his long hair was a mixture of gold and silver. Trinkets and the skulls of mice and birds had been braided into his locks, and he made a soft, rhythmic clacking sound as he walked.

The figure came to a halt before Will, his face unreadable.

'Few dare to call to us,' he said in a voice as dry as summer bracken.

'You know me?' Will asked. He felt curiously calm in the face of this stranger.

The stranger thought for a moment, and then said with a wry smile, 'I know of your kind.'

'And you speak for the Unseelie Court?'

'Ah,' he said, still smiling, '*unholy*. Yes. You may call me Deortha. I am . . . an adviser.' With his right hand, he appeared to be plucking words from the aether in order that Will could understand. Finally, with a nod, he settled on, 'I am the Court's equivalent to your Dr Dee.'

The wind soughed through the grass. 'You know Dee?' Will enquired.

'Oh, yes.' Deortha gave a strange smile.

'A sorcerer, then. An alchemist. A wise man.' Cautiously, Will eyed the brooding, still-motionless sentries.

Deortha's pale eyes twinkled in the moonlight. 'You have a request of us?'

'You know?'

'You would not be here otherwise.'

'What you are is anathema to humankind,' Will began. 'You are the madness in the night. The shadow on the family hearth. In the very nature of your being, you tell us that however much we order this world to make it sane, it is not, and will never be, and we are nothing. We have no control.'

Deortha nodded. His smile became wry.

'Some who come too close to you are burned to ashes, like moths approaching a lantern's flame.' Will watched Deortha's face for any hint of manipulation, or sign of an impending attack. He knew his own life had hung in the balance since the

575

moment he set foot on the tor. 'I have a friend and he is one of those. His wits are gone. He could not cope with the secrets that lie behind your eyes.'

'Unlike you. You would revel in the knowledge of our secrets,' Deortha challenged.

Will ignored him. 'My own people cannot help him. You have at your disposal great things unknown to us . . . charms . . . potions . . .' He shrugged. 'Can you help him?'

A faint glint shone in Deortha's eyes and then was quickly gone. Will knew he had bared his throat for an attack.

'And why should we aid you?' Deortha asked.

'I killed several of your own. I helped bring about the death of Cavillex, one of your leaders. Help my friend regain his wits, and I will give myself to you for whatever punishment you see fit.' Will raised his head to show he was not afraid.

'Are you sure you are prepared to lay yourself open to our attentions? Our punishments are fierce.'

'Nevertheless. Yes, that is my offer.'

'Even though you will never see your kind again? Even though you will plead for a death that will never come?'

Will looked up and nodded. 'I am ready.'

Deortha was intrigued. 'If you are ready, then those punishments have no value.'

'Tell me about Dartmoor,' Will said.

# CHAPTER SIXTY-ONE

*Five carriages trundled along the rutted, muddy ways in the last light of the sun. The gale had finally blown itself out. From the window of the second carriage, Walsingham watched the shadows pool over the bleak Dartmoor uplands, his sense of apprehension mounting with each moment of the day that passed.*

*'You are still convinced this is the correct course?' he asked.*

*On the opposite seat, Dee kneaded his hands together, an anxious habit that had begun to irritate Walsingham as the journey from Plymouth drew on. 'I am not convinced of anything in this world,' he replied. 'We fumble around, making what progress we can in the pitch dark of our existence, and hope for the best.'*

*'Hope for the best,' Walsingham repeated. The crack of anger in his voice was born of his uneasiness. 'How do we know they will not try to trap us?'*

*'We do not.'*

*'And we take the Queen into this danger, still?'*

*'Elizabeth took the decision herself. There is too much at stake for England to let an opportunity like this slip by. She has courage. You cannot deny her that merely because she is a woman.' Dee cast a critical eye over Walsingham.*

'She could be dead by the time the sun rises.' Elizabeth's spymaster leaned back in his seat. 'As could we all.'

'I hope . . . I hope I have done enough to convince them of our intentions,' Dee said, now tugging at the hem of his cloak.

'I hope so too, Doctor.' Walsingham had always considered himself a good captain steering a steady course through the turbulent seas of his life, but at that moment he could barely contain his fears.

Promising more rain, the lowering clouds brought the dark in too soon. The carriages came to a halt four miles east of Yelverton on the western edge of the moor, and the guards in their gleaming helmets and breastplates laid down their pikes and swords and busied themselves lighting lanterns to guide the way.

Wrapped against the autumn chill, Elizabeth held her head defiantly as she climbed down from her carriage, though Walsingham could see the fear in her eyes.

'Is all ready?' his Queen asked him.

Resisting the urge to voice his own doubts, he nodded and bowed.

'Then let us be done with this business. I dream of a warm fire.' She strode out across the moor with the guards hurrying to keep up.

After a short time of steady walking, they came to the cairns and menhirs that stood so proudly against the darkening sky. Elizabeth cast a contemptuous look at the ancient monuments and turned to Walsingham. 'This is the place?'

'It is. It was chosen with great care. The preparations have been made.'

'And now?'

'We wait, Majesty.'

Darkness came down hard upon them. Around the standing stones, the lanterns flickered in the harsh wind, offering little comfort. Then, finally, the moon broke through the clouds and they were there.

Walsingham almost cried out in shock, but the Queen showed no sign of surprise. She rose from the velvet travelling stool upon which she'd been sitting to greet the newcomers. Forty of them stood on the edge of the circular indentation beside the standing stones, more than he had anticipated. His apprehension increased. Most had the look of guards, akin to the tight knot that now surrounded Elizabeth, but two tall male figures carried themselves like aristocrats, heads held at a haughty angle. Their clothes seemed refined, though about them was a hint of decay.

And there, in front of them all, stood the Faerie Queen.

Her green eyes blazed with such a terrible light that Walsingham could not look into them. But all could feel the heat that came off her, a magnificence that took the breath away. Two English guards fell to their knees, so dazzled were they by her splendour. She was tall and slender, and a gown of a green that appeared to reflect the night-dark grass around her clung to her form. Brown hair tumbled in ringlets around her shoulders, and her flawless skin appeared to glow with a faint golden light.

'An angel,' one of the guards whispered in awe.

A devil, *Walsingham thought.*

But her beauty captivated him in a way no earthly woman had, and as her gaze fell upon him, her full lips curved in a knowing smile. Walsingham felt sickened by the feelings that had been stirred within him. He muttered a prayer and crossed himself, but it did little good.

Yet beneath her appearance, something unsettling waited. Watching her, sensing the power she radiated, Walsingham dreaded what lay ahead.

'I am Elizabeth.' Walsingham watched his Queen stride forward confidently to address her opposite number.

'I know who you are.' The Faerie Queen smiled seductively, her voice mellifluous. Her tone appeared to entrance the English guards near her.

'We meet here as equals,' Elizabeth said firmly.

The Faerie Queen gave a slight bow, but did not show any sign of agreement.

'You have preyed on my people for a great many years,' Elizabeth continued.

'As you have preyed upon the animals of the field.' The Faerie Queen caught herself, paused and smiled slyly. 'We have been like shepherds, guiding you over the rough ground of your existence. At times you may have encountered . . . difficulties. At times we were not as cautious in our dealings as we should have been. You yourself know this. Your encounters among your own kind have proved . . . turbulent.'

'England will no longer tolerate . . .' It was Elizabeth's turn to catch herself. 'The time for predators and victims is past,' she continued, choosing her words carefully.

'I speak to you as one queen to another,' the Faerie Queen said. 'Our intermediaries have agreed the terms of our meeting. Members of the High Family are here to observe.' She indicated the two aristocratic males who both gave thin-lipped smiles in response. 'There is an opportunity for a new relationship between our two nations. Peace, even.'

'Would you have responded so positively if our strength had not increased? Our defences? Our ability to challenge you for the first time?' Elizabeth asked.

Walsingham winced; the English queen's words were too bald. He was suddenly afraid they would only drive the Enemy into an unnecessary confrontation.

The Faerie Queen's eyes flickered towards Dee. 'Indeed, you have gained a great deal under the auspices of your wise and honourable counsel.' Smiling, she gave Dee a respectful bow. He nodded in return.

'We feared you would use this opportunity to attack us,' Elizabeth said.

The comment seemed to sting the Faerie Queen. 'We are an honourable people.'

'You can afford to be,' Elizabeth responded.

It was then that Walsingham made his move. 'Now!' he yelled.

From their hiding places in covered trenches, the fifty-strong force rose up as one, their pitch-covered arrows ablaze in an instant. As Elizabeth's guards rapidly led her away from danger, the archers fired into the mass of startled Enemy. Many figures caught ablaze, their cries terrible to hear. Others retreated in the face of the onslaught.

In the confusion, a small group of English men-at-arms grabbed the Faerie Queen and dragged her to Dee. Forcing her mouth open, he emptied into it the contents of a small phial. As her eyelids fluttered shut, the regrouping Enemy attempted to reach her, but Walsingham's soldiers blocked their path and drove them back with yet more arrows. As the Enemy retreated to the grassy ground next to the standing stones, Walsingham knew they were preparing an assault that would no doubt be devastating.

But the thin covering on the ground gave way beneath the Enemy and they plunged and tumbled into a gaping hole. It was a pit once used by the local tinners for lodeback work. The mine was not deep, but it would serve its awful purpose.

From their hiding place, the soldiers dragged the barrels of pitch and sulphur, setting light to them and flinging them into the pit one after the other. The reek of burning flesh filled the air, and the screams of agony, of anger and of fear that rose up would haunt all present for the rest of their days.

The flames soared so high the soldiers were forced to back away from the inferno's edge, and eventually the dreadful cries died away.

Shielding his eyes from the blaze, Walsingham turned towards Elizabeth. 'You said you dreamed of a warm fire, Your Majesty.'

'Enough!' she said, eyes filled with fury. 'This night has blackened the history of England! Oh, how can I live with the memory of our treachery!'

Walsingham recoiled at her tone – it was not the reaction he had anticipated. Chastened, he replied, 'The ends will justify the means.' He thought to protest more, but gestured to the unconscious Faerie Queen, whose wrists and ankles had been bound under Dee's direction. 'She will be our prisoner for all time, locked away at the top of the Lantern Tower where she will serve as the crux of Dee's magical defences for our country. The Enemy will be kept at bay, their power muted.'

Elizabeth did not appear convinced.

'This dark night will fade against the golden days that lie ahead,' Walsingham went on. 'England . . . finally free of the grip of an Enemy that has hounded our people for sport, slaughtered them, mutilated them, defiled their lives and spoiled their dreams. The English people have always deserved peace, and now they will get it.'

'I do not share your conviction, Sir Francis.' She glanced back at the burning pit and then quickly averted her gaze. 'I fear this night will echo down the years for ever, and none of us will know sleep.'

# CHAPTER SIXTY-TWO

SHAKING HIS HEAD, WILL STOOD SPEECHLESS FOR A MOMENT.
Numb with shame, he was convinced he could smell smoke
on the wind.

'You understand now,' Deortha concluded. In the moonlight, a thin mist drifted across the lonely grasslands and there
was a chill in the air.

Will shivered, gooseflesh rising on his arms. He could not
bring himself to defend the actions of his countrymen. In
Deortha's pale eyes, Will saw the true depth of emotion. Now
he understood much of what had troubled him; of what was
kept in the room at the top of the Lantern Tower. Now he
knew why the Unseelie Court had risked so much to attack
Whitehall and why they needed the Shield as protection when
they unleashed the Silver Skull's plague. All made sense now:
Cavillex's words in Edinburgh; and why the Enemy was so
determined to destroy England.

'This madness of ours will never end,' Will said, his voice
almost a whisper. 'Each atrocity driving each of us to commit
another in a spiral of horror.'

'It will end,' Deortha said firmly. Will shivered at his words.
There was no doubt as to their meaning.

'Yet no one can win,' Will continued. 'There is no good here. No evil. Everything is tarnished. Do we even remember why we fight?'

'We remember.'

'We continue this war, then, like the dogs tearing at each other in the pits in the inn yards of Bankside?' Will's bitterness made the words catch in his throat.

'What you did that night can never be forgotten, nor forgiven,' Deortha said coldly.

'And what you have done to Englishmen for generation upon generation—'

'Then you understand fully. There can be no peace. We are too much alike.'

Will felt as desolate as that dark landscape stretching out into the night.

'And there is worse to come,' Deortha continued. 'The death of Cavillex is a bitter blow to the High Family, which has already suffered greatly in this conflict. His brothers and sister burn with the desire for vengeance. Your nation will soon feel the heat of their response.'

'And so it never ends,' Will said as if to himself. He held Deortha in his gaze. 'Then commit to my request. Help my friend and let them take me and punish me for their brother's death.'

Deortha's laughter was filled with clear contempt. 'Your arrogance never ceases to amaze us. You think you are a fair exchange for a member of the High Family? If all your country-men were put to death, your nation burned to the ground, it still would not make amends. You mean . . . nothing.'

Will set his jaw. 'Then you will not help my friend?'

Deortha considered for a moment and then nodded. 'I will help.' But his smile chilled Will.

'The conditions?'

'You must make a choice. Aid for your friend . . . or an answer to the mystery that consumes you: what happened to your lost love.'

Will was stunned, and struggled to stay upright. It was not that Deortha had presented such a dilemma, but that he knew about Jenny. The slyness around the Enemy's eyes showed that he knew exactly the effect his offer would have.

Fighting to contain his shock, Will replied, 'Why? You refuse to punish me, yet you offer help if I make a simple choice?'

'Choose.' Deortha was relishing the torment that consumed Will. Knowing the truth about Jenny had been the only thing that had mattered for so very long. It obsessed him, spurred him on to do everything he did. How could he turn his back on what might be his only chance to know the truth? Yet how could he abandon Nathaniel to the horrors of Bedlam? Will saw the elegant cruelty in Deortha's offer. Either answer had the potential to destroy him. Not a sudden end at the hands of the High Family, but slowly, inexorably, over years, a cancerous agony that would eventually consume him. Either he was responsible for Nathaniel's suffering, or he was responsible for never knowing the truth that would finally give him peace.

'I choose . . . my friend,' he said, reeling.

'Very well.' The triumph in Deortha's face sickened Will. 'There are worse things than death,' Deortha continued. It was as if he knew the phrase had been uttered before. 'For the rest of your days, you, William Swyfte, will be haunted by the knowledge of this night, as we are haunted by the knowledge of that other night. You could have solved the mystery that wrenches your heart. You could have found the one answer that will allow you to sleep at night. Perhaps you could have even brought your love back to you.'

'Enjoy your small victory,' Will said. 'What I have secured for my friend is worth my own suffering.'

'Now, perhaps,' Deortha agreed. 'But in a week's time? A year's? At the end of your days, lying on your deathbed, knowing that your entire life has been wasted by the never-knowing?' He shook his head.

Will's confidence was slowly returning. 'You think you know our ways so well,' he said, anger carrying his voice out into the night air, to the silent sentinels. 'But you do not understand hope. I have hope that I will find my Jenny, and I will do everything I can to bring that about.'

'Exactly.' Deortha smiled one more time, and then indicated for Will to wait. Without Will's being aware of the moment when he went, he disappeared from view, and when he returned he held a small glass phial. 'Give this to your friend. One drop, on the tongue. He will forget his contact with the flame of our being, and he will recover. And should it happen again,' he added knowingly, 'one more drop again. It will only work for him.'

Taking the phial, Will held it tight in his palm, suddenly afraid Deortha might snatch it back once he had finished his taunting.

'You make all your choices with such a poor vision,' Deortha said. 'Your kind see a week ahead, at best a year. We are long-lived. Our plans move cautiously over years, decades, centuries. Connections that are invisible to you fall into relief only when seen from our perspective. You cannot hope to succeed against us when your reactions to our schemes are based solely on the here and now. Who is to say that the things you do are not aiding us? That everything you consider a victory is but a manoeuvre we expected and factored into our plans, leading inexorably to our ultimate victory? Think on this, Will Swyfte . . .' he nodded and added pointedly, 'and enjoy this moment.'

As he considered Deortha's words, Will looked down at the phial in his hand. When he looked up, the Unseelie Court was gone. Yet something glinted in the grass in the moonlight. A meaningless object Deortha had dropped while basking in the warm glow of his cruel victory.

For a moment, Will stared at it, barely believing. A small flame of hope flared in his heart. Stooping down, he plucked it up and began to make his way back across the desolate, empty moor.

# CHAPTER SIXTY-THREE

THE STAGE WAS SET, THE PLAYERS READY, IN COSTUMES OF GREEN
and gold and scarlet, trying on their expressions for a good
fit, their true selves long since forgotten. Yet their private
conversations carried subtle, conflicting notes. The dress
rehearsal was a pivotal point, the end of the prelude. They
were filled with apprehension at how their performances
might be received, yet also jubilant at a new start filled with
possibilities.

The yard at the Bull Inn was flooded with early-morning sun
and crisscrossed with shadows cast by the pennants and banners
that had been strung haphazardly from window to window
overhead. It seemed the whole of England was celebrating the
news still coming in of the end of Spain's armada, its ships
wrecked by storms all around the northern coasts of England,
around Scotland and Ireland.

All yawns and lazy gap-toothed smiles, doxies hung
from windows to watch the players run through their final
preparations. Scents of honeysuckle and rosewater mingled
with the sour aroma of beer that drifted from the shadowy
interior of the inn.

Leaning against the cool stone in the shade, his arms folded,

Will Swyfte watched the proceedings. It was going to be a hot day.

Marlowe sauntered over in a brighter mood than Will had seen for a long while. He was in the company of a young man who shyly left before he could be introduced to the great hero of England.

'Is this one of yours?' Will nodded to the group of players running through their lines.

'A shine on the speeches here and there. Nothing more.' A dismissive shrug. 'I am filled with passion for a greater work. The one we spoke of? About a man who makes a deal with the Devil for rewards which prove only fleeting.'

A chill ran through Will, but it quickly dissipated in the summer warmth. 'I am sure it will be well received, Kit.'

Shielding his eyes, Marlowe studied the players approvingly. 'I feel better times lie ahead, Will. With the Spanish so roundly defeated; the Enemy pushed back once more. We can get on with our own lives, and there is much I wish to do with mine. Great plays to write. I see years of productive activity lying ahead.' Embarrassed, he looked to Will and laughed. 'You will think me an impostor.'

'I am glad your spirits are high. You deserve some pleasure.' Will watched Marlowe's young friend squeezing into a dress prior to making his entrance on stage; a role upon a role upon a role. 'I will speak to Walsingham,' he added, 'and smooth this disagreement that lies between you.'

'No one has any control over Walsingham.' Marlowe sounded doubtful.

'I do.'

Will ignored the playwright's probing gaze. He had yet to decide how to use what he knew about Dartmoor, and how far he could go with it before he became a liability.

They were interrupted by a carriage thundering into the inn yard. Onlookers scattered as it came to a halt near the stage, much to the annoyance of the players. Nathaniel climbed out and then offered a hand to Grace.

Marlowe glanced at his friend.

'He is well,' Will said, but offered nothing more.

Two players involved in a furious argument dragged Marlowe away to consider their lines, and he left Will with a wink. Will was pleased to see him at peace; he hoped it would last.

However, he couldn't contain his own troubled feelings as he watched Nathaniel and Grace approach. He feared what lay ahead for both of them and doubted whether he could continue to honour his vow to keep them safe. For a moment, he wondered if he was no different from the Unseelie Court – a too-hot flame that burned all those who came close. He pushed away such thoughts. For now they were safe and after the threat that had hovered over them, that was a victory he could cherish.

'Is this the end of a long night, or the beginning of a long day?' Nathaniel eyed Will and the open door to the inn.

'Neither, Nat. I am simply enjoying the sun and the peace of a day away from my duties.'

Nathaniel raised an eyebrow in disbelief. 'The Spanish defeated, the country in the mood for celebration, and you are not already three drinks ahead? Something is amiss.'

'There is time enough for that. And you might care to know that I have been spending my time considering a new assistant, for the old one has a sharp tongue and I feel he mocks me when my back is turned.' Will grinned and slapped his man on the shoulder.

'To your front only,' Nathaniel said indignantly. 'I am not a spy – I am open in my ways.'

590

'And we are all thankful for that, Nat,' Grace said warmly. 'No news of Jenny?' she asked Will, hope in her voice. She paused then, her brow wrinkling as she struggled with what Will knew to be the gap in her memory. 'Have I asked you this recently?'

He smiled at her. 'No, not recently. Do not worry, Grace. The physician says the blow to your head has left you in good health, if a few memories short. You will soon make new ones. And the answer to your question is, not yet. But I continue my endeavours.'

'It warms me that your love for my sister was so strong it still burns brightly even after she has gone. But sooner or later you must let someone else into your life, Will. You deserve warmth, and comfort, and the love of a good woman.'

*I deserve Jenny*, he thought.

His smile and a nod was enough for her. Pleased, she took her leave and went to tease Marlowe, who was caught in a huddle of bickering players.

'You will break her heart, Will,' Nathaniel cautioned.

'What do I do, Nat? I must protect her from harm. I cannot keep her at arm's length to do that. She mistakes my care for love and will not hear anything other.'

'She may be right, though. She loves you—'

Will's warning glare stopped him in his tracks.

'Yes, yes, I know. There is only room for one woman in your heart.' Nathaniel shook his head in frustration. 'But do not complain to me in your bitter, lonely old age. You work a cold business in sour times. You need some warmth to prevent your heart from becoming as hardened as the world you inhabit.'

'You are like an old fishwife, Nat.' And although a part of Will feared his friend spoke true, in his hand he clutched on to hope. He unfurled his fingers to reveal the glint of gold.

'What is that?' Nathaniel asked.

'Something I found on Dartmoor.'

'A locket?'

Jenny's locket. And within it was a fresh rose petal, mark of a love that had not died in all the years apart.

Although the High Family would be inflamed by their loss and there would be no respite in the long battle, Will now harboured a hope that he scarcely dared believe in.

On stage, the players put away their true selves and the theatrics began. Intricate layers of trickery and emotion unfolded in the subtle spin of their words. The crowd laughed at the conceits, applauded the deceits. Standing at the side of the stage, Kit Marlowe nodded in approval at how the players danced to the strings he pulled.

Will clapped a hand on Nathaniel's shoulder. 'Our Sir Francis Walsingham muttered something about more work, in France. In Krakow. And in fair Venice. And on the Spanish Main. It seems there is to be no rest for the swords of Albion, ever. But for now the sun is shining, and time runs away from us. There is wine to be drunk, and women to be romanced. Whatever lies ahead, the here and now is good, Nat, and we must make the most of it. Let us celebrate our great victory and drink to a world made right.'

FINIS